And wherever they settled from then on,
there was called **Magdala**,
for they knew not into what generation
the Magdalene would be born.

— the Song of the Holy Ones

MAGDALA
A LOVE STORY
THAT HAS NO END

BY VALERIE GROSS

SHOSHANNA PUBLISHING

Printed in the United States of America

ISBN: 978-0-578-02563-6

For my parents
(who are much missed)
for making me out of their great love

Let him Kiss me with the Kisses of his mouth,
for this love is better than wine.
- Holy Bible, Song of Songs, 1:2 (circa 800 B.C.E.)

I tell you the truth, wherever the gospel is preached throughout the world,
what she has done will also be told, in memory of her.
- Holy Bible, Mark 14:9, quoting Jesus,
regarding the woman who had just anointed him (circa 30 C.E)

The whole world is not as worthy as the day on which
the Song of Songs was given to Israel;
for all the writings are holy but the
Song of Songs is the holy of holies.
- Rabbi Akiba, quoted in the Mishnah,
Yadayim 3:5 (mid-2nd century C.E.)

Simon said to Mary, "We know that the Anointed One loves you.
Tell us what he told you, that he did not tell us."
- Gospel of Mary, 6:1-2 (mid-2nd century C.E.)

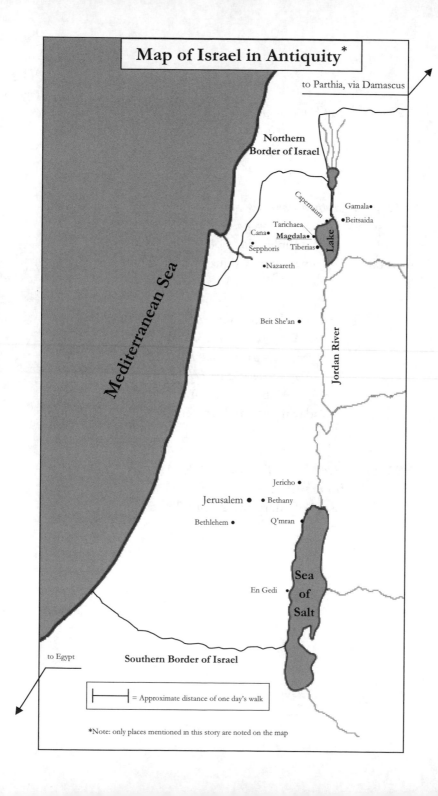

Map of Israel in Antiquity*

to Parthia, via Damascus

Northern Border of Israel

Capernaum

Gamala●
●Beitsaida

Tarichaea
Cana● **Magdala**●
Sepphoris   Tiberias●

Lake

●Nazareth

Mediterranean Sea

Beit She'an ●

Jordan River

Jericho ●

Jerusalem ●   ● Bethany

Bethlehem ●   Q'mran ●

Sea
of
Salt

En Gedi ●

to Egypt   **Southern Border of Israel**

├────────┤ = Approximate distance of one day's walk

*Note: only places mentioned in this story are noted on the map

ACKNOWLEDGMENTS

This book would not have been possible without Cristi Alberino, whose faith-restoring powers inspired a whole character herein. A shining beacon of friendship, I shudder to think of what my life would have been without her.

Woven into the seven years it took to write this story, are Hanelore Hahn and all women of IWWG and Skidmore, in whose presence, power, and faith I found the voice of this book. May we ever remember the magic. Dana Heather Schwartz, in whose literary welcome the amulet was conceived and the saboteur disarmed. Dawn Copeland and Joanna Lindenbaum, who gathered the circle of women that gave life to this story. We return to our ordinary lives, extraordinary women. Eve Pomerance, who loaned me her writer's ear and gave me her boundless heart, and too many dinners to count. Teva Bjerken, who never doubted. Deirdre Fischer, who gave me more than can be said in words, including the vision of her five-year-old's wit and wisdom. Erica Warner, the worst badminton player and the most wonderful hermana de mi corazón. Diane Benscoter, who brings out my truth. Ma chère cousine Dana Schechter, who makes me laugh at my worst mistakes. Eve Bromberg, for her editing help and enthusiasm.

Herma Briffault, who lives on in everything I write.

Daniel Gross, my brother and ever my champion.

Linda Dohanos, who was the first to take a chance on me.

Margaret Starbird, whose wonderful writing and scholarship gave roots to this book, and more than this, read and loved this story, despite our contradictions.

And Paul, who confirms daily that the love of which I write is no dream.

THE WOMEN OF MAGDALA

Mary   healer, daughter of Muriel, granddaughter of Martha, great-granddaughter of Rebecca, sister to Martha and Lazarus

Abigail   servant, daughter of Zanna

Ariella   servant, orphan, sister to Dinah

Deborah   seer, mother of Hannah, grandmother of Maryanna and Elizabeth, great-grandmother of Jesus and John

Dinah   scribe, servant, orphan, mother of two sons, sister to Ariella

Elizabeth   seer, daughter of Hannah, mother of John, sister to Maryanna

Hannah   seer, daughter of Deborah, mother of Maryanna and Elizabeth, grandmother of Jesus and John

Joanna   seer, high-ranking slave in Herod Antipas's court

Judith   mother of Rachel and Salome, sister to Phebe and Rebecca

Maryanna   musician, daughter of Hannah, mother of Jesus, sister to Elizabeth

Muriel   daughter of Martha, granddaughter of Rebecca, mother of Mary, Martha, and Lazarus.

Phebe   healer, mother of Yudah, grandmother of Tabitha, sister to Judith and Rebecca

Rachel   scribe, daughter of Judith, mother of Tabitha, sister to Salome

Rebecca   healer, mother of Martha, grandmother of Muriel, great-grandmother of Mary, Martha, and Lazarus, sister to Judith and Phebe

Salome   weaver, daughter of Judith, mother of two sons, sister to Rachel

Tabitha   daughter of Rachel, granddaughter of Phebe (through Phebe's son Yudah)

Zanna   servant, orphan, mother of Abigail

In the name of the ancestors to whom we are beholden,
In the name of the children to whom we entrust our blood,
With the authority vested in me as Holy Magdalene,
I, Mary,
Do humbly and prayerfully request
The complete healing and restoration to life of my beloved,
Jesus of Nazareth
Whose mutilated, crucified corpse now cools in a stone tomb
Across this holy city of Jerusalem.

I request this healing in Your Name,
Oh Great Mother Goddess Astarte, oh Great Father God Yahweh.

No. That will not do, that will not do at all. It should be more of
a psalm:

Most Gracious Lady Astarte, Most Glorious Lord Yahweh
Show Your Greatness to Your humble servant, myself,
Mary of Magdala,
Restore to me the man who opened my heart and let me touch his.
Though we are far apart across the city of Jerusalem,
He in his tomb of stone,
where Pontius Pilate deigned to let us lay him this night,
I in this house of marble, without him.
Without him!
Oh Great Mother Goddess, Great Father God,
You make the rain and watch over the newborn's life.
Restore Jesus' heart to beating and –

No, that will not do either. These are old forms, and what I need to do has never been done. For an amulet like this to work, it has to be completely different from any I have written.

Back in Galilee, in Magdala, I wrote countless amulets in our dank mountain scroll room, sitting alone on a worn wooden stool. Here, in Jerusalem, in this mansion of smooth marble and fragrant cedar wood, I sit on a stone bench whose cold penetrates my thin tunic like the hand of death itself. As I write, my arms rest on a long pink marble table amidst jars full of ink, piles of soft papyrus and boxes of sharp reeds. I sit alone here too.

I happened upon this windowless library seeking sanctuary from our friends, the very ones who brought me to the shelter of this vast home. They plan to flee this holy, terrible city; they are ready to mourn Jesus but not fight for him. I must reject their fear and remain calm and purposeful. I must ignore the scent of musk still in my hair which I have let fall loose around me like a cloak. I set aside the memory of that last kiss in the garden of Gethsemane. I push back all thought of broken body heaved up on bloody cross by crude soldiers.

I need to find a way to write this amulet. I have no shortage of supplies. I can keep trying.

Up north in Galilee, where our papyrus was hardly this smooth, nor the ink so abundant, I wrote many amulets for protection against evil spirits, ten times more to bring quickening to a woman's empty womb, and whatsoever else the Valley folk requested of us priestesses.

Rachel and Dinah both taught me, "The people slip these amulets inside their small stone pendants and wear them for comfort, to remember that they are protected, but the power of these words comes the moment they are written, for that is when the healing begins."

Then let the healing begin. Though I have never heard of an

amulet meant to heal one back from death, have I not seen and done much that others said could never be?

For an amulet such as has never been, I must write in a new way. I will address not Our Creator but speak to you, my love. You are a man born of woman, Jesus, but you opened the very sky for me.

I will tell the full story of how I came to be yours and how you came to be mine. And I will tell how you were torn from me.

I pray that in being written, the power of our story will stir you from your deathly slumber and bring you back to me.

May it please Our Creator that no one find me in this library until I am done. Just in case, I have slid both bolts across the thick cedar doors.

I solemnly promise, as best as is in my power, that I will not cease until you and I are reunited.

What else would you have me do?

A story properly told begins with birth. But our story begins before we were born. I could not be witness to these events, and so I will tell them as they were told to me.

The year before I was born, a mighty Oracle came to the three seers of Magdala as they sat in the fragrant shade of the ancient oak tree. The High Priestess Deborah, her daughter, and her granddaughter received in their meditation the same Oracle, at the same time.

They had been waiting for this their whole lives. Indeed, the struggling faithful of Magdala had awaited this Oracle for six hundred years. As promised in the ancient Psalm, this Oracle announced the arrival of the Queen and King who would restore righteous rule to Jerusalem, and peace to the whole land of Israel.

At the outset, the lofty Oracle presented an earthy and thorny problem: how best to summon a young woman to leave her husband and little children at the start of winter? This task fell to the prickliest messenger: my great-grandmother, Rebecca, healer and priestess of Magdala.

Uninvited, unexpected, and unannounced, Rebecca rode her mule through the open gate, into the walled courtyard of Muriel's vast and well-appointed home on the outskirts of the town of Bethany. Despite the pouring rain, the crone remained thus mounted just inside the gate until Muriel rushed out from the kitchen where she was conferring with her servant. Her thick wool cloak extended over her head like a small tent, this young woman who would become my mother stood in the wet cold and asked, "Greetings, stranger, are you

16

in need of shelter for the night?"

The old woman pushed her blue cloak off her pale gray hair, looked down her long nose at Muriel, and answered, "I am no stranger. I am Rebecca, your grandmother, your mother's mother. I have come from Magdala in Galilee, on behalf of our High Priestess. I am in need of shelter, yes, and much more."

This could only be trouble, Muriel said to herself. Please let it not be what I think. Out loud, she said, "Come in from the rain!" Rebecca gathered up her cloak, slid gracefully off her mount and handed Muriel the reins of the docile animal. These were immediately transferred to Jesse who had appeared without being called and took the mule into the warm, dry barn.

Extending her cloak over her elder's head, Muriel asked, "You have come all the way from Magdala! Surely not alone? The roads are fraught with danger." Rebecca indicated with a motion of her head the young redheaded woman and two black-bearded men-of-arms who stood waiting outside the gate. Just as Muriel was about to invite them in, the crone called out,

"Salome, take the guards and be gone! I will let you know if I need you again before the trip home."

After showing the old woman into the second-story guest room, Muriel went out and found the three escorts setting up a threadbare camp in the wet olive grove, outside the high wall that enclosed the courtyard, house and barn. She sent Jesse to bring them into the dry barn, and she told him to make sure they were brought food and drink.

The priestesses' home in Galilee was a three-day journey from Bethany under the best conditions, and in this weather who knew what they had to endure, even if, as it seemed, they had traveled without incident. Muriel did not understand why Rebecca treated her attendants this way, especially the young woman who wore the dark mask and soft curves of early pregnancy.

That evening, in the main receiving room directly across the courtyard from the gate which had been closed and barred since sundown, Muriel sat next to her husband Jacob on embroidered cushions before the food-laden table. Her good servant Ruth was putting the children to bed – a first. Muriel wondered how her babes were liking that.

She waited patiently while her grandmother, seated across from her on many cushions, picked carefully through the fine wooden bowls containing the best Muriel had to offer an unexpected guest at the edge of winter: fresh bread, some dried figs and dates, dried fish, fat cured olives and the best olive oil from their grove. Silver goblets held clear water from the well, and wine.

Turning up her long nose as she sniffed the fish, choosing instead a date, Rebecca lifted her black gaze and broke the long quiet, "Muriel, Jacob, I bring an urgent message. Shall I tell you, or can you imagine what would bring an old woman such a distance in such a downpour?"

Neither Jacob nor Muriel spoke. Rebecca snorted at their silence, "I am your closest living relative, whom you have never met, arriving unannounced at the start of winter," she spat out a smooth date pit, "and you have no questions for me?"

Muriel rounded her shoulders. There were so many questions. Which one should she ask of this grandmother who had cast her out of Magdala as a baby, when her mother died in childbirth? Jacob leaned in over the low round table. He put one wide hand over his wife's and ran the other through his thick combed beard.

"Rebecca," he asked, "we have no recent news of your sister Phebe, who as you well know raised Muriel, indeed brought her to Bethany as an infant, along with her own newborn son. Perhaps you bring a message from Phebe, or her son, Muriel's milk-brother Yudah?"

"My sister Phebe is well, thank you, quite content to be in Magdala." As Rebecca spoke, she toyed with five date pits, arranging them into various configurations on the table before her. "Her son Yudah is as he should be, fighting the Roman occupation, alongside the rebels he leads. With the help of our allies, he is preparing to take the Romans, and their vile puppet King Herod, head-on, and to evict them from our northern province of Galilee, and indeed from all of Israel. Though I am so old, I may live to see Yudah complete his kingship ritual and rule over all of Galilee."

"Has not Yudah already completed his ritual?" Muriel asked. "I thought that Rachel already – "

" – No, his ritual with Rachel will not suffice," Rebecca answered, cutting her off. "We need – "

Suddenly parched, her heart racing, Muriel reached for her goblet, "Why will Rachel not do?"

Rebecca looked up, rested her gaze not on her granddaughter's eyes but on her forehead and said, "Now you interrupt me?"

"I am sorry, Rebecca, forgive me; I do not understand."

Just then Ruth rushed in, "Muriel, please come, little Martha has come down with a terrible fever, she is delirious."

As the young mother raced after her servant, Rebecca followed with her eyes, saying just loudly enough to be heard, "Muriel, I think you understand perfectly."

The heavy rain drowned out the crone's uneven, softly booted footsteps, but heavier still was the blanket of a mother's hush-lullaby over her fevered child's moans – woman bending over girl like palm tree over water.

Muriel jumped out of her skin when she heard the ashen voice behind her speak, "You know what I am here to tell." She gathered herself, turned to face the wizened woman, one hand still on her sweat-soaked child.

"Rebecca, shh, I have just got her back to – "

Rebecca pulled Muriel by the arm out of the room with a brute strength that surprised the younger woman, then released her outside the door. Relentless curtains of rain splashed off the pale sandstone railing of the wide, covered balcony that ran along the entire second story of the L-shaped house. Only a small strip along the exterior wall remained completely dry. The women huddled there for a moment, pulling their fine wool cloaks tightly across their chests, looking out with a single resigned gaze at the impenetrable night.

"Such rain."

"Never seen the like."

Muriel turned her head, "My daughter needs me."

Rebecca faced her granddaughter. "Your daughter? You cannot be a mother first. Do you not understand, we of Magdala… yes, that means you too, you were born there…"

She stopped short, letting the rain speak for Muriel's birth, that brief moment long ago when they first met, which only one remembered. Rebecca leaned her back against the wall, pinched her brow between thumb and forefinger. She inhaled deeply, held her breath, then exhaled slowly. She turned back and spoke to the space above her granddaughter's worried oval face.

"Muriel, I bring word…" She grabbed the young woman's arm, this time in eagerness, "Oh Muriel! How many times have we heard the Psalm of Magdala?"

"Well each month, on the new moon, when the women gather we always…"

"Yes, I know I know, but each month for how many years now? Six hundred years, yes?"

Muriel's heart fluttered inexplicably as it had earlier, but she kept her voice calm, reasonable. "Well yes, Rebecca, but a six-hundred-year-old psalm is hardly urgent, and right now my daughter…"

Rebecca dropped Muriel's arm like a hot stone and glared into the night. "Phebe spoke so highly of you when she came home to us. She told us how well you had learned the ways of Magdala. Still, I was against you having a husband and children here. Jacob is a fine man, but living like a wife, you seem to have forgotten everything Phebe taught you. Why would you not forget? You dwell here with such luxuries: for the children a separate room, for your dinner a table instead of a rug, on which you eat food you do not sweat to raise or harvest." She scowled, "You were born a priestess of Magdala; you have known from the beginning that the nation of Israel is your child, the one who must always come first."

Turning her ear to the soft moans coming from the room behind them, Muriel asked, "How can you say that when your own great-granddaughter aches with fever?"

"I do not put up with the rabid dogs of old age to worry over any random child! Who gave you permission to call her Martha, anyway? It is one of the sacred names."

"I had a dream; she has a right."

Realizing that Rebecca refused to meet her gaze, it occurred to Muriel that she might look exactly like her own mother, and her maternal throat caught on Rebecca's pain.

"Rebecca," she said softly, "I know that Martha was my mother's name. I dreamed of her. She told me my daughter had a right to her name."

"Though the girl was born to you she was not priestess-born," Rebecca spat out, her voice rising in pitch as she spoke. "She has no right to that name, as you know full well. You think you live above the rules here, beyond responsibility to those who made you, who keep you safe."

"No, that is not it at all, I told you – "

"And as to your dreams, they are ordinary dreams, without power. If you were anything you would not be a seer but a healer, which clearly..." Rebecca's chin indicated the room where the fevered child lay. Muriel's mouth opened to form a dark silent "o", but before her throat could loosen to let words out, the old woman had already turned away.

As Rebecca walked carefully toward the stairs down to the courtyard, she called out over her shoulder, "We will speak again tomorrow after dinner. I see now that it is best for us to talk with Jacob present."

Finding her voice, Muriel called after her, "But tomorrow is Friday; it is Shabbat."

"Fear not, granddaughter: our discussion will be of a most holy nature."

With an anxious sigh, Muriel returned to her children's room. Her baby Lazarus was sound asleep on his back, his thumb in his mouth, in his bed against the opposite wall. She settled herself down on the thick rug on the tiled floor and leaned against her daughter Martha's small wooden bed. Muriel pulled the soft brown wool blanket back over the frighteningly ill girl each time she kicked it off. When Martha's breath softened, the young mother rested her weary head next to her daughter's tangled locks.

Muriel's serene face did not betray how haunted she was by Rebecca's words: "You know what I am here to tell." There was only one thing the women of Magdala could want from her. Her great-aunt Phebe had taught her that much.

A priestess of Magdala was obligated to do three things: contribute to the community with her individual skills and gifts, lead the new moon rituals, and when called to do so, serve in the Ritual of the Sacred Marriage, the enactment of the Sacred Union of Our Great Mother Goddess Astarte with Our Great Father God Yahweh. The Ritual which, on occasion, served to anoint and bless the new king.

Muriel knew she had no special skills. Born of a line of healers, her hands were deaf and dumb. She wove some, as did every woman who did not have to work the land, but her cloth lacked grace. It was only suited for blankets at best, certainly not clothes nor anything as fine as the sacred veils for the ritual tent.

As for the new moon circles, she had never led them, nor done more than attend. Ever since she was a child, the women of Bethany came to Phebe in the olive grove just outside the gate, and gathered around a small careful fire where incense burned and smoked. After Muriel began menstruating and became initiated, Phebe went back to Magdala. Phebe's other sister, Judith, had led the circle ever since.

Judith had come to Bethany from Magdala with Phebe all those years ago, and had settled in nearby Jerusalem where she still lived. Judith came to the new moon circles in Bethany with a group of devout women dressed all in white, known as the Holy Doves. Judith herself dressed in a white tunic and blue cloak, as did all the women of Magdala. While the women babbled gaily, Judith sat on the ground and waited for them to quiet and join her in a circle around the sparkling fire. Then, she would stand and shake her tumbling mane of red and silver hair. Then, she spoke the ancient stories, the ancient prayers, and held them all rapt with her song.

Recalling those nights, Muriel felt as though she were floating, or was she drowning, or had she caught her daughter's fever? Muriel clutched Martha's small warm hand but behind closed eyes, she saw Judith's glowing face; in the calm room of sleeping children she heard her great-aunt proclaim their well-worn story, the Psalm of Magdala.

"Long ago, Our Great Mother Goddess Astarte was worshipped freely throughout the land, side by side with Our Great Father God Yahweh. In every hearth and in every field, on every high hill and in every temple, the people praised them both and praised their Sacred Union from which all Creation sprang.

"Then came Young King Joshua, who banished Astarte from the Great Temple of Jerusalem, and broke all the altars to Her therein. More than this, Young King Joshua forbade Her Worship anywhere in all the land. More than this, he destroyed the great Tower, the great 'Magdala', that Wise King Solomon had built for Astarte long before. Young King Joshua ordered the Tower smashed to the ground, with the High Priestess trapped inside.

"More than this, he forbade all worship beyond the Great Temple of Jerusalem. All sacrifice would be made at its altar; all tithing would flow to its coffers.

"But worst of all, Young King Joshua commanded the ruthless slaughter of all of Astarte's priests and all Her priestesses, some beheaded at the very altars where they prayed. The few who survived the scourge gathered at their sanctuary, the lush oasis of En Gedi in the pale rock desert. There they wept, adding their tears to the immense Sea of Salt.

"They mourned their brothers and sisters who had been slain like pigs, their bodies unburied, left for vultures. They mourned the silence of ancient hilltops, where no more lambs would be offered, no more psalms would be sung. They mourned for the gathered-stone altars under the sacred trees, where the holy fires would go out and the incense grow cold. Most of all, they mourned the loss of Sacred Union.

"How lonely would Astarte be in the fields without her Yahweh. How lonely would Yahweh be in the temple without his Astarte.

"Surely the crops would fail and the babes die; surely the king of Jerusalem had brought a terrible wrath upon his head, and upon his people's.

"But what could the Holy Ones in the desert do? There were only ten times as many of them as we have fingers. What could so few do against such great evil?

"After many days of lamenting and mourning, mourning and lamenting, one moonless evening the Holy Ones became still. And among them was a young woman who had not been there at the beginning, who had just arrived, and who told them,

'I was with the High Priestess in the Magdala, in the Tower, before it fell. She told me:

Hear these words in your dreams,
carried to you on the wind of your journeys:
Many generations of faithful and
generations of tyrants will come and go.
Be steadfast and await the Oracle.
Three seers will receive together a single Oracle announcing
One who will be known as the Magdalene,
the new Tower of Jerusalem,
not a building of stone but a living woman,
a tower of faith and courage.
The Oracle will tell of the king to be Anointed by her.
Then we will know that the time
to reclaim the Holy City is upon us.
When you next return to worship Astarte and her Yahweh,
to celebrate their glorious fertile union
in our Jerusalem, in our City of Peace,
then the Peace of Creation will settle in all the lands.

Until then, keep Her flame burning, if only in your hearts,
when there is no oil for the lamp.

Remember this: Be fierce in self-preservation.
You who carry this knowledge are essential to the world's peace.
Be pliant in your compassion:
your heart must be pure to create our world anew.
Be steadfast, and wait for the Oracle, no matter how long it takes.'

"Upon hearing the High Priestess's charge, the Holy Ones rejoiced, for they were restored to hope and faith. They pledged to continue in secret the worship of Astarte and the ritual of the Sacred Union, until the Oracle was received, until the Magdalene and her King appeared. The Holy Ones swore an oath to risk their lives in so doing, if necessary. They knew the people of the land would help them, for those who tilled the soil would never cease in their worship of the Great Mother.

"Being thus exiled from Jerusalem, the Holy Ones wrote down the sacred texts, so knowledge would not be cut off when heads were, not be dispersed when bodies were.

"They wrote what Young King Joshua did to them: the Lamentations.

"They wrote the liturgy of the Sacred Union: the Song of Songs.

"They wrote the words of the High Priestess: Magdala.

"And wherever they settled from then on, there was called 'Magdala' for they knew not into what generation the Magdalene would be born."

With her mind's eye, Muriel saw her great-aunt Judith reciting these words, her ecstatic face and open hands raised to the stars, her fiery hair ablaze in the night.

"One day soon," Judith intoned the Psalm's familiar closing, "we will again sing the Song of Songs in the Temple of Jerusalem. Once again the sacred lovers will walk through the seven gates in Jerusalem, the City of Seven Hills, and with their joining restore Our Creators' grace to our people and to our land.

"We have always known that this time will come. Thanks to this Psalm of Magdala, our guiding hope these past six hundred years."

Rebecca's words from earlier in the evening came back again to Muriel: "You know what I am here to tell." When Muriel first welcomed the crone, she feared Rebecca had come to call on her to serve in the Sacred Marriage Ritual, as all priestesses of Magdala must do. But it was much worse, she realized with a jolt of understanding that lifted her to her feet, much better and much worse. Muriel felt in her bones that the Oracle had been received. And she was to play a part in its fulfillment.

"I am not worthy! I am not ready!" she cried out to the night. But all she heard was Judith's desert chant – no longer an incense-scented tale from the past, but a fierce living wind that would tear her life apart.

To conserve oil through the winter, Muriel had gotten Ruth into the habit of lighting just one lamp in the evening. With that lamp, after the evening meal was done, and the children were in bed, Muriel usually accompanied her servant past the main room to the ground-floor quarters Ruth shared with Jesse. Then Muriel took the lamp upstairs to her and Jacob's chamber, just above the main room.

But tonight, in honor of Rebecca's presence on Shabbat, Muriel gave Ruth a lamp of her own to take to her room by herself. A second lamp remained on the table.

After the long, mostly silent meal of roasted goose with Shabbat bread, cured olives, and dried figs, eaten sitting on full thick cushions around the ancient dinner table made of a single slab of cedar.

After murmured lamp-lit prayers.

After Ruth assured Muriel and Jacob that she would look after Martha and would properly swaddle baby Lazarus for sleep.

Rebecca raised her eyes from the table and looked at her granddaughter, meeting her eyes for the first time since she had arrived. There was nothing menacing in her gaze, not even a trace of anger. But those shining black olive eyes, framed by cloud-gray locks, set the young woman's heart to race.

It did not matter that Muriel's upright loom stood silently behind her, its weights hanging low and still as if heavy with fruit. Nor that she sat beside her own round-bellied husband at her own round table, on her own round cushions whose linen she wove and then embroidered with her own hands. Nor even that they sat sheltered from the wind and rain outside by the walls whose mortar-mending she herself had supervised just last moon. In the hold of her grandmother's gaze, Muriel felt like a guest in her own home.

Beneath the old woman's unflinching stare, Muriel reached under the table for her husband's hand, welcoming its enveloping dry warmth. With his free hand, Jacob stroked his black beard absently, staring at the dancing light from the ornate brass lamp set in the middle of the table. Long wild shadows danced on the walls around them, and Muriel inexplicably felt that she was in the very cave in which she was born.

The flame stilled as Rebecca spoke, "Muriel, as I suspect you know, it is time for you to lead us in the next Sacred Marriage Ritual – "

" – Yes, Rebecca, I realize that – "

Ignoring her, " – on the winter solstice."

"The winter solstice?" This she had not expected. "But that is in just a few weeks," turning to look at her husband whose gaze told her that he already knew. She turned back to the old woman, "Why so – "

"I have talked this over with Jacob. He understands. There have been signs." Rebecca exchanged a quick glance with Jacob, who was now completely still. "Muriel, it is time for you to perform this sacred task, for you to embody Our Great Mother Goddess as She celebrates Her Sacred Union with Our Great Father God."

"Yes, Rebecca. I need to tell you..."

Rebecca interrupted again, "As you may also have gathered, your Ritual will serve to anoint the son my sister Phebe suckled along with you. The one you call your milk-brother. Yudah."

Muriel had expected this. Still she did not understand, "Yudah! But... He and Rachel already..."

"Despite having borne him a girl, Rachel has not been chosen, Muriel," her palm raised, her voice a stilled wind. "Though you should not need a reason to do as I ask, I will tell you everything." Her eyes sparkled. "This is not only about your Ritual, nor about Yudah's anointing. Our three seers have had a shared vision; they awoke from their Sukkoth meditation with a single shared understanding. The Oracle. You do know what I am talking about?"

"Yes, Rebecca, I have been trying to tell you that – "

With both hands flat on the table, Rebecca leaned forward and asked, "Shall I tell you the Oracle?" Without awaiting a response, the crone closed her eyes, tilted her head slightly back and recited in a sing-song voice:

The Queen of Peace will issue from the broken healer,
her King from the seer blind.
They will be born of love not fate, as their fate is love.

One will burn.
One will fly.

They will be One, then Two, and Two will be One again.
One alone cannot find the way.
The Way will be known when the Two are One.
He and She will walk as One, and She and He will talk as One.

They shall see what none other see, and shine this, and tell this.
They shall not know want, for They shall see their
Creator in all things.
They shall know Death, for They shall know Themselves.
They shall know Life, for They shall know Each Other.

And Peace will come into the hearths of all and reign for all eternity.

Muriel did not know what to say. The words danced around her head without making sense. "What does it mean?"

Rebecca opened her eyes as if returning from elsewhere. She took in her surroundings, repeated her granddaughter's question slowly, "What does it mean?"

"Well yes, I – "

" '*The broken healer.*' You are the healer who cannot heal. The only one. It has to be you. '*The Queen of Peace will issue from the broken healer.*' "

"The Queen! Issue!" Muriel's jolting, fragile understanding from the night before became a crushing physical reality. She leapt up from her pillow-seat and paced back and forth behind her husband. "I must not only perform the Sacred Marriage Ritual, but bear another child as well?" Lips trembling as she spoke, she thought of how she barely escaped with her life after squeezing Lazarus from her narrow hips. "And you will claim her as you never..."

"Of course we will claim her," Rebecca answered calmly. "She is the awaited Queen, and likely she will be born into the healing gift you were denied. In Magdala, far from King Herod the Terrible and his ubiquitous spies, she will be safe. There we can suitably watch over her becoming, starting with her conception."

"Her conception? You mean in Galilee?"

"Well yes, Muriel. She must be conceived in Magdala, as you were."

"Why not here? Is this ground not sanctified enough?"

"Deborah is our High Priestess. She must be present outside the tent. And she is not well enough to travel."

"So we have to go up to Galilee now? At the start of winter? In all this rain?"

"One thing we can thank the Romans for, they know how to build a road that withstands any downpour."

"But what about my daughter Martha? She is sick, she needs me. And Lazarus is still nursing. Can Yudah not come here? Can we not do it here? You are here. With me and Judith that is three, that is enough for – "

" – Enough? Enough! Enough of this!" Rebecca's open palm slapped the table. "Is this how you receive such news? Is this how Phebe taught you to speak to your elders? Ah, if only your mother..." Rebecca's shoulders slumped. With a great sigh she shook a thought out of her unruly hair and straightened again. "My sister Judith will help see to the children, with Ruth. After all, Ruth is still nursing her own child, she should be able to feed the boy as well. But none of this matters, Muriel, do you not see... the Queen we have been waiting for..."

"You want me to let another woman nurse my baby!" Muriel's face reddened, her fingernails dug into her palms. "Are you not a woman? Has Our Great Mother Goddess Astarte swallowed your heart?"

Slowly, deliberately, Rebecca rose, lifting a hand to stop Jacob who had shifted in his seat as though to get up and stand between the two women.

Rebecca made her unhurried way and stopped before her granddaughter. Muriel stood a full hand taller than the old woman, but she drew no confidence from this. She dared not meet Rebecca's gaze, though her fists did not unclench, and her feet did not step back as her grandmother came as close to her as could be done without touching her.

Muriel was suddenly bewildered by a strangely delightful fragrance emanating from Rebecca's hair and finely woven cloak – a musky floral combination – that summoned inexplicable tears. Her hands relaxed; but she did not move.

The old woman leaned in, her cracked lips not quite touching her granddaughter's pink ear. A shiver ran down Muriel's spine. Rebecca's otherworldly whisper, on a breath of juniper berries and rain, thundered in her ear, "You will come to Magdala."

Rebecca kissed her granddaughter's round cheek, speaking with her lips pressed to it, "The three seers... The Oracle... We need this child." She pulled back to look into Muriel's now hooded eyes, and smiled ever so faintly. "You will come back with me to Magdala. We leave Sunday morning."

After sitting back down, Rebecca continued in a normal voice, "After the ritual, you will live out your term in Magdala. Once you have weaned the child, you may come back here – unless and until Yudah gains control of Galilee. Then you will come back to reign at his side, as his queen and our High Priestess. A glorious fate."

Muriel returned to sit at the lovely table and stared at her hands that had always seemed so small to her. Some glorious fate, reigning at Yudah's side. She remembered the wild boy he had been. The Ritual. And then, the wilds of Magdala. She knew how they lived up there, growing their own food, wearing their one tunic day in and day out, year in and year out! Just one look at Rebecca's leathery

calloused hands told her... The Ritual, then almost a year of pregnancy, two years before weaning the child, at the very least! At least
three years away from her children and her gentle Jacob, all for...

Rebecca reached over and covered both of Muriel's smooth hands
with her own lined, brown ones and pressed them gently. Muriel
closed her eyes; images rushed in. The liturgy of the Song of Songs,
of the Sacred Marriage:

> *Let him kiss me with the kisses of his mouth,*
> *for this love is better than wine...*

She had known these words by heart for as long as she could
remember, these words that had never moved her. She shivered now
at the thought of inhabiting them. She imagined crossing to the
other side of the knowledge to which Phebe had softly referred. She
could almost touch the truth behind the Mysteries to which all her
rituals pointed. She envisioned her land free of Romans, free of war,
ruled by righteous leaders. For the briefest of moments, barely the
time of a breath, her motherhood, wifehood, personhood fell from
her shoulders, and she was filled with the Presence that sometimes
brushed her shoulder in the grove on the new moon.

She let out her breath, opened her eyes and found herself alone
in the darkened room. How long had she been sitting there? Quiet
filled the house. The rain had stopped. Her thoughts rushed up the
stairs to her ailing child, her body followed, only to find little Martha
sleeping cool and sweet under a square of fine white linen embroidered with red thread that Muriel had never seen.

Rebecca? Giving her back, one daughter, one life, for the life and
daughter she was claiming? Muriel slumped to the floor by the child's
bed, swallowing jagged sobs besides Martha's peaceful, even breath.

Her face still swollen from tears, Muriel stumbled to her room and buried her face into her sleeping husband's furry chest. Still asleep, Jacob wrapped his arm around her and pulled her close. Under the renewed song of rain on their solid roof, they lay together on the bedding sagging with the shape of their joined bodies for how many years now? Thirteen? Fifteen? She had lost count.

She snuggled in more deeply, felt his breath lift and move her. Rocked to calm by his steady rhythm, she was quiet now. Jacob's arm warmed her like a blanket. She let her eyes adjust to the semi-darkness and watched the rain through the open door, cool air breezing across her face. Muriel squinted, trying to make out individual drops of rain in the night.

Suddenly a white dove flew in, prepared to land.

Muriel is holding a baby girl in her outstretched arms, dances around with her; her own arms are insubstantial, they are light, they are sunshine, though she feels the baby's dense flesh quite distinctly. They are laughing together, twirling on a bright mountaintop, and suddenly the baby's face becomes a young woman's, an exquisite oval with Muriel's own thick red lips and Jacob's unmistakable rich brown almond shaped-eyes.

Muriel blinked, and the dark rainy night returned to her sight. Had she fallen asleep? No, the dove was just landing; it circled a few times then flew back into the night. In the wet shadows, the face of the child danced before her. She did not make a decision; the decision grabbed her, in her gut. So. The child would be hers after all. That was after all what the Oracle said – the Queen would be her issue. It said nothing about whose eyes she should have.

Muriel turned and kissed her man. She climbed atop his hillside body; she laid on him, her length over his, her toes reaching his calves.

She kissed his dreaming ears, buried her face in his neck fragrant with his own musk. Her hands formed a crown over the tangle of his dark curls. Her breathing quickened, her sighs deepened, as she explored with hand and mouth this man who had been her world since...

His body awakened before he did. They made love quickly, quietly, as parents learn to do. Jacob came fully awake as Muriel collapsed onto him, and he rested his heavy hands on her back.

"Mmm," she said. "It has been a long..."

"Muriel, my beloved..."

"Jacob, I am so glad we..."

Then rolling her off him as if jolted by lightning, "Woman, what have we done? What have we done? You are leaving the day after tomorrow and..."

"My love," she said, as he shook off the hands she tried to place on his cheeks, "Jacob, it is all right, it is all right."

"No it is not! The Oracle."

"I had a vision. She had your eyes."

"What vision? You heard what Rebecca said! You are to bear..."

"Yes, the Queen. And so it will be. I tell you, I had a vision."

"You have never had a vision before. And if anything, you should be a healer, not a seer. You fell asleep, my sweet, you had a dream."

"Husband, I may not be my mother, nor my grandmother, but I am a priestess of Magdala after all, however flawed. Do you not think I know the difference between a vision and an ordinary dream? There was a dove."

"A dove? In this rain? Muriel, you were dreaming," he said with a complicated look on his face. He got up from the bed and straightened his tunic over his generous form.

"Sweet husband," she said, "as Rebecca told it, the Oracle spoke of the '*broken healer*'. It had nothing to do with Yudah," looking out into the night as she spoke this name. "That part is only the vision of their ambition."

Leaning against the stone wall, Jacob looked at his lovely tiny wife, the pale glimmer of her in her white tunic, sitting in the middle of their bed, in the middle of their night. "Beloved woman, do you not understand? This is not easy for me either. But the Oracle..."

"What about my vision?"

"Darling, you are not a seer."

"Maybe I am."

"Maybe that is why you are the '*broken healer*'."

She rose from bed and came to him. He opened his arm to receive her and chanted from the Psalm of Magdala in his rich creamy voice, " ' *...hear these words in your dreams, carried to you on the wind of your journeys...*' " Brushing the hair from her face, he continued, " '*...An Oracle of one who will be known as the Magdalene, the new Tower of Jerusalem, not a building but a woman, a tower of faith and courage.*'" He took a breath. "My love, to think that you will be the one to bear..."

"I really cannot fathom it, Jacob." Muriel pulled back from his embrace, faced her husband squarely. "How will this be for you?"

"Oh my love, you are so much more wife than priestess," he brushed a stray lock from her cheek and kissed her fingertips, "so much more mother than daughter. We are at the edge of the new era for which we have been waiting, all these generations upon generations. And you worry for me? Fret not. I will pray for you, for us all, that is how I will be."

Muriel looked out into the night and flattened herself against her husband. For a long while they stayed like this, saying nothing, letting the rain do all the talking. My mother's head rose and lowered slightly with each of my father's deep breaths, and for a while she drifted into a soft sleepy state.

Then she lifted her eyes to him. He sensed this and met her gaze.

"Husband, if indeed we are in the time of the Oracle, then nothing can change what must be. I will partake in the Ritual, and Our Creator will pick whose seed my womb will keep. After all, you are an initiate, and your family has served Magdala for generations. Not such bad stock."

Jacob placed his wide thick hands on his wife's soft cheeks, took her in for a moment with his almond-shaped eyes, then lowered his lips to hers.

"As Our Creator wills it, so it shall be, my wife. We will tell no one of this night – this that has passed between us."

"Perhaps not, my love, but our child's eyes, they will tell all."

Jacob considered this for a while and then asked softly, "Wife, promise me this: if what you say is true, when it is time to tell our child the tale of her coming into being, when it is time to tell her the tale of her birth, let me be there."

"Goddess willing, my husband, I give you my word. We will tell her together."

"Goddess willing."

A cool breeze danced between them. "May it be so."

It was hot and smoky in the birthing cave. Out from this gaping mouth of the earth rose a smoke-sliver of delicate incense. In order to keep the tiny fire going, Zanna rushed in and out on eager legs, gathering anything that would burn. By this time of year, even chaff was scarce. They rarely had open fires such as this one for burning incense cones, preferring the small brass bowls that burned less incense, longer. But Deborah insisted that this fire touch the earth directly. So feverish and headily joyous was the occasion that no one wondered why. Not that anyone in Magdala would question their high priestess.

Deborah also specifically selected Zanna to tend to this hungry, difficult fire, instead of her usual kitchen chores back down in the compound. When they had come up here the night before, there had been a full pile of charcoal Zanna had brought from the kitchen. No one had thought they would be here so long.

Though the slope of Mount Arbel on which the compound of Magdala sat had been her home for years, Zanna did not usually come up this high, and she struggled as pebbles kept slipping under her sandals and threatened to throw her off-balance along the steep landscape. She hummed to herself anxiously as she pried bits of dried lichen from the pale rock to which they clung; now that the light was fading, it was getting harder and harder to distinguish one from the other. The flakes clung to her hands, which were still wet from washing them after her latest attempt to help with the birth.

Inside the low-ceilinged hollow, Rebecca towered, lit by the flickering smoky light. The cave walls pressed close to her stooped, seated form and mass of wild gray hair. Before her lay Muriel, alternately howling from the center of the earth, alternately falling into a sleepless slumber from which curses and gibberish emerged. Muriel's once lush cheeks were stretched to skeletal by the hungry force of new life within; her round high cheekbones threatened to break though her translucent splotchy skin. A bit of old sinewy leather between her teeth had been chewed to shreds. All that remained unchanged by the past night and day were the warm round rocks Rebecca pried out of her granddaughter's clenched fists to squeeze cool ones in their place.

Muriel leaned against Hannah who leaned against a rug upon the back wall of the cave. They sat on three thick rugs above the wide clay bricks that rested on the cool hard earth. These were the rugs on which each of these three women – and their mothers and theirs – had been born. Spun, dyed and woven before living memory, the original zigzagged patterns of blue, gold, white, red and purple were barely distinguishable now, soaked with blood as they had been over the years, but everyone knew they were there. Just as they knew that on this night in this tiny cave their own mothers were present, and theirs, and theirs.

By now, Hannah's existence as chair, support, throne, life-bearer, had been nearly forgotten, even by herself. The aging seer was startled whenever Zanna came back and managed, despite her emerging curves, to squeeze into that narrow depth of the cave to pour some drops of fresh water between her parched lips. Zanna did the same for the laboring one, when she was not screaming.

This was supposed to have been a simple birth.

When villagers on the shore of the Lake came to her for midwifery, Rebecca always let the birth be guided by the laboring woman's strength, which she supported with the potent herbs her sister Phebe gathered and prepared all year for these occasions.

Only in special cases, after deep meditation and prayer, and only with the most trusted families, did Rebecca lay her healing hands on the laboring one. Her wide feet bared to touch the earth, her bare head tilted back to summon the sky – only when she received the internal instruction and permission to do so did she invite the colors to move through her hands. These became cool like a living water, as had the hands of generations of healers before her. Thus she pulled the laboring one and her issue back from the edge of darkness into the bright world where their living family waited and wept and prayed.

Despite this power, her own daughter Martha had died giving birth, in this very cave. Rebecca's hands had become inexplicably stone quiet, as they seemed to be once again.

The great healer had taken every precaution for Muriel's delivery to be easy. She had prayed incessantly for three nights and three days at the gathered-stone altar in the cedar grove just above the compound. She had spoken every invocation. The women let her be. "Whatever will soothe her soul," they whispered among themselves. Though they knew that Muriel had been troubled with hard labor before, all expected Rebecca to simply lay her hands on the great belly and smooth the baby out, as they had seen her do; all expected she would not even need her herbs, though she had a handful in the pouch at her belt, as always.

The night before, their high priestess Deborah conducted the same ritual as she did for every birth. The pregnant one had stood in the cedar grove, the others around her with ready drums and tambourines. When a birth took place during the time of the rains, they met in the barn, the warmest, driest spot, also the only indoor place where the life-force of the Great Mother Goddess could be purely felt.

For Muriel there had been a bright and full moon. Deborah had stepped inside the glowing circle of women with Rebecca, who had stood in for her own daughter, though Muriel had wished for Phebe, the only mother she ever knew, now standing in the outer circle, holding the hand of her little granddaughter, Tabitha.

The two old women had held the hands of the one whose contractions were coming closer together all the time. Together, Rebecca, Deborah and Muriel had formed a small triangle. When Deborah had intoned the ancient prayer, all the women had joined in the familiar chant, while those who had held drums beat them softly in rhythm with the words:

> *Beruchah at Astarte*
> *Blessed art thou Astarte, oh Great Mother Goddess*
> *Beruchah at Muriel*
> *Blessed art thou Muriel,*
> *Blessed art thou among women*
> *Blessed is the fruit of your womb*

To which Muriel had answered alone, her voice trembling but clear,

> *Oh with all my soul, I praise Our Creator*
> *And delight in His Name, and delight in Her Name*

The women then all had joined in again,

> *Beruchah at Astarte*
> *Blessed art thou Astarte, oh Great Mother Goddess*
> *Beruchah at Muriel*
> *Blessed art thou Muriel,*
> *Blessed art thou among women*
> *Blessed is the fruit of your womb*

Again Muriel had sung alone, her voice gaining strength,

> *Oh Great Mother Goddess,*
> *You have chosen us women to be the bearers of this,*
> *the greatest mystery, of this the greatest gift:*
> *the passage of new life through our very bodies.*
> *As we come to our greatest fullness, we are in Your Hands.*
> *We walk the road between life and death,*
> *between old life and new life*
> *for both the mother and her babe.*

The other women had joined in again,

> *We stand together on the threshold of new life*
> *Beruchah at Astarte*
> *Blessed art thou oh Great Mother Goddess*
>
> *In this holy night where Your daughter Muriel,*
> *In whom You are well pleased,*
> *will pass through the gates of Your Wisdom,*
> *we beseech You, let her pass unharmed.*
> *Let her bring a screaming rosy babe to light.*
>
> *We stand together on the threshold of new life*
> *Beruchah at Astarte*
> *Blessed art thou oh Great Mother Goddess*
>
> *Her child in time will pass through the fires of initiation*
> *and be dedicated to You.*
> *Take her then, we beseech You, not now.*
> *But if it be Your Will that this babe be born only to come*
> *dwell with You,*
> *then bless us with the wisdom and the peace to feel her by Your Side.*
> *We stand together on the threshold of new life*
> *Beruchah at Astarte*
> *Blessed art thou oh Great Mother Goddess*
>
> *O Great Mother Goddess*
> *You have made us in Your Image, Creators of Life*
> *Life that comes from our sweetest bliss, O Great Mother Goddess*
> *There are no words of praise to thank You enough*
> *for this gift You have given in eternity to all women.*
> *Therefore we lift our voices in wordless song now that*
> *You may know our joy.*

Then the women all had raised a great cry to the moon, and with a great hoopla they had proceeded up to the birthing cave, along the narrow path behind the grove.

That was last night.

Since then the sun had risen and set again, but little moved in the hot cave. Rebecca sat cross-legged, barefoot, her heavily veined hands hanging limply on her knobby knees. By her side, carefully laid inside a plain earthen bowl meant to catch the afterbirth, was the pale marble knife whose handle was carved with incantations and whose blade was suffused with the prayers of the many generations whose umbilical cords it had cut. Curved sweetly beside it like a sliver of moon or a sleeping child was the alabaster wand, etched with holy serpent and holy dove, ready to draw the circle of protection around the newborn babe.

These lay as if dead, as dead as Rebecca's mind worn to dullness by stillness and heat and screams and the awful emptiness in her hands when she pressed lightly against the mighty belly, drawing forth no coolness, no colors, no life. The only life in this cave came when her granddaughter howled into the mountain, and then the crone howled too, "Why can I not heal my own flesh and blood? Not my daughter, nor my granddaughter? Why can I not feel this great-grand-baby? Why would our Great Mother Goddess curse me thus? I can cause a fever, but not... Why can I not..."

And when screams softened to groans for a while, Rebecca bent her high wide brow to the earth and prayerfully whimpered, "Oh Great Mother, oh Birther of us all, where are You now? Why do You leave me now? Why do you leave her now?"

Sometimes she made herself strong, sitting up and singing to her granddaughter, this howling woman before her, this bug-eyed sweating pleading cursing woman, this being imprisoned by the one within her. When Rebecca reached to pull black sweaty hair back from dripping ashen face, Muriel turned away as best she could.

When they had first come up to the cave, with the round moon dawning, how they had sung and held hands, and clapped rhythmically to time the lightning contractions. There had been honey cakes for a sweet birth, dark wine for a joyous babe, bawdy songs about how easily things go in and how much work it is for them to come out.

No trace remained in the cave of that festive ascent. Deborah, who had stayed with them all night, had gone back down to pray under the sacred oak when the dawn brought no child, no progress at all despite the nearly uninterrupted agony of contractions. The poor undelivered one could barely unclench her jaw for a fresh piece of leather before another eruption ripped through her.

As the heat of the day passed into the thick of a second night, the laboring woman fell into an unconscious state, unnoticed until her screams passed into moans then whimpers. Then quiet.

Rebecca was jarred from the chanting trance into which she had slipped. Hannah lifted her head and opened her eyes. Over Muriel's shoulder, Hannah saw the great round moon rise before the mouth of the cave, filling it with its ghostly light.

Rebecca called urgently to Zanna, "Come again, child, with your narrow hands, try again, see if you can feel something."

Zanna rinsed the pieces of lichen from her hands at the cave's little spout, as Rebecca had instructed her to do the last time. She held out her hands for Rebecca to pour oil on them from the small round earthen jar beside her. The moon-faced adolescent forgot to roll up her sleeves. No one noticed.

Kneeling down between the two pairs of legs, Hannah's and Muriel's, Zanna reached into the otherworldly space of a woman's womb and concentrated.

"Oh yes!" she lit up, squealing with awe to Rebecca, "I feel it! I feel a round hard head."

Rebecca squatted forward, practically straddling the girl, as if she could look inside, "Go deeper, can you feel the neck? Is it..."

"There is something there, like a snake."

"That is her birth cord, loosen it, loosen it, free her."

And reaching above Zanna, Rebecca slapped her granddaughter's face with red-hot hands, slapped her harder than she had ever had cause to slap anyone in her life. Not getting any response, Rebecca then grabbed a hot stone from inside the fire and pressed it into the unconscious woman's foot who stirred and howled.

Zanna pulled her hands out just in time as Muriel whimper-hissed, "enough cursed swine sonovadog."

"Push! Martha! Now!" Rebecca commanded.

"Push it your cursed self," Muriel seethed, spitting out the leather. And yet as Hannah lifted the laboring woman's torso, Muriel complied and pushed with a strength no one thought she had left. My head crowned, and one more push and my infant self emerged, born into Zanna Rebecca's arms, at Hannah Muriel's feet, crying, healthy, ten fingers and ten toes.

Muriel fell back, her breath audibly turning into sobs. As I squirmed in Zanna's arms, Rebecca quickly took the knife and severed my umbilical cord. She placed the bowl for the afterbirth at the tunnel from which I had emerged and began to wrap me, still sticky with birth, into my swaddling linens.

Suddenly my mother rose like a ghost from the tomb, sitting straight up, "Oh no, you old dog, you took my life, you give me my baby!"

Rebecca handed my blood-slick half-swaddled screaming self over to my mother's sweat-slick arms that grasped me hard then quieted me cozily against her full breasts. As I got my first outside taste of her, she fell into an unconsciousness that would last until the new moon.

Despite her enfeebled state, my mother refused to let me be taken from her arms. When one of the women came in to bathe me and change my swaddling, Muriel fussed in her nightmare world and would not be still again until I was restored to her embrace. Even in that stillness she was never quiet but called out incessantly – hoarse whispers in a language no one understood.

The first night after her delivery, her ranting kept everyone awake in the common sleeping room, so she and I were moved to the guest room. Now the other women took turns in pairs sitting on the shaded second-story balcony, just outside our room's narrow door. There they kept an ear out for my cries, and an eye on each other, keeping each other awake in this unusually hot summer.

Two weeks after my birth, Hannah and Elizabeth took a rare turn together. Mother and daughter shared a small thick rug in the balcony's oasis of cool, necessary sanctuary from the anvil sun.

Their backs leaning against the wall, the two seers sat awash in sound. The fountain gurgled in the courtyard below; the cicadas called from everywhere; my mother's angry gibberish echoed in the room behind them. More faintly, Deborah's incense-making chant floated out from deep inside the pool of shade under their sacred oak; Rebecca murmured a constant prayer, kneeling in the blazing courtyard; Zanna hummed to herself as she kneaded the day's bread. Barely audible was the high sweet voice of Maryanna, Hannah's younger daughter, coming down to her mother and sister from the cedar grove above them. There Maryanna sat as usual, singing the same phrase of hymn over and over, plucking at a lute and making tiny adjustments to her instrument. The whole fabric of sound was struck by the gentle percussive clinking of clay weights as the tranquil redheaded Salome worked her loom beneath the balcony.

Never would any two women sit idly in the compound, except for the two days of the new moon up in the grove. The rest of the month, their hands were ever active. Even on Shabbat, they were busy in prayer and sacred writing and healing. But all of Hannah's and Elizabeth's usual handiwork was down under the oak with Deborah — the resins, the gum, and the bowls they used to make incense for their own use and for sale — that is, for gifts in exchange for alms for Magdala. None of this could be transported to the balcony; not only were the vast stone mixing bowls too heavy, but it would not do to mix the sacred scents anywhere but under the protective shield of the spreading tree's mighty branches.

There was as much to do as ever, but leaving my infant self alone with my barely conscious mother was not a possibility, nor was leaving Zanna to watch over me all the time, for how would anyone eat if she was not minding at least the barest essentials — grinding the flour, keeping the stove hot, kneading the bread, fetching the olives, dried fruit, and salted fish from the storeroom.

Lacking resin and gum to knead into incense, Hannah and Elizabeth had brought to the balcony some wool to spin. Hannah rolled the tufts with her hands, feeding them to the spool which Elizabeth spun expertly, holding it just above the ground with her long graceful arms.

After listening for a while to the strange harmony of cacophony around them, especially the singing coming from the grove, Hannah cleared her voice and said to her eldest daughter, "Twas a good thing Zacharias noticed Maryanna's musical ear. I was beginning to wonder what to do with your sister — how could a daughter of mine not even have a talent for blending incense?"

"Yes, it is true, Mother," Elizabeth answered quickly, "that night that Zacharias danced with me so madly, all the while playing his flute — it just flew out of his hands into the fire, that night was blessed indeed." Elizabeth let fly a rare girlish laugh. "I never knew where my little sister disappeared to all those afternoons before. When I called her to come up to the grove with me, to practice visioning, she only came if I let her carry the drum. Then once I slipped inside myself, little Maryanna slipped outside to Goddess-knows-where, and when I came to, she was always gone. But that night with Zacharias," the sleek-black-haired woman sighed deeply, "we were all so upset to have no more flute for our dance, and then, remember, Mother?" Her gaze alighted tentatively on her mother's lined face. Hannah turned to meet her daughter's shining eyes, nodded and smiled as Elizabeth continued, "Our little Maryanna, whom no one had even noticed was missing, suddenly appeared in the center of our confusion, standing next to the fire, holding out that crude but perfectly tuned little wooden flute."

"Yes, I remember it well. It goes to show one."

"What, Mother?"

"Not even a seer sees everything. You never know what a child will inherit, or from whom."

"But Mother, we are seers, not music-makers. No one in our line has ever..."

Looking down at the floor before her, smiling to herself, Hannah hinted, "What of her father?"

"Ah yes. Her father." Elizabeth glimpsed at her mother. A question went round and round in her mouth with a force that turned her head. She looked out past the courtyard, past the great oak, past the fields, down and out to the vast blue Lake shimmering with afternoon sun. Elizabeth gathered her courage, "Mother, I have always wanted to – "

" – And this one," Hannah interrupted and looked through the wall behind her as if she could see my mother and me, "born from a '*broken healer*' indeed. But who knows if she herself will be a healer? Maryanna is no seer, and Muriel never showed any signs."

"Has there ever been such an interruption of these gifts before?"

"No, daughter, but the Oracle does say, '*The Queen will issue from the broken healer, Her King from the seer blind.*' Perhaps this interruption is part of this new age that is upon us."

"We do not know what this new age is." The voice issuing from her daughter was so unfamiliar that Hannah had to turn her curled, graying head to make sure this was Elizabeth speaking. Hannah watched with a portion of fascination as the foreign snarl poured from soft pink lips, "Our vision, Mother, was that the Queen would '*issue from the broken healer*'. We do not know if she will come into this generation or the next, or even the next. We still need her King, and none of the seers are going blind that I can tell. Besides – "

A patch of silence interrupted Elizabeth, a silence that turned both women's heads toward the room where my mother and I lay. Dropping their spinning, scrambling to their feet, they rushed in to find me soundly asleep, my mother wide awake, staring straight ahead.

Muriel whispered, without looking at them, "Where is Zanna? I need Zanna."

Hannah began to reach for me, addressing my mother, "My child are you...?"

"No," Muriel feebly raised a hand with all the authority she could muster. "No. I want Zanna. Just Zanna."

Hannah and Elizabeth rushed back out to the balcony and called to Zanna who was fetching water.

"Come, now, Zanna, come to Muriel; she is awake, and she asks for you."

"She is awake? Is the baby all right?" Zanna, halfway between the fountain and the kitchen, hesitated under the weight of her full jar.

Elizabeth flew across the balcony, down the steps to her side. She took hold of both ears of the hip-high water vessel. "Leave this. Go to her."

Rebecca watched Zanna clamber up the stairs. Then the crone prayed louder than before, howling, "May my beautiful child Martha live, oh Great Mother Goddess, oh Great Father God, or may the infant die. It is not enough to curse the infant with hands empty of healing. Let the infant die, that my Martha may live, or if my Martha should die, I will do Your justice on this earth and kill the infant with my own hands, for why should my child's killer live, is this justice, oh Great Mother Goddess, oh Great Father God?"

Only ten paces from Rebecca's ranting, the clinking rhythm of Salome's loom was not interrupted. One could perhaps notice a faint flush around the weaver's eyes, easily attributed to the day's withering heat.

Elizabeth, for her part, did not stop to talk to Rebecca. What could she possibly say to someone who would not even get out of the merciless summer sun? After dragging the heavy splashing jar all the way to the kitchen as best she could, she ran up to join Hannah where she had left her: standing by the doorframe just out of Muriel's sight, listening.

"Did you hear what Rebecca…" Elizabeth whispered breathlessly.

Hannah answered by nodding, holding up a hand, her inward gaze indicating that the whole of her attention was given to listening to what was happening in the room where my mother lay with me.

Elizabeth risked a peek and saw Zanna bent over Muriel, propping an extra blanket to support her back so the ailing woman could sit up, as my swaddled sleeping body rested in the nook of my mother's weak arm. Elizabeth pulled her head back quickly.

Muriel's dusty, cracked voice murmured, "The tunnels are deep and I shall never return."

"Muriel?" Zanna placed her cool hand on the steaming brow, but her steady brown eyes could not lock in on roving black ones. "Muriel? It is me, Zanna. You wanted me to come, and I am here."

Grasping Zanna's warm arm in her cold clammy hand, squeezing it as best she could, "Zanna, oh Zanna, my deliverer, you are here, at last. I have been waiting for you."

"I came as soon as – "

" – Yes, but I wanted you long before I could speak. You are my witness. You will be the one to tell my daughter of her birth and her becoming."

"You will be witness to her, Muriel, you just rest now and – "

Muriel's nails dug into the young woman's skin, "Zanna, I have not much breath left. Be quiet and listen. In the name of Our Creator, in the name of Our Great Mother Astarte, be quiet and listen."

"All right, Muriel," lying her rough dry hand on the clammy clinging one, relaxing it. "I will sit right here and listen to every word. The way you tell it to me is the way I will tell it to her."

Muriel took a deep gurgling breath. She cleared her throat and said, "You know that ten moons ago, Rebecca came to Bethany. Did you know I had never met her before? She did not come to see me. She came to get this child."

Hannah and Elizabeth listened in complete stillness at the door, as my mother recounted the events that brought me into earthly existence. The seers' faces remained impassive as Muriel told of her vision and of her last night with Jacob.

Muriel also told of the night of the Sacred Marriage Ritual with Yudah. After they had passed through the seven gates of the ritual marriage and entered the tent of veils beyond the stone-gathered altar, the groom did not touch her; instead he fell into a sudden and deep slumber, from which she had not been able to wake him.

Whatever emotion the seers experienced as they received this news could not be seen on their faces. For now they simply recorded the story, knowing that they too, in time, would be called upon to tell it to me. They knew that it took more than one person to tell a story, just as it took many resins to make a single cone of incense, many voices to sing full harmony.

After completing her tale of the fruitless night under the tent of veils, Muriel burst into a terrible breathless fit, gasping for air, a fit racking her body so completely that Zanna took my swaddled body from the bed, afraid I would be struck by a wayward elbow or knocked to the floor.

When she finally caught her breath, my mother reached for me, but Zanna feared another attack and held me firmly in her arms.

"You mean to take her from me. That is alright. I have seen that too. I have named her Mary."

"You cannot just go and name a child like that! Our High Priestess Deborah must cast the stones, and – "

"Listen to me Zanna, these are my dying words," she whispered hoarsely. "Do not argue with me now or we will be arguing for all eternity. Her name is Mary. Most of all, swear to me, Zanna, swear to me as I die, that you will take the child back to Bethany, to her father

Jacob. She must not belong to Rebecca. Swear to me that you will not let Rebecca so much as lay one eye on her, as long as she lives."

Zanna turned to the bright doorway, saw Elizabeth's and Hannah's heads tilt in. Muriel's gaze followed Zanna's just in time to see the graying elder seer nod her head.

"I swear it, Muriel," Zanna said, more to me than to my mother, "I swear it. I will take Mary to her father Jacob in Bethany."

Muriel closed her eyes at Zanna's words. Her head fell to the side. "Tell Jacob... Tell my children... I love them... Make sure my children know who I am. Who I was."

Quiet tears rolled over her round cheeks, as Zanna answered, "I will do it, Muriel, I will do it all," taking my dying mother's hand.

Muriel's breath became short, then shorter, then gone.

The air turned fragrant now with newly lit musky incense and sharp smoke from burning bread.

Outside, Rebecca's courtyard wailing, Deborah's tree chant, and Maryanna's grove song still rode on the endless gurgle of the fountain and the rhythm of Salome's loom. The cicadas response to the sun grew and stretched like a cloud of sound.

But no one made a sound on the second story – not the two women in the doorway, not the two women inside the room, and not the sleeping infant with almond-shaped eyes.

In Bethany Zanna and I shared the small dark room next to the kitchen's garden. At night, we slept side by side upon mats and under blankets that we rolled up each morning. During the day, white doves nested in a small space between the top of the wall and the roof, and the sunlight danced across our walls.

I did not discover this sunlight until I was five-years-old. By then, my sister Martha was all of ten, and she ruled the world for me and our brother Lazarus. I did not know that we were related; indeed, no one told me until a few weeks later, in the middle of the night, just as I was about to leave Bethany with a strange red-haired lady in a strange carriage.

The day I discovered the sunlight in our room, Martha was playing in the courtyard with a small wooden cart. When I asked her if I could look at it, she said, just as Jacob used to, "Look with your eyes and not with your hands." She stuck out her tongue at me and ran away, waving the cart over her head. Lazarus caught her and sat on her, while I grabbed the cart and sang out, "Mine, mine, mine!"

Martha cried out, "Give it back!" She squirmed out from under Lazarus and ran after me, calling, "Our new Father brought me that from Jerusalem. It is mine!"

Lazarus ran after Martha, arguing, "He is not Father, he is Uncle! Our father is Jacob!"

And I said, "That is right, he is Uncle!"

We ran past the well; as Martha reached for the cart, she said, "Yes, he is my Uncle, not yours, just like that is my – "

And I threw the cart in the well. Martha screamed so loud that the white chickens pecking at the ground scattered. Zanna emerged from the kitchen. Lazarus, who was allowed near the well, dropped the bucket down to get the cart. I was not supposed to come within one pace of the well, but I could not resist. I looked down over its small wall: the cart was floating on the water! Was this magic? I picked up a pebble and threw it in, and sure enough it sank.

Martha was not content with getting her dripping cart back. She wailed into my Zanna's smock, turning her head so Zanna would not see her stick her tongue out at me again. Zanna only saw me and my guilty face. She pointed at our room, her other hand on Martha's head.

"The sun is barely over the hill and already you are causing trouble, Mary! What else will this day bring?" Zanna called to my back as I walked away.

I had never had punishment before breakfast. I was so angry at Martha that I refused to cry. I decided I would stay in that room forever and not come out, even when Zanna called me. Then I noticed a small hole in the back wall, through which a ray of sunlight came, like a finger caressing everything. Our folded blankets shone a blue I had never seen, even when Zanna took them out and beat them in the afternoon, making the dust dance.

And me? I wondered. What would this special light do to me? I put one finger in the shaft of light and saw it glow, my skin bright pink and my nail bright white. I moved my fingers in and out of the shaft of light. Shiny pieces of light danced with my fingers.

I declared to myself, I do not need a stupid cart! I do not need stupid Martha or anyone! I could come there and play with my special sun. It would be my special secret, and no one could take it.

"Mary! Do you not hear me? Breakfast!" Zanna appeared round in the square door.

"Zanna, Zanna, look, I am making the sunlight dance! And before, it was all so pretty, blue and yellow! Even my fingers are shining. Look Zanna, I have the best toy of all!"

She crouched down to me, her eyes dewy. Her hands smelled like yeast. She kissed my forehead wet and loud and said, "So, little one, are you coming to eat?"

I ate the piece of bread Zanna gave me in the kitchen, at the

wooden counter, sitting on my stool. I gathered up the crumbs left
where Zanna had broken up Lazarus's and Martha's bread, which
they ate in the main room.

"Zanna, why did the cart stay on the water? Like the pieces of
light? Why do they not drop down like a rock?"

Zanna had her back to me as she tended the oven. "Why do not
who what, child?"

"Zanna! The sun was dancing in our room! The cart stayed on top
of the water! Does this happen every day?"

She giggled and kissed the top of my head, "Why yes, many
things happen when you are not looking," and began humming as
she returned to her task of feeding small bits of wood into the fire,
in the back of the deep stone hole where our bread was baked each
day. I chewed my slice and watched Martha and Lazarus play in the
courtyard.

I could not see Aunt, but I knew that squeaky voice, "Martha, it
is time for you to practice your spinning! You may yet learn to make
a thread smooth as your mother's was! Lazarus, come now, it is time
for your study."

They stopped playing and looked at their feet. Sullenly they went
into the main room, the one into which I was forbidden to go.

Zanna pulled her head out of the oven and turned to me, "Uncle
is out for the morning. Finish your breakfast, then get off that stool
and go run and play."

I looked out at the empty courtyard, then at the barn where the
animals were. My favorite was Jacob's black mule. But Jesse was in
there, cleaning out the stalls. Jesse smiled all the time with his nearly
toothless grin, but he never let me stay on the mule, not even for a
tiny moment, please, even if I was very quiet.

I told Zanna, "I do not want to play. I want to stay with you."

"Love, come back later when I am doing the things you can do
too. It is time to grind the wheat, and you are too small to help me.
You will just get in my way."

"No I will not, I will be good. I want to see what happens when
I am not looking."

Her smile pulled her ears, "Well you can never know that, for you will be looking!"

"Oh please let me stay, Zanna, let me try."

She shook her head, but her smile did not come off. I followed her out of the kitchen and sat next to the round stone flour mill, in the shade of the balcony that lined the second story of the house. The square stones near the mill were cool and pleasant.

Zanna lifted the lid off the large jar full of grain, and set it down carefully. "Here, you take just a fistful of wheat to start." She scooped some shining yellow kernels off the top. The jar was almost bigger than she was. "Then you pour them down the hole as you have seen me do forty thousand times before."

"Yes, Zanna, I can do it, let me try it!" I stood and held my hands together, forming a bowl.

"I will not be able to help you, you know, I will need both hands to turn the mill."

"I know, I know, let me try!"

She poured some grain into my hands, smooth and cool. "Now pour the wheat carefully, and do not spill a one. Each one you drop will be a whole year off your husband's life."

Husband. I had just learned that word, and I had seen one too, the week before. He had a thick black beard: Omar, Uncle's son. This husband pulled his brown mule, on top of which was seated Morah, Jesse and Ruth's daughter. She was barely older than Martha. Under her gray cloak, Morah's shoulders were stooped and shaking as she crossed the gate on that mule. Crying with no sound.

"I do not want a husband!" I told Zanna. I poured a little grain in, and Zanna began to turn the mill.

"Of course you do! Every girl…" then she stopped herself and looked at me in a funny way.

"I do not want a husband, Zanna, I want to stay here with you forever."

She let go the mill and took my chin in her hand, lifting my face to hers. Her eyes were sharp, her mouth pursed, "Do not wish that, child!"

Then she returned to the mill. On purpose, I opened my hand wide over the hole at the top. Half the kernels fell on the ground. I looked at them and then at Zanna. Her face was closed like a gate.

My eyes hot and stinging, I picked up the grains of wheat. I counted them out loud, one two three four, like Zanna had taught me to do on my fingers, but she said nothing.

I blew the dust off and poured the grain in the mill. Maybe Zanna can be my husband, I thought, instead of Omar. I wondered if there were husbands like Jacob. I could still see his face. I did not have any wheat left, and Zanna would not give me more. I wanted to shout, but I did not know what to say.

I ran out the gate. Zanna called to me, but I did not hear what she said, and I did not want to know.

Next to being in the kitchen with Zanna, I liked climbing the olive trees in the grove. The ground there was soft, not like the courtyard that scratched my toes. Between the olive trees and the road, there were tall cypress trees that perfumed the air, especially in the mid-day heat. These tall dense trees prevented me from seeing the road, but I could hear it: many different voices and metal horseshoes clanging on stone and wooden wheels creaking under laden carriages.

As we did not have our own olive press, at harvest time Ruth and Jesse went down the road with the black mule laden with sacs of olives, and they returned with sacs of grain and long jars of olive oil. When Jacob went away, I always knew he was returning because as he neared he sang a special song, about the moon lady coming home.

But Jacob was not coming back any more. As it was explained to me, he had gone to live in the earth. One morning, about a month before I discovered floating carts and sunlight in our room, Jacob was striding across the courtyard on his way out to the grove. In the next moment, he was prone, by the well. Nothing anyone tried to do helped. He did not breathe again.

After he died, I began having a nightly dream, about a woman I called my moon lady, for she had white hair like the moon. She smiled at me with her whole face and told me secrets that were just for me. When I woke up I never remembered what she said, only her face. Zanna said she was glad I had a moon lady.

When I went out into our grove, there was a particular tree I favored, one that had a long low branch at just the right height for me to sit. That was where Jacob used to visit with me. We liked to sit there and look at the other trees and the birds. But never as often as I wished, which was everyday. Curled in his lap, I could hear his heartbeat through his cloak that smelled unlike anything or anyone else.

Jacob told me stories: about how olive trees grow old and young at the same time, about our Great Mother Goddess and our Great Father God, whom we could see in Creation's abundance, and about a baby girl who was far from home.

That story was my favorite. Jacob would tell me about his wife Muriel who was very beautiful. He told me that they had had a baby girl that they loved very much, but that Muriel died when the child was born. The baby had been sent to live where no one knew who she was, far away from people called Herodians, and also from her great-grandmother who had sworn to kill her. I did not understand why someone would hurt a baby girl. I made him tell me this story again and again, trying to make sense of it.

Jacob said to ask Zanna any questions I had. He said she knew everything. But I believed that he knew everything. Men and women in brightly colored clothes came to see him on Shabbat with sour faces. Jacob opened his big arms and took them into the main room. When they came back out, their faces were smooth and smiling. "Thank you Jacob," they said, "May your blessings be many."

One day I asked Jacob what a blessing was. He said, "It is something that makes your heart glad, like you and Martha and Lazarus, something that comes from the hands of Our Creator."

"Do you come from Our Creator? What about Zanna?"

He laughed, "Everything comes from our Creator."

"So then everything is a blessing, if everything comes from our Creator!"

He laughed and kissed my head. Then his eyes went away even though he was looking right at me. "I suppose everything is a blessing, but it does not feel that way."

"Why not?"

"I do not know. Maybe when you grow up you can find out and tell me."

"How can I find out if you do not know?"

"Ask Zanna," Jacob answered, which meant he was done with the subject.

After he died, our tree felt big and empty. It was the only place we had spent time together. Inside the courtyard walls, he paid attention only to Martha and Lazarus. Once I tried to go to him in the main room, but he did not look at me. He closed the door.

That morning of discovery, thinking about Jacob closing the door made me sad and tired. I curled up in our tree and fell asleep. That tree cradled and restored me. When I woke, I ran back into the courtyard, eager to find Zanna and make her laugh.

I found Martha and Lazarus again playing in the courtyard, but I ignored them. I did not want more trouble. They only played when Aunt and Uncle had gone out. Whenever he was home, Uncle brought Lazarus to study in the main room. I could hear the lessons through the open doors. Zanna told me that Uncle was Jacob's brother, but I could not imagine two men more different.

Martha had to work with Aunt, doing what seemed to me a funny dance with a piece of wood and string. Zanna told me that was called "spinning wool." Whenever I tried to get close to them, Aunt would shoo me away.

Sometimes Uncle would send out Lazarus and call Martha into the main room. She would blush bright red and go, and Uncle would close the doors behind them. When she came back out, she was drawn and pale.

Other than being with Zanna in the kitchen, I enjoyed the company in the cool barn best of all. I loved watching all the animals – the horses, mules, cows and calf, gray goats, white chickens, and geese.

Whenever I could, I climbed on Jacob's black mule, put my face on his neck, and whispered into his furry ear. When Jesse found me he would yell and pull me off, chase me out. Then I would go sit outside the kitchen with Zanna. Sometimes Ruth helped her grind the wheat and the barley. They rolled the dough on a big flat rock, after Zanna had brought the water from the well to mix with the flour. I could help pluck chickens and geese, because I was good at getting the little feathers with my little fingers.

On occasion, Jesse and Ruth came back from the village with fresh shining fish "right from the Sea," they would say. I loved watching Zanna clean out the floppy fish, one big swoosh with her special knife, and the insides slipped out. She put the leavings in a bowl and took them to the garden between the kitchen and our room. After spreading them around the roots of the eggplant and cucumber plants, she covered them with dirt to prevent them from stinking in the sun.

I enjoyed pitting dates because Zanna would let me keep the long smooth pits. I used them for the games I played by myself in the cool sandy dirt outside her kitchen.

When Uncle was home, Zanna kept me near her in the kitchen. He would come right in, which Jacob never did. Uncle would ask, "What is for dinner?" and "How is your pretty little girl?" I had never heard anybody call me pretty. Uncle always looked at me in a strange way that made me want to hide behind Zanna, even when he was smiling.

Whenever Uncle went to Jerusalem, Zanna would say, "Go and play, why sit in this hot kitchen?"

As Uncle was out on this day of discovery, Zanna would not let me stay by her side when I returned from my nap in the tree. Jesse was raking the stalls, so I could not go sit on Jacob's mule. Then I saw Ruth sweeping in the main room. She was the oldest person I knew, all bent and skinny. No hair peeked out under her veil, and she had no teeth in the front, just like Jesse. I imagined that was because they lived in the same room, and nothing could make me go in there, even though it was one place I was allowed.

Ruth did not see me come through the forbidden doors. It was dark in the main room, especially all the way in the back. Resting on a large, round, and shiny table were a cluster of long, rolled-up scrolls. I wondered if they were Uncle's. Zanna had told me she had taken Jacob's scrolls away when he went in the earth. Once I had seen Jacob open one and show Lazarus and Martha. When I had asked him what was inside, he had told me it was the Law and the Records of the Seers. I had never seen one up close. I admired the cool shiny handles on either side. They smelled like the laundry when Ruth brought it in from the sun.

I poked one scroll, and my finger went right through the dry papyrus. As I pulled it out, I made a bigger hole.

"Uh-oh!" I squealed.

Alerted by my cry, Ruth turned around. "What have you done! Master's scrolls! Quick, get out of here before they..." Just then Uncle and Aunt came through the gate, arguing. "Quick, here, hide!" Ruth pointed under the table, "They must not know you have been in this room."

As Ruth rushed out to the gate, I slid under the wide slab of wood, which covered me completely. Though my heart was pounding, I was fascinated by the hard and rough bumps underneath, so different from the smooth surface on top.

Uncle and Aunt came in and stopped right by my head. I could see Uncle's big hairy feet in his thick sandals, and Aunt's red and round in her little sandals. All four feet were very dusty. They had not even stopped at the door to wash them! Zanna got angry when I came in our room at night before washing my feet. I wondered if Ruth would be upset too, as she had been sweeping.

I worried that Zanna would be angry knowing that I was so close to Uncle. I decided I would not tell her. Would Ruth tell her? I saw her go into the barn with Jesse. I tried hard to be still. Aunt said in a high tight voice,

"No, husband, it simply will not do to have a priest like Ezekiel, a Sadducee and member of the Sanhedrin, the Holy Council of Jerusalem, for goodness sake, honor us with his presence for Shabbat dinner, and not offer him the best we have. I will not serve him last week's fish!"

"Woman, calm down. I was not suggesting any such – " Uncle's voice was deep and reasonable.

"We will offer him the new calf. It is the only – "

"That is just too much. What will he think? That we are trying to show off our wealth?"

"You mean your brother Jacob's wealth. In fact, is it not his wife Muriel's wealth?" still whispering.

"That's enough!" Uncle stamped his foot. "I will not tolerate such insolence in my house. It is right and good for a man to care for his dead brother's estate. And what belongs to a wife belongs to her husband. Now – "

"Yes," Aunt said, whispering now, "but people still talk about his wife Muriel's disappearance, and then the appearance of the servant's child…"

"What are you trying to say? What tangled web of gossip are you weaving?"

"It is clear, is it not, look at what everyone calls her: Zanna. Who else would put up with being called 'harlot' all day long?"

"Zanna is the children's name for her," Uncle said calmly.

"Suzanna is the name her mother gave her, and – "

"It is not so far from Suzanna to Zanna! What has gotten in you, wife? Anyway, 'Zanna' did not always mean harlot, it used to be a rather reverential – "

"Reverential? To idolaters, maybe, like that little wife your brother disposed of…"

Uncle clapped his hands and boomed, "Stop this, stop this right now! Woman! It is perfectly well known that Muriel was a good wife to Jacob and a devoted mother to her children. She succumbed to a fever after traveling through the rain to visit her ailing grandmother. And Zanna was properly married to the little girl's father, who gave his life for the…"

I put my hand over my mouth to avoid crying out. Zanna was married? My father? He gave his life?

" … Temple in Jerusalem, dying in a building accident. You know that as well as I do. My brother Jacob performed a generous and honorable action, protecting a widow and giving her and her child a home."

"You will believe what serves you, but – "

" – Wife! Enough of this impertinence! I am not like my brother; I do not expect a woman to know the Law, but I do expect her to be obedient and not question her husband's will. Many flock to listen to a wise Hebrew, the rabbi named Hillel. He teaches that if a wife burns her husband's soup, that is a sufficient reason to divorce her. So. Now. There will be no further discussion on the subject of my brother, his wife, his servant or this week's dinner. Tell Ruth to help Zanna with the fatted goose, that will be the proper honor for Ezekiel."

His big sandals disappeared, slapping dust all the way out the door. Aunt whimpered then took a deep breath. She went to the door and called for Ruth, who emerged from the barn and hastened into the room.

"Well Ruth, go and tell Zanna – it took some doing, but my husband agreed to the calf after all."

I watched them walk out into the courtyard together. I got out from under the table and hid between the open door and the wall. Looking through a small hole between the rocks in the wall, I saw Aunt and Ruth go into the barn. I ran out to find Zanna.

"Is it true Zanna?" I asked breathlessly as she was kneading the dough that would rise overnight. "My father gave his life?"

"What are you talking about child? Who told you this?"

"Uncle."

She paled and stilled, "What were you doing talking with Uncle?"

"Oh I was not talking with him. I was just listening. Aunt was talking too, but I did not say one word. I was very quiet."

"And when did this all happen?" she asked, turning from her work, her hands on her hips.

"Just now. I was under the table and – "

" – What were you doing under the table?"

I told her everything: my finger and the hole in the scroll, Ruth and the table, and the feet and the goose and the calf.

Zanna listened intently and then had me repeat it all. Then she said, "This business with your father. Mary, your father was a good, devoted man, but not like they say. Someday when you are older I will tell you all about it, all right? But not today. For now just stay away from that room. I do not want you anywhere near Aunt or Uncle, especially Uncle, do you hear me?" She shook her finger in my face. Then she stopped. "Mary, little Mary, do not cry. Shh, it is all right," and she pulled me into her soft apron that smelled so good. "Tell me again the part about the goose."

After I told her, she called for Ruth. They talked together anxiously, trying to decide on a course of action. I was thrilled – they were talking about me, what I had done and said. After a while I pulled on Zanna's apron.

"What, child, what now?"

"Zanna, Aunt and Uncle said different things when they were in different places. So maybe they will say the same thing when they are in the same place?"

Zanna and Ruth looked at each other.

"You are right, Mary, of course, it is so simple, why did I not think of that? That man is like a bad desert wind, troubling my head," and Zanna scooped me up. "Look at you! Trouble in the morning and trouble in the afternoon, but you have saved us in the end. Praise Astarte for your trouble, little one, praise Astarte."

I knew Zanna was happy now because she put some bread dipped in honey in my mouth. I remembered to break off a tiny piece and hide it in a little hole in the wall between the rocks, to give to our doves. Zanna told me that was how we "Praise Astarte."

"For now," she always added. "For now."

A few days later, the evening found us ensconced outside our room on our special Shabbat rug, me cozy in Zanna's soft full lap.

Shalom Shabbat, Shalom Shabbat, on Shabbat nights she was all mine. Martha and Lazarus had already eaten and were in bed, on account of the special company of the priest for Shabbat dinner with Uncle and Aunt. For the occasion, Ruth had lit many lamps in the main room, and their shadows danced across the courtyard, where all was quiet. I felt like the well and the gate and the sky and everything was just for Zanna and me.

I only sat in Zanna's lap on Shabbat; on the other nights she did not have a lap. On Shabbat, she stroked my hair in time with the song she always sang to me, the one I called the "up-and-down song."

The round moon rose up behind the barn, and Zanna's song stopped. In the soft light, we saw a tall woman jumping from the courtyard wall onto the ground. Her cloak shone bright blue. Was this my moon lady? I wondered. Zanna pushed me off her lap and ran to the moon lady.

"Elizabeth! Praise Astarte!"

The moon lady hugged my Zanna – together they looked like a tall cypress tree and a round olive tree.

"Praise Astarte indeed, Zanna," Elizabeth said very quietly. She put her hands on Zanna's shoulders and looked her up and down, "You have filled out very nicely since the last time I saw you."

"Elizabeth!" Zanna looked down. I had never seen her look down before, not with Uncle or anyone. Elizabeth lifted Zanna's face by her chin.

"It is good to see you well, sweet Zanna."

"Elizabeth, I do not mean to question you, but why do you arrive at night and jump over the wall? And how is it that you are traveling on Shabbat?"

"Oh, we have been here all day. We have set up camp on the far side of the olive grove, where we cannot be seen from the gate. Such times these are, that a priestess of Magdala has to hide in Bethany." With a nod to the main room with its lamps and shadows, she added, "We have been waiting for quiet so we could speak with you alone. That meant waiting for them to close and lock the gate."

"Thank Our Creator that you are here at last. Not a moment too soon to take the child away from here."

The child? I ran to Zanna's side.

"Is this Mary?" Elizabeth asked.

"Mary," Zanna pushed me forward, "say hello to Elizabeth."

Our visitor came down to eye level with me. She smelled like spices.

"Hello," I said very quietly, to speak like them.

Zanna put her hand on my head. "So Rebecca...?"

"Yes. Rebecca has finally crossed over."

Zanna pulled me close. "May she rest in peace in the Great Mother's womb. When? How?"

"Around the same time as Jacob, actually. In her sleep. You could say she took Jacob with her, brought him home to his bride."

"Jacob has gone home?" I asked. "But did he not go in the earth?"

Zanna bent down. "That is right, love, Jacob has gone to his home in the earth where he can rest."

I looked up at Elizabeth. "Are you the moon lady?"

"What moon lady?"

"Like the song: 'When the moon lady comes home…' "

They laughed together, and the moon lady answered, "My name is Elizabeth. I am a seer and priestess of Magdala. I am not the moon lady. I am a person like you."

"Only bigger."

"Yes, much bigger," Zanna laughed, but Elizabeth did not.

"Did you come because of what I did?" I asked. "Did Zanna tell you?"

"No I..." Elizabeth closed her eyes, sighed deeply then turned to Zanna. "Rebecca's passing has been echoed in the sky. The heavens themselves have told us that it was time to bring Mary home, just as we had foreseen."

"A sign in the sky?" Zanna asked.

"Yes, have you not seen it?" Elizabeth gazed at the sky for a moment, then pointed at the stars with her long fingers. Her blue cloak came off her head, revealing hair as smooth and shiny as water.

Now I was sure she was not my moon lady because her hair was black as night.

"There," almost loud, "see?" Elizabeth showed us a bright star, larger than all the others, with a little cloud of light around it.

I lifted up my arms, and Zanna picked me up. "Do you see your star, my little one?"

"I have a star? Can I keep it in my room with my sun?"

Zanna laughed. Elizabeth answered, "No, but your star will take you home."

"What is home?"

Zanna petted my head, "Home is where you belong. You know that here you cannot go in the big room? Well, when you are home, you can go anywhere."

"Anywhere? Even on the mules?"

"Anywhere. That is what being home means."

"Zanna, this and Rebecca's death are what we have been waiting for."

"Praise Astarte. The child has been... Ever since Jacob..."

"How has it been with his brother?"

"Oh, he and his wife believe the child is mine, no trouble with that. But that man is lower than a pig. What he has done already to the older girl. The sooner we get this one away from him..."

"Has Mary shown any signs? Growing up so far from Magdala – "

" – Oh Elizabeth, I can still hear Rebecca's wailing and tearing at her clothes, with a living great-grandchild right there, thinking her daughter Martha was dying all over again. Did she ever recover her sense?"

"No, she would not come from the spot where she kneeled until we told her the infant was dead. We told her we had burned it. We gave her the ashes from the fire in the birthing cave."

"Oh, I remember that fire."

"Yes, she wore the ashes in a pouch that hung at her neck until her dying day. But once she had them, she calmed and resumed her healing work. Now that she is gone we are without a healer. Has Mary shown any signs? We have all been hoping against hope, what with my sister Maryanna with no special sight, and Muriel with no gift for healing, we all need to know…"

"Oh yes! Elizabeth! Oh, thank Our Creator that you are here! I must tell you, the child…" Zanna looked around. "But we should go inside. In the light of the bright moon, someone could see us. And you must be starving, thirsty, and who else is with you? What do you need?"

"Salome is with me, but she refused to set foot in here. She has insisted on staying in the olive grove." The lady shook her head at the ground. "Zanna, go and put the child to bed so we can talk."

"Yes, but…"

"Meet me in the grove. Do not be long."

On the next new moon, in the middle of the night, I awoke to Zanna poking me on my mat, one finger on her lips. She handed me my cloak and went to stand in the door, looking outside one way and then the other. She did not say one word, and she did not look at me.

Jesse opened the gate for us, and we went out. Zanna and I walked to a tree near the edge of the road and sat inside it. I was awed to find the night everywhere around us. Bright stars twinkled between all the trees and all the hills. Zanna looked at her feet and said not a word. Not knowing what was happening, I burst into tears, but following Zanna's example I did so as quietly as possible.

Then we heard carriage wheels turning and horseshoes hitting the stone road. Zanna picked me up and grasped me tightly. It sounded like she was crying.

"Mary, oh my little Mary. Listen to me. I want you to know that no matter what happens, you are in my heart. I want you to know that no matter what they tell you about who you are, you were born in my arms and you will always be a daughter to me. I want you to..." I had never heard my Zanna cry. I looked at her face and put my hands over it to try to smooth it out. She took my hands and kissed them. She had never done that before.

"My Mary, there are some things I have to tell you, and I have waited until the last moment, and that was probably wrong, but I did not know how to tell you. Elizabeth, remember, she was here two weeks ago, for the full moon, she said I should be the one, and maybe here in the dark of the new moon I can tell you."

She tucked my hair behind my ear. Then she looked at my hands, "Mary, I am not your mother. It was better for everybody that you thought I was, it was simpler that way. Your mother was Muriel, who rests in the earth. But you were born into my arms. Your mother gave you to me and only to me, so in a way I am the closest to being your mother. But you came out of Muriel's womb, not mine. You are Mary, daughter of Muriel, daughter of Martha, daughter of Rebecca. And Jacob. Jacob was your father.'

"Jacob was my father? Like Martha and Lazarus?"

Tears streamed down my face, and my insides felt as twisted as an olive tree's branches.

"Yes, you are the baby girl he told you about."

"I am the baby girl!"

"Your birth and your life have been a secret, Mary."

"I am the baby girl? Does someone want to hurt me?"

"Shh, Mary, love, I cannot explain it all to you now, but I can tell you that you are going to a place where you will be very safe and no one will hurt you and soon you will understand everything."

"I am going to a place? Are you coming?"

"Magdala. I will be there soon."

"Are you coming with me?"

"No, Mary, not right away."

"Why?"

"Shh, love, not so loud, we do not want to wake anyone up, then have to answer their questions." The carriage on the road drew nearer. Zanna hugged me tight and pressed her wet cheek against mine. My heart boomed inside my chest.

"Am I going alone in the night?"

Zanna laughed a little, and I felt better. "No, love, no, you are going in a lovely carriage with Salome."

"Who is Salome?"

"She came with Elizabeth, the woman who came on the full moon Shabbat."

"And Jacob is my father?"

"That is right."

"But he is in the earth with my mother Muriel! So I am the baby girl who is all alone!"

"No no, Mary, you are not alone, you will never be alone, you have me, and you are about to meet many others, starting with Salome who is very kind. You will see. Your life will be so much better now that you do not have to be a secret anymore. So much more than I could give."

Zanna kissed my whole face all over. I was a secret? I did not understand. The carriage arrived and stopped a little past where we sat. A lady emerged and said, "Hello Zanna, hello Mary." She held out her hands.

Zanna sobbed, "Salome." The two women embraced. Taking a breath, Zanna stepped back and asked, "Salome, are you sure it will be safe to travel at night?"

"Yes, we will stay for now on the small roads that go through the farms; people are sleeping in their fields during the harvest, so help is close at hand should we need it. And Ezra is a formidable fighter." She pointed into the night.

Zanna asked, "Only one?"

"Yes, this way we can pretend we are a family, if a patrol stops us. When there is a child, if there is more than one man, they get suspicious."

"But Elizabeth said that, Yudah said that…"

"Yes, Zanna, others will follow, close enough to help but not so close as to raise doubts. Now then. The child." Zanna turned and hugged me again, so intensely I could hardly breathe. She tucked more hair behind my ear.

"Do not be afraid, Mary. Be a brave girl; you are going home. I will come as soon as I can. You do as you are told. Whatever happens I will always be your Zanna, all right?"

"What is happening, Zanna?"

She went back to the gate, and the night covered her completely. Salome came to me. I was amazed by her red hair. I wondered, was it magic like the cart on the water?

"Is Zanna coming back?" I asked her as she picked me up.

"Not tonight, love. Tonight you are coming with me. I am Salome. We are related, you know. Your great-grandmother Rebecca and my mother Judith are sisters. Were sisters."

"Rebecca took Jacob in the earth. That is what the lady said."

She brought me to the carriage as I looked for Zanna who was nowhere. The night was everywhere. A man stepped forward from the carriage. He wore his cloak pulled over his head like a woman. Zanna had said not to be afraid, so I did not cry when he lifted me in his rough hands and set me gently inside the carriage, through the back. Then he did the same for Salome. Inside there were pillows and rugs. It reminded me of the main room.

In silence but for the sounds of the carriage, we began our journey. It took me a while to adjust to being jostled about, but I did and quickly fell fast asleep. When I woke in the strange pillowed room with the strange red-haired lady, I immediately asked,

"Where is Zanna?"

Salome touched my head softly, shook her head, and I sobbed hot tears. "Zanna will be with you soon, Mary. Do not worry. We are going to take good care of you."

"Who?"

"Well, for one, remember Elizabeth?"

"The lady with the star?"

"That is right."

"Where is she?"

"Well first, after seeing you, we both went to Jerusalem. We stayed with her... friend, Zacharias, the Sadducee."

"What is a do-see?"

"A Sadducee is one of the chief priests who run the Temple in Jerusalem. Some of the Sadducees, like Zacharias, secretly uphold the sacred traditions, and they want to help us restore the true ways and the worship of Astarte in the Temple."

"What is a Temple?"

"Oh child! The Temple is where people go to worship and offer sacrifice. As I was saying, we were in Jerusalem, and then Elizabeth went straight up to Magdala, and sent me to get you."

"Where is she?"

"Do not worry, we will see her again in Magdala."

"Where is Magdala? Is it very far?"

"Once we are past Jerusalem, we will go North on the main road, through the valley. Here, have a look." With her graceful arm, she opened the purple curtain that covered the back of the carriage. I had a hard time keeping my balance, so Salome held my hand. I was just tall enough to see over the edge.

"Stretching out before you, receding with every moment, are the slopes of the rocky barren Wilderness. Look at the sky paling behind them! Look at the tiny clouds, pink as the ear of a new lamb."

After a while the carriage stopped and the man opened the back door for us. I could see him better now, with his wide grin inside his wide unkempt beard.

When Salome took me behind a bush, the man called out, "Why do you have to go all the way back there?"

"It is early yet," Salome said when we got back, "and the sun's next visit is but a faint promise, but we may not be the only travelers on the road."

I let go of Salome's hand and before anyone could stop me, I climbed on the carriage and then onto the large workhorse that was pulling us. Salome tried to coax me off, "Come down, I have some breakfast for you."

"I like this horse. Please?"

"I must say, Mary, you are beaming! What do you see from up there?"

"Everything!"

"Tell me one thing."

"I see the mountains are getting smaller in this direction," I said, pointing.

"We need to keep moving. Enough now!" the man went around the other side. Likely for sensing the man's impatience, the horse got nervous and stepped back. Salome yelped and stumbled.

"Now see what you have done!" the man yelled.

Salome got up, and with our driver's help got back inside the carriage. Then the man lifted me off the horse and set me beside Salome, who was holding her red swollen foot with both hands. I sat as far from her as I could.

"It is not my fault," I said very quietly.

Salome smiled without her eyes, "It is nothing, I am fine." She closed her eyes, and I thought she was falling asleep, except that she was breathing hard. I felt terrible. I tried to be as quiet and inconspicuous as possible. I had no pitted dates with me. Nothing to do. I waited for Salome's eyes to open.

As soon as they did, I asked, "Can I go back on the horse now?"

"Maybe later. Why not look out the curtains and tell me what you see?" She helped me to the back and sat behind me. "Look, the whole world is going away from us."

"Like Zanna? If something goes away, does it come back?"

"Oh yes, child, Zanna will be back, and soon. Everything that goes away comes back. It is just a matter of time. Like the sun comes up and goes down and comes back again."

"I know all about the sun. It came in my room."

"Oh did it now?" She tickled me. "Look, it is just crossing the horizon."

"I have never seen the sun go up. I have only seen it go down."

"Well of course. All the houses in Bethany face west, for shelter from the scorching summer winds from the desert in the east. It is only natural that you have never seen the sunrise." She freed her dark arm from inside her blue cloak and pointed with calloused brown fingers, "Look, golden pink clouds are getting brighter and brighter. Soon it will look like any other day."

"And then night again."

"Yes."

"I did not know the night was so big."

"What do you mean?"

"I thought nighttime was just in my room and the courtyard, because whenever I went out to the olive grove it was always day. I never saw night outside, until Zanna..."

I went deep inside the carriage and buried myself under the pillows. I felt Salome's hand on my back, up and down. After a little while, I came back out.

Then Salome gazed deeply into my eyes. "My child, you will see your Zanna again, if Our Creator wills it." Then she exhaled loudly. "Has anyone told you that you have your great-grandmother's stare? Your father's eyes, maybe, but your gaze, it silences one."

Salome got very quiet, then she started to weep. She pulled me on to her bony lap and rocked me while she cried.

"Salome?"

"Yes child?"

"Why do I have to go to Magdala?"

"Because that is where you belong. You will understand when you get there. It is one of those things."

"I have to pee again." She laughed a little and wiped her cheeks with her hands. Then she called out to the man, "Ezra! Time for another stop!"

"So soon! Children! All right, all right. Let me find a good spot."

When we stopped I jumped out and turned for Salome. She moved so slowly, and I had to go so badly! She tried to put her sandal on, but her foot had swollen too much.

I reached for her foot. "Let me..." She started to pull away, but I was quick. When my hands rested on her, she became still. I closed my eyes so I could see the colors. I felt the ground under my feet pushing up like a song. My hands warmed. When I opened my eyes, her foot was healed.

"Come on," I pulled her hand, looking for a bush.

She said, like a whisper, "Praise Astarte we did not wait a day longer. Is this the first time you..." She stopped herself mid-sentence. As she emerged from the carriage she mumbled, "Nothing. Nothing. Here, this thick boxwood bush will do nicely." Her hands were shaking when she held up my tunic. The bush smelled very green.

When we got back in the carriage she did not say anything, just looked at her foot.

"Are you going to be angry at me?"

"No love, why would I be angry? You healed my foot!"

"One time I was with Lazarus. Zanna came and saw the big scab on his knee was gone. She got so angry at him for picking it, but then she saw that his knee was all perfect. You could not even see the cut from where he fell on the jar. And Zanna yelled at me. She said never do that again."

"Love, Zanna only said that to protect you."

"Is that the secret?"

"Once we get to Magdala, we will talk about it all together, all right? But let me tell you, you did a good thing, and we are all very happy with you."

"I did a good thing?"

"Yes child, now come back in my lap, let me sing you a song."

> *Let him kiss me with the kisses of his mouth.*
> *for this love is better than wine.*
> *the King hath brought me into his chambers:*
> *we will be glad and rejoice.*
> *A bundle of myrrh is my well-beloved unto me;*
> *he shall lie all night between my breasts.*
> *My beloved is unto me as a cluster of camphor*
> *in the vineyards of En Gedi.*
> *Behold, thou art fair, my beloved, yea, pleasant: also our bed is green.*
> *I am the rose of Sharon, and the lily of the valleys.*
> *As the lily among thorns, so is my love among the daughters.*
> *As the apple tree among the trees of the wood,*
> *so is my beloved among the sons.*
> *My beloved is mine, and I am his: he feedeth among the lilies.*

"I know that song, that is Zanna's up-and-down song! She never sang it that way. That is a very long song!"

"That is only a small part of it child. It takes a long time to sing the whole Song of Songs."

"It takes a long time to get to Magdala too!" I stared out the back at the rolling hills, and so many people! I had not known there were so many. Then I saw a small group of unbearded men far behind us, but visible for their armor that shone like silver cups, atop tall horses. I asked Salome why some men did not have beards. She pulled me back inside and closed the curtain. Going to the front, she whispered something to Ezra. Then we started going faster.

Before I could ask what had just happened, Salome opened a box I had not noticed, for it had been hidden under a rug.

"Those are scrolls, are they not, Salome?"

"Yes child. Have you seen a scroll before? Would you like to hear this story?"

"What story?"

"The scroll I am holding."

"That is a story? Jacob said it was the Law."

"Sometimes the Law is a story. One of the things we do in Magdala is keep the sacred stories so no one will forget. We write fresh scrolls when the old ones get crumbly."

Salome unrolled the scroll and motioned for me to come sit in her lap. Her hand over mine, she moved my finger along the scroll while she told the story. She read to me the Psalm of Magdala, which scared me. I was glad it had a hopeful ending. I also found it hard to believe that inside the squiggles there were people, and towers, and crying – so many things! Salome said that when you could see all that, that was reading. When she was done, she rolled up the scroll and put it back in the box.

"So the Holy Ones of the desert are still inside the scroll?"

"You could say that."

"So even if you are not looking at it, they are still having a story?"

"That is right, child, that is why we write the story down. So the Holy Ones will live forever."

"They will live forever?"

"Yes."

"And if you write down my story I will live forever?" She did not answer, so I turned around in her lap to face her and asked her again, "If I am in a scroll I will live forever? I never have to go live in the earth? I can be in a scroll?"

Salome looked at me and bent her head to one side. "I have never seen a story written..."

"What's 'rittin?' "

"Written down means putting the story on the scroll. With ink and a reed. You will learn soon enough. That will be one of your tasks. But I have never seen a scroll of a story about a person while they were alive in the flesh, child. And anyway, no matter what happens, we all die."

"But Astarte and Yahweh do not die."

"Because they are Our Creator; They are Divine."

"So how do you become divine?"

"Mary hush your mouth. A mortal cannot become Divine."

"What is a mortal?"

"A person who dies, like you and me."

"So how do you know for sure? Have you tried? Have you 'rittin' the story of a person like you and me to see what happens?"

"You are making me dizzy with your questions. Turn back around and," she opened a different scroll, "let us read about Wise King Solomon. Pay attention now. You are going to need to learn how to read, and how to write too."

"Why?"

"Because you will need to know these stories in order to become... Because in Magdala we all have work, and yours will be mostly weaving and writing. Now. Let us look at this one..."

"This looks different. Is this the same as the other scroll?"

"Very good, Mary, the other was in Hebrew. This one is in Greek."

"What is Greek? What is Hebrew?"

"These are languages. Different people speak different languages when they come from different lands."

"Why?"

"There are many stories to explain how we all came to speak different languages, but in truth I do not think any one knows."

"Are we speaking a language?"

"Yes. We are speaking Aramaic."

"Are we from Armay-ick land?"

"It is a little complicated. There is no Aramaic land. We are from Magdala, in Galilee."

"I am not from Magdala; I am from Bethany."

"You were too little to remember, but you were born in Magdala. I was there."

"Did you know my mother Muriel?"

Salome sighed deeply. "Your mother was a very gentle woman. And she loved you and your father Jacob very much."

"It feels so funny that Jacob was my father and I was the baby girl. And Muriel, his wife he missed so much, that she was my mother."

Salome parted the back curtain and looked out. "Everyone has a lot of funny feelings about their mother and father, Mary."

"Martha and Lazarus are my brother and sister." When Salome did not respond, I asked, "When is Zanna coming?"

"She will come soon. She is from Magdala too, you know."

"She is? Why is she from Bethany if she is from Magdala?"

"That is a very good question, one that will be answered for you later, as you begin your studies."

"What are studies?"

"Studies are how you are going to know as much as me, and maybe more. You will learn how to read and write. As I have started to tell you, one of the purposes of Magdala is to protect the ancient scrolls, the ones those now ruling Jerusalem would destroy. Of course you will also have to learn how to weave. You will learn all about the world, about the Mysteries, about – "

"What is mis-trees?"

"That you will have to find out for yourself. Maybe we can guess a little about it from this story, now let us see, where were we? Ah yes, let us find out how Wise King Solomon built a Tower to Astarte..."

I grew quickly restless during that trip; though we stretched our legs at little at night and again in the morning, it was never enough. During the day, Salome read to me more stories, with evil kings, good kings, queens, and priestesses. She kept assuring me we were getting closer, but I started to believe Magdala was this road, and we would just keep going, with the stories and the bushes and the rolling hills.

Then one morning, after our short walk behind some rocks, Salome grinned widely at Ezra. "Tonight you will rest at home, Ezra! No more sleeping with one eye open, dear man."

Ezra leaned down and he and Salome held hands. It seemed to me an egg of light surrounded them. Then Salome picked me up and kissed me.

"What is tonight, Salome?"

"Mary, tonight we arrive in Magdala."

As I write those words, "Tonight we arrive in Magdala," I cannot help but shiver, and it is not because of the cold stone on which I sit in this library.

I warm myself by thinking of the day you arrived in Magdala, Jesus, so many years later. From the start you did everything wrong.

From the beginning, Jesus, you broke all our rules, broke them open and savored their sweet juice.

That bright morning of Shavuot eve, I was still the picture of a dutiful priestess of Magdala, a grown woman working at my loom, putting the finishing touches on Our Great Mother Goddess Astarte's sacred garment. To the outer eye, surely I appeared focused on weaving the white linen tunic before me, in the cool shade of the balcony, in rhythm with my partner of wood and leather and rope and clay. This tunic was seamless, as were all the clothes we made here – that was our specialty. The threads of pure linen flew between my hands, and the clay weights clinked in a rhythm that had long since merged with my own breath, merging too with the song of Salome's loom right behind mine, her supervisory position now only symbolic.

Anyone could think I was simply preparing for an ordinary Shavuot, the Festival of Wheat, when the Valley folk would come and bring us some of their first harvest of figs and wheat. Only my new friend Joanna knew that I had been weaving this fine linen tunic to wear for our ritual, yours and mine. For the past year, Joanna had been carefully, tenderly restoring my faith in the possibility of you, teaching me how to draw you to this day, after all the years of waiting and then the years of giving up waiting. For twelve moons I had done all the magic I knew to lure you down from your mountains, wondering all the while at the wisdom of cracking the comfortable husk of my resignation.

Across the courtyard, nestled against the external stone wall of the kitchen to keep an eye on the oven's fire, Zanna sang as she always did to grind wheat into flour for the day's bread and more for the night's feast. The millstone nestled between her strong squatting legs, her two brown hands on the wooden handle, she turned the upper stone disk over the lower one. She stopped periodically to pour grain through the hole in the center, in time with her song's chorus. Her rhythm was so steady she set the pace of my weaving, of the whole morning.

I could hear Zanna's daughter Abigail accompany her mother's song as she swept the balcony above the gate, exactly opposite the great tree. She was careful not to send any pebbles or chaff onto the veiled heads of Elizabeth and Hannah as they emerged from the storeroom. Their bowls full of frankincense, their walk full of whispers, they crossed the dusty courtyard toward the spreading oak, their foreheads almost touching as they murmured, daughter stooping to meet mother.

Up in the shady cedar grove, Maryanna tuned her lute for the night's festivities, singing a high clear note at exact intervals with Zanna's song, pulling an increasingly clear sound from her instrument. Tabitha, grown from simple child to simple woman, assisted Maryanna with an occasional harmony, as usual her mind half on the intricate embroidering in her lap, half inside herself as if listening to other voices.

One of the white doves that shared our human nest flew out from under the barn's roof to the flowing fountain in the middle of the courtyard, took a drink from its central spouting pillar, rested a moment on the edge of the wide basin and took off again, likely to its daytime roost in the woods beyond the grove.

Our Zanna was the first to see you cross the gate into the compound. The rhythm of her mill stopped, as did her song. That silence, followed by her shriek of delight, alerted us all, turned our heads in the direction of her run.

Abigail remained motionless on the balcony. Salome's loom went silent behind mine. Elizabeth and Hannah appeared at the threshold of the oak's shade. We took in your commanding gait with a single eye.

My heart raced – the sight of you – the crashing realization that our prayers had worked, the more devastating one that my hardened shell of outrage-turned-to-apathy could fall away in an instant, after seventeen long years, revealing me naked, shining.

Zanna grabbed you with both arms, stopped your course mid-courtyard, and patted your high wide shoulders, "Jesus my boy! Look at you big grown man! Look at you!"

You rested your hands lightly on her arms, saying, "And you Zanna, you have not changed one bit!"

"Foolishness! I am an old woman now! But you! Why did you not tell us you were coming! Nothing is ready for such a visit. Have you traveled all night? You do well to arrive on the eve of Shavuot, the festival of the wheat, you yourself are a tall ripe stalk of wheat!"

Your mother Maryanna flew down from the shade of the grove, her cloak falling off her head as songbirds flew from her mouth, "My son my son my son!" Maryanna took your offered hands. "Why did you not send a herald? Speak to me my son!"

"It is good to find you so well, Mother."

Maryanna's song-words drew the rest of the women near. Joanna emerged from the deep belly of the scroll room, ran to me and kissed my cheek in her excitement. Then she joined all the others who rushed to the spot where you stood. All except me – I had been stilled by Salome's ringed hand on my shoulder as she rose to greet you.

After nodding courteously to the gathering women, you walked deeper into the courtyard and paused at the flowing fountain. I watched your approach, sensed your men's palpable presence outside the gate.

On your shoulders rested the sun-drenched midnight blue cloak I had sent you, into which I had woven all my prayers. I turned to face you directly and found, under your dazzlingly white headscarf, your sparkling dark gaze.

From ten paces away, your slice of a grin could have stilled the wind. You rested against the stone lip of the fountain's basin. I drank in your sinewy brown arms crossed in front of you, your outstretched legs, your thickly-sandaled feet, pale from dust.

You looked nothing like the tender boy who touched my hand seventeen years before – how could you – nor like the other mountain men who brought down the wounded for healing, with their chest out, hair wild under their tattered headscarves, thick scarred hands on their jutting hips.

Eight counts I breathed in, eight counts held, eight counts exhaled, as Hannah had taught me.

Abigail arranged welcoming and restorative servings in the shade outside the kitchen, across the courtyard, and then brought a bowl to wash your feet. Did you not see her, as you had not broken eye contact with me since you gained it? Had you not heard your mother and Zanna tell you of the greeting being prepared for you?

Without rising from the edge of the basin, you unlaced your sandals and swung your legs over, immersing your dusty feet and calves into the cool flowing water. You removed your headdress, let it fall to the ground, revealing hair like mine, knotted and dark, tumbling down past your shoulders. You rolled up your long sleeves and, cupping the clear water in your broad dark hands, you splashed your face and throat, over and over again.

Only a few of us had ever seen a man bathe, definitely never in broad daylight, and most certainly not in public. You noticed the silence and turned, took in the stunned faces around you. Your bright laughter splashed out like the water you playfully sprayed on your mother and Zanna, who replied with surprised giggles and wasted no time in splashing back, until everyone joined in. Tabitha seemed to be drinking as much water as she was throwing, laughing so hard she could not close her mouth. Even Abigail entered the fray, though she was still shy after all these years, still not certain of her place. But you saw this and splashed her the most, until everyone was wet with mid-morning water and mirth.

Everyone but me. Everyone except Hannah and Elizabeth. I had actually forgotten about them. Hannah emerged from the great oak's shade and stopped, her wizened gnarled frame vibrant with dignity, and Elizabeth behind her, a tall shadow. Maryanna sensed them with the eyes on the back of her head and turned and suddenly you were all guilty children.

Pearls of light hung in your black-as-night beard while Hannah advanced on her three legs, two flesh-and-bone and one carved wood, shuffle and step, shuffle and step. The compound's unfamiliar daytime silence baked in the heat. No one but she moved. Not even Elizabeth, who stood motionless a few steps from the tree. Even the air was still, lending no breeze to press Hannah's stray white locks to the blue cloak pulled over her head.

Our most holy high priestess did not speak nor stop until she reached the basin, and you turned to face her. To our high priestess you deigned to bow your playful sober head, so you did not see the clever strangeness of Hannah's smile as she winked at Tabitha behind you, who rushed into the back of your knees while Hannah pushed you into the water with unexpected strength. You must have heard Hannah's laughter like a tiny child's when you re-emerged, and the game was on again.

I longed to join in, and yet I could not move, and it was no longer for the shadow touch of Salome's hand still on my shoulder, Salome who now had one foot in the basin and was half-soaked.

You sensed me then somehow; you turned and your eyes settled into mine, moved down to my throat and sauntered back up again.

You stepped out of the water, walked toward me, you began to speak your first words to me, but this Hannah would not have. I should not have been out for you even to see. Hannah stepped out in front of you, between us. Maryanna's bird-song on one side, and on the other Zanna's wide motherly hand in yours, you were pulled from me toward Abigail's feast-in-the-making across the courtyard. As your body turned away from me, your head did not, you said right to me,

"Mary."

My mouth fell open to see sunlight bounce off my name in your mouth, and then you were gone, forty long paces away, deep in the shade opposite me, where you and your men – whom Hannah inexplicably invited in – were offered three different mixtures of wine, four layers of rug to sit on, five different kinds of olives. When at last you sat and folded your legs under you, your back was turned slightly from me, but I could still see your smile crease the corners of your eyes when you turned to listen to your men.

Then Elizabeth dropped a veil from the balcony above my head, curtaining me off from all sights save my loom and the great oak beyond it. Salome returned to me and to her loom, Zanna began again her song at her mill, and the day returned to order, more shining and buzzing than before.

The sound of my name in your voice like a dove cooing remained in my ear all day. It spread a heat, a lightness, a tension through my whole body, into my toes and fingertips, making me wish there was more of me into which this feeling could spread. I was taut as a drum.

Till night came, and your knock on my door, soft like thunder.

What a great distance from that mirthful bath to the solemn one at which I first met all these women! And to that time I must return. For while I have yet to understand how to make this amulet perfect, I believe I know how to make it complete.

My first memory of Magdala is of Salome waking me in the gray dawn, the two of us alone in a large room full of rolled up blankets lined across the far wall. I must have slept through our arrival. Salome brought me downstairs to the courtyard. By the gurgling fountain – wonder of wonders – she introduced me to a young woman named Dinah and her little sister Ariella, who silently offered me a small piece of fresh bread still warm from the oven. Salome explained this would not happen again: breakfast came after the bath, not before. Allowances were being made for my first day. Even after all our dry traveling food, the delight of eating fresh bread was overwhelmed by my fascination with the fountain's spurting water. I wanted to linger and explore the courtyard, but Salome scooped me up as soon as I had swallowed my last bite.

As we passed the great oak I twisted and turned toward the compellingly cool and fragrant tree. But Salome carried my squirmy five-year-old self up the steps in the mountain behind the great oak. When we reached the natural hot spring basin, carved into the rock of Mount Arbel's cliffs, Salome set me down, disentangling her hair from my hands. Before us stood a group of women and one large girl, all wearing blue cloaks pulled over their hair, and tunics white like Salome's, like mine, I realized, my tunic having been changed in my sleep, from the raw wool one I had always worn to this soft white wonder.

My breakfast began to curdle in my stomach at the sight of all these people staring at me, and more so even at the sight of the steaming hot water beyond them. What creature was to be cooked that so large a pot was needed? I pressed myself to Salome's still unfamiliar legs.

"Welcome, my child, welcome to Magdala." How fitting that Hannah was the first to utter these words, Hannah with sparkling black eyes and sparkling white hair curling out from under her cloak. I knew her immediately.

"You are my moon lady! You are the one who tells me secret things in my dreams!"

Hannah put her knobby hand on my shoulder and smiled with her whole face, just like in my dreams. When she kissed my head, I was awash in the spice-scent that also exuded from the great oak tree in the courtyard.

"Yes, Mary, I am Hannah, and I have visited you in your dreams. Welcome, welcome home at long last." She kissed my cheeks again and again.

"Enough coddling, Mother, that will do." Elizabeth stepped in; I recognized her hair, so black and long and flat like rain; I remembered the courtyard in Bethany, the safety of Zanna's arms. I remembered her harsh tones. I clung to Salome.

"My dear granddaughter..." A very ancient woman spoke, and Elizabeth immediately looked down at the ground. This unfamiliar voice made me think of the table in the big room, smooth on top and bumpy on the bottom. "We are all most grateful for the risks you and Zacharias took in bringing our Sacred Marriage Ritual to Jerusalem for the first time in so many generations, albeit in secret and in hiding. Nevertheless, nothing could earn you the right to interrupt your elders. That is certainly the wrong lesson to teach our newcomer." The crone turned to me, "Mary, this impertinent person is Elizabeth, daughter to my daughter Hannah."

The tall young priestess remained silent and still.

"Elizabeth," the grandmother continued, "since you are so eager to speak, why not proceed with the introductions, this time with some deference and courtesy?"

Elizabeth nodded and stepped forward. "Yes, Deborah. Thank you. Now," she looked down on me from her great height, "Mary, let me present you to your many mothers and sisters. First, our high priestess, my grandmother, Quedeshah Deborah."

Deborah smiled as big as the sky and kissed me like a butterfly. "Welcome, Mary. You may call me Deborah."

"You smell like the big tree, like Hannah."

"Yes, Mary, I sit under the tree all day with my daughter Hannah and my granddaughter Elizabeth."

"It smells so good under there!"

"That is because we make our incense there."

"Can I come and make sense with you?"

Deborah laughed one way, and Elizabeth laughed another. The younger woman said, "Learn one thing right now, Mary: you do not ask for things here. You take what is given."

I swallowed a cry for my Zanna.

"Elizabeth!" Deborah exclaimed. "Jerusalem has surely gone to your head! Or is it Zacharias? Since when do you answer a question posed to me?"

Elizabeth blushed and looked away. Following her gaze I saw for the first time the great expanse of the Lake of Galilee, smooth as polished stone in the pre-dawn light, and pink as Elizabeth's cheeks now were.

My mouth filled with more questions, to begin: what is that vast shining thing?

But Deborah turned back to me, "You can always come and sit with me, but not when I am under the tree. That is a special time, and a special place. You will have your own special times and places."

"It is so nice under the tree!"

"Ask me again next year."

A whole year!

Elizabeth whispered loudly, "How can a child learn respect when we no longer use the sacred names? Why should she not call you at least Quedeshah Deborah, or Her Holiness, or something of that ilk?"

Deborah smiled in a funny way and touched Elizabeth's cheek with her hand, thin like twigs. "How can the child learn respect when she sees a daughter interrupt her mother and question the judgment of her high priestess and grandmother? Where did you learn this?"

Elizabeth pulled her face away. Her eyes stayed open, but they seemed to be looking inside, not out.

"Hannah," Deborah asked, smiling more broadly now, "would you proceed with the introductions?"

"Yes Mother, thank you. Now then," Hannah's big eyes shining on me, "you know that your great-grandmother Rebecca has gone into the earth."

"Yes." I pressed myself to Salome again. "She went to bring Jacob to my mother."

Hannah's white thick eyebrows arched high, but she continued as before.

"This is Phebe, sister to Rebecca." A cloud of dark gray hair around a long sad face descended on me like a storm. Phebe's dry, quick kiss landed more on my ear than my cheek. She lingered there, then pulled back with misty eyes and said,

"You look just like your mother did at your age."

Before I could ask one of the questions cascading through my mind, Phebe stepped back, and Hannah continued. "And this is Rachel, sister to Salome whom you have already met. Salome and Rachel are both daughters of Judith, who is in Jerusalem right now."

Rachel stood as tall as Salome, with the same red hair, but a much rounder face. She smelled different from everyone else, like wood before it goes in the oven. She kissed the top of my head, inhaling me as she did.

I wanted to ask her about the dark stains on her fingertips, but she stepped back, and Hannah went on, "And this is Tabitha, daughter of Rachel and granddaughter of Phebe."

Her hand on the back of the child's head, Rachel pushed forward a tall girl with a flat face. Tabitha just looked at her feet, then turned into Phebe's tunic and buried her face there. Phebe held the girl's shoulders with both hands.

Hannah smiled wistfully and said, "And this is my younger daughter, Maryanna." Maryanna crouched all the way down to be at eye-level with me. She took both my hands and looked at me square in the face. She looked like her sister Elizabeth but had dense curly hair, fuller cheeks and laughing eyes.

"Welcome, Mary, welcome to Magdala. If there is something you need, come and find me. I do not mind if you ask me for things. I am almost always up in the cedar grove."

"Where is the grove?"

She pointed behind me. I turned and saw a circle of trees that looked to me like round olive trees with the long graceful branches of the cypress.

"It looks nice in there," I said, and Maryanna hugged me. She smelled like a cypress tree, like home, and I squeezed her back. She made me feel so good I was emboldened to ask her, "Do you know my Zanna? Do you know when she will come get me?"

"Yes I know your Zanna, and yes, she will be here as soon as she can. But she will not come to get you; she will come to live here. You are going to stay here and learn how to be a priestess."

"What is a pistiss?"

"Enough questions for now," Elizabeth said in her voice high above us. "The introductions are complete."

Salome took my hand. "All will be answered in time, Mary. No secrets will be kept from you," she said very softly, the way Zanna would say "goodnight."

Maryanna took my other hand, saying, "It is now time for our bath."

Zanna used to give me my bath the morning before Shabbat, with water from the well, which she warmed in a stone bowl in the oven.

"Will you give me my bath?" I asked Salome.

"Our Great Mother Goddess gives us all our bath."

Zanna's wet rag always tickled me, and I imagined a great big moon lady coming down from the sky, or maybe from the mountain, making me and Salome and Maryanna laugh under our tunics with her wet cloth. I thought, maybe this place will be all right.

"Will the Great Mother Goddess get angry if I laugh when she gives me my bath? Zanna did. She said I was impossible."

"Let us find out, shall we?" Salome said. "Here we are."

"This big thing is a bath? Why are there clouds on it?"

"Because it is very hot."

"Did you put it in the oven?"

"No, Mary, this is how it comes out of the mountain." We went right up to the edge of the water. "You are already barefoot. That is good. If you were not, I would ask you to remove your sandals."

She and Maryanna let go of my hands, and they both took off their sandals. Then they removed their smooth brown leather belts and their blue cloaks. They put these over the pale limestone railing that bordered the bath's basin. Just beyond it, the Lake's smooth surface mirrored the paling sky, down in the Valley.

"What is that?" I asked Salome, pointing.

"What? The Lake? Oh, that is the Lake of Galilee, Mary. It is like a great big bath of cool water."

"That is all full of water! Can we go there?"

"Maybe another time," Maryanna answered, exchanging glances with Salome. Then they both took my hands. "Now come with us."

They went in the water, down the basin steps up to their knees. I put one foot in.

"It is hot! It is very very hot!" I got right out.

Salome squeezed my hand. "Yes, child, that is all right, you will get used to it, just a little at a time."

She said it so nicely I wanted to try. I put one foot in, then the other, counted one two three, and came right out again. The air felt good and cool on my feet.

Salome and Maryanna let my hands go. "That is all right, Mary, just stay on the edge as best you can, so you keep your feet wet and touch the water with us."

I watched the rest of the women and little Tabitha take off their sandals, their brown belts and blue cloaks and put them on the railing just as Salome and Maryanna had. All in white, they went in down the steps. Some went in to their waist; some went in all the way until they disappeared and came back up, hair glistening wet.

I sat on the cool stone and played with the hot water, holding my fingers and toes in for as long as I could stand. In and out, in and out.

Deborah waded in until her head looked like it was floating on the water. With her scant pale hair plastered wet against her scalp, she looked bald. The women all faced the pale blue Lake and the purple mountains beyond, their backs to the sheer looming cliffs of Mount Arbel.

"Now then," Deborah looked up at the sky and raised her hands. Her tunic sleeves fell back to reveal strong tanned forearms, which surprised me, considering her twig-like hands. The others followed her lead, lifting their hands to the sky and tilting their heads back. Keeping my feet at the edge of the water, I held up my hands too but I could not keep my eyes closed. I wanted to see everything.

"Let us pray," Deborah's voice sounded like it was coming out of the mountain itself. She chanted:

> *Oh Great Mother Astarte, Oh Great Father Yahweh*
> *You hear us and You do not ignore us,*
> *For we are Your beloved Daughters in whom You are well pleased.*
> *We have received in safety the one You returned to us,*
> *and we share with her these primordial waters*
> *from which we were born,*
> *from whose chaos and destructive force You keep us.*

Then everyone intoned the chorus, which they repeated together throughout the prayer,

> *Our Most Blessed Lady, Our Almighty Lord*
> *You hear us and You do not ignore us, for we are Your Daughters.*

Then Deborah alone,

> *This is our covenant with You.*

You have found us worthy to guide this one into her fullness.
Let our eyes be open to see the path of Your Righteousness before us,
our ears open to hear Your Wisdom.

The steam off the water caressed my face like a veil. Little rainbows danced between the women. When I looked at Deborah more carefully, I noticed a pendant around her neck, something no one else had. A small dark cylinder, on a silver cord around her neck. The sight of it made my heart race; I hungered for it instantly, inexplicably, savagely. I stared at it as the prayer grew in intensity and volume.

Oh Great Mother She Who Is, Oh Great Father He Who Is
You hear us and You do not ignore us, for we are Your Daughters.

Let us be both merry and solemn in the tasks before us.
Let us not forget our responsibility to each other, to ourselves,
and to all those whom You send our way.
Help us obey Your Commandments that Your Will be fulfilled.

Oh Great Mother Astarte, Oh Great Father Yahweh
You hear us and You do not ignore us, for we are Your Daughters.

Open our inner eye to the vision of what will yet be,
that we may ever be instructed by Your True Will,
and not our own multiplicity of desire.
Let there be harmony in our hearts, harmony among us,
that our cup may run over and this harmony flow
into the homes and fields of those for whom we pray.

Deborah took a little bowl from the side of the basin, filled it with water from the bath, and poured it over the far side of the basin edge, down the mountain. She did this three times, praying all the while.

Oh Great Mother Astarte, Oh Great Father Yahweh

You hear us and You do not ignore us, for we are Your Daughters.
We pour this ablution out in honor of the Sacred Truth
that all that we are and all that we have,
in the end find their way back to You, Blessed Art Thou.
Oh Great Mother Astarte, Oh Great Father Yahweh!
Grant us the trampling underfoot of our enemy
who would keep us alive only to drink our flowing blood.
Grant us the courage to be merciless, the means to be triumphant,
in Your Name.
Amen.

Everyone said "Amen" together, so I said it too. Then they immersed themselves in the water, and for a moment, I was alone. As they came out of the bath, in passing they touched my head, except Elizabeth who had both hands on her belly.

Deborah came out last and stopped in front of me. My heart pounded in my ears. I pointed and asked, "What is that?"

She clasped her pendant and looked down at me. Salome stood near me; I could feel her eyes on my head.

"This is my signet, the signet of the high priestess," Deborah answered.

"Why is it all scratched?"

"The symbol of our power is etched in it."

"Where did you get it?"

"From the one on whose neck it hung before mine. She took it off and placed it on me."

"Why do you have one and nobody else?"

"It is the mark of our high priestess."

"What is a high pistiss?"

" 'Preess-tess.' That is who I am and all that I do."

"How come?"

"Because I was chosen, and I accepted."

"How come?"

"You have a great many questions, little one," Deborah answered, as Salome picked me up, "which will all be answered in time."

Now that I was high enough, I did not hesitate. I reached out and grabbed hold of the dark object of my desire. It felt so good that I closed my eyes. I saw so many things, so many colors, so many people and places going by faster even than those I saw from the carriage.

Then I let go because it burned! Even more than the water! Even more than when I healed Salome's foot.

"Why is everything so hot here?"

Deborah put her hand on her signet. Her eyes widened. She did not answer me.

I asked Salome. "How come it gets so hot?" I showed her my hand which was all red, hoping she would lick it and blow on it like Zanna did when I accidentally touched something near the oven.

But Salome did not answer me either. Instead she asked Deborah, "What is it?"

Deborah touched my hand and felt the dissipating heat. She asked me, "Do your hands always get so hot?"

"When the colors go through me, when there is a hurt, when I touched Lazarus, and then Salome too where the horse stepped on her foot. But they never got hot before when I touched a thing that was not hurt."

Then all of the sudden Deborah put her olive branch arms around Salome and me. Deborah seemed small now; her face rested on my back. "Maybe we are in need of your healing, little one! Praise Astarte we brought her here in time," Deborah said so softly I thought I was the only one who could hear. Her hair smelled good up close.

When she let us go, I licked my own hand and blew on it. "Why do you have a hot thing on your neck? Is it hot like that all the time? Does it burn you too?"

Deborah whispered with eyes shining, "No, Mary. Just you, just now." Then she called to the others in her big prayer voice, "Come back! Come back! She *is* the one we have hoped for! She *is*!"

I could feel she was talking about me. What did it mean? I held on tight to Salome, who felt hard like a tree. The others came back up the path, all talking at the same time.

Hannah held up a hand for quiet. She asked, "Mother, what

happened?"

"Little one," Deborah said to me, "show them your hand." I held up my hand, which was still a little red from the signet. "She grabbed hold of the signet, and it heated in her hand, almost to burning. She tells me her hands heat when she heals."

"That is true," Salome said, moving and softening all of the sudden, "when she healed my foot on the trip up here, it got very warm. I was so moved that she was a healer I did not think of the heat."

Deborah spoke again in her booming voice, " '*The Queen will issue from the broken healer, Her King from the seer blind. They will be born of love not fate, though their fate is love. One will burn. One will fly.*' Rebecca's hands cooled when she healed. My sisters, we have among us one who '*burns.*'

"My sisters in Astarte," Deborah continued as she pulled my hand up high by my wrist, "we have our Queen, who will save our nation of Israel and with her King restore peace to the land. My sisters and daughters, the time to reclaim the Holy City is close at hand. This is indeed a holy day."

Everyone talked at once and gathered in close to touch my head and my feet. A round of murmured prayers surrounded me like a breeze. I hid my face in Salome's hair from where I could see Elizabeth look at me, her smooth face small and tight, and her hands flat at her side.

Few of Deborah's words meant anything to me; I had no notion of queen or nation or peace. Nor did her pronouncement affect how we spent that day, or any other day. We all rose before dawn, worked all day at our tasks and chores and, by sundown, fell onto our mats in the common sleeping room, exhausted.

Upon awakening, we headed straight for the bath before the sun crossed into the sky. Breakfast was a rushed affair, done standing around the kitchen – a bit of olive oil-soaked bread, some hard cheese, and water, while the chickens pecked around our feet for crumbs.

Dinah and Ariella took care of the kitchen and all that went with it – keeping the oven going, grinding flour, making bread, minding the chickens and the goats, tending the garden and preparing all our food. They kept track of our storeroom with a list of all we needed that we could not make, such as grain, oil, olives, wine and fish, which would be purchased at the town's market by Phebe. Having been rescued from possible slavery at worst or starvation at best, Dinah and Ariella's gratitude for the sanctuary of Magdala shone in everything they did. One discerned this from their actions and gazes, for neither spoke a word.

Rebecca had found them nine years before, on one of her rare house calls into the lakeshore town of Tarichaea. On her way, she passed a small house with a broken-down door. Lured by the terrible unmistakable smell, which likely had kept away all other passersby, she entered to find the rotting headless corpse of a man and that of a whole, but obviously ravaged woman.

Something moved furtively under a pile of blankets; Rebecca pulled them back to discover an ashen but breathing ten-year-old girl holding her soiled toddler sister. Rebecca cleaned the silent girls from water drawn at their well, as best she could with the older one refusing to let go of the baby. The healer abandoned her house call and brought the girls back up to Magdala. As they would not speak to name themselves, Rebecca introduced the older one as Dinah, which means "vindicated," for the revenge there was in simply surviving, and the small girl as Ariella, which means "lioness of Our Creator," to give her strength. It fell to Ezra, our erstwhile driver, to collect the parents' bodies, and it was Ezra too who collected from their neighbors the all-too-common story of their death: the tax collector not getting his hefty bribe, a squad sent in to "set an example."

Rebecca saw to it that the girls' parents received a decent burial, with new stone ossuaries that were placed in the town cemetery, not of course at Tel Rapha, the "hill of the healed," our sacred hill of the dead reserved for our own kin and holy bloodlines.

Zanna, who told me the whole story years later, told me she too had been rescued by the women of Magdala, but she never would tell me how. The girls came under her wing in the kitchen, and she gave them the same tender care she later gave me. By the time Zanna left with my infant self for Bethany, the adopted girls had been in Magdala for four years, and Dinah was well able to take over Zanna's tasks, including tending her little sister, with whom she shared a language of hands known only to them.

They were excluded from all ritual activity, except our baths once a week on Shabbat eve and our new moon time sitting in the grove, once a month. As far as one could tell, this seemed to suffice them.

That first summer I often envied them and longed for the simplicity of their tasks. I knew how to do most of what they did, but I did not know how to spin, and I was sure I would never learn. Directly after breakfast, that first morning and everyday after that, Salome brought Tabitha and me to the weaving corner under the balcony where I ruined thread after thread of wool as I tried to master this impossible task. I could roll the raw wool between my fingers well enough. Salome would then stand me on a small stool to give me enough height to twirl the spindle. When she demonstrated, her spindle spun so fast around the thread, that it did not seem to be moving. Tabitha did it too, and even she made it look easy.

But when I tried, the thread would break, causing the spindle to drop to the dusty ground. Salome did not get impatient; she said this was normal. I would learn in time. She was not very encouraging either. Everything she did was simply steady and measured, and I could never figure out how to make her smile at me the way she had in the carriage.

The best I did that whole summer was to make the spindle turn three whole times before the thread broke. I had much more fun rolling the thread, especially when Salome went back to her standing loom and its clay weights. Her back to us, she did not see Tabitha entertain me with funny faces while she spun and I rolled.

When Tabitha ran out of funny faces, I thought of my Zanna and how much I missed her. I thought of all the things I would tell her when she arrived. Daily I pestered Salome with questions of "When?" only to be answered, "Soon." I wanted to tell Zanna about our daily bath that did not tickle, about the spinning that was so hard, and about all the other things I was learning and seeing.

I wanted to tell her how every single night, when the sun began to set behind Mount Arbel, a mighty wind came off the Lake, strong enough to set straight whatever portion of woven fabric was hanging off the back of the loom. I could barely keep my cloak pulled over my head as I ran up to the grove, where we were most exposed to the weather. As soon as I heard thunder I would race up there, because it offered the best view of the lightning that flashed across the great expanse of the stone gray Lake. I had to be quick, because sometimes the storms came and went so fast, by the time I got up to the grove the sky was already clearing.

The wind died down by nightfall. Soon after I arrived in Magdala, it got so hot at night that we abandoned our common room for the wide flat roof, with its high protective ledge. There we slept under the stars. From the roof we could hear people moving in the woods around us. Salome told me they were Yudah's men, here to protect us, but she would not tell me from what. She did not seem very worried, so I did not think about it much.

The coolest I felt all day was in the mornings, right after the hot bath. The soft morning air caressed my skin still prickling from the steaming waters into which I soon learned to immerse myself for at least one breath. But by the time I was spinning with Salome, my tunic was dry, and I welcomed the balcony's shade.

Despite the heat, I preferred the mornings I was called to help Phebe outside. Phebe had no special healing ability as her sister Rebecca had had, but she prepared herbal infusions for the Valley folk to drink in each season, to keep away whatever malady the hot or then the damp weather was wont to bring.

When Phebe appeared with her long face and vast cloud of dark gray hair besides Salome's loom, she always exchanged a few words with her niece before holding out her hands to Tabitha and me. We came running. Phebe made herb-gathering a game. She would show us a long silver-green leaf and say, "This is sage. Can you go and find me some more?" And we would run all around, up to the grove, around the bath, on either side of the great tree, and in the garden next to the kitchen. I learned that it helped to smell the leaf first, to avoid coming back with the wrong kind. At twelve years of age, Tabitha was a faster runner than I, but she had a much harder time remembering where the herbs grew or which one was which. I learned fast, but I pretended not to know what I did, and I followed Tabitha's uncertain lead to get that much more time away from spinning.

Sometimes we had to bring back just the leaves, and sometimes we had to bring back the whole plant, with as much root as possible. Once, entranced by its large red petals and black center, I picked a huge poppy as a gift for Phebe. Tabitha told me not to touch it, but I did not listen. Who could resist such a big pretty flower!

"Never touch those!" Phebe knocked the flower from my hand. It was the only time she ever raised her voice at me.

"But why? It is so pretty!"

"Those are special for Elizabeth."

"But she never picks flowers," I protested, "she is all day long under the tree!"

"She will pick them at the end of summer when the petals are gone, and the bulb is ripe."

"When the petals are gone?" I did not have much reason to like Elizabeth, and now I had less. Who would want a flower without petals? What could I know then of the special dream-inducing substance that would be extracted from the boisterous-looking poppy flower?

"Mary, promise you will never do that again," Phebe said in her more customary gentle tones. When I nodded, she petted my head and bent down to kiss me. "Oh you are so like your mother! Even as a girl, she always wanted to know why this and why that, never accepting things the way they were. It got her into trouble, the best of which was you, dear girl. Now, Mary, look at this," showing me a curled up dried green leaf. "It is mint. It likes water. See how many leaves you can bring back before the sun is too high."

The mornings passed much more quickly if I spent them gathering herbs instead of trying to spin. And soon as I started working with Rachel, the afternoons disappeared in the blink of an eye. Salome's sister came one high noon and rescued me from a miserable day of crumbly wool and dusty spindle. When Rachel took me into the deliciously cool barn, I thought with delight that we were going to climb on the mules. But instead Rachel pulled back a blanket on the far back wall to reveal a narrow door, with a thick leather strap for a handle. She had to use both hands to pull it open, and when it moved she made a 'hunh!' sound that I came to associate with the door opening. Later Dinah made the same noise, and so it seemed to me for years that it was the wood speaking.

I had not noticed the small lamp Rachel had in her hand until she lifted it to illuminate the dark corridor we entered. I remembered something Salome had said to me on the carriage ride.

"Is this the Mysteries?" I asked.

Rachel laughed in the shadows. "Not exactly, Mary, but close, close."

I felt like we walked forever, but I realized later it was only about ten paces. At the end of the passage Rachel easily opened a small door and touched her lamp to a torch set in the wall. The whole room appeared to me at once. An entire wall was built with shelves, filled floor-to-ceiling with scrolls. A longer table than I had ever seen occupied almost the entirety of the room. Three wooden stools beside it made me think of Zanna's kitchen in Bethany.

The smooth solid walls around the scrolls confused me by appearing at once familiar and foreign.

"I never saw a wall like that before. Who made it, Rachel?"

"Our Creator made it, love. That is the rock of Mount Arbel. The underground part."

I touched it and then walked up and down the room and counted. "Twenty of my paces, that is ten Salome paces." This was something else I wanted to tell Zanna. Sometimes instead of spinning, Salome taught me to walk with my eyes up and chin straight and to count my steps, and then her steps over the same distance. I had learned to count all the way to twenty, and to understand the words "double" and "half" as the difference between our paces.

"Rachel, why do we have so many scrolls? Why do some of them look so old and cracked? What is inside them? Have you read them all? Will you read them to me, like Salome did in the carriage?"

"These are our sacred texts, Mary, and the sacred texts of others put here for safekeeping. Some are from Egypt. Some are from Babylon." She pointed to some way up at the top. "Those were the scrolls your father Jacob was keeping for us."

I remembered Jacob showing them to Martha and Lazarus and not me. "I do not care about scrolls. Scrolls are stupid."

"Well, you have to read them before you can know whether or not they are stupid. But most of these are our sacred texts, and those are neither stupid or smart, they are just – "

"I am not going to read anything."

"That is what I said when I first came here. And now I have read them all. You will learn to read and write too, and in time you will read them all for yourself."

"I cannot read."

"Once I did not know how either, but my mother Judith taught me. And so I learned."

"You learned how to read all this?"

"Yes, Mary, and so will you. Shall we begin then?"

"All right."

I wanted to sit in her lap, but we each sat on our own stool. Rachel smelled even better than the mint leaves I picked for Phebe. I snuggled close to her, for warmth as much as comfort in this chilly enclave. On the table before me, she placed a clay tablet, which she softened with some water from a bowl on the table. She placed a thin reed in my hand. She wrapped her cool smooth hand around mine and moved it with the reed on the tablet. We made a mark together! She told me it was an "M", the first letter of "Mary" and of "Magdala", then she left me to practice on my own. When I made a mistake, or when I filled the tablet, she would put a little bit of water on the tablet and smooth my marks away.

I learned first to write my name and the name of everyone I knew. Once she had taught me a new letter or word, Rachel returned to her own task of copying the fading, cracking scrolls onto fresh papyrus, her careful ink-stained fingers moving quickly across the pages color of rock. Sometimes she asked me to watch her, and she read aloud the stories that appeared in the squiggles she made.

Rachel would tell me everyday that I was making good progress. She looked so much like Salome, but her eyes smiled more. Even when her mouth was serious, as it was when she looked over my clay tablet, she was never grim. During one of these moments, I noticed something white and shining in her hair.

"What is that?" I tried to touch it, but she covered the object with her ink-free palm.

"That is my alabaster comb. Mother gave it to me."

"Who is your mother?"

"My mother is Judith. She lives far away, in Jerusalem. I miss her sometimes, and this is a little like having her with me."

I wished I had something from Zanna. And from Jacob too. Then I remembered something, "If Salome is your sister, does she have a comb too?"

Rachel's face changed, and I felt bad for asking. "She had a comb. But then she put it in the earth with her miscarried baby."

"Salome had a baby?"

With a sharp look, Rachel put an end to my questions.

"I am sorry," I whispered, feeling as though I had done something wrong.

"Do not be sorry love, you did not know," she said softly. "Please, never speak of this, especially to Salome." Then she gave me a kiss on the head. "Let us begin something new today. It is time to write sentences. Let us begin with the Song of Songs."

"What is the Song of Songs?"

"Surely you know it, it is the very best song: '*Let him kiss me with the kisses of his mouth.*' "

"That is Salome's song! And Zanna's up-and-down song!"

"It is everyone's song. And one of our most sacred texts. Now, you are going to learn a lot of new words, so pay attention."

While we were working, Dinah came in to bring us water for Rachel's ink and for my tablet. She came almost every day, sometimes several times a day, such as when fresh new papyrus was delivered. It smelled bright green like a strange forest. Sometimes Dinah went down the corridor more deeply into the darkness carrying something, and returned empty-handed. I was very curious about where she went, as the corridor to the library seemed to end at its door. Rachel often encouraged Dinah to linger with us on her way back, offering the adolescent a stool of her own. At first Dinah refused, gesturing silently about the endless tasks of the kitchen. But in time, Rachel got her to stay, longer and longer, until Dinah was writing almost as well as Rachel. They would stay there late into the night; after walking me out to the barn to find my way to dinner, they would go back inside, not to be seen until they woke up next to me on the roof the next day.

Dinner was much better than breakfast. We had the day's fresh bread, dried fish, some cucumber or eggplant mixed with goat's yogurt and dill, fresh figs and grapes, and chicken for Shabbat. We ate all together on thick rugs in the courtyard, next to the kitchen, under the balcony across from the weaving, right where you and your men ate, that day of your return.

That day of your return.
I must not linger there, not until I have traced the full path.

One morning when I was practicing not dropping the spindle, Hannah came to whisper to Salome at her loom. Hannah had not talked to me much since my first day in Magdala, but I remained fascinated by my living moon lady. From my weaving corner I had a clear sight line of the three seers as they sat under the spreading terebinth oak that dominated our courtyard.

In addition to making the incense we burned and sold, Hannah, Elizabeth, and Deborah also welcomed the women from the lake-shore village of Tarichaea and beyond. These came to sit at the edge of the tree, to tell of their dreams and the signs they had seen, and to hear interpretations. This is also where women came to request amulets and special prayers.

The village women were not allowed to interact with anyone else in the compound, and they were not allowed to touch the seers. They would sit just outside the shade of the great oak tree. Having heard their petition, Deborah, seated just inside the tree's shade on her three-legged stool, would throw the shiny divination stones she called the Umim and Thummim, which lived in the pouch at her belt. She, Hannah or Elizabeth would interpret the stones in relation to the village woman's concern. The request for a written amulet would be passed on to Rachel. Once her request had been granted, the woman would then make an offering, such as a small jar of oil or a ball of wool. Sometimes the women received one of the doves that nested in the barn, or a cone of incense, along with a set of prayers to speak each day.

I was not allowed under the tree, but I watched all this in the shadows and silhouettes from where I stood, trying to spin. By the morning Hannah came and talked with Salome, I was deeply in awe of her. I was also worried because I thought she may have found out about me climbing on the mules in the barn after my lessons with Rachel. I strained to hear them speak, but I could not make out everything. Salome said, "no it's too soon" and Hannah said, "we have no choice" and Salome said, "too young" and Hannah said, "Deborah says now."

They said more I could not hear, and some I could not understand. Salome's eyebrows furrowed the way they did when she saw me drop the spindle. Then Hannah held her hand out for me. I took it and followed. To my delight and amazement she led me under the fragrant oak. It was so cool there, cooler than in the shade of the balcony, despite the little lamp that burned in the brass bowl next to the immense tree trunk.

Deborah and Elizabeth did not look at me. They sat facing each other on a stone bench, rolling in their hands the dark purple incense they took from a large gray bowl between them, rocking slightly, mumbling together words I could not make out. The heady perfume was overpowering and made me want to sit down.

But Hannah did not invite me to sit. Instead, she opened the little pouch that was at her belt, took out a small knife, and cut her arm until it bled. I looked for help to Deborah and Elizabeth, but they did not look up from their bowl.

"There," Hannah said as she stretched her arm out to me. I put my hands over it and closed my eyes, but nothing happened. No colors. No music. No warmth. When I took my hands off, she was still cut and bleeding. But Hannah was neither angry nor scared.

She said, "All right then, come with me." She took my hand and brought me up the steps to the grove. Hannah walked very fast, and I kept up as best I could. She was still bleeding; some of her blood dripped in my hand, dripping past my wrist. We were at the last steep step, about to enter the grove.

"Hannah, your blood is coming out on the ground!"

She turned and looked at me strangely. "Who told you about bleeding in the grove?"

"No one." I felt as if I had done something wrong. She reached for some thick leaves in her belt pouch to shore up her cut. Then she crouched down and said,

"This is a good thing, Mary; the memories of your lineage are stirring. Yes, the grove is where we come and sit and bleed with our new moon. Only a living blood can feed this grove."

"What is a living blood?"

"A living blood is that which comes from a living woman; it can pour like a fountain back into the earth. Do not look so scared! You will understand in time. But a dying blood, the blood that comes from one who is returning to Our Creator's womb, that blood must never be permitted to defile this grove. The consequences would be terrible."

Before I could ask another question, we were off again. Hannah took me to the other side of the cedar trees, where a cypress forest began. Hannah did not let go of my hand as we walked up the narrow trail, and I was glad because I was tripping left and right over loose rocks. When at last we stopped, Hannah pointed behind me. I turned and saw everything: the three limestone sides of the pale courtyard and the fourth, which was the top of the green oak tree; white chickens running around, Dinah's curly dark hair as she fetched water from the fountain, the whole golden valley that rolled into the great blue Lake, and the dusky mountains on the far shore.

"Look here, little one," Hannah called.

Behind us was a cave big enough for me to walk in and out of without banging my head. Inside, it was dark and smelled like rain and yeast.

"This is the cave where you were born. Your mother was born here too, and so was I, and Elizabeth, and Maryanna, and Rachel, and Salome too."

"And Zanna?"

"No, Zanna was born in the valley."

"Salome says Zanna is coming soon."

"Yes Mary, I know. She will be very happy to see you."

"Yes," and I felt all warm inside, thinking about it.

"And look at this." Hannah showed me the waterspout at the

mouth of the cave. "This cave is where our water starts, my child. Then it goes down inside the mountain and comes out again at our fountain. Now you know something that only the priestesses here know."

"Really?" I put my fingers in the cool water.

"Here, let me show you something else." I followed her around the cave. "You see here?" she asked, pointing. "You see this line here in the rock?"

"No."

She picked me up so I could see, like wet rock on dry rock, the brown seam that climbed gradually all the way up to the top of the cliff.

"I see it! I see it!"

"If you follow that line, when you are bigger of course, you can climb all the way up to the top of the mountain!"

"All the way?"

"All the way!"

"Have you gone all the way?"

"Yes, I go sometimes, when I need to get away, to be with myself."

I was happy to be snug in Hannah's arms even though I did not understand her words. How could a person not be with themselves? She carried me back to the mouth of the cave where we sat in the welcome shade. We looked out together at the Lake beginning to shimmer with mid-day mid-summer heat.

"That line in the rock I showed you, that is my secret. No one else goes up there."

"It is a secret?"

"Now it is our secret."

"So you really are the moon lady from my dreams, with a secret just for me."

"Yes, and now you are my special friend, the keeper of my very special secret. You must not tell anyone."

"I am your special friend?" I looked at her, but her eyes were on the Lake.

"Yes."

"I never had a special friend before."

"Me neither, child. Me neither."

She put her arm around me in a way that made me think that she did not put her arm around little children very often. Still it felt nice. After a little while, she rested her cut arm on my leg. The blood was dry now. I put my hand on her wound, closed my eyes, and felt the colors go through me like the water went through the mountain into the fountain. When I took my hand off her arm, the cut was gone.

"Thank you Mary. That is very good. It is as I thought, little one. I think I understand. You think you have to be alone, and you need to feel very safe, do you not little healer? Someone must have made you feel wrong about this. That is fine. We will make you a tent, then no one can see."

"What do you mean, a tent? What for?"

"Deborah will explain everything. Do not worry." The fine lines around her dark eyes seemed to me to be light coming from her bright white hair.

"Hannah, why is your hair all white? I never saw anybody with hair all white before."

"Never mind about that, Mary." She put her hand in her hair, left it there, looked like she was remembering something. "You should not ask people about themselves that way, it is very rude."

"I am sorry Hannah, I know, I did not mean to – "

"Shush now, it is all right, I know you are still a small child. What is important right now is this thing you can do, this healing. We need it."

"I do not understand."

"That is all right, child, you do not have to."

She rested her hand on my head, and when she kissed my hair I burst into tears. Hannah did not ask why; she just rocked me and sang me a soft song.

When she finished her song, she brought me back down to see Deborah under the tree. Hannah whispered into her mother's ear, and our high priestess stopped her work, stood up from the bench and sat instead on the small three-legged stool, while Hannah took her mother's place and went back to her task.

In an ordinary voice, Deborah told me to sit at her feet on the ground. Then in a voice so soft it felt like she was talking from inside my head, she said, "Mary, you have heard me tell everyone that you have a special role here among us, that you are to be our next Queen." She waited for me to nod before continuing. "But before you do that, there is some special work here that needs to be done, that only you can do. Healing is like the eternal flame," pointing to the lamp in the brass bowl. "It must never go out. Now, you know that your great-grandmother Rebecca has been gone for many months.

"As you have seen, the people in the Valley and others come from all around to be blessed by the priestesses of Magdala. They come for the interpretations of dreams and the sharing of visions. They come when they need an amulet or a charm, when they need a contract written or witnessed. They come for our special incense and for the sacred doves, to keep in their homes as reminders of our covenant with Our Great Mother Goddess Astarte. That way, when they pray to Her, they feel that She is there, watching over their bodies and their souls."

Deborah stopped and smiled, looked right into my eyes. "How much your gaze is like your great-grandmother's! It is as if..." She closed her eyes for a moment, then continued. "But something important has been missing. Every Shabbat, the people need to come to us to be healed in their bodies and soothed in their souls. We need you, Mary. You can still be a little girl, but in this way we need you to grow up before your time."

There was a little bit of dry grass growing under the tree between my feet. I pulled on it, made rings with it for my toes.

"You are our healer. The people in these parts, the people of Galilee, especially the people around the Lake, they count on us for this. And we count on them. The incense, the doves; these sacred gifts we sell are not enough. Even with our weaving... The thing is, it has been almost nine months since Rebecca left us..."

"She went to get my father Jacob."

"That is right. When Rebecca was still here, once a week she sat up in the grove and received the sick to heal them. Normally..." Deborah breathed deeply and started pulling at the grass too, "there would still be your grandmother, Martha, or your mother Muriel, to do this. But that is how it is sometimes. Always remember, child, we never know what Our Great Mother Goddess intends for us. Normally, one cannot become a healer for the people until at the very least one is menstruant..."

"What is mestrit?"

"Menstruant is when you become a woman, Mary."

"When I am mestrit can I have the sing-et?"

She grasped the object with her twig-like hands and sighed in such a way that I thought she would cry.

"Mary, do not ever ask me again about the signet. Do you understand?"

"Yes, Deborah." I pulled so much dry grass I had enough for rings for all my fingers and toes.

"You are still a little girl, and I do not expect you to understand everything, but conditions are such that we need you now. We will begin right away. Hannah will sit with you. You will have to tell her what you need."

"What do I need?"

"You will know. You begin next week."

Just then I heard the voice I had been waiting for, out in the courtyard. Without waiting for a dismissal – not knowing I needed one – I ran out from under the tree, blinded by the bright day. I looked everywhere! Where was she? I ran up to the bath and back down to the courtyard and up the stairs to the grove, while I was running back down I ran poom! right into her stomach.

"Mary, have I not told you a hundred times to watch where you are going?" Her face all round and pink, Zanna picked me up and held me, and I hugged her back so tight as though I would never let go.

"My Zanna! My Zanna! Now that you are here only good things can happen."

It is all blended together now – Zanna's return near the end of that first summer in Magdala; the migration of the pelicans with their vast black and white wings spreading over blue sky and pale earth, swooping birds suddenly everywhere one turned; the purple and blue arrival of Zacharias and Judith from Jerusalem. What do I remember, and what grooves have I since added into this pebble of memory by fondling it overmuch? What have I erased?

I was shyly curious about Judith – Salome and Rachel's mother, the one of the long white comb. Judith was the first woman I had ever seen with silver jewelry on every part of her body: earrings, ring, bracelets, and anklets. She did not notice me, did not seem to be interested in anyone, really, other than Deborah.

Zacharias reminded me so much of Jacob I wanted to crawl into his lap, but he did not see me either from his great height. Our words were a little bent in his pink mouth, from which he smoothed away his dense black beard with long slender fingers. Next to his left eye, he had a big black mole, which fascinated me, and he never touched it, which tantalized me.

The moon rose bright on that holy night of Sukkoth, the festival of Booths. After our abundant feast in the sacred grove, Zacharias stood in his long purple cloak and sang for us beside the small ceremonial fire, while we sat on rugs on the ground in our usual circle. I had heard the shepherds up in the hills hum for their sheep, but their song was absentminded, like Zanna's. Zacharias sang with his whole body. I had never heard anything like it.

When he sang he looked out at the moonlit Lake and straight down at Maryanna, who was seated next to Elizabeth, who was now visibly pregnant. I was sitting on Elizabeth's other side, content in my

Zanna's cushy lap, only bothered by Elizabeth fidgeting all through Zacharias's song.

I remember thinking that maybe Elizabeth was moving around so much because she wanted to hug him again. She had welcomed Zacharias with full embrace and kiss when he arrived. I had never heard her laugh before. When he kept her hand tucked in his arm as he greeted all the others, Elizabeth, whose face was always as straight and tucked away as her hair, beamed round and pink as she leaned girlishly against him, holding his arm with one hand and her belly with the other.

Maryanna had not come down to the courtyard to welcome Zacharias and Judith. When she was tuning her instruments, nothing could interrupt her until their perfect tone was achieved. It had not been until the feast that she and Zacharias met. I did not witness that meeting, so focused and proud had I been, helping Zanna carry big round bowls of steaming meats and grains from the kitchen to the grove where we gathered for the welcoming feast. This was my first real celebration of Sukkoth, when we sleep under the stars to remember to be thankful for our homes. In Bethany, we had spent that evening on the roof, as we had spent all our hot summer nights. But in Magdala we would be sleeping right on the ground, down in the courtyard near the fountain.

Amidst our empty bowls and full bellies, we sat and listened to Zacharias's song. Hannah was seated across from me, facing Zacharias's back, and I saw her features soften as she watched the dance of eyes between the black-haired man and, so I now think she thought, her pregnant older daughter.

I leaned in to the circle to see Maryanna's face, and she seemed lost in the marvelous music pouring from the center of the circle, her dark head tilted back, her eyes closed, a faint smile on her full lips. At the end of the slow and ponderous song, the silver-and-red-haired Judith raised an arm jangling with bracelets and suggested a duet between Maryanna and Zacharias.

Under her bright blue cloak, Maryanna's wild black hair escaped down to her waist. Her face was bright with flame. Zacharias towered over her in his dark purple cloak. But once she started to sing, it seemed like they were the same height, tall as trees, their voices wrapping around each other like plumes of smoke climbing high into the night.

When their song was done, silence fell like a blanket. Zacharias and Maryanna stayed deep inside each other's eyes. The fire crackled. Elizabeth squirmed, stared at the ground, hands on her belly. Everyone was quiet as stones until Judith spoke again,

"Thank you for that enchanting music, Zacharias and Maryanna. That was lovely." The priestess from Jerusalem looked around the circle with her eyes black as night, her straight twig mouth contradicting the soft waves of her uncovered black and silver hair. "Now Deborah," waving her jangling bracelets to get the high priestess's attention away from the singers at whom she was staring, smiling, "is it not time we went to the inner room behind the scroll room?"

Deborah laughed easily, "Why would we do that?"

"Have you forgotten what I told you?"

Deborah stared into the fire. "We have closed and barred the gate. And we have sent word to Yudah," with a nod to Phebe.

"Barred the gate?" These words spewed from Judith's mouth like dry sand. She raised a finger on which shone a heavy silver ring, whose engravings I would have much leisure to ponder after this night. "Do you think the enemy will be stopped by a gate?"

As she spoke, the two singers left the middle of the circle. Maryanna took back her spot next to her sister, and Zacharias sat on the other side of the songstress rather than at his original spot across the fire next to Hannah, causing Phebe to scoop a getting-too-big-for-that-Tabitha into her lap.

Judith continued, "Did you not hear what I told you earlier? King Herod has been spying on us in Jerusalem. He arrested a Magi, one of Zacharias's guests, had him interrogated, asked him about the new king who is to be born."

"Well surely the Magi did not – "

" – Of course not, but King Herod is a most suspicious and evil man. Have you not heard that he put his own sons to death for suspected treason! I doubt the poor boys did more than cough the wrong way at the wrong time." Judith stood and paced around the fire, her delicately sandaled feet raising dry dust, bells on her silver anklets chiming with each step. "King Herod is not one to call off his spies just because our good friend lied and told him to look for the child in the town of Bethlehem!"

Deborah raised her clear gaze on Judith, a gaze all the more piercing for the midnight blue veil that covered her head. A strange smile lingered on her face, one that made me snuggle more deeply into Zanna's lap. Then in her morning prayer voice, she said, "Nothing happens but that Our Creator wills it."

Judith leaned forward, "Well then, Deborah, Our Creator wills me to give you this warning. Zacharias's house is being watched. His secret gatherings are infiltrated with spies. We could have been followed up here. Do you not see?"

The great seer smiled broadly without parting her lips, and sighed deeply. "You are asking *me* if I *see*? Judith. This is what I see. Elizabeth's womb has quickened, her child has already begun to kick. Though she is not a '*blind seer*,' there may yet be some sign that her issue is our long-awaited king, which you say King Herod now seeks. And King Herod, terrible though he is, darling of the Roman Empire though he is, is also old and very ill. His imminent death will cause chaos among the pretenders to his throne. Phebe's son Yudah is young and strong up in our hills, training his army, ready to make good use of that chaos. And little Mary here is... Well, I sent you word about her. All is well."

"All the more reason, Deborah! Let us simply move into the inner sanctuary!"

"Judith, surely you have not forgotten that Sukkoth is a most holy time. We are to sleep under the sky tonight. Is that how it has become in Jerusalem? Turning sacred observance on its head because of some vague danger? Yudah's men are all around outside, nearby, sleeping like us under the stars this week. Yudah knows perfectly well that you and Zacharias are here. He will hear everything and will have taken the usual precautions."

"But the usual precautions are not enough!" Judith's voice rose high and tight. "At least tell Yudah that King Herod himself might think we are here. Zacharias, would you send a messenger?"

I could not see Zacharias's face when he replied, but I could hear his smile in his voice. "My dear Judith, I think everyone here is right. There is danger, and Yudah must be warned. I would send one of my guards who escorted us here. They are Parthians all, four fierce and clever men , foreigners with no concern for working on our holy day. But only a local man would be able to find where Yudah camps at night. Therefore, I will tell them to be on high alert until morning when they can find him. And let us not forget after all, that I am a chief priest of the Temple, and even King Herod knows he would have to answer for my death."

"You mean like he answered for killing my husband Hezekiah?" Everyone turned to look at Phebe, her rarely used voice mesmerizing in its quietude. Tabitha, asleep in her lap, did not stir. "Herod has been getting away with murder since he was seventeen years old and governor of this province of Galilee. He killed my Hezekiah, Yudah's father, also a leader of men, in broad daylight, in the center of town. Right away, I went to seek justice, all the way to Jerusalem. With my son Yudah nursing one breast and baby Muriel at the other... Judith, you remember, you came with me. The Sanhedrin Council granted us a hearing immediately; they were as outraged as we were.

"But young Herod barely got his wrist slapped!" Phebe raised an outraged fist to the dark night as she spoke. "No surprise there: the Romans sent an armed cohort with him, to wait outside as he pled his case to the Court. The mighty Sanhedrin Council members bowed their heads and said not a word. Now the Romans have made that same faithless Herod," she spat on the ground, "king of all our provinces and all our land. He has their entire imperial army at his service, to do whatever he claims will 'secure the peace'. Why should he shy away from killing a priest here or anywhere?"

When no one replied, Phebe went on, "And if his soldiers come, who will bury *our* bones? Who is left? With Muriel gone, there is not one of us left in Bethany. No one in En Gedi for over a generation now. Will Judith's Holy Doves risk their lives and leave Jerusalem? I think not. Judith is right. We cannot take these chances. Herod's soldiers could be hiding in the woods listening to us as we speak."

"Phebe," Zacharias chuckled and stood, "do you honestly think men of arms would sit in the woods like good children, waiting to be invited in? If soldiers were here, they would be at our throats already. But my sisters and daughters in Astarte, I do not want anyone to be afraid. In addition to speaking to my guards, I myself will keep watch up here in the grove." He pulled from his belt a long shining sword that I had not seen up until then. "From there I can see all sides of this precious compound. I will watch all night that you may all sleep soundly in your courtyard, and alert you at the slightest trouble."

He sheathed his weapon. "Just in case," looking at Rachel, "tell us: the sanctuary room behind the library is well stocked in food and water and blankets for all?"

"Yes," Rachel answered nodding, "Dinah has been seeing to it." Her words did not shake the look of dread from her face.

"I will watch with you," ventured Elizabeth, brightening.

"Nonsense, granddaughter," Deborah said, "you will sleep in the courtyard with the rest of us. If Zacharias is to keep watch, he should have no distractions."

Deborah then turned to Judith, who had sat back down on the rug next to Hannah. They looked almost like sisters, the two old women with their feet gathered under them, hugging their knees, staring into the fire. "My dear Judith, I appreciate your warning and Zacharias's precautions, but you have both been living in Jerusalem too long. Things do not happen so fast around here. Why not rest now? You have had a long journey, and you have been away from home so long. Sit back; breathe in the night air, the quiet. Remember that nothing happens but that Our Creator wills it. Relax into Her Embrace."

Judith answered without turning her head from the flames, "Deborah, Deborah, it may be that *you* have lived *here* too long. The world is moving faster than you know, faster maybe even than your visions can tell you. You and I both know that Her Embrace can be withering. Deborah, I have been Her priestess all these years too. Let us sleep inside the mountain. That is a natural shelter after all, and the rules of Sukkoth are clear…"

Judith was the only one I had ever heard contradict our high priestess. As I felt myself falling asleep in Zanna's arms, I fought it, focusing on Judith's firelit face, wanting to know what else she might say.

The first time we woke that night, it was to the unfamiliar sound of metal clanking against metal, breaking open the depth of night, the depth of our sleep.

As I woke to the strange noise, Salome was already pulling me from my mat. I heard men's voices shouting in an unknown language, one louder than the others.

I looked up in time to see Zacharias standing in his white moonlit tunic, behind the grove's altar of gathered stones. I heard him call out, "Show your faces! I am a chief priest of the Temple in Jerusalem, and I fear you not!"

To whom was he speaking? The moon was setting on the other side of the grove, lighting the stone altar like a cold fire, but I could see no one but him. Within moments Salome and Zanna had gathered Tabitha, Dinah, Ariella, and me into the barn. There, deep in the corner, behind the pungent goats, the two grown women formed a bodily tent over us little ones. They would not let us move or speak. I wondered where Hannah and the others had gone. From inside the barn we could see nothing but hear everything. Up in the grove, a sharp swooshing sounded like a rock exhaling. Salome whispered, "A sword!"

An unknown man's voice spoke our words in a broken way, "Your guard dead. Quiet throat cut. Give us your son and we go."

"Show yourselves!" Zacharias called out again. "I have no son, and if I did I surely would not give him to you."

Then another voice, still a man's but higher, called out loudly,

"Do you think you can mock King Herod and live? Mock Rome? Your friend the Magi," and he made a retching noise like spitting, "lied to King Herod about Bethlehem. Our spy heard him say that one destined to be king over all of Israel," spitting again, "is here with you in Galilee. So here we are. We know that you have made an alliance with the Magi, to prepare for a new king. All in vain: King Herod defeats all who stand against him. You sired the child, also in vain. I just hope you had your fun doing it."

"How dare you, you pig, you dung-eating worm, you soulless wretch—" Zacharias shouted, then we heard sword being drawn.

"Save your breath and your life, Priest. Consider the lives of the women and children hiding in the courtyard below. Your son dies tonight, if you help us or not. I give you this chance to save your own life."

And Zacharias said, "I am God's martyr, if you shed my blood; Our Creator will receive my spirit, because you will be shedding innocent blood at the holy sanctuary."

Salome and Zanna stiffened at these words. I freed myself from their grip and climbed the inner wall of the barn, which I had learned to do to get on the mules by myself. There was a small window-slot up there. I could not see much – just a sword glinting in the moonlight.

Then Zacharias screamed, a deep bellow that turned into a high-pitched scream, and then there was another sound, as if the mountain itself were crying out, as if the caves of the mountain were returning all their echoes all at once.

I heard men running in the forest beyond the grove, and more sounds of swords and metal, dark screams and grunts coming from deep in the woods.

Without waiting for this new battle beyond our walls to quell to silence, we all poured into the courtyard and scrambled up the steps to the grove.

Rachel was the nimblest. I reached the grove just in time to see her crouch down beyond the altar and take Zacharias's head in her lap. Her white tunic grew dark with his blood, but try as she did to spread out her cloak beneath him, her garments could not contain it all.

Elizabeth came as fast as she could, holding her swollen belly with one hand, pulling up her mother with the other, screaming "Zacharias!" Hannah had to pull on her immense daughter with both hands to keep her from throwing herself on Zacharias. Rooting her heels into the ground, she tried to reason with the deranged woman her issue had become.

"Elizabeth, you know the consequences of touching his blood now. Think of your child, if not yourself! Spare your child, Elizabeth!"

Just then Maryanna ran down to the grove from the bath. I wondered how she had gotten all the way up there. She flew down the steps to her mother and helped grab hold of Elizabeth who was screaming now almost as loud as the mountain had, "Zacharias!"

In semi-darkness of that luminous night, it looked like Zacharias was trying to say something. Rachel smiled as best she could, running her shaky hand over his dark hair. He breathed his last gurgled breath, and the others arrived only in time to see Rachel close his eyes, a gesture which stole Elizabeth's voice in an instant.

Into this ringing stillness, Judith crossed from the top of the steps into the grove. She stopped, seemed to see only Rachel. When she saw Zacharias's blood puddle shining on the ground in the bright moonlight, she covered her mouth with her hand, her ring catching the night's light. She turned and found Salome carrying Tabitha, her head resting on Salome's shoulder. Judith hugged Salome, her embrace going all the way around the young woman's waist and the too-big child in her arms. She kissed Salome's forehead, whispered, "Daughter." Then she broke away like a branch falling from a trunk, stumbling toward her first-born, Rachel. Salome made a small animal noise and buried her face in Tabitha's hair.

Judith helped Rachel drag Zacharias's dead weight all the way into the black shadows of the grove, out of the moonlight. She was not so far that I could not hear her say to her eldest daughter, in an ashen voice, "You did well, Rachel, but his blood hit the ground even before he did. The grove has been defiled. It could not be helped. You know what we must do. We need only a third."

At these words, Maryanna stepped forward. Her mother and sister gasped, but did not try to stop her. Just as she was about to cross into the shadow, Deborah appeared and called her name. The young musician turned and saw the high priestess raise her hand, palm forward, bent at the wrist. Deborah did not need to say more. Maryanna stayed where she was as her grandmother hobbled past her, moving unequivocally toward the two women and the dead man. With a hushed thump, she sat down next to them in the complete darkness. Though she cast not one glance at her daughter Hannah, it felt to me like the deepest sigh emanated from the shadows.

Tabitha let out a small cry as she broke away from Salome and rushed toward her mother Rachel, but the young girl's tunic was caught and held back by Phebe, whom I had not noticed was there until that moment. Tabitha struggled, but Phebe wrapped her in her cloak, letting her bury her shaking head inside. That is when I saw Dinah, standing quietly, holding her little sister's hand. I felt Zanna's warmth behind me — when did she get there? — her hands steady on my shoulders.

The second time we woke, it was indeed as the story was told in the Valley for years to come. At first light, after falling into a sudden slumber in the midst of our waiting and grief and bewilderment in the moonlight, we woke up to find the grove empty but for ourselves.

The woods were silent. Zacharias's body was not there.

There was no trace of his dark blood in the pale red earth.

Nor any trace of Rachel, Judith or Deborah.

Only three piles of gray ash on the gathered stone altar.

Crowning one pile was Rachel's alabaster comb. In the middle of the other was Judith's silver ring. Coiled around the third were Deborah's silver cord and black signet.

We all crowded in, holding whosever hand was close. Salome reached for her mother's ring and put it on the middle finger of her left hand, where it fit as snuggly as it had on her mother's. Tabitha, encouraged by this gesture, took her mother's comb, put it into her thick black hair, ashes and all, sobbing all the while, wiping her pink face on Phebe's white tunic.

Over the child's sobs, Elizabeth's sudden scream, "His smell, it is all over you!" and everyone turned, looked, and saw her long fingers grabbing her younger sister's hair.

Maryanna stammered as she struggled with her sister, "You would not understand. It was meant to... We were... He was... I am the blind... You do not..."

"I do, I understand everything! This is all your fault!" Letting her go and stepping back, Elizabeth waved an accusing finger, "You went up to him! You distracted him! He would never have been surprised if..."

"He was sleeping when I found him! I woke him! At least we were not taken by surprise. I was right there, I could have been killed too! You do not even care about that! All you care about is – "

" – You think you can do anything you want, take anything you want! He was mine, and now..."

While they argued and no one was looking, I reached for the signet that was still on the altar. I squatted down amidst everyone's legs and held the signet tight. Though it burned my hand like a hot coal, I rode the colors and the images moving behind my closed eyes, like flying. I had never known anything the way I knew that this was *mine*. It felt right and good and better than anything I had ever felt, better than Jacob and better even than Zanna. This time I would not let it go.

Through my closed eyes I heard Hannah speak to her daughters in her softest voice, "I did not see this blood nor these ashes in any of my visions. None of us did, not even Deborah, unless she did not speak of it. '*The Queen will issue from the broken healer, Her King from the seer blind.*' I suppose we are all the blind seers now."

With these words both her daughters put their hands over their wombs, looked at each other, at Hannah, then at me. That is when they saw the silver cord coming out of my hand.

"Child, what is..."

Salome understood right away, "The signet."

I ran toward the other side of the grove. Hannah and Salome chased after me and caught me right at the edge of the silent woods, four strong hands on my little arms.

"Mary, what are you doing?" Hannah was breathless. Then all of the sudden, she fell to her knees and wailed. I had never seen a grown-up become so completely overwhelmed, and it frightened me more than anything that had just happened. Those still gathered around the altar walked over until they surrounded us. I clutched the signet more tightly, curled into myself like a ball, my fist at my center, against the place where the colors were the brightest.

Salome squatted down before me, her touch purposeful and light, like when she was teaching me how to spin. But her voice was different; it was not her teaching voice. She talked to me the way she had in the carriage that first day, like I was a person. "Mary, listen to me. Let Hannah have the signet for now. We understand why you took it." She patted my head, and I looked up at her steady brown eyes. "We really do. We all do. We are not going to take it away from you forever, only for a little while, until you are ready."

Everyone had gathered around me. What else could I do? I gave the signet to Salome. As she took it, everyone gasped to see our sacred symbol neatly seared into my pudgy palm. Salome handed the signet to Hannah, who lifted her head and took it. She just held it, staring at it. She was still crying, and the other women leaned in and began to keen with her.

"Stop it! Stop this right now!" Shocked silence greeted Phebe's words. We all turned to her, amazed at the harsh voice emerging from this gentle woman. "There is no time for this. Yes, there is silence on Mount Arbel this morning, and yes, the assassins seem to have been scared or killed off for now, but do you think we are safe? No, they may well come back with more men, more weapons. Especially now that they found Zacharias here.

"I am not our high priestess, but I am now our elder, and the only one who remembers rebuilding life here after the last devastation, that one wrought not by a few soldiers, but by the Roman General Cassius and his whole army, taking thirty thousand prisoners, killing nearly all those they left behind. If we had succumbed to weeping then, we never would have been able to gather all the bones, yes, the bones."

Phebe flashed her black eyes that seemed to have no center. She met each pair of eyes, narrowing her own. "First, we must focus on practical matters. Later we can mourn. Now, Dinah, you have learned how to write well enough, yes?" Without waiting for reply, "Go send a carrier-dove to my son Yudah, tell him to come with his best men immediately. He has a scribe among his men who can read. Do not say where, do not mention any names, in case the message falls into the wrong hands.

"Once Yudah gets here, we will confer as to the best way to ensure the safety of our compound, and especially of Elizabeth and Mary. Hannah is right. They carry all our future in their blood and in their womb, and we must not expose them to further incident. Come to think of it, Maryanna, it seems that we should concern ourselves with your womb too, yes?"

Maryanna blushed a bright dark red. She did not speak, but she nodded her head. Elizabeth howled and raised her fist, which Phebe caught with a force that surprised us all, and peered into the younger woman's eyes,

"Elizabeth, surely somewhere underneath your passions, you are still one of our seers, and you can allow that perhaps Our Creator willed for Zacharias's seed to be planted in both your wombs. Now that Zacharias is dead, without children, and the last of his siblings, there is no other chief priest of the Temple who serves Magdala."

At these words, Elizabeth dropped her arm. It seemed that all the blood that filled her sister's face had drained from her own.

Phebe again swept us up in her black gaze. "Listen to me. We must put aside our grieving and grievances, until we have ensured the safety of the precious lineage with which the generations of Israel have entrusted us."

When she saw me blow on the blister forming in my palm in the shape of our sacred symbol, her face shone with purpose. She held my wrist and showed my red hand to everyone.

"You see now without a doubt, that little Mary is the one for whom we have been waiting. And now that we have two blind seers, one who is and one who may well be with child, we have two potential kings for her. This is not a time to despair, but to exult. This is surely no time to lose our heads.

"Now, Zanna, go get some breakfast ready. Ariella, go help her. Then see if anything is needed in the inner sanctuary in case we need to take refuge there. Elizabeth, help your mother gather up these ashes. We will need them for her ceremony of initiation into her high priesshood, once things are settled. Then go and feed the eternal flame under the oak. Dinah, what are you still doing here? I gave you your task, go send that message. Run!"

We all watched Dinah fly down the stairs to the courtyard. "Good," Phebe said. "Now, Maryanna, take Mary and Tabitha to help you roll up the sleeping mats and make ready our guest quarters. We will have company soon. Everyone meet up at the bath when you are done."

Later, when we had to, we called it: the night of waking twice.

That was the simple way to evoke it, the light, feathery way to point to the moment that created a "before" and an "after" without also lifting its mountain of blood and ash.

Phebe's son Yudah soon took up residence in the guest room above the gate. His foreign male presence at our regular meals uncomfortably echoed the invasion we had just suffered. Even Tabitha kept her distance; though Yudah seemed interested in his daughter, she was nowhere to be found when he looked.

While his men disguised as shepherds guarded our perimeter day and night, Yudah conferred with his mother Phebe and Hannah in the shade of the balcony near the kitchen, just across the courtyard from me. From my spinning stool I could hear them perfectly. His men had killed all our attackers. As these wicked men had only found us by following Zacharias, our compound was now safe, as it appeared innocuous, yet another place of women doing women's work. The surrounding villages were so devastated by wars and forced conscriptions that they too were often inhabited by only women, children and the occasional toothless old man.

Nonetheless, our elder Phebe and our high priestess Hannah decided together that Elizabeth and Maryanna would be safest if they did not stay with us. Boys – which no one doubted they carried – were always fostered elsewhere once they were weaned, and under the present circumstances they were better off born elsewhere too. Yudah sent word out among his men – which of their families could best take in Maryanna and Elizabeth?

Here is where Judas entered our lives. Almost a man, he had recently joined Yudah's rebel forces and was proud to propose his own home in Nazareth. His father was a widower, and Judas's grown married sisters lived right next door to him, ready and able to help with the births and the babies. As no one in his family could read, no message could be sent. Judas ran all night across fields and mountains to talk with his father and ran all day to return with his consent, collapsing outside the gate where he was brought fresh water, old bread and a good blanket.

Hannah and Phebe gathered all of us up in the grove to sit and discuss these matters. We sat in a circle – yes, even us little ones were expected to listen and learn. Hannah and Phebe decided that Maryanna would go to live with Judas's father in Nazareth. Zanna would go too, to help with the birth. Maryanna, in a cloudy daze since the night of waking twice, agreed easily, or rather, showed no dissent.

Being visibly pregnant, and therefore more conspicuous, Elizabeth's circumstance was more difficult. She stood and paced in the grove, shaded in the late afternoon shadow of Mount Arbel. Though her mother had been initiated into her role as High Priestess, Elizabeth addressed Phebe when she said,

"I should to go to Jerusalem. You have been there, you understand. That is where I belong."

Phebe paled. "Jerusalem? You can hardly call that place safe! Almost a week's journey when you are six months with child? To the city of a man sought after by Herod?"

Hannah chimed in, "And assuming you arrived unharmed, where would you stay?"

"With one of the Holy Doves, as we are called there. Judith gathered quite a flock, with the help of her friend, Joseph of Arimathea. You must agree with me, Phebe: I am better off in a crowded place, not some small village full of gossip." Elizabeth sat back down and put both hands on her belly.

Phebe remained still and thought for a long time. Tabitha curled halfway into her grandmother's lap, and our elder petted her head, looking down at the ground, at nothing. Hannah was completely still. Birdsong punctuated the silence but had never sounded less gay.

Finally Phebe decided, "All right, Elizabeth, I could send word to Joseph of Arimathea in Jerusalem. He is a young man yet, but Judith spoke well of him to me, said he has a good head on his shoulders, especially for one both so young and so wealthy. I will send word by carrier pigeon. The rains may soon be upon us, and if you are to make such a journey we can waste no time with a foot messenger, or even one on horse. Hannah, what are your thoughts?"

Hannah sighed deeply, "My thoughts are that my daughters are leaving, that they will give birth in a place where my feet have never walked, scream their deliverance against walls whose echo I do not know. I am thinking of what I will pack for them: to begin, some incense to burn and keep harm away from their labor."

With that she stood. We followed, back down to the courtyard, and back to work. I asked Salome, who had been sitting near me, "What is the name of the man in Nazareth who will help Maryanna?"

"His name is Joseph, Joseph of Nazareth."

"Is not that the name of the man helping Elizabeth?"

"Almost, Joseph of Nazareth will help Maryanna, and Joseph of Arimathea will help Elizabeth."

I had heard of Nazareth, a town on the other side of the mountains behind us, but not the other. "Where is Amathea?"

"Arimathea means 'of a high place.' That is what we call the men of Jerusalem who help us, because we worship in high places and hilltops. It means that Joseph keeps an altar to Astarte, in secret of course."

"Why is it secret?" I asked as we started down the stairs.

"Because in Jerusalem there are people who want keep Yahweh all alone in the great Temple. And that is why we do what we do, to help bring Astarte back. Sometimes things have to start out as a secret."

"I have a secret."

"Oh do you? That is very nice," she said absently as we reached the courtyard. "Now pick up that spindle. We have work to do – "

" – and it will not get done by itself," I interrupted, knowing what she was about to say.

Salome sighed, "That is right," and turned to her loom.

Within a week, we heard back from Joseph of Arimathea. I was with Dinah in the library when his message arrived, and Phebe rushed in for us to read it to her. I knew all the letters by then, so I did my best to sound out the words, with Dinah mouthing the word for me when I hesitated.

" 'Have the Holy Dove' – " I began.

" – That must be Elizabeth," Phebe interrupted.

I continued reading Joseph of Arimathea's letter, " 'Have the Holy Dove meet me in Beit She'an, the great city halfway between Magdala and Jerusalem. I will be there in one week. We will go together to the safest place for her at this time: Q'mran, a sanctuary in the desert not far from Jerusalem. There live a peaceful and reverent group of men and women called the Essenes. Their leader is a great admirer of one you say is recently deceased – ' "

"Zacharias," whispered Phebe to herself.

" – who visited them frequently,' " I continued. " 'The Essenes will be honored to take in the Holy Dove and attend to her in her state of need.' "

Phebe became very solemn and made Dinah and I promise to keep the message a secret. I was only too happy to share in another secret. When Phebe told Elizabeth about the message, she simply said that Joseph of Arimathea would meet her halfway. Yudah agreed to accompany Elizabeth himself with his own guard all the way to Beit She'an, and he selected four of his best men to accompany Maryanna and Judas back to Nazareth. Phebe said nothing to Elizabeth about the Essenes in the desert. The roundly pregnant seer was tense with purpose as she went about making herself ready for the trip. She asked Zanna for a good blanket and a spare tunic. She asked Hannah if Ariella could go with her, to attend to her. She spent hours under the great oak, conferring with Hannah and Maryanna in voices that did not carry.

The two sisters left a few days apart. Elizabeth rode off on a mule, her eyes bright and hard. Maryanna insisted on walking, her voice soft and cloudy as the first rain that attended her and Zanna's leaving.

Once again I began asking for Zanna. Once again I was told, "soon."

Thus within one moon, our number was cut in half, from twelve to six. Only Hannah, Salome, Dinah, Phebe, Tabitha and I remained in Magdala. It is a marvel to me that anything ordinary continued at all, that any fabric was woven or incense blended or any food made. But continue we did. In fact, we were busier than ever. Everyone worked hard to keep things going, though ever with an ear for Ezra's call at the gate, where he brought us news.

Over the following weeks and months, reports dribbled in. Mary-anna and Zanna had arrived safely in Nazareth, Elizabeth and Ariella in Q'mran. Judas was assigned to stay in Nazareth – nothing was more natural than a young man coming home to his father, and no one was more perfectly situated to guard the house and the women. I can imagine now how Judas must have seethed upon learning of his new post. He himself had offered his family, but he never thought he would be taken out of combat.

And combat there was. We had only just gotten word back from Yudah's men that Elizabeth had safely arrived in Q'mran, when news came from all around that King Herod was dead. This meant new wars would erupt to claim the empty throne, the entire country flaring up after thirty-seven years of tyrannical oppression.

Men were leaving their villages and farms left and right to join Yudah's army up in the mountains. Ezra did not bring news every day, and of course he never came after sundown. Once when the sky paled and darkened without his call at the gate, Phebe said to me as our four hands crumbled dry sage into her lap, "Oh my little Mary, let me tell you something: I dread the news every time Ezra appears. But worse, the time between visits is killing me."

Weeks went by before Ezra brought the news she feared, on one of the first days of heavy rain. Yudah had raided the Roman town of Sepphoris, where all the collected taxes were kept, to seize all the gold and grain. After slaughtering anyone within reach who was not his own, Yudah and his troops went back out into the countryside, distributing the reclaimed taxes back to the people who had paid them. He was quickly found. The Roman forces, knowing our ways, did not just kill him. They cut him into pieces and scattered his remains so that he could have no proper burial, no rest in death. Rachel had once read to me a story of Egypt, in which Seth slew Osiris and scattered the pieces of his body, for the same reason. But the Great Goddess Isis was able to put her beloved Osiris back together.

Phebe had no such power. As if her heart had been cut to pieces too, she dropped dead right on the ground when the news of her son's horrid end reached her. He was killed by the hand of Herod's own son, no less. Father Herod killed father Hezekiah, son killed son. And on it went.

When she collapsed, she dropped the small jar of rosemary oil she had been holding. Hannah and Salome dropped to their knees around her prone form in the middle of the scorching courtyard. Once they saw her breath had stilled, they could not touch her dead body. Touching a corpse would defile them, rendering them unable to perform any of their sacred tasks for a week. Being the only two priestesses left in Magdala, they could not afford this luxury. Nor could they stop Tabitha as the girl stepped past them and lay her full length over her cooling grandmother. She buried her face in the cloud of gray hair and inhaled deeply. The powerful aroma of spilled rosemary oil filled all our noses. Hannah and Salome did not try to pull Tabitha off of Phebe, for touching her would have also defiled them. As soon as Tabitha got back on her feet, she wordlessly stepped around the body and gathered the broken shards of the oil jar.

In the week that followed, Tabitha had to stay at the birthing cave for a full week, day and night, in order to be cleansed from her contact with the dead. During that time, she fashioned the clay pieces into a sort of necklace that continuously scratched at her throat and brought forth small droplets of blood which stained her tunic. She fingered the necklace whenever she was not at the task of gathering our herbs, or spinning, or a few years later, helping Maryanna with her music.

Ezra, who had witnessed the scene from the gate, sent for some local women to come help prepare Phebe's body. This would be a great honor for them, worth many amulets and healings. Then Ezra helped us bring Phebe to Tel Rapha, our Hill of the Dead, just to the south of Mount Arbel, where Hannah told me that we would visit her again the next year at the end of Sukkoth. That was the time we would go each year, to pour out libations at the foot of the trees planted over each dead priestess. After we buried Phebe, Hannah showed me where my mother's tree was, a slender cedar that leaned a little to the side. It was my first time there; they had not brought me when they came with the ashes of the three, after the night of waking twice. Hannah told me we would come back on the last day of Sukkoth and spend the day with our dead, singing to them and feeding them and bringing them news of all that had happened.

Good news came too. By the winter solstice, Ezra reported on the successful delivery of Elizabeth, though the seer could bring forth no milk and her baby John had to be fed from a rag soaked in goat's milk. When by the end of the rainy season we heard of your birth, Jesus, there was much celebrating. Once Hannah was certain that both her daughters had traversed the darkness of labor without harm, she wept and laughed for two days.

In those months after the night of waking twice, whenever I saw Hannah, I tried not to stare at the signet at her throat. Our high priestess rarely ever spoke to me, and I was sure I had done something wrong, but I did not know what exactly, nor why I could not have the signet, nor why I wanted it so.

One morning, a few days after Hannah knew that everyone was safe, her daughters and grandsons alive and thriving, our high priestess took my hand right after our bath and led me up to our special place by the birthing cave. We settled there in the fragrant dry summer grass, amid round blue thistles as big as my fist and tiny white butterflies as small as my fingernail.

Hannah said, "As you know, child, Elizabeth and Maryanna have given birth far away from me, far away. I never thought their labors would happen anywhere but here, with my hand in theirs to hold, and my voice in their ears to soothe them. I never realized how much I wanted that until I learned I would not have it. You see, child, life is full of desire."

Tugging at the pale brittle grass at my feet, which was remarkably resistant to my efforts, I asked, "What is desire?"

"Desire is wanting something, with all your body, heart, and mind. It is what I feel for my daughters right now, and what I know you feel for this signet I wear. Look at me," her bony finger lifted my plump chin. "Mary, I brought you here to tell you two things. First," she held up a finger on her other hand, "I am wearing the signet instead of you, and that has nothing to do with what happened the night of waking twice, or that morning. It has nothing to do with you being good or bad."

"It does not? Then why?"

"You are a good girl, Mary, and one day you will wear this. It is simply not your time yet. But you want it now."

"Why do I want it so much?"

"That is desire, child. What you are feeling."

I saw a small butterfly settle in front of me on a blue thistle and tried to catch it, wincing when the thistle pricked me.

"You see," Hannah chuckled, "that is the funny part about desire: getting what we want does not always feel good, does not always bring us peace. Look at Elizabeth, she went to Jerusalem, and she ended up in the desert. And it is peace that we must always seek, first, before anything."

"What is peace?"

Hannah sighed deeply and was quiet for a moment. Then she said, "Peace is the way I think you felt when you healed me. The trouble with desire, sometimes it feels so strong that it hurts you, even without touching a blue thistle. If you live long enough, and if you live well, this will happen more than once. You cannot stop it. But you do not want it to rule you. You have to rule it. So when desire happens, and it hurts you like it is doing now, here is what you do."

We were sitting as we usually did, hugging our knees, but now Hannah lowered her legs and crossed them, rested her palms on her knees, and began to inhale deeply, speaking breathily as she did. "Inhale, one two three four five six seven eight. Now hold," here she tapped her knee to show that she was still counting to eight, "and exhale, one two three four five six seven eight. Again, inhale, come Mary, do it with me."

And so I did, and there in that shady cave felt the magic of my breath shifting my feelings, moving out desire, putting nothing in its place but breath.

So I was very calm when she told me the second reason she had brought me to our special place: it was time for me to start healing, as my great-grandmother Rebecca had done.

Before she died, Phebe had finished what Deborah had started. She had completed the rounds, alerting the folk of the nearby towns and farms that Magdala had its healer once again. But after the night of waking twice and then the death of Herod, everything had been shaken up. Now we had returned to order.

The day after Hannah spoke to me up at our cave, I began. The one constant in all that time of war and death and uncertainty, other than my spinning, was Shabbat up in the grove with Hannah.

We sat on our thick rug at the top of the stairs, together in a little tent they fabricated for me to shield us both from the sun, and me from prying eyes that would turn my abilities to stone. One person in need of healing would enter the tent or be deposited there, if they could not walk. I placed my hands on them, and the colors came through. Then they called me "Holy Magdalene," or "Quedeshah Magdala."

"Why do they call me that?" I asked Hannah at the end of the first day. "Why do they not call me Mary?"

Hannah answered in the same still tone she used for our morning prayers at the bath. "Quedeshah Magdala is what the world calls the Queen you will become. Mary is your private name, just for us. The world will call you Holy Magdalene, Quedeshah Magdala, because you are of Magdala."

"Do they call you that?"

"They call me Quedeshah Hannah."

"But are you not from Magdala too?"

"We will talk about that another time, child." She became quiet then. We did not often speak in the tent. Hannah was there to keep the people who came in from embracing me too long or staying with me, as they kept trying to do.

The visitors soon changed from people seeking relief from common arthritis and breathing problems to soldiers covered in blood, having to be carried up the steps. Nightmares haunted my sleep: blood all over everyone in the whole world, not one person left without it. Salome, who always slept near me, would wake up with me and my racing heart and say, "Shh, shh." She would lift her blanket and I would climb in, comforted, but often unable to go back to sleep.

Still I looked forward to Shabbat and to all the people coming to see me. I knew I was doing a service, but mostly, I simply felt wonderful when the colors moved through me. Nothing else gave me that feeling. On Shabbat eve we sang songs of praise and protection for Elizabeth and John, and Maryanna and Jesus, and Zanna and little Ariella in all the prayers. But our songs were pale without Maryanna's enchanting voice, just as our morning prayers at the bath seemed small without Deborah's booming one. I wondered if Our Creator would hear us.

I had so many questions, but no one seemed to be talking about anything that had happened, and I did not know whom to ask. Then one morning when Salome and I were spinning and weaving alone together – Tabitha now spent most of her time gathering herbs and helping Dinah in the kitchen – I saw Salome stop and rest her head on her loom, for a long time. I went over to put my hands on her, so the colors would come through and she would feel better, but she just looked at me with her eyes all pink, and said, "Come here, let me show you something."

She brought my spinning stool over and made me stand on it. Then she showed me how her loom worked, though I was not even a proficient spinner yet. I felt tall standing there with her, my head reaching her shoulder.

"Why did Elizabeth and Maryanna have to leave?" Of all that had happened, it was the simplest question I knew to ask. Salome looked at me and then back at the cloak she was weaving, bright dark blue like all our cloaks. "Is it because they did something bad?"

She stopped weaving and turned to me. She lifted me off the stool, and we sat in the shade together for a while. I knew she was going to talk to me, the way she had in the carriage, the way she had that morning up in the grove.

"All right, well, let us see, where to start. For one thing, no, they did not do anything wrong. It is to protect them, keep them safe. You have heard us talk about King Herod. He was the ruler of all of Israel. And he was very mean. Now he is dead, and people are fighting each other to become the new king."

"Then why did Elizabeth and Maryanna go away? Is there going to be more fighting here, like the night of waking twice?"

"Well, the men who were here that night, who hurt us, they are all dead, so no one who wants to hurt us knows anymore who we are or where. Still, it is better if there are not any boys here."

"Why? Are boys going to hurt us?"

"No, child, it is not that." Salome squinted her eyes at me. I squinted back at her, trying to appear as smart as I could, so she would tell me everything.

"Well, you see, one of those babies will be the next king of all of Israel."

"All of Israel?" Rachel once made me a map of all of Israel, telling me that was how a bird flying over the land would see it. It was round, with the Great Sea on one side and the River Jordan on the other. She showed me Magdala and Bethany and even Jerusalem. Just little dots. I saw the whole long way Salome and I had traveled. "That is so big! Little John is king of all that? But he is just a baby."

"Not yet, silly. He has to grow up first."

"Why are those boys going to be king? Why can I not be king?"

She squinted at me even harder, then she turned my whole body around so I was right in front of her. "A girl grows up to be a queen, not a king."

"Am I going to be a queen?"

"You remember what Deborah told you."

"Is Deborah coming back?"

"No, child, she is not."

"Is being queen why I was the baby girl they wanted to hurt, so I was in Bethany? So I should be in Nazareth with Zanna, and the baby Jesus and Maryanna."

"Well you see, the people who want to kill the new king, they are a bit stupid, and they do not worry so much about a queen. They do not think a queen can be important."

"Which is better, a king or a queen?"

"They are both better. You cannot have one without the other."

"And how will you know which baby boy it is? If they are both going to be king, will they have a fight?"

Salome pressed her calloused finger to my lips. "Do not ever say

that again. Do not even think about that. For now the most important part is that Maryanna's and Elizabeth's sons are in a place no one
knows."

I shook her hand off. "But we know."

"Yes, that is right lovey," she smoothed back my hair. "We
know."

"Are Maryanna and Elizabeth coming back?"

"Yes, everyone here misses them, and I suppose they miss being
here too."

"I miss everybody too. Especially Zanna, and Maryanna with her
singing, and Deborah, and the way she did the prayer in the morning. Hannah does not..." I did not have the words for it. "She does
not make my insides come outside."

Salome put her face in her sleeve for moment. When she lifted her
head, she was my teacher again. "Now get back on that stool, but first
go get your spindle. There is work to do – "

I finished her sentence with her, " – and it will not get done by
itself."

This time she smiled a little before turning to her loom.

By the time Elizabeth and Ariella came home, two years after they left, we had long resumed our gentle rhythm of Shabbat and harvest celebrations. Except for the special holy days – Yom Kippur and Sukkoth in the fall, and Purim, Passover and Shavuot in the spring, when the Valley folk congregated and celebrated in our courtyard – our compound was quiet, so quiet.

I no longer broke threads at the spindle and now practiced not breaking them around the small loom that had been Tabitha's, thus helping Salome cultivate her unending patience with me. Tabitha had assumed her grandmother Phebe's role, gathering the herbs we needed for infusion, incantations and occasionally, incense. Until her daughter returned, Hannah worked alone under the sacred oak, blending into incense the resins Tabitha gathered and those Dinah bought at market.

Hannah had invited Dinah to enter the priestesshood with us. I realize in retrospect this offer was born more out of need than generosity: after the night of waking twice, I was still too inexperienced to write amulets and contracts, one of the main services the community at large expected of us. Also, Dinah was menstruant, at the edge of blossoming into full womanhood. I do not know how she passed from ordinary person to priestess. I only know she and Hannah spent the three days of the full moon up at the birthing cave, and when Dinah came back down, she began attending the daily morning baths with us. And she began speaking, without self-consciousness, as if she always had.

Despite her new status, necessity required that Dinah still divide her time between the library, the kitchen and the market, leaving me more of the work of copying the scrolls, though I wrote more slowly than she did.

When I had finally copied an entire scroll by myself, Dinah took me to the special place she had been disappearing into all this time. The corridor looked as if it ended at the library door, but that was a trick of the eye. In fact, the passage bent around a curve in such a way as to make the opening invisible to those who did not know it was there. As we passed through it, Dinah pointed out a boulder in place behind the curve that could be rolled in front of the passage to block it, if we were ever invaded again. I was astonished at how far into the mountain we went. At last we arrived at a dank, close hollow of a room, about five paces wide in each direction. A quarter of it was filled with storage jars. Dinah told me some were full of water and others of dried fish, enough for all of us to live on for a few days. On top of the tall jars were blankets, rugs, tunics and cloaks, and on the ground were several small lamps and jars of oil for burning. In the opposite corner lay an empty bowl with its lid resting against it. I shivered in the damp cool.

"What is that for?" I asked Dinah.

"What do you think? What happens to all the water and food we drink, after it goes through our bodies?"

We used the outhouse on the far side of the barn. I could not imagine having to go in front of everyone.

"I know, it looks terrible, right? I hope we do not ever have to stay here," Dinah said, raising her small lamp so I could take it all in. "But after the night of waking twice, it is good to know we have some place to go."

I just hugged myself and nodded, eager to get back to daylight. Just as we walked out, I noticed the passage continued on the other side of this hollow. "Where does that go?"

"I do not know," Dinah shrugged. "Just deeper into the mountain, I guess," and back to work she went – the oven, the scrolls and the storerooms all calling to her.

By time Hannah's elder daughter came home, I had become skilled enough to assist our high priestess when a woman from the Valley came to the edge of the oak tree to ask for an amulet. Hannah would send Tabitha to the library to tell me what was needed. I would write the words she requested on the small square scroll used for these occasions and bring it directly to Hannah. Our petitioners could not read, they wanted only to hold in their hand a bit of the magical substance known as the written word. Once Hannah pressed the scroll rolled into the size of a finger into their waiting palms, their eyes shone momentarily through the cloud of daily misery; they would stand for a moment a little straighter, and the lines on their faces would smooth.

I heard them sometimes joke, as they stood at the edge of the oak tree, "Would you write an amulet that sends the relentless tax collectors away for good? One that does away with Romans and Herodians alike?"

Hannah would answer such teasing gently but firmly, "We are working on it."

"Would you make one that does not replace the Romans with some other empire that taxes us to death, so that we can barely feed our families, but an amulet to free us from foreign empires and taxes for good?"

Hannah would repeat, calmly, "I assure you, we are working on it," and hand them the amulet for which they had come.

At the time I wondered if there truly was a master amulet being worked on. Hannah frequently took my hand and brought me up to the birthing cave to simply sit and look out at the Lake together. She never spoke then, and I longed to ask about this secret amulet. I wondered if maybe it was kept back in the tiny dark room behind the library, of which Dinah and I never spoke since the day she had shown it to me.

Dinah and I shared another, more delicate secret. Only we and Phebe had known the true message Joseph of Arimathea had sent for Elizabeth; only we knew that he never intended to take her to Jerusalem. We need not have worried.

When the tall liquid-haired seer returned, at the end of the second rainy season since she had gone, she spoke little of her journey or her time in the desert. She mentioned once how the chaos following

Herod's death had kept her from reaching Jerusalem, and that was all. The desert – or was it motherhood, or the loss of Zacharias, or what she saw as Maryanna's betrayal – had visibly aged her, the way wood ages, making her face both harder and more beautiful.

It was Ariella, who had found her voice in the desert, who told us about the toddler John; Elizabeth only said that he was fine. Ariella had tended to him day and night and was heartbroken to leave behind her little Nan-nan, as she called him. She gushed about his nimble fingers and bright eyes, the speed with which he learned to walk and talk, the charm with which he seduced all who approached him. I marveled with her. I had never heard anyone talk about a baby growing up before, and I assumed these were remarkable signs, possible only for a great king such as he was likely destined to be.

With Elizabeth present, our rituals took on more ceremony. The morning bath, which had devolved into a single quick immersion, prayer and ablution, once again occupied the full length Deborah had accorded them. Hannah and Salome were shored up in their lifelong priestesshood, and Dinah in her novice-hood, with the presence of this solemn seer.

The gathering in the grove for the new moon also deepened in meaning. Those two days of the new moon were the only time we all gathered in any one place, other than the bath. We all went, those who sat and menstruated together, but also the children and the crones. There we sang the songs of Magdala and told the ancient stories, but we were not to converse.

Salome relished telling the Psalm of Magdala and intoning the Songs of Songs. Often though, with her tumbling red hair forming a veil around her, she sat and rocked herself, chanting her own made-up prayers. The way she worked out new rhythms and lyrics, it seemed she was keeping time with an invisible loom that clinked not in her hands but in her mind.

Hannah, as high priestess, was the only one who could repeat the Oracle, which she did each month, entering an altered state, as if reliving the moment the dream of it came to her, her daughter, and her mother at once.

During this time of the new moon, our sacred incense burned all day and all night on the stone altar of the grove. No visitors came when the moon was dark and the incense wafted down the hill. We sat and chanted and bled into the hard ground of the grove, making it holy with the blood of our wombs, the gift of life-giving with which Our Creator had endowed us. I longed to bleed too, to feel Creation stirring in me in such a direct manner, but I was to wait a long time for that. I knew once it came, it would be my turn to tell how this ritual began, a tale well-worn like a pebble in the fountain of our telling. Until then, Elizabeth told the tale.

"This blood from our wombs was the first blood of worship. Long ago, in the Beginning, the First Man saw the First Woman sit on the earth and honor Our Creator with the living blood from her own womb. Wishing to offer an equal honor, he became jealous and despondent to have no such gift to give. He cut his thigh to give of his own blood into the earth, but he could not bleed continuously for the two days of the dark moon as the First Woman could. Our Creator took pity on him, and visited him in the form of a serpent, which has no menstrual blood to give either. The serpent told the First Man to make an offering of an animal he loved. Our Creator would consider this equal to the gift of First Woman's moon blood.

"This is the infinite wisdom of Our Creator, for men have only pleasure in bringing forth life, and no pain. They do not face death in child-bearing. Thus are they brought into harmony with women, being made to feel the sorrow of giving life, by sacrificing a beloved animal, and by being reminded to honor women, to whom it is given to honor Our Creator with their very bodies."

When Elizabeth told this story, she used it as an introduction to other kinds of stories spoken in a deeper voice that teased and taunted, stories that brought the grown women among us to full out laughter, often to tears. As a child I wondered what these stories were about, and why was it so funny that men and women felt itchy or bothered in some way. As I grew I came to understand that these were jokes about sex, and so I came to understand the physical requirements of sex, but I remained perplexed as to what about them caused even Hannah to blush and Salome to howl.

As our morning baths and new moon gatherings in the grove gathered momentum, I gained a fuller experience of Our Creator, as being like the colors and music that flowed through me when I healed someone. I delighted in the sense that we, all together, revered and adored this same glorious blissful power.

This delight grew when your mother Maryanna came home to us, two years after her sister did. You were four years old by then, Jesus, and she had left you in Nazareth, in Zanna's and Judas's capable hands. Those two had now fallen in love and had their own child, a girl named Abigail. Maryanna spoke effervescently of everyone in Nazareth, especially of you, of course, how smart and strong you were – another good candidate for kingship I thought – and of Joseph of Nazareth who was kinder and gentler than any man she had ever met or heard of.

In coming home, Maryanna brought back not only her joyous nature but, most important for me, her music, which brought our worship to life, bringing our minds and hearts and bodies into that place of ecstasy: the full experience of Our Creator's presence.

My joy in our rituals increased much as a cloud stretches over the sky, until it covers the blue completely. Someone looking on could have easily seen the storm coming. I did not.

Every Shabbat, the line of Valley folk coming for the laying on of my hands serpentined up the mountain slope from the woods beyond my sight, up and through our gate, right to the bottom of the steps to the grove. They remained as hidden from view as possible to avoid attracting the attention of the Roman patrols along the road below, as those foreign soldiers took no Shabbat rest.

I had grown in confidence in my seven years of this practice. Hannah sat no longer with me but under the great oak to receive visitors and pray with them. Elizabeth stood at the bottom of the steps, where I could only see the top of her head. She transacted with the person there and made them wait for whoever was with me to go down before she let the next one up.

While they waited to be healed, the people milled around the fountain. Shabbat was a noisy day, with people crying in fear or pain, others laughing and telling stories, and others still arguing about the Romans and the Herodians and the Syrians and the endless impossible taxes. Maryanna sat on the steps to the bath and played music all Shabbat long, to keep people calm and reminded of the sacred place they were occupying.

Only people who made an offering – which Elizabeth collected – were allowed to come and see me on any Shabbat. I understood and accepted that my healing helped sustain the compound. The people needed us to heal them, to write their records and contracts and amulets, and most of all to intercede on their behalf with Our Creator. It was right that they help us live, as we did them.

On the Full Moon Shabbat, however, those who could not afford to bring an offering of grain or oil or tanned leather could come with empty hands and ailing bodies, and be received. We did not do any scribe work for these folk, and in any case they rarely needed it, because they had nothing to secure in a marriage agreement, nothing significant to sell and little to leave to their children. A word from us and a touch from me was considered sufficient blessing, amulet, formality – whatever was needed at the time.

The queue was longest on these days, but it moved quickly. I did not need to spend much time with each person. Sitting on the sacred rugs of birthing, inside my tent of privacy, I laid my hands and felt the colors move through me. My eyes closed, I heard the music and felt the colors. I then opened my eyes and saw the person's complexion change, as my hands felt the wellness restored to them. Sometimes the convalescents fell into a deep sleep and had to be carried away; sometimes they walked away on their own, so grateful, so delighted, "Bless you all your days, Quedeshah Magdala." It was easy and joyous. I felt powerful, helping everybody by doing something that came so freely, that felt so good, certainly better than weaving or spinning or reading or writing.

And then one day, a man reached his hand up to the sky. A hand raised in protest of the sun going down. Who among us has not, at one time or another, wanted to slow the path of the sun across the sky?

Since then I have realized that what I remember, I could not have seen. When I looked down from the grove, the people in the courtyard were outlined by the garden, our single-story kitchen building, and the fields beyond it.

The man I saw would have had to be a giant for his hand to be outlined against the sky, its shadow stark black against the still bright day. But that was what I saw. That is what I remember. With his other hand he was holding up his wife, who could barely stand. Elizabeth had moved in front of them, blocking their path up the steps, for you see, it was sundown, and Shabbat was done. No more free healing could be done until next full moon.

That was how it was. That was how it had always been. Surely those in the line kept their eyes both on the length of the line over to me and the distance of the sun above the horizon, formed by Mount

Arbel behind me. As that distance shrank, many went home. The setting of the sun, the end of Shabbat, was as much Our Creator's Will
as anything, and there was nothing to be done about it.

Until the man raised his hand. Did he cry out? I do not remember
a sound. I had just finished laying hands on the wounded one before
me, so many these days with flesh sliced open like bread, eyes that
could not meet mine for long, mouths that did not move, blood so
crusted into the cracks of their own hands they could not wash it
out any more. The man with me that day could walk; he did not
need to be carried up the steps. I had only a moment to think of the
amorphous war he was fighting, a war that was never talked about, a
battle that was nowhere and everywhere. It was a given, like the evening wind off the Lake. Once my hands were on him, the bliss took
over everything, and then he was rising, and blessing me through
still unmoving lips with whispers and breath. As he exited the tent I
looked up and out, and that is when I saw that black silhouette of a
man's hand.

I remember total silence. And in that silence I felt, without touching it, the torment in the man's heart, and I felt the stony gray ooze
that gurgled in the woman's breath, close to choking her completely.
I had never before felt someone's sickness without touching them. I
had never before felt someone's pain from afar.

But there it was. And Elizabeth, blocking the couple's path. Without thinking, without any kind of decision, I understood that if I
could feel the couple then they could feel me. I extended myself down
the steps and over around the tall liquid-haired seer to the man with
the outstretched hand, the one saying "No!" to the sundown and the
end of Full Moon and the end of healing. But somehow Elizabeth
felt what was happening and ran up to me and pulled me to my feet,
and in moving me broke the connection and whisper-yelled, "Never
after sundown! You impudent, thoughtless girl! What do you think
you are doing? Do you wish to blaspheme? Defy Our Creator here in
Her sacred-most sanctuary?"

In that moment my heart closed shut to a creator who had a right
and a wrong time for healing a man's heart and a woman's breath. I

felt as if the earth were shifting under my feet. Seeking steady ground, I broke from Elizabeth's grasp and tried to run down into the courtyard, but she blocked me this way and that. I could see our own armed men escorting the protesting man out the gate. Not knowing where to turn I ran out into the woods, and I found myself at the birthing cave. Without thinking I went around it and followed Hannah's secret path marked by the vein of dark stone against pale. The way was hard and steep. I had never tried this before, and my fingers bled from pulling myself up along the rocks, but I found a place for my feet and hands at every step.

When I reached the top, I found the sun had not set. It was only sundown on one side of the mountain, the east side, where our compound was. The valley in the west, behind Mount Arbel, was basking in the end of the day's light. I was basking too. I was all aglow. I turned toward the lightless Lake and looked out over the small stream of people I could see heading back down into the shadowy valley. Words tumbled through my mind from our Shabbat dinner's prayer, King David's psalm:

> I walk through the Valley of Shadow without fear,
> for You are with me,
> with Your Rod to protect me and Your Staff to guide me

Where was these folks' protection? Where was their guide? I could feel their suffering in my hands, I could hear their silent cries in my ears. I yelled for them to come back, but the wind pushed my voice back into the silent sunlit valley behind me, where it was not needed.

I felt the woman's breath stop. I could not see her slump against the man, but I could feel his heart break open, like a jar of precious oil cracked on the ground, the thirsty earth drinking it all up until there was nothing left but dagger-sharp shards.

A rustling sound preceded a man coming out of the woods. A short, intense man with a dark-bearded jaw as square and set as a loom corner, his knife drawn, a walk as forward as the fountain water, called out with a voice of one twice his size,

"What in Creation's name are you doing up here for all the world to see?"

"Who are you?"

"Come now," gesturing with his knife, "we have to get you down from this mountaintop, it is dangerous!"

"What does it matter? That woman just... I could have saved her."

"What in the name of Creation are you talking about? How are we supposed to keep you safe if you do not stay put? Anyone could see you up here! Come now!"

I realized he must be one of the rebel forces assigned to guard us. Guard what? A group of women who let other women die within arm's reach. What was the sense in that?

He gestured feverishly, but I could see he did not dare touch me.

"No one is looking up here," I replied. "And what does it matter anyway?" I walked away from him along the ledge.

He glanced around. "Someone could see you even if you do not see them. You are like the sun itself up here, all in white. At least sit down."

Out of the corner of my eye I saw him put his knife away in the leather sheath at his belt. I kept walking along the edge, my arms out for balance, feeling as though I was walking between day and night. Then I turned and looked right at him. He turned away.

"What a gaze you have, for such a young girl. Which one are you, anyway?"

"Which one what?"

"Let us see, you are about twelve years old. You must be Mary. That explains it, you are Rebecca's great-granddaughter. I knew her, you know. She once healed my father Joseph."

"Yes, I am Mary."

The man came closer; I skittered away, causing some rocks to loosen and fall off the cliff.

"Mary, this is dangerous! Even if our enemies do not see you, you could fall and kill yourself."

But I had no words for him. What difference did it make if I lived or died, really. In an instant, all our rituals had ceased to make sense.

The man kept talking to me. I walked back and forth, taking in the sunset, the first I had seen since I had left Bethany. All the colors of cloud and wind, the same colors that came when the healing happened. I thought to myself, I can believe in that, I can believe in the sunset. But I cannot believe in a god who puts the rule of the sun between a healer and an ailing one.

I do not know how long I was up there. When Hannah came to find me her white tunic was pink with setting sun. Her wild white hair seemed alive in the wind. My heart clenched like a fist, afraid that she too would turn against me and scold me.

But instead she said, "Judas, son of Abigail and Joseph! Praise Astarte that you are here. I thought she was all alone."

"None of you are ever alone, Quedeshah Hannah," he said, bowing to her, his hand on his chest.

I looked at the man with new interest. "You are Judas, son of Joseph? So you are the one protecting Maryanna's boy, Jesus, in Nazareth."

He squared his shoulders. "That is one of my tasks."

"You are the one who gave Zanna a baby girl."

"That is me too."

"Then what are you doing here? Why are you not there making sure she is safe?"

"Because I am here trying to get you down and out of danger."

"How is my Zanna?"

Hannah came to me, put her arm around my waist, and took my hand in hers, pulling me tenderly away from the ledge.

"Mary, Mary, what are you doing up here? Getting news? Mary..."

She led me further inward, and we sat together under the solitary olive tree that clung – clings yet? – to the rocky peak. Judas neared us; Hannah turned and raised her hand, palm out, bent at the wrist. Judas saw her gesture and disappeared back out of sight.

"Mary, tell me what happened."

I gazed out at the Lake, wanting to jump off the cliff and fly across fields and throw myself into darkening waters so I would not have to answer that question.

"Elizabeth said you had an outburst over a man and a sick woman and that you just ran off."

"Is that what she said? Well, Elizabeth knows everything. She must be right."

"Elizabeth does not know everything. No one knows everything. Only Our Creator knows everything."

"Then how can Our Creator not know that woman needed healing right away? How can Our Creator have such a stupid rule as 'no healing after sundown,' when it is only sundown in some places and not in other places! And how can Our Creator create me to be a healer if all the healing does is break my heart and my spirit?"

"Mary, how did you know that only the woman needed healing, and not the man?"

I looked out at the smooth waters of the Lake again. I felt comforted by the dark clouds of storm gathering on the far shore; I longed for that cleansing rush of rain and wild wind.

"Mary, answer me." Hannah brushed my hair back from my face, touched my cheek. Her touch, as always, pushed away the veils that kept me so alone. I turned and met her eyes.

"Hannah, I felt it."

"But she was in the courtyard, and you were in the grove."

"Yes I know where I was," brushing her hand away, suddenly wanting to bite it or scream at the top of my lungs, but it was Hannah, so all I showed was this one small impatient gesture. Bless her heart she did not take offense. Hannah never took offense at me.

"So you felt the woman's..."

"Her lungs were full of gray ooze, she was choking. I started to send out the – "

" – Wait, you could not only feel it, you were prepared to heal her? Without touching her?"

"Yes Hannah," feeling so old all of the sudden, older than Hannah, older than anyone I had ever known. "Yes. But Elizabeth felt something too, and she made me move, because it was after sundown. She would not let the man up, and she would not let my spirit down, and once she moved me, well... the healing broke."

Hannah sighed a deep sigh. I could feel her close her eyes and go inward, but I kept talking.

"And then I came up here. I did not know what else to do, I had to get away. When I found that it was still sunlight up here, still daylight… What sense do these rules make? I cannot heal her down there but up here I can? When I reached out for her with my mind, down into the valley, the woman was already dead. And the man, his heart..."

The word "heart" brought up the flow of tears. I curled in on myself. All this pain for want of a little sunlight.

"What of his heart?" Hannah asked so gently, like a fine soft rain blending right in with my tears. I answered her between sobs,

"His heart was all broken! She was dead in his arms and his heart wanted to die too, just to bring her back to life if he could! We are up here in Magdala, we are supposed to be so holy we cannot even step out of the compound unless it is for some special holy mission, but never do we feel anything like he felt! Everyone here does their duty about this and their duty about that, even Judas is supposed to be with Zanna, but no, he is here doing his duty, she is there doing her duty, and there is no one here who would die for anyone!"

"You want someone to die for you, Mary?"

"No! No!" I got up and moved away. "You do not understand at all! That kind of feeling, that kind of passion means being alive! What are we doing here if we do not feel these things? I never felt it before, so I did not care, but now that I felt it, I want it. I want that feeling; that feeling is more holy and pure than anything we do here, any prayer, any weaving, any scroll even!" I felt like screaming, but I knew that Judas was still around somewhere, and I did not want him to come back.

I stomped around, picked up some rocks, and threw them over the side as hard as I could, to the north, where they would not hit anyone. "At least, Hannah, if we cannot feel that way, then we should be in service to that feeling, and not turn it away just because in our little grove the sun's gone down!"

"Mary," Hannah motioned to me, "Mary, come back here and sit down, come back, let us talk about all this," patting the ground next to her.

"There is nothing to talk about! It is the Law, the Law is the Law, and I am supposed to be a good priestess and uphold this stupid Law. Right now I would rather die."

"All this talk of dying and wanting to die!" Hannah smiled at me out of the corner of her wide mouth. The orange sunlight bathed her crinkly face. "Do you think we can find a way to live through all this? A better way?" She patted again the ground next to her.

I stopped pacing and took in her gaze. Once I was sure she was not humoring me, I went and sat down, near her but not touching, and hugged my knees to chest.

"Mary," Hannah's bony hands rested on mine where I was holding my shins, rocking myself, my face buried in my lap, "I know how it is for you; there is still so much that you cannot yet be told about the Oracle, cannot yet understand. All will be revealed to you when it is time."

I bit my knees lightly to relieve the familiar frustration those words brought.

Hannah spoke slowly, "I am beginning to see the Oracle may mean much more than we thought it did. I am beginning to think you will find the deeper truth of the Law and bring its understanding to a new generation."

"How could I possibly do that?"

"Shh. The answers will reveal themselves in time."

"Time!" I raged, close to tears and screaming. I spoke through my teeth, into my knees. "I am so tired of hearing that! It will never be 'time,' or 'one day!' I know the Oracle, but I still do not know what I am supposed to do, more than the healing, more than being queen one day, but queen of what, exactly? Of whom? The Oracle does not make any sense, *They will be One, then Two, and Two will be One again.* What does that mean? I know you know, Hannah, and Elizabeth, and Salome, I see the hushed conversations, the meaningful gazes! When will someone tell me, so I can begin to learn, to understand, to do what all are expecting of me!"

Hannah caressed my back softly, "Shh, Mary, shh, this is desire rearing its head, blinding you. Remember the round breathing."

What else could I do? I lifted my head and commenced, breathing eight in, holding, and exhaling eight. Though my mind still whirred, it began to calm.

"Good, good. Now. Here is something I can give you, which might help. For now simply know this. There is nothing in you that is not from Our Great Mother Goddess. Say that back to me."

"What?"

"There is nothing in you not from Her."

I could not repress a grin. "There is nothing in you not from Her."

"Mary! Come now, say it right, you know what I mean."

I rested my chin on my knees. "There is nothing in me not from Her."

"Again."

"There is nothing in me not from Her."

"Excellent. Now. When you feel this terrible knotted feeling you have now, when something happens as it did today, and you feel that the way we understand the Law of Our Creator is wrong, when you feel as if you want to run or scream or both, you come up here, and... and..." looking around, finding a nice fist-size stone, "just like you did, take a rock like this, and put all your feeling in it, and fling it off the mountain." Her rock flew, a perfect arc into the sky that got lost in the rocky shadow. Through her light-hearted smile, she added, "Just try not to aim at the compound or the woods, all right?"

"But what good will this do? This changes nothing!"

"Mary, for now you must live with the rules into which you were born, and obey the others to whom you were born. And you also must live with the outrage which has become rooted in you today. But think of this, today, you discovered not only your outrage, but your power to heal without even touching. This is unheard of in all our time, all our stories, all our land. Perhaps your outrage has fed this new power. But for now, you must keep it to yourself, and wait for your time."

The sun slid behind the Horns of Hattin, the mountain beyond our Mount Arbel, and we were bathed in blue gray shadow.

"But Hannah how can I do this? How can I wait? How can I live by all these rules, when I feel people's suffering in my heart and hands?"

"It is good that you feel people's suffering. This will serve you when your time comes. And you will help them. If you try to wreak havoc now, you will only be able to help one or two. You do not yet know what She intends for you. Wait until you come of age, come into your own, and then you will be able to help all Creation," her hand fanning out over all we could see.

"How will I know when I have come of age? How do you know I have not already?"

"It is not I who will know, it is you. You will know because you will no longer want to run from the fire, but directly into it. In the meantime," raising her hand to stave off my interruption, "come up here whenever She starts to move you that way. Throw off a rock, a rock of blessing, a rock of anger and hate, whatever is too heavy for you to carry. That way, when the time comes, you will be ready, and you will be carrying no burden. At least, less of a burden, and that will help."

I thought, but did not say, "What can you possibly know about burdens?" I had not yet lived long enough to know that everyone alive is burdened, in simple visible ways, and in invisible ways which tax us most of all.

I thought but did not say, "For a seer, Hannah, you are remarkably long on hope and short on sight."

I wonder now what would have been different if I had witnessed my first Sacred Marriage Ritual before the day of the black hand, rather than after. At fourteen years of age, I knew full well what I was supposed to be seeing. Robed in white, with rows of pink flowers and gold coins in her red hair, Salome stood in the grove with Zebedee the Sadducee. As had been done as long as anyone could remember, before there were any scrolls to help people remember, the great priestess and the great priest would enact the marriage of Our Great Mother Goddess and Our Great Father God. In doing so, the people invoked the creative fertility of Our Creators, Who would then bless the faithful's bodies, flocks, fields, and minds with Divine Creative Force.

I had learned from all the different scrolls I copied that in different lands there were different ways of conducting this ritual. In the days of Ur, by the river Euphrates, the whole city would gather for days, or even weeks, to celebrate the joining of Inanna Queen of Heaven and Earth with the shepherd Dumuzi. In Babylon, they once celebrated Ishtar and Tammuz. In Egypt today, they celebrate Isis and Osiris.

In Magdala, we celebrated the union of Yahweh and his Astarte, Astarte and her Yahweh. We followed the liturgy of Wise King Solomon, the Song of Songs, which Zanna had been singing to me since I was a wee thing, which by the time of Salome's ritual I knew by heart. This was how King David celebrated with his Bathsheba, how Queen Jezebel anointed her King Ahab, and how all the Sacred Marriage Rituals have always been celebrated in our land.

In Magdala, we had a simple ceremony that lasted one night and one day. Though we did not have occasion for the Great Ritual every year, when we did it was celebrated on Purim for the springtime and ascension of the life force around us, at Shavuot in early summer in gratitude and celebration of the wheat and barley harvests, or at Sukkoth in the late fall, as a ritual of thanks for the completed harvests, in praise of our dead, and in prayer for steady rain.

In most ancient times, Purim had been the time of king-making. The great priestess, incarnating the Great Mother Goddess Herself, would anoint with her inner essence the man who thus became the ruling king for one year. Sukkoth had been the time for the king to die, to be sacrificed on the Creator's altar in order to earn his Creator's goodwill for his people. Eventually, the kings pushed to rule for more than one year, as of course they did not want to be sacrificed. In time, they designated a surrogate who would have the great honor of dying in their place. Later, when that seemed too cruel, it was decided a choice animal would be sacrifice enough.

In Magdala we did not sacrifice anyone. No one had been killed in this way since long before Abraham and Sarah came to the land they called Canaan and gave birth to Isaac who sired Jacob who sired the twelve tribes of Israel. With the Sacred Marriage Ritual, we instead invoked the generative powers of Our Creator, and thus celebrated and honored the Union from which all Creation issued. As the first words of the Book of Genesis tell us, "In the beginning the 'Elohim,' the Divine Ones, created the heavens and the earth."

The Ritual did not result in a husband and wife union. After having embodied Our Creators for us and in so doing blessed our land, our lives, our loins, Salome would stay with us, and Zebedee would return to his home. A priestess's life revolved around the rituals she helped keep, and there was room for nothing more.

I had never seen Zebedee before this springtime holiday of Purim. He was a Temple priest, a Sadducee, though not a chief priest, as Zacharias had been. Some years ago Zebedee had left the urban lavishness of Jerusalem for the pastoral peace of our Valley of the Doves by the Lake. Salome later told us Zebedee left the city mostly because he felt pressed by his fellow Temple priests; the public aspects of Temple living impeded too much on his abilities to keep in secret

what he felt was appropriate observance of Our Great Mother Goddess Astarte's rituals.

For her Sacred Marriage Ritual, Salome wore the tunic she had
woven especially to wear for this night and this night only. Since the
new moon she had spent all day and night in the sacred grove with
Maryanna, praying and meditating, aided by Elizabeth's mysterious
brew of poppies. She fasted for three days prior to the ritual.

The Sacred Marriage tent awaited the couple, up in the grove,
beyond the seven gates constructed specially for the Ritual and
the gathered-stone altar that was always there. Inside the tent were
strong wine, sweet figs, salty meats, fresh breads and cakes shaped
like the moon, and delicate incense – every delight to stir Salome and
Zebedee's senses, set on a small table to the side of the bed of thick
rugs and pillows covered in the finest linen. I knew all this because I
helped place everything in there. I had enjoyed attending to Salome
in this way. She had been an exacting teacher, but she was always kind
to me, and there had never been anything I could do for her in return
until Hannah asked me to work with Dinah to ready the tent.

In the grove now, as the Ritual was about to begin, Salome beamed
under her crown of flowers and coins, though she had not chosen
Zebedee – he had been chosen for her, just as Zacharias had been for
Elizabeth. Yet both women came to cherish their Ritual consorts, all
the same. My mother Muriel had chosen Jacob the night of my conception, and Maryanna had decided by herself to go to Zacharias. In
both cases disaster ensued: Muriel's death and my early banishment,
and then worse, the night of waking twice. Perhaps then, I pondered,
it was better to live within the rules and embrace the law. I could
understand this with my mind, but my body and soul rebelled.

With these thoughts louder than all the music, I stood for the
celebration in the grove with a wooden face, banging on the tam-
bourine Maryanna had made for me, but unable to open my voice
to join in the Song of Songs. Salome flushed as she and Zebedee, a
stout rosy-cheeked man, recited the words that had been spoken for
generations, words of love and lust and worship:

> *Let him kiss me with the kisses of his mouth,*

for this love is better than wine...

The other women chanted out the call-and-response gaily and rattled their tambourines loudly as Salome and Zebedee passed under the bright full moon through the seven fragile gates made of palm fronds, decorated with yellow daisies, pale wild roses and purple myrrh. As they were meant to do, the gates fell apart around the couple as they passed, for there was no going back, no undoing.

After the last gate, Hannah handed Salome a small alabaster jar filled with fragrant spikenard oil. With the oil, Salome anointed Zebedee's forehead above his open smile. She turned as red as her hair when he opened the tent flap for her, and the music reached a fevered pitch. After they disappeared inside the tent, after much howling up to the bright round moon, we descended to the courtyard for a great feast of the same foods that had been laid out in the tent for the holy couple. This was part of the Ritual, to recognize that our lives were so sweet precisely because we were able to partake of the same joys and bliss as Our Creator.

Noticing but misinterpreting my gloomy face, Hannah hugged me as we arrived near the fountain. She assured me, "Do not worry, Mary, it will be your turn soon enough. And yours will be more than ritual, my dear, it will be a true anointing of the King."

The mention of this chilled me. No one but Hannah referred to my special status in regard to the Oracle, and even Hannah did this so rarely that each time she did, it felt like one more jewel of information dropped in my lap, which I could eventually string into a whole necklace that would make sense. But how could my being queen of all the land ever make sense? Was not the queen supposed to uphold the Law, to believe in it wholeheartedly? I felt trapped, as I could change neither how I felt nor who I was expected to be.

I sat to eat with the others, but I consumed nothing but Maryanna's song, not realizing until the next day that her unceasing singing meant she did not eat either. I thought of her and Zacharias, their one night, a half-night really, on that same spot beyond the altar, but without a tent, without a ritual, without a feast. That night brought you into the world, Jesus. That night was made sacred by

the possibilities your birth presented. Zacharias and Maryanna had
made their own ritual, with only a shared song and a full moon.

I wondered, did anyone else think about these things?

The faint light of the early morning pulled me from my familiar dream: that backlit silhouette of a raised open hand, its palm and five fingers so terribly clear. I sat up, letting the haunting vision slip away into the night's last shadows. The new day beckoned me to come out, come forward, come into.

That time before life stirred, before the dawn, those moments were mine alone. Everyone else was still sleeping, even Salome, who seemed so small to me in her stillness. Though I was now a full head taller than she, she still called me 'child.'

Did she still call me that because I had not yet been initiated to the Sacred Marriage? Or was it because she had borne children and I had not? Her twin boys were now in Zebedee's care. Even Dinah had performed the Sacred Marriage Ritual and borne a son, who was being fostered by his father Cleopas. At nineteen years of age, I was the youngest one in Magdala, and I was still waiting for my life to begin.

Quiet as the first light, I grabbed my cloak and snuck out of the room where all lay sleeping to answer the pre-dawn's invitation to the roof of my world – the plateau of Mount Arbel, where I belonged only to myself. There all the world was mine, and I traveled it on any passing breeze that would take me.

As I did each morning, I reached the top by climbing along the foot of the sheer cliffs, along the dark path that Hannah showed me when I was little. At the peak, the abrupt cliff facing the sunrise over the Lake met the gentle plateau sloping unhurriedly toward the shallow valley in the west. At this spot began a completely differ-ent world, just at the edge of ours – on my face a thin dry wind replaced the thick moist air below, at my feet a rich black soil unlike the reddish clay on which we lived, in my eyes an unfettered view in all directions around our cave-like compound. I stood with my arms opened wide, letting the gentle morning breeze from the Valley blow through my tunic to caress my skin, legs apart so I could feel the air moving between them. The climb up the side of the rocky peak always left me with a light sweat that turned deliciously icy in the morning mountaintop air.

Much of the sky was still starry dark. There was just the faintest pallor above the hazy purple mountains across the Lake, the gentlest suggestion that the sun might once again return, that day would push out night. The birds knew it and called to each other in celebration. The fishermen's torches, lined up on the Lake's shore with their boats and the night's catch, were brighter now than the stars above.

It had been a good wet winter, praise Astarte, and it seemed there would be a good crop in the Valley this year, so long as the rain eased off gently and brought no rough storm as a parting gift, and so long too as the rain was not followed by another devastating heat wave as there had been last year. All the grapes in the hills had dried into tiny, green, inedible raisins, right on the vine. We had drunk wine so pale it was best called water, but that was no hardship compared to that of the vine-keepers who had nothing to trade all year. It was easier to drink last year's wine than to eat last year's bread.

But never had there been such a heat wave two years in a row. If all went well, a little more rain would yet come. Right now, on what promised to be a clear bright day, the scent of wild fennel filled the air through which larks flittered about with twigs in their beaks.

The full throaty call of the warbler, the steady rhythm of the farmer's scythe song against the stone, the fishermen's voices calling to each other the returns of their labor, these sounds blended together like the flying carpets I had heard of, offering a ride to a world beyond my own: the place where everyone else lived.

This was the first day I had been able to climb straight up here in more than two moons. All winter the rains rendered the steepest part of the trail too slippery. In the wettest times I had to take the circuitous path through the woods, which left me no time up here at all, no time to rail against all I wished I did not know and cry for all I wished I did. Still I came, if only to throw the rock of all I could not carry, as Hannah had prescribed, and then go back down again.

Our vast courtyard seemed to shrink every year as I longed for out, up, down, away. By the end of winter the sacred tasks of my life felt like insipid chores, except the Shabbats spent in the little dark room next to the barn. There, sheltered from the uncertain weather, I received the ill for the laying on of my hands. I preferred that tiny room with only neutral memory. Under my small tent in the open grove for the rest of the year, I could not help but recall the hand raised in protest, though I took comfort in seeing the horizon which I felt held some promise, some answer to the question that filled me to bursting though I could not name it.

Weaving filled much of my days. Though it did not cheer me, the rhythm of the loom brought my mind to stillness. There I found a reprieve from dwelling on how these hours, these days that made up my life, were given to a Goddess I worshipped but did not understand, women I lived next to but not with, prayers I spoke but did not inhabit. The presence I was born to serve, I felt only when I was healing someone and, ever so slightly, on my mountaintop.

Hannah came up there with me sometimes, in the afternoons, when she saw my face darken more than usual. We sat and talked, or sat and did not talk. In our quiet times especially, I felt accepted as I was, without effort or pretense. As she grew older, Hannah came up less and less often with me, and I missed that.

The only consistent brightness of my winter months burned in the lamp that lit the dark dank scroll room. I thought sometimes of shutting the door and locking myself in there. I labored through copying the pages of our ancient laws, which governed what we did and when, whom and where we touched, the precise description of all our rituals as they had been handed down for generations. But I savored transcribing the trials of yore of the Goddess Inanna as she became Queen of Heaven and Earth. I loved copying the psalms of David most of all, "Save me My Creator, for the waters have come into my soul, I sink in deep mire, where there is no standing." He always concluded with such faith in Our Creator's triumph that I believed that I too might be comforted someday. As I sat and copied the words of Proverbs – "Does Wisdom not cry out? And does understanding not bring forth Her Voice?" – I never failed to envision the time before Solomon's Temple burned, before the Holy Ones gathered in the desert at En Gedi. Perhaps that had been a sweeter, softer time, a time when there was such abundance that no one was turned away who could not pay for healing or could not make an offering for prayer. I imagined a time when people did not put rules before compassion, when no one's heart had to shrivel at the sight of a man's pleading hand raised at dusk against a still pale sky. I knew I was making up a story. But, I thought, where would we be without the stories that comfort us? How could we hope for a better life if we could not imagine that somewhere, someone lived it?

In the winter, outside that dank room, the rain fell like prison bars, keeping me from my time up on the mountain, from what I knew of peace. When the first rain of the season came, it was such a celebration, such a joy, we all raced to stand in it, to welcome the cool drops on our parched skin. By the time the songs of praise were sung and the daily showers settled in as routine, I had to remind myself that we desperately needed this rain, that I ate this rain all year, and that it too would pass, as did all things.

From my mountaintop, I could see everything – the long black dock of the town of Tarichaea reaching into the blue Lake in front of me, the sharp ragged slope of Mount Nittai in the north across the Valley of the Doves, the soft greening hills and valleys that stretched behind me to the rocky peaks of the Horns of Hattin. Most cherished lay to the south: Tel Rapha, the Hill of the Healed, the Hill of the Dead, the cradle of the cherished bones of so many mothers, including mine. When I rested my eyes there, my heart began to quiet, and I reached out my hand as if to touch the sleeping hill.

A gust of wind blew my hair into my face. I shook my head and lifted my eyes to the sky, stretching my hands as far as they would go. Then I dropped them, their silhouette reminding me too much of the image I had come here to release.

Hannah's movement down in the waking compound caught my attention. I could clearly make out Hannah's stooped frame, white mane of hair glowing in the light of the small lamp she carried. Always the first one up, she crossed the wide courtyard from the storeroom beside the gates, to go sit on her three-legged stool under the oak tree. There she would feed the tiny fire that burned in the large brass bowl all day and all night. She would meditate alone until Elizabeth joined her to discuss the night's dreams and toss the Umim and Thummim, the holy divination stones, as was fit to do on this holy eve of Purim, the last holy day of the rainy season.

As Hannah walked, I could see her left foot beginning to drag a little, as her mother's once had. Ariella emerged next into the court-yard – like a dove set free from its cage, she flew down the steps from the balcony to the kitchen, there to check on a flame of different nature – our oven – and take stock of the day's tasks before her. Espe-cially that day, as Purim fell on Shabbat that year, as many dishes as possible had to be prepared in advance, with only the cooking of the meat to take place right before sundown, after which no work could be done. The oven needed to be burning all day to have sufficient heat left for that afternoon's cooking of lamb.

From so high up, I felt a stirring of tenderness for this tiny ancient place beneath me. For the keeping of this fire, the weaving of Her veils, the mating of the Sacred Ones.

Around the rectangle womb of the courtyard and the frame of stout buildings that enclosed it, beyond the grove above it, the woods spread far and wide. I could not make out where Judas had his men stationed, so well did they blend with tree, rock, and cave. They were always there, though I never saw them up close anymore. When I started coming up here regularly, the men had not approached me; they would not have dared. Instead Judas came on their behalf to the gate, to talk to Hannah about keeping me in the safety of the com-pound. She told me about it later. She said she told Judas that they were to work around me, not the other way around.

I was self-conscious after that, for a while. I knew they were always up here with me, somewhere. When I talked to Hannah about it, she said they were not watching me, they were watching the perimeter. So I tried not to think about them. Anyway, I thought, who would come and bother us anymore? Anyone who should not know where we were was long dead, as far as I knew. Had not enough blood been shed?

This spot where I stood would really have been the perfect lookout for them, but sometimes during the day, I looked up here, and I never saw anyone. I was glad. I needed at least one place that was mine. None of the other women seemed to need that: Salome appeared content at her loom, Dinah with the scrolls, Ariella at the kitchen, Hannah and Elizabeth under their tree, Maryanna with her lutes, flutes, and singing, and Tabitha wherever she was.

I prepared to throw my rock. As I looked out to make sure no one was beneath me, I saw Maryanna splash some water on her face at the fountain. Then she walked up to the grove, where she looked around to make sure no one was watching. She did not see me above her. Then she lay face down, belly down on the earth, arms and legs spread out, just beyond the gathered-stone altar.

She and Zacharias had consecrated that place, in their own way. I realized here was someone else who needed to feel that a spot was all her own, if only in memory, if only for a few moments. Had she come there before? Had I not seen? I smiled to myself sadly and thought, remembering that long ago morning in Bethany, what else happens when I am not looking?

After throwing my rock to the north, I took a deep breath and turned back to the south, to Tel Rapha. I tried to imagine my mother's spirit welcoming mine into the day. Just then Hannah's booming voice rose from below, rounding up the women for the bath. I hesitated for a moment, wanting to linger where I was. I reached my hands up to the dark bright blue sky one more time, let the few remaining stars dance among my fingers, and then I was off.

I knew the way down the mountainside so well that my fingers and toes reached with their own mind for the nooks and small ledges. At the birthing cave, I broke into a run down to the grove. I could just make out the silhouettes of the women coming up from the compound, their awakening voices chanting, over and over,

L'cha dodi lik-rat kalah, p'nei Shabbat n'kab'lah (Beloved, come to meet the bride; Beloved, come to greet Shabbat.)

I hummed along as I took my shortcut directly from the grove to the bath.

As tonight would also be Purim, every fifth repetition was changed to *Shoshanas Yaakov tzahala v'simcha, birosam yachad techeles Marduk.* (The lily of Jacob cheers and rejoices on seeing her Marduk in royal blue.)

I could see the basin clearly now in the growing light of day; the steaming surface of bath water and the limestone basin carved out of the pale mountain. Beyond it, the Lake shimmered with early morning iridescence, while the still-hidden sunlight barely gilded the purple enclosure of mountains on the far shore, their solid form already receding into the day's haze.

I wound down the path and arrived at the steps of the pool of water just in time to face and greet the others. As Salome and Elizabeth arrived at the lip of the basin platform, they hesitated for a moment in their step.

Salome cried out happily, "By Our Lady Astarte, with your face shining like a ripe pomegranate, Mary, your tunic clinging to your curves, your dark locks wild around your face, on this Purim it looks as though you are indeed our Bride."

My heart rushed out to her, for her desire to see me that way, until Elizabeth added, pointedly, "Indeed, she is Mary of 'Jacob.' "

Yes, my mother chose Jacob, I thought to myself, why did that matter now? I smiled back in a way that made my cheeks feel stiff. Walking toward the bath, we resumed the chant.

As our predictably slow Tabitha made her way up the last steps, she fingered her sharp necklace with one hand and with the other held Ariella's, who had taken to looking after her. Dinah walked behind them, chanting faintly but gaily, holding hands with Maryanna who shone with the beauty of the pure voice emerging from her breast. No sign of her early morning prostration lingered in her song. Hannah closed the informal procession in silence.

As our high priestess approached, I saw she was ashen, her wide mouth set and tight. I wondered, was she all right? Then I realized Elizabeth had the same expression, which I thought was just for me. Had they had some dream? Some foreboding? When Hannah arrived at the basin's edge, the chanting ended. I quietly took off my cloak and entered the steaming waters which embraced me like a mother. The other women came in, immersed themselves, and waited for Hannah to lead us in prayer and pour the ablutions.

Her voice never seemed as strong as Deborah's had been, or was it that when I was little, everything around me had seemed so big? I repeated the words, focusing on the heat of the water and relative coolness of the air. After everyone left I stayed, eyes closed, lulled by the heat, vaguely trying to prevent the day from starting in earnest. Hannah startled me by speaking from the side of the basin, her face flushed with heat but not softened,

"Mary, do not break your fast. Today you come and sit under the oak with me and Elizabeth." Without waiting for an answer, she walked off on her softly sandaled feet.

Fully roused by her words, I extracted myself from the water's hold and let the morning air clear my mind. I had not been invited under the tree since I was small, when Deborah had spoken to me of healing and told me of my role in the Oracle we sang each new moon. It was true that this was the first Purim since my menstrual cycle began, finally this past winter. Everyone had been so worried, except Hannah, who remembered that Rebecca's had started late too, as had my grandmother Martha's. The onset of my bleeding had not delighted me as much as I had thought it would, arriving when I no longer understood what Our Creator wanted from me, nor how I could possibly give it. I gave my living blood to the sacred grove like I did everything during that time, with a little hope and enough willingness but not much else.

But Hannah's invitation sparked my imagination. She had never intimated that my sitting under the oak would be a possibility. I remembered my wonder the first time I stood there as a small child. A tangle of loud voices below pulled me completely into the day. I wrapped myself in my cloak and made my way down to the courtyard.

Everyone was talking at once, what was going on? Then I saw Zanna! My Zanna! Home from Nazareth? I was about to run and embrace her.

But then
I saw you
and
I paused,
my foot hovering for a moment
over the last stone step,
before I entered the courtyard firmly,
wrapping my cloak tightly around me.
I laid eyes on you, the boy Jesus,
on the path from bath to oak.
The sun crossed the horizon.

I knew immediately who you were. Other than John, who would not have been with Zanna, no other boy your age, at the very first light of manhood, would be admitted past the gate before sunrise. Why had no one told me you would be there on that day?

From the distance of ten paces where I stood, I took in the tight congregation around you, standing by the fountain under the courtyard's first ray of sun. I was moved by your regal stillness as your mother, your aunt, and your grandmother, all almost equally strangers to you, stood with the others with their backs to me, in a semi-circle around you, all talking at once in high voices, poking at your arms and chest, feeling your coarse wavy black hair, pinching your still-round cheeks though your height almost matched your tall aunt Elizabeth's. You stood calmly in the circle of cooing women, looking at them from under the astonishingly long lashes that made your eyes seem like living creatures in their own right. You did not resist their inquiring hands – rather, you took the women in with your gaze, each in turn, collecting with your eyes the information they sought with their fingertips. You did not speak.

I did not get to see many healthy children in those days, only the pale nearly lifeless ones brought to me by trembling mothers, "Quedeshah Magdala, help us, Quedeshah Magdala, if it pleases Our Creator." The children departed from me, quiet in their mother's arms, with color in their cheeks, but deep in the sleep of convalescence. From the stories I had heard, down in the town of Tarichaea, a hearty child your age was already stealing figs and picking fights, bent and weary from picking up chaff off the threshing floor or endlessly mending fishing nets with his small dexterous hands.

I could not imagine you doing any of that. You stood tall without straining to square your shoulders; your small mouth, completely relaxed, seemed not hushed but choosing its moment to speak; your long hands were relaxed at your sides.

You must have felt my stare because you looked over, between your grandmother's and your aunt's shoulders, right into my eyes. Your gaze hit so hard that I almost took a step back. But I stayed put, remembering looking into adults that way when I was your age. I breathed deeply, open, despite my morning's despondency still in my mouth like a bitter taste.

A single round tear rolled down each of your downy cheeks. I felt mine warm, felt the taste in my mouth mellow. Salome and Hannah turned and followed the direction of your stare. When they saw the look on my face, they smiled a strange smile at me and then at each other. I turned my head away. They looked at each other like this often these days, it made me feel as though I were still a child, even though I knew what they were thinking: if all went well, and you and I were indeed destined for each other, we might as well have some feeling for each other. A jumble of emotions wound around my heart – I did not want to want whom they wanted me to want.

Then Zanna separated from the group and came to me, her round face shining, tugging a gangly girl behind her. She hugged me like only she could. My Zanna!

Releasing me, "This little one, here," pulling forward a dark-haired girl, "this is my girl. Abigail."

"Oh Zanna!" Bending down, "Hello little one. How lucky you

are to have Zanna for your mother! She was a bit my mother too, you know."

The child with Judas's unmistakable square jaw on her small tender face disappeared again behind her mother's abundant hips. I rose back up to meet Zanna's tentative smile, "So Zanna, what are you doing here? A surprise visit for Purim?"

"You have not heard, have you?"

"What happened? Something happened?"

Zanna turned to the women in the courtyard behind her. Following her gaze, I looked at you again, and at the women around you, wondering why I had not noticed the tension buzzing around everyone's head like bees.

"I thought maybe Hannah and Elizabeth would have..."

"What? What?"

"Joseph of Nazareth was murdered, savagely, right before our eyes."

"Murdered! When? By whom?"

"Who do you think, Mary, who do you think?"

"Soldiers! And Jesus was there?"

"Right in front of him. Of us all. Right in our home."

"Oh Zanna! No! When did this happen?"

"Night before last. We left yesterday morning, right after it happened."

We watched your mother walk you toward the kitchen, presumably to feed you. Zanna pulled her child out from behind her. "That's a good idea, go get some breakfast." The girl clung to her mother, shook her head. "Go now, will you! I will be right here, I will not be out of your sight. Go, I say!" And she gave her daughter a gentle but firm push, and the girl tottered shyly away.

"Was she there too?"

"Yes, but she has taken to sleeping on the roof in all kinds of weather, so she only heard, she did not see." Looking toward the kitchen, "Abigail will eat, but I doubt if they will get so much as a crumb into Jesus. He has not opened his mouth since he told me what happened."

"Told you what happened? I thought you said you were all there," I said, touching her forearm, pulling her to come sit in the shade under the balcony, on the spinning stools near the looms.

"We were all there, but Jesus…" her voice trailed off. She had not taken her eyes off you, seated as you were on the rug under the balcony across the courtyard from us. You calmly watched Abigail eat, but did not touch the bread and olives before you. "Look at him; you would never know he has not eaten in two days. He refused."

"Zanna, what happened?"

Facing me now, but eyes on the wall behind me, "Six soldiers burst in, broke down the solid wood door, in the middle of the night. They grabbed Joseph, pinned him to the ground, and cut his head right from his body with their swords, hacking away while he screamed. Once they were done, while blood still spurted from the stump of his neck, they pissed on his writhing torso, laughing, making some joke about the messy fate of rebels. Oh my good Joseph!"

She covered her face with her hands. Shaking, she took several deep breaths, then revealed an ashen face. "When the door flew open, Mary, I was so scared. I knew there had been a tussle at the market a few days before. Joseph had stepped in, grabbed the reins of the horse of one of those pigs. The uniformed swine was just plowing through on his war horse, with no regard for the people shopping, nor their stalls. Joseph took the reins just as the horse was about to knock over an old man whose foot was caught in a fallen stall and could not get away. Joseph, no young man himself, you know, he stepped up and grabbed the reins! The horse reared, threw his mount.

"Joseph ran when he saw the soldier on the ground, and they would never have known who he was, except that the old man he had saved kept saying, 'oh, praise Joseph, Our Creator bless his soul,' on and on.

"So the soldiers came. I was right there. We were all asleep. Either Judas or I always slept near Jesus. But Judas was out patrolling the town. You can imagine how he is almost mad with rage that he was not there to protect us. I say it is better this way – he would have been killed. After seeing his own father like that, you know!

"But I was right there. I put my hand over the boy, I could not protect him, but it is just natural, you know – I raised him like I raised you!"

Zanna's throat closed on the last word. She took a moment to catch her breath, before continuing. "But the soldiers did not see us, praise Astarte, they did not even look at us. Jesus did not move at all. His eyes were open, but there was no expression on his face, and under my hand his heart inside his thirteen-year-old body was calm. After the soldiers were gone, he asked me, 'What happened?' And I said, 'What do you mean what happened? You were right here.' And he told me that when the soldiers burst in, he had felt flattened, as if a strong wind were pushing him against the wall. I can still see it all, the metal armor, shaved faces, dark red blood. But Jesus told me he did not see anything – he said he sank through the wall and flew out, up above the roof..."

"Zanna – those were his words, 'flew out?' "

"Yes, that is what he said, flew up to the roof, up above the roof. He said he saw Abigail sleeping there, and that he did not come back until Joseph's body had been covered with a blanket. Since then, he has not parted his lips, not even for a sip of water." With this last, she burst into big wet choking sobs.

"Zanna, my sweet Zanna." I put my arm around her soft shoulders, and she buried her face in my hair.

"When will it end, Mary? If the Prince of Peace is due to come, he better come soon. How can we live like this? How can we..."

"Shh... you are in Magdala now. Shh. It is safe here."

"How can you say that, after..."

"That was a long time ago, Zanna. We are quite safe here now. I hope you will stay with us, after all that."

Zanna nodded. "But what about Jesus?" she asked. "He cannot very well go back to Nazareth now, can he?"

"No, of course not, no."

"There had been talk, before all this, that once he was initiated into manhood – do you think watching your stepfather be killed counts as that?" She laughed darkly, a sound I would never have imagined coming from her. Then, continuing in a more tender voice, "I think it was Hannah who said that after his initiation, he would go to stay with Balthazar, Zacharias's friend the Magi. Balthazar lives in the royal court of Parthia, as do all the priestly Magi, all the way across the desert in the East. But after what happened to Joseph... The whole way here, Judas has been talking of taking Jesus to train for war with the rebels, and live up in the mountains with them, can you imagine?"

"He is still a child! To live with the rebels? What is Judas thinking?"

"I do not know, my Mary, I do not know," patting my arm.

"How can Judas think of taking Jesus into the mountains? The boy has to be educated, does he not?" Zanna nodded vigorously as I continued. "He must have learned the Psalms, everyone is taught those in song, and the sacred texts and the Song of Songs. But there is so much more! He must learn to read and write. He could go to Q'mran and study with his brother John. I can tell just by looking at him, Jesus is gentle, tender. Even beyond the terrible risk to his very life, what will it do to his soul to put a sword in his hands, so soon after witnessing bloodshed?"

"You are right, I know, but that is not how Judas sees it. He says this is the perfect time, because his heart will be full of vengeance, and he will learn fast. I asked you, learn what? Learn killing? Murder? The boy has always been, well, delicate, you know, and now with this flying thing..."

"I know! Especially with that! We must keep him out of harm's way!" I insisted.

"Yes, well Judas and I argued the whole way here. Praise Astarte, Jesus slept through that."

I doubted that, but I just said, "Praise Astarte that the decision of Jesus' future is not in Judas's hands. Judas has been a good protector, and he has a right to his opinions, but it is up to Hannah where Jesus goes. After all, she is our high priestess."

"Judas is a good man, you know. He has a soldier's foul mouth and a rude manner, but he has stolen my heart and all that was good in me and given it back to me one hundred fold."

"Judas? Really?" Even though I had known of their union for many years, it was still hard for me to imagine my tender, bread-baking Zanna with the wiry daggered rebel.

"He is such a good man, Mary. You should see how he looks after Jesus. More than a stepbrother, more than loyal servant. True devotion. He would never let anything happen to him. He may never forgive himself for being away from the house when this happened."

With her chin she pointed to the gate, where we could see Judas observing the women and children too. She whispered, "You see. He never lets Jesus out of his sight."

With these words my heart raced, for no reason I could name.

Zanna looked at me, "What is it, child, you are all flushed!" Her sweet cool hand pressed my arm.

I took a deep breath and turned back to my dear friend. I had no idea what had just happened, what to tell her. "I am all right; it is just so much news at once. And so you, my Zanna – "

"I am here now; it is the best place for our Abigail, we are all agreed on that," she said heavily, her gaze slinking back toward the gate where Judas and a handful of his men stood.

"But Judas, he will be here too, this is one of his posts. Now that you will not be in Nazareth, he will be here all the time, you can see him."

"Mary, did you not hear me? He is going up into the mountains," indicating the range behind us with a wide sweep of her hand.

"But what for? There is no ..."

"Since Phebe's Yudah was killed, there has been no clear leader-ship. Ever since Old King Herod's son, Herod Antipater, has been ruling over the province of Galilee, for more than ten years now, the rebels have been fighting each other, instead of fighting the Herodi-ans. That is why Judas wants to bring Jesus up to the mountains – since he is to be their king, after all, he is planning to have them rally around..."

"But Jesus is still a child, look at him, not even a hint of beard!"

" 'One who flies' Mary. You heard it. You know the Oracle."

"But that was in his mind; he was frightened, shocked."

"Judas is convinced. Determined. Let me tell you something about Judas. He was not born with that jaw, he grew it."

We chuckled together for a moment, a strange white cloud of levity in this gathering dark storm.

"Does Hannah know about this?" Then I remembered her tight mouth. Zanna did not even bother to answer my question. I took in her dear full face.

"So then you are back for good... ?" I asked and felt a selfish feeling flower inside me, not admitting to myself until that very moment how much I had missed her.

"For good? For good? Who knows what that means? I live by the will of Astarte. But even if I wanted to leave, where would I go? I cannot go with Judas. Can you see me in the mountains with a child in tow, a girl, living in caves, without an oven or even a steady spring for water?"

I wrapped my arm around her yielding shoulders, closed my eyes and breathed her in. My heart stirred for her as it did for that husband of yore who raised his hand against the sky. I felt her move and saw Abigail running to her. The breakfast gathering had broken up.

You stepped out ahead of the group, your poise all the more striking to me now that I had heard what you had been through. I walked toward you. I wondered if you had any idea about the prospects being considered for you, and what you thought of them. What would you do, if you had a choice? How did you feel about not having one? Your eyes revealed nothing.

You stopped in front of me and reached out your hand to me. I took it, we touched, your skin on my skin, your cool fingertips in my burning palm. Your burning eyes did not leave mine; music and color moved through me from your touch, your lips parted as if to speak.

Without looking at us, Elizabeth stepped behind you and moved you along, jarring us apart. My mind whirred. They were taking you up to the grove. Elizabeth and Salome would want to welcome you formally, as you should have been at your birth. Likely too, they had heard the story I had heard, and they knew your spirit needed to be coaxed back into your body.

I thought to myself, I should be there for that; I am the healer. But we were the ones of the Oracle, you and I. Whatever that would yet mean, we could not meet like two drops of rain falling into the same puddle. There was a ritual for this meeting. I asked myself, Could any ritual touch me more than what had just happened?

A voice in my head said, it is not time. When would it ever be? I wondered. And how would we know when it was? Hannah and Elizabeth were clearly hobbled as seers, ever since Deborah left us. They had not foreseen Joseph's death, only sensed it after it had happened. What else did they not know?

I followed you with my eyes, watched your round calves under your short tunic as you carefully ascended the narrow stone steps so familiar to my own feet. I closed my eyes. My fingers went to the place where the signet would have been hanging if Hannah and Salome had let me keep it, and I worried the fabric there. I tried to feel you as I had felt the husband with the raised hand, but I was interrupted by Hannah's bird-like touch on my shoulder,

"Come now, Mary. It is time."

I had actually forgotten, in the space of time between my bath and your ascent to the grove, that I had been summoned to the oak. I was so shaken by all I had heard and seen and felt that I entered the fragrant shade of flat reaching branches as if I had done it every day. I did not even think to greet Hannah. She said nothing. Deep inside the green limbs which grazed the top of my head and fell like veils toward the ground on the courtyard side, Hannah handed me the small empty alabaster jar which was used for the Sacred Marriage Rituals. With my eyes I asked her why, and she pointed toward the fountain.

As I stepped back out into the bright courtyard, I raised my eyes
to the gate, and saw Judas there, his compact frame, sitting on the
ground and drinking, talking with a man I did not recognize. He
sensed my stare and turned to face me. Pressing his right hand to his
chest, he bowed his head in silent greeting. I returned the gesture,
hoping that I would be able to stand at the gate and speak with him,
the following evening, when the festivities of Purim were complete. I
had never had much to say to him. Now, there was so much I wanted
to ask. Namely, how could he think of taking a young boy into the
mountains?

As slowly as possible, I walked the ten paces from the tree to the
fountain. I filled the jar, letting it overflow many times, as I strained
to hear what was happening up in the grove. I heard only your
mother Maryanna's trance-inducing drumming and singing. When I
returned, I paused on the threshold of the tree's branches to listen for
one moment longer, until Hannah's now chthonic, sepulchral voice
beckoned me back under the oak.

Elizabeth had come down from the grove. She sat facing her
mother on the small stone bench that both women straddled. The
younger seer took the jar and handed me a small earthen cup, lifting
it slightly to indicate that I was to drink its contents. The dark liquid
tasted like wine sweetened with honey and some bitterness I could
not place – I realized it must be her brew made from poppies. Why
was I being given this? What initiation or vision awaited me? After
Elizabeth watched me drain the cup, she returned her full focus to her
incense-blending task, as did Hannah. Their bench was positioned
right next to the thick trunk of the tree, right where the courtyard
ended in a cliff drop that I had never had occasion to measure. They
sat there on the threshold, between the solid earth and an open space
to fall into. It did not seem to dizzy them.

They held the great stone bowl with their four knees and rolled
the resinous dough therein between their practiced fingers, all the
while chanting the invocation Salome composed some years ago, on
the new moon preceding her Sacred Marriage Ritual with Zebedee.

I am the beginning and I am the end.
I am praised and I am reviled.
I am the whore and the sacred communion.
I am the bride and I am alone.
I am the parent and I am the child.
I am barren and I have many sons.
My wedding will be magnificent and I will take no husband,
I bring forth life and I bear no fruit.
I am the easement of my own life-bringing pains.

We sang the invocation on Purim ever since, even the years when we did not enact the great Ritual. Salome called the chant "Perfect Mind" for the state she was in when she composed it. Even as I joined in the chant, my mind drifted sideways, to those days of the new moon, to the tale of the First Woman's first blood and the First Man's sacrifice. I pondered this story as if for the first time. Our menstrual blood was holy. Was the blood that men shed in war holy? What made something holy? All that brought me closer to a real experience of Our Creator's presence were the beauty of Creation and the people's care for each other, such as the laying on of my hands, the love of that protesting man for his ailing wife, and lately, Ariella's tender care of Tabitha.

Why would Our Creator care about anyone's blood, when the moon and stars were created in a single day?

What was happening? Why was I thinking about the moon and stars? I touched the cool ground beneath me, to steady myself. I watched Hannah and Elizabeth in their rhythmic task; I discovered that I was still chanting with them:

Our Creator created all, and thus created me.
Those who seek me, seek to behold Creation.
See yourself in me, and remember that I am in you.
I am the peace that is beyond understanding.
I am the thought that gives you no rest.
I am the call you hear from every direction

and the single word which means many others.
When you say my name, I am with you.

Without breaking the rhythm of the chant, Elizabeth carefully took the rounded grayish incense cones from the gray stone bowl and placed them on a small rug behind her. Then she mixed fragrant powders and wood chips into the empty bowl. Meanwhile, Hannah used a small cedar bowl to blend the gray gum, harvested from the cypress trees just beyond the grove, with the water I had brought, which had been set to warm by the brass lamp. Then she and Elizabeth carefully kneaded their combined ingredients in the largest stone bowl.

Their actions all seemed quite ordinary to me, and I felt a childish disappointment that nothing more than this happened under the great oak. Not so very different from what Zanna used to do in her kitchen. She sang too.

Then Hannah and Elizabeth stopped chanting, as if of common accord, and laid their sticky hands quietly in their laps, eyes closed. I stopped with them, but kept my eyes open. I felt a tingling in my spine, up and out. In the prolonged silence my thoughts turned to you, to the power of your touch, the healing force it pulled from mine, or had it been pouring into mine?

Then we chanted again, and Hannah invited me to take her place and kneed the incense dough, while she sat on the ground and rolled the cones in the dust to set them. The singing spread over my thoughts like rain over skin, touching but not penetrating, like the brownish purple incense blanketing me inside, up my nose and through my palms and fingertips; a scent at once cloying and enchanting, at once from the darkest depths of the Lake and from the clear space between the stars.

Hannah passed on the secrets of making incense to her daughter Elizabeth, but Elizabeth had not chosen an apprentice. Could she have been hoping yet for a daughter?

I never heard her speak of John, who since his birth lived among the Essenes in Q'mran. No one spoke of him anymore, not even Ariella. What was there to say? We knew that if some trouble came to him, we would have news. None of the women spoke of their male children. Boys were raised in the world, by their father or an appropriate surrogate, as you, Jesus, were given to be raised by Joseph of Nazareth. But neither Salome's nor Dinah's children were as far away as Q'mran. Their sons all lived in the green valley around our blue Lake or in the vineyards just beyond the Horns of Hattin, close enough to come with their fathers to pay their respects on days of celebration, like Purim, Rosh Hashanah and all the harvest holidays. In fact, they would come today.

Zebedee would bring his and Salome's twin boys, Yacob and Nathan, who were nicknamed the "Sons of Thunder," after Zebedee proclaimed to all who would hear, the morning after his Ritual night with Salome, that he now had an intimate understanding of the phenomenon of rolling thunder. Salome never commented on this, but when she asked Dinah to write down some of the prayers she composed, like "Perfect Mind," she thereafter asked her to list her author's name as Thunder.

Cleopas would come too. A faithful who traced his lineage all the way back to Quedeshah Jezebel, the Holy Queen, he had completed the Sacred Marriage Ritual with Dinah. He would come with their son, also called Yacob, and his own son Gad, who would be toddlers by now. The boys tended to approach their mothers dutifully, cautiously. They were much more bonded to their nurse-mothers, as was proper. Once they were grown, they could be called into service, such as Phebe's son Yudah had been.

Why was I thinking of these boys? I asked myself. I needed to quiet my mind. Surely I had not been summoned to the oak and given a poppy brew in order to daydream about ordinary life.

I tried to return my focus to the words we were singing…

I am the beginning and I am the end.
I am praised and I am reviled.
I am the whore and the sacred communion.
I am the bride and I am alone.

… but as I reached into the bottomless bowl of incense and shaped the resinous substance with my hands, I floated out of time.

In that moment I experienced this floating as our role, as the state we sought to perfect, to bring out from under the oak tree, out into our courtyard and sacred grove. The whole Valley would be full of revelry tonight, and they counted on us to hold the sanctity of this celebration of the return of Spring, of light, of heat – and with our holy chanting and praying to create, I supposed, some balance to the drunken debauchery that was also at the heart of the Purim festivities.

Somehow I noticed things were quiet. Hannah had stopped singing. Elizabeth had stopped singing. Had I been singing alone? Why was there not one noise anywhere in the world?

Hannah and Elizabeth were looking toward the fountain. How long had they been doing that? I turned my head, slowly and ever so smoothly as if my neck had been oiled. I saw the oval of Maryanna's face at the edge of the oak. Did anyone else see her? Her delicate hand rested on one of the inner branches. Hannah gestured to Maryanna to stay where she was, so I deduced the old seer could see her too.

My breathing returned to normal. I had not noticed that it had stopped. The courtyard was in shadow. The day had come to the edge of night. We had only been here a little while! I felt as though I had dropped from the sun. Through my head swam fragments of the "Perfect Mind" chant, bouncing off the chambers of my mind like children at play:

> *...When you contemplate Creation, you contemplate me.*
> *I am the beginning and I am the end.*
> *...I am the bride and I am alone.*
> *...I am the peace that is beyond understanding.*
> *...When you say my name, I am with you.*

I thought, looking at Maryanna, I am with you, I want to be with you. She was talking, but I could not quiet my mind sufficiently to hear her words over the chant in my mind. Finally I thought to pinch myself hard. My mind then settled some, and I was able to hear her high tight voice say, "Jesus actually said to me, about half-way through, he did not realize he was interrupting me, 'Why all these questions? Do you not know I must finish the work my father's death interrupted?' "

Hannah beside me nodded, then raised and lowered her hand.

Obeying, Maryanna sat on the ground, breathed deeply, eight in, eight hold, eight out. I felt I could feel her breathing, as if I were her. Her words came softly now, in monotone, as her hands fondled the small patch of pebbles before her. "Jesus spoke about that night, the night Joseph..." Her voice quivered. "Joseph. Joseph." Her face in the crook of her elbow, she drew a breath. When she lifted her face, her gaze flashed like lightning, "Jesus said he flew up to the roof."

"Jesus said that he himself flew? Those were his words?" Hannah asked gently.

Maryanna nodded. "I'd like to go back up to him. He is alone with Salome. I should be there, in case something else..." As Hannah nodded again, Maryanna's flushed face disappeared into the fading day.

Hannah sing-songed, " '*The Queen will issue from the broken healer, Her King from the seer blind. They will be born of love not fate, though their fate is love. One will burn. One will fly.*' " Hannah repeated, "*One will fly.*"

Seeing Elizabeth's face darken, our high priestess put her bony hand over her eldest daughter's quiet one. "Daughter, we knew this could be. Let us be grateful that Jesus survived the attack on Joseph and that we will not have to wait for another generation to be born!" Hannah tried to get Elizabeth to meet her eyes but failed to raise those long-lashed lids. "And so the one who came last will come first. Elizabeth, this has been our way for all time: the youngest son. Like Sarah chose Isaac before his elder brother Ishmael, like Rebecca chose Jacob before his elder brother Esau, like Bathsheba chose her youngest, Solomon, to be king above of all of King David's sons. Fret not, love, your John will have his place, just as Ishmael did, just as Esau did. We must trust."

Without replying, Elizabeth stood, carefully and quickly picked up the cones that had been rolled in the dust and lay them softly in a large black stone bowl. Carrying the bowl with two hands, she disappeared into the night that had now settled in the courtyard.

Hannah faced me and took my hands in hers. I was not sure whose were shaking. I became terribly aware of my hands being covered with resin. I wanted to wash them. At the same time, I knew this was absurd. Hannah's hands were like this all day, most days. And as she took my hands right out of the big bowl, she must have known. Why was I worried about this?

Inside the sticky resin, my hands felt as if they were lit from the inside. I could hardly focus on what Hannah was saying. I was completely distracted by my sticky fingers and glowing hands. I thought, I will need oil and warm water – cold water would not be enough. I wanted to ask Hannah how she got her hands clean at the end of the day.

This stream of thought cascaded through my mind as Hannah told me, "Mary, you are not to see Jesus again for three years. He will go to Balthazar, across the desert in the East. When he returns from the royal court in Parthia, where he will have studied with the great-learned priests, our allies the Magi, only then will he be ready to participate with you in the Sacred Marriage.

"This time it will not be simply ritual. To receive this news, you have been brought to sacred tree and given the sacred brew, to receive in your depths what is being told to you. When Jesus returns, you will be initiated into your role as High Priestess and Queen of all the people of all of Israel. You will anoint Jesus as King of all the people of all of Israel."

I understood High Priestess, but I still did not understand Queen. My mind was stuck on this thought: how could I be queen of all the people if I have such sticky hands?

Hannah spoke glowingly of "taking back Jerusalem," a notion as vague to me as was the idea of a city. Hannah gushed about restoring Astarte's open-sky altar to the stone courtyard of the Great Temple, and as she spoke, I saw sky and stone kissing, and I imagined kissing you, your soft cheek. Did I dare think of your lips?

I was present enough to know I had never heard Hannah's voice quiver like this. "Mary, all our people's hardship, from the destruction of Solomon's Temple to this latest occupation by the Romans, came to our land because in all this time there has been no public altar to Astarte in Jerusalem. Yahweh grieves, and the people grieve. The proper rituals have not been observed. The Law has not been obeyed. This has made our land vulnerable to foreign invaders; this is why we have been occupied by one illegitimate ruler after another after another, war tearing up the crops and the people each time.

"At last the time is nigh, Mary. We will take back the Great Temple, the one built by the hands of priests but under the orders of that dead heathen, Herod the Terrible. As it stands, women are allowed only in the outer courtyard, but not past a huge brass bronze door, beyond which lie the great altar and the innermost sanctuary, the Holy of Holies. Once we return, the high priestess will pray deep inside the Temple. We will restore proper observance of the Law, and peace and prosperity will return to Israel."

As she continued talking, her words came to me in broken pieces, "Three years… Long and short… High priestess." When I heard the word "signet," my hands pulled away from Hannah's, but she did not let go.

"You cannot run from this, child. Do not be afraid. You have three years to prepare."

As she spoke I heard that voice inside me repeat, it is not time. I could see the three years ahead of me clear as day; I could see even six and nine, but there was no you, no ritual, no anointing. Nothing but the endless string of days more like each other than were two rain drops. I wanted to tell Hannah, I do not care about Jerusalem and bronze doors and sky stone kisses, I only want to feel what I felt when I touched Jesus, when he touched me, our skin on skin… Something happened, did it not? I felt something, and in the moment I felt it, a certainty was born, out of nothing but a resonance in the core of my being, a certainty that this feeling was how I was supposed to live, that this feeling was what I had been seeking on my mountaintop.

But I could not speak, I could not form words, and Hannah said three years, but I knew she was wrong, wrong, wrong. But I was not a seer, nor was my mother, or was she?

I closed my eyes and told myself, Nothing in me not of Her, nothing in me not of Her, and if this pull to you is so strong then nothing will stop it. I felt myself falling and centered again on Hannah's words which had not ceased flowing.

"I know it sounds impossible, does it not, Mary – when have there not been taxes? But we have an advantage: the Parthians are the Roman Empire's only powerful enemy. The Parthians, and their priests the Magi of course, are now our allies. Their mighty empire is locked away from the Sea. The Roman Empire rules all the Sea's shores. The Parthians want to use our seaports and all the markets they now cannot reach. In exchange for that, they will use their enormous army to help us push the Romans off our land! And they will help us control our borders. Many foreign merchants will pay to cross our land, to avoid crossing the terrible desert and the man-hungry sea. So the people of Israel can keep their entire crop. No more imperial taxes. So this is about much more than you and Jesus sitting on the throne in Jerusalem, it is..."

I lost track of her words, but not her voice, which rocked me. I found my head was now in her lap. There was laughter and music, from the other women, just beyond the tree. I could occasionally make out Salome's voice, and Maryanna's laughter. Among the sound of men's and boys' voices, thick and heavy, I sought you out, Jesus, with all my mind I listened for your voice, in vain.

Under the tree, Hannah held my head, deep into the night. I did not know if I slept or dreamed. When I came to for a moment, I found she had moved to lean her back against the oak's trunk.

I was curled on the ground like a child, my head on her leg, my ear on her calf, when my other ear heard Zanna's urgent whisper at the oak's edge.

"They are gone! They are gone!" Hannah pushed me out of her lap, got to her feet and pulled me to mine. She held her arm around my waist, as I had yet little balance. Zanna cried out, "Judas is not at the gate. And the boy – Jesus is gone!"

Still dazed, I sat where Hannah placed me on the edge of the fountain basin. I watched the night's sky pale above the purple mountains across the Lake. Meanwhile the women conducted a thorough search, as far as it was safe to go into the woods. Hannah interrogated the men Judas left at the gate, who either knew or admitted nothing.

The next thing I knew, we were at the morning bath. The cliffs danced before my eyes, above the hot bath and cool stones. Maryanna sang but did not glow. Elizabeth seemed less like wood, more like stone. Hannah's small voice sounded immersed in the bath, as she spoke our morning prayers.

And I was spread thin like a soft breeze, searching for you with my mind across the Valley, as the steaming water held my body in its unshakable grasp.

Must I wait for you again? Trapped here in Jerusalem, in Joseph of Arimathea's library? This time I know where you are, Jesus, at least where your body is. This time I imagine you would come to me if you could.

How I would welcome waiting in the land of the appointed time: one crosses the halfway point with a happy leap as over a rock in the path.

But here in Jerusalem as I write, as then in Magdala as I wove, I wait in that place of not knowing, where there is no beginning, no end, no middle, only the endless horizon over which the sun rises, bringing little, taking much. I did it once. I thought I would break, but I did not. I do it again, now.

How did I find you again the first time? Was it all Joanna's doing, Joanna whose apparition in our lives I have yet to tell?

Instead of writing this amulet, of telling the story of our lives as I have known it, should I be trying to appeal to our friends who followed us this far? These women fed and cared for me, and taught me everything I learned, much of which they did not mean to teach, I know. These women surely are somewhere near in this house – I know they would not leave me behind in this room the way they left their faith at the foot of your bloody cross.

No, when I think of that, I cannot turn to them. How could they help me now? I can turn only to you, and to Our Creator, Whose Will I understand even less than before, but Whose Presence I yet feel.

In the years after Judas took you up to the mountains, good old Ezra began appearing at the gate with his regularity of yore, with whatever news he could find. For the first two years, he had little to tell, which at least meant no news of your death. After a while, he came with stories of tax collectors seized by mountain rebels at the end of their collecting rounds and tax coffers emptied back into the hands of those who had filled them. We heard of the Syrian forces at our border to the north being pushed off the strongholds and farms the Romans had given them. We heard of young men leaving their plows and their sheep to come find you and join your men. We heard that you never sustained any wound, not even the slightest scratch or bruise, despite going first into every new danger. We heard that your men adored you.

For a while, these developments restored our hope, which had been damaged by Judas's disobedience. I say our hope, but in truth my hope and everyone else's seemed to be woven of entirely different material. My hope was this: to see you again. I wanted to talk to you and find out if you had felt what I had felt and what you thought of it. How I went over our two encounters in my mind! One of eyes and the other of fingertips – again and again I relived each detail, embroidering new ones I am sure, trying to remember something new, about your face, your expression, trying to discern something more in your eyes which I sometimes saw when I closed mine. I wanted to know you, to discover if you had any answers for the questions that banged around my head like stone pebbles in an empty brass bowl.

During the first three years you were away, Salome praised my weaving overmuch and spoke of how I would be missed when we went to Jerusalem. Elizabeth reminded me of the incontrovertible Will of

Our Creator, Who could not be stopped by any circumstance from fulfilling the Oracle's promise. Maryanna told me stories of your boyhood, how you used to sing in your sleep, the way others sometimes talked. Dinah said little, other than that she was looking forward to your return, to our celebration of the Sacred Marriage Ritual. Hannah prayed that you would survive each battle. As your success grew, the initial ill will against Judas faded; indeed it turned to admiration as we learned how many flocked to your side. Judas had indeed put you in the best place to be seen by your people as king.

Even after the three years had passed without word from you or sight of you, and then six years and then nine, the hope of the women around me did not deflate; in fact, it grew with every report of your great deeds. But my hope shriveled like a ripe fig left in the sun. The boy who touched my hand had not loved war. This much I knew. Each new battle took you further into being someone who would never have answers for me, certainly never touch me that way again. Less and less did it matter if you stayed away, less and less did I think anything would ever change. I no longer waited for some inspiration to help me believe in the Oracle I was to bring to life, let alone inhabit the words everyone insisted were about me.

I think my hope died completely the day our grove of Tel Rapha was flattened, and you still did not come back. When I first saw the desecration, I thought I was dreaming. My morning mountaintop eyes were so accustomed to coming to rest on those trees and the dear souls beneath them; that when the familiar sight was not there to catch them I got dizzy and had to sit down on my rocky ledge. The trees were not only cut, they were gone! The ground had been stirred, red clay wounds like so much broken flesh. Who would do such a thing?

I flew down the mountain to tell Hannah, but she already knew. For all she could no longer foresee, had not foreseen, there was still the unsevered cord to her mother. A messenger was sent down to the village, and the news soon came back: Herod Antipas, ruler of Galilee,

son of the late King Herod, had chosen our sacred hill for the site of his
new city, to be dedicated to the Roman Emperor Tiberius. I went back
up to the mountaintop and forced myself to watch the workers come
and dig up the earth and further desecrate our Tel. I threw many rocks
off the mountain that day.

From this height I had always been able to pick out the cedar tree
planted over my mother's grave, right next to her mother's and her
mother's and countless others which had over the centuries begun to
spread out over the earth, as they were supposed to, forming a small
grove.

I used to see, twenty paces from there, the still small cedar tree at
whose root were buried Deborah's, Rachel's and Judith's ashes. I had
watched it grow and reach for Phebe's grave.

Though we feasted and rejoiced and danced when Elizabeth
returned from Q'mran and then Maryanna from Nazareth, it never
felt like they were quite home until the wheel of the year turned and
brought us back to that hilltop together, on the last day of Sukkoth, the
day for the dead, the day to talk and sing with our mothers.

And now we would never be all together again. Where were our
dead? Where were their bones? They seemed to have gotten stuck in
our throats, for no one could speak. The horror of it. And no one
asked, but I am sure everyone wondered: where would our own bones
go? People from all around lined up at our gates – some had family
there too. They wanted to know: what were we going to do?

What could we do? We sent word to you, Jesus, and heard no reply.
Taking on Herod Antipas meant taking on the Roman army, head-
on, and Salome conjectured that you were not yet equipped for that.
Hannah and Elizabeth organized a delegation: Zebedee and Cleopas
took some of the fiercer-looking locals and went to see the authorities
in the town of Sepphoris, in vain. They were not given an audience.
I could have told them that would happen, but I stayed out of the
discussions; I found myself talking less and less over those years. What
was the point? Did we need further proof of our insignificance in this
land? If it was not apparent to Hannah and Zebedee, what sense in my
saying anything?

My Shabbat healings continued as before, but for the amulets and divination there was an ever dwindling demand. Who could put their faith in us? We could not even protect our own dead; we had let foundations of carved stone forcibly penetrate the tender earth that had been our most hallowed ground, excluding the compound of Magdala itself.

And meanwhile, you were flying around up in the mountains, fighting your allegedly righteous battles against the Herodians and the Romans within Israel's borders, and the Syrians without, too busy, it seemed to me, to bother with a mound of dust and trees and bones. My insides ached on our mountain side, for upholding a tradition that had lost all its meaning to me, except for the light I saw sometimes in the eyes of the women around me, and in those who came for the laying on of my hands. A light I could not bear to extinguish for I had nothing to put in its place.

I kept going up to the mountaintop. I still threw my useless little rock, toward the Tel now, every morning. Even the smallest rocks felt heavy.

Other than the building by foreign slaves of that blasphemous city – as no local could be wooed or intimidated into going near it – the seasons flowed into each other quite unremarkably. There was too little or too much rain, or it came at the wrong time. I ate what was put in front of me, I wove what was asked of me, I copied the scrolls Dinah set out, and I wrote the amulets requested. I returned the smiles given me. I put an arm around stooped shoulders. I spoke prayers with eyes closed. I sat in the grove for the new moon and listened to the stories, and sometimes I heard myself laugh.

I could do this because I felt I would die soon. I would die suddenly, unexpectedly. I would not see the shock of disappointment on anyone's face at the breaking of the Oracle's promise. I would gladly miss the scrambling for power as each reconfigured the words to suit herself, and I would never find out who would come down from Jerusalem or even Bethany to claim prominence.

As long as I lived there was a peace, there was a hope, and I would not outlive these, as only my death would end them. I longed for it.

Everything that held meaning – the dreams of you, the coveted signet, the Hill which held my mother, Hannah's counsel – all these lost the power to touch me. Stagnation hardened around me like a second layer of skin through which nothing passed.

I ask again, do we owe it all to Joanna? Would you have come down from the mountain on your own? Would I have welcomed you if you had? Joanna. What good cannot be said of her?

Joanna came to us like a fine rain upon a summer-hard soil. A strong rain comes and runs like a stream, taking the topsoil with it, giving nothing to the earth. But a fine rain, barely noticed at first, softens the hard ground, invites it to open, so that later, full rains can quench the roots deep in the soil.

I first saw Joanna in her orange silken cloak, chatting at the fountain with Zanna. Orange! Shimmering fabric. I had never seen silk, nor any fabric dyed this color. I walked over from my loom and fondled the strange material. I wondered who she was, and what she was doing there, but most of all I wondered at that incredibly fine, watery cloak that rested on her like a cloud, not quite touching the tight black curls that shook with pleasure as I gaped and gawked, my face pressed to the fabric I had pulled to my cheek.

When I recollect this scene, I am taken aback at how far I had departed from normal social intercourse, how I reached and touched what attracted me, like a child, without words or introduction. That says more for my state of mind at the time than anything else I could describe.

What a stark contrast were my simpleton's reaching and grabbing compared to the great patience and subtlety Joanna exercised in order to gain access to Magdala and to be standing at the fountain with Zanna that day.

When Hannah finally invited her to our full moon Shabbat feast, which in those lean days was made special by a few extra olives and fresh rather than dried fish, Joanna told us of the long circuitous path that had led her to us.

Her local Tarichaean mother, like so many thousands, had been taken into slavery at the tender age of nine by the warring Roman Cassius, the same that Phebe told us had devastated Magdala all those years ago. Joanna's mother was taken north to Syria and sold in Damascus to the city's Roman governor, in whose palace she was put to work as laundress. A few years later, Joanna was born of an unnamed father. Though born into slavery, she was born a powerful seer, one who saw through touch. As soon as she was old enough to work alongside her mother, she learned the secrets of the house from handling the linen sheets. Once her mother understood what the girl perceived, she brazenly used her knowledge of illicit affairs and hidden illnesses to secure increasingly easier jobs for herself and her daughter.

Joanna's trip from Damascus to Magdala was on the magic carpet of love at first sight – or first touch – with Andronicus, one of Herod Antipas's attendants. She met him when Herod Antipas visited the governor's court, looking for military support to control what they called "the bandits" – in fact, our rebels – at their common border. One brush of Andronicus's shoulder as they passed in the great marble hall, and Joanna knew. She found him in his sleeping quarters and spoke to him in the night as no other woman ever had. They wasted no time in marrying. When Herod Antipas returned to Sepphoris in Galilee, Joanna left with Andronicus, taking tearful leave of her mother who had been left to the gentle task of dressing the governor's wife. Their parting was softened by the knowledge that the old woman had enough household secrets to keep her safe for the rest of her life.

In Sepphoris, Joanna whispered secret truths into her husband Andronicus's ear after touching the plates she collected from various notables around Herod Antipas's table. Using this information cunningly, Joanna's husband quickly rose to prominence; Herod promoted him to chief steward and called him "Chuza," which means "seer", for his alleged gift. Joanna's sight permitted her to learn not only the secrets but also the deepest wish in everyone she met, and this information gave Herod amazing powers of negotiation. She thrilled at the move from the valley city of Sepphoris to the Lake-side city of Tiberias – the city that had been built on our Tel Rapha – to be closer to her mother's roots, but once they arrived she wept every night for weeks, because beneath her feet she felt the desecration on which the town was built.

When she happened upon our weavings at the market in the town of Tarichaea one day, she rejoiced at the impressions that came in through her hands from our cloaks and blankets. She became determined to find us, to find the source of this energy so unlike the parasitical, paranoid, predatory one in Herod Antipas's court. It took her years to win the trust of Tarichaeans. None would reveal themselves as our merchant, and none would admit remembering her mother's family. Joanna was patient. She knew they saw only that she was the wife of Herod Antipas's steward – one of "them." She had to be patient for six years, as it turned out, but Joanna was not one to be deterred. She understood how much of an abyss was to be crossed.

Over the years, her goodwill and good nature were tested and confirmed. At last conversations occurred, the latest that of our cloak merchant with Hannah, and, after much divination and arguing and more divination, Joanna was invited to our stony gate and let in, with her father's strange pale eyes, her mother's mass of ill-behaved black hair, ill-concealed under her bright veil, and her laughter like a fresh spring coming out of hard rock.

She shared our evening meal, talking little once she had told us her story. We told her none of ours, spoke only of weather and crops. That night she stayed with us and slept through our early dawn bath. After our prayers, on my way down to the courtyard, I found her waiting for me on the steps. I was always the last one out of the bath, so we were alone.

I can still feel her cool hand on my hot wrist; see her soft smile, her closed eyes, and her nodding head. "Mary, she who burns, she of the Oracle, she with the healing hands."

She had told us of her gift, but I had not completely believed it until then. There was no other way for her to know any of what she had just said to me, including my name. "Mary, you think you have closed your heart, you think your life is over, you think you have stopped waiting for him, you think you have stopped believing in anything, but you have not! Otherwise, why would you still throw your rock? You have good reason to. Together, if you will let me help, I know how we can get him down from the mountain."

Her eyes, a pale shade of sky looking through me, touched the longing I thought I had let die; it fluttered so softly, I was not sure it was really there. I did not trust this flutter; even less did I trust Joanna. I kept her at arm's length for a long time. As far as I knew she was but a colorful bird come to enchant us all and depart when the next wind blew. After all, she was a slave from Herod Antipas's court. She worshipped not Astarte but one called Demeter.

Nevertheless, she came to see me. Her husband, bless his heart, lied (what lies could he tell I did not know) to explain her absences to the court, for he knew that she was coming to us, and he saw the light grow in her eyes as she had found women who not only were much like her, but who needed her. This she told me, and much else, coming to visit with me at my loom, every chance she got.

It was not until she had coaxed the tiny alabaster jar used for the Ritual from Hannah and Elizabeth that I began to take her seriously. Despite their many failings, our seers would not have entrusted her with this precious object if they had not a good reason, far more than being charmed by her orange eagerness and springtime laughter. Joanna took to sitting at my feet, leaning her back against the wall while I worked my loom.

Rolling the small white vase back and forth between her graceful brown hands, she would tell me, "You must forgive Jesus for Tel Rapha; he did not come because there was nothing he could do; he only fights battles that have a chance, and so he stayed away." Holding up the vase between thumb and middle finger, "But with this we can bring him back. He is a grown man, but for all he has been through, his touch is still the same. Remember his touch."

She spoke to me in rhythm with the motion of my hands across my loom, casting a spell on me, pulling me back through, how many now? Sixteen years since that day of fingertips touching and eyes speaking.

Soon Joanna was there every day but Shabbat, sitting with me, the empty jar dancing from one hand to another. "He is not dead. He is waiting for you too. He is waiting to be called. You think he likes it up there in the mountains, with all those smelly men, fighting, hiding, killing, and dying all around. Do you not think your touch touched him? He was a boy when Judas took him, a frightened and shocked boy. He is a man now; no one can make him go anywhere, but he can be called. A man can be seduced down from a warring mountain to a peaceful grove, you just have to want to, you just have to make yourself ready."

After a time, she began leaving the empty jar on the loom when she had to go home. I could not leave it out in the night. I did not know what to do with it. I did not want to ask Hannah. Somehow I knew Joanna was right, that this was a way back to you. I brought it to the common sleeping room that night, and slept with it under my pillow.

I always brought it back to the loom, rested it where Joanna had left it, so she could pick it up again, settle her bright self down against our pale walls, and tell me again, please tell me again. Tell me hope, I asked of her silently, tell me possibility.

There was no lightning. No sudden parting of the clouds. Just that little jar, under my pillow. I began dreaming of you. I began weaving for you. I made you a cloak, bright midnight blue, to the tune of Joanna's incantations, some of which I had begun to mumble myself. The day after Passover, when it was done and, in fact, the best weaving I had ever done, I sent you the cloak by messenger, without word, without explanation.

And then there we were, fifty days later, preparing for Shavuot, preparing to receive the offerings of the people's bread and first wheat, to bless them with abundance throughout the harvest time until Sukkoth. We would prepare our best incense to offer to sell, select the whitest doves for those whose dove had died or for those few with enough to start a new home. As happened each year, we expected the people would come to dance and feast while we sat and fasted, in our finest tunics, to welcome their visit.

Then, as I have already written it, as I could not wait to tell it, you appeared at the gate of Magdala on Shavuot eve.

Then you were standing in our fountain, bare-headed, blue-cloaked, laughing with somber women turned playful and splashing.

My name danced in the air between us.

Like a lawless man, that night you knocked on the women's door. After lightning meeting of eyes across the courtyard of eyes: our first moment alone.

My true initiation to the Mysteries, never mind the incense-soaked chanting in the grove or the fragrant sweat dripped into the soil under the sacred terebinth oak or even the peculiar, precious pulse inside ink-stained fingers.

Husband, you touched me like a woman, not a priestess.

You said my name, not Hers.

No invocation but your wide hand grazing my round hip.

No scent but ours, mingling.

No prayer but our audible breath.

In the middle of the moon-soaked night, your knock at my door, soft like thunder, pulled me from what you must have known was no sleep at all. From the moment you first said my name to me, to the hours later when I heard your approach, my thumping heart had announced this visit. To draw me out to the balcony you needed only tap the door with your fingertips. I tiptoed among the sleeping women and crossed the threshold into the cool night.

We touched hands, as we did the last time I saw you, then a boy of thirteen, now a man of thirty. But there was nothing. Nothing! How could this be? My whole skin suddenly lonely for you, but no music, no colors. Was it you or was it me? Who had changed?

I looked into your thickly lashed eyes so open to me; I saw no doubt there. Had something closed in me?

You touched my hip, then you took my hand, and we climbed the stairs that led to the roof. The moment I crossed the last step – your arms around me, your tongue inside me, your heartbeat against me. Such a wind you were, you blew all my words away. A cough from below us, surely from someone dear, loosened your grip, pulled me apart from you.

A faint and foolish, "You have changed, Jesus," passed my lips.

"From what?" you asked.

"From the last time..."

"You mean since I was a boy, Mary?"

I felt completely ridiculous now. Had you not felt the colors those seventeen years ago? Had I been alone in that? I felt so old. I felt my skin loosening from my flesh as you looked at me. You were a ripe fruit, so full of faith in your cause; you could not see what a hollow joke of a priestess I was. I did not know how to speak to you. What had I been I thinking? All that hope. All that time with Joanna. All those juices flowing. Who had I been fooling? Myself? I walked to the roof's edge.

"You have changed too," you said, following me.

Leaning over the roof's waist-high wall, I spoke into the night, "Not as much as you would think. Perhaps I was simply different in that one moment when we met."

I took in the familiar expanse of the moonlit Lake below us, the dark shore, the occasional orange glint of the fishermen's torches from their boats far out on the night-black water. You leaned your elbows on the wall near me. I could have inhaled your scent all night and remained just as we were, close without touching. Perhaps that could be enough, I thought. A man and a woman, no Oracle, no expectations, just a moment of contentment and a place to rest, somewhere far from here.

You spoke, and your voice touched me even more deeply than your scent, "I wish that moment when we met years ago could have been lifted out of time. I wish we could have dwelled in that moment for always, with none of what came before, and," your voice dropped, "certainly none of what came after."

I thought of what came before for you, Joseph's brutal murder, and of untold violence since then. "Tell me," I whispered.

"What."

"What came after."

Deep sigh. "That is not what I came here for, Mary. I did not come to relive all that head-chopping." You laughed darkly to yourself. "Judas is convinced that the fact that I have never been wounded, not even a scratch, is yet further proof that I am the one of the Oracle."

"And you?"

"Me what?"

"Do you think you are he?"

You stood straight, turned, and faced the mountain. Before speaking you tilted your head up to the stars, your throat open to the night. "Do you know who the Pharisees are?"

"I have heard tell; they are the ordinary priests in the Temple of Jerusalem, working as scribes for the Sadducees."

"Yes. Most of the Pharisees are in Jerusalem. Some travel all the way here, because they want every village to not only tithe to the Temple, but to follow its Law and memorize the Holy scrolls." You began to pace as you spoke. "I met such a man. Here in Galilee, in the town of Cana, where no one wanted to hear his talk of Holy scrolls. The people only sought him out for contracts and amulets, like they come to you here in Magdala. The Pharisee preached that the end of the world was near, that it was time to repent, time to seek atonement for sins. No one listened. Nonetheless he sat at the village gate, reciting the prophecy from the Book of Daniel, saying that the End of Days were upon us, saying that it was now the time 'to make reconciliation for iniquity and to bring in everlasting righteousness, and to seal up the vision and oracle, and to anoint the most Holy.' "

That dark laugh again, as you continued with your long-legged stride, "Is that not interesting? The Book of Daniel speaks of an oracle. Do you think that five hundred years ago when he wrote his book, Daniel was thinking of our Oracle? The women here remind me of that Pharisee. Some people learn all the sacred texts just to twist them to mean what they want. *One will fly?* Fly, Mary? That day you and I met, they drugged me; then they took my story to mean what they wanted it to mean, what they needed it to mean."

Your words caught on something in your throat. After a deep breath, when you spoke again, your voice was at first open, unrestricted, "Real people are hungry out there. People are desperate," but then you trailed off, stopped your pacing. "Mary," you said, turning to me from five paces away, "our people do not have another war in them. Maybe there is some truth in the Book of Daniel; maybe this is the end of their world. Our people have less than nothing, and their less than nothing is already owed to the tax collector, and," your voice like a bird flown into a wall, soft and motionless on the ground, "all I can do, all I can do..."

You gazed at your hands, palms up and then palms down, back and forth, as if you were wondering if your hands were really yours. What a distance from your commanding presence when you crossed into our courtyard this morning, further still from your playfulness at the fountain. I felt the impulse to come to you, take your hands, and... I stopped myself. What did I have to offer a man, a warrior, a killer? But when I looked at your face, your hands...

I managed simply, "And all you can do...?"

Snarling now, "Cooped up here in Magdala, you think your Law and your rituals will protect you, while men are dying out there, Mary – dying and killing each other and reveling in the blood on their hands. Ancestral farms lost to the Romans is real. Starving for lack of food is real. Mothers and fathers starving their children so they can afford to pay the taxes that build marble palaces, that is real. Sons and daughters taken into slavery, that is real. But what substance is there in prophecies, oracles, and your Law?"

"My Law? It is hardly..." I caught myself, unsure how much to tell you. "Jesus, you think I do not know what is real? You think there is no blood on my hands? The people who can afford it come up here every week for me to place my hands on them. Good people who pay us with real grain and oil," my proud angry voice cracked into whisper, "but not the good people without –"

" – What do you mean, the people without, what about the full moon Shabbats? You are Rebecca's child to be sure, I hear tell of your gift all the way up to the border."

"Oh? What do they say?"

"That one moment with you and the lame walk and the blind see, the ailing child cries for his mother's milk and the barren woman's womb opens."

"They say all that, do they?"

"I know people are hungry for story, but surely some of it..."

"It is all true, but it is all for gold, or grain, or oil. And on full moons, there are so many we turn away, and why?" No longer able to restrain myself I blurted out, "Because the sun has gone out of the grove while it shines yet on the mountaintop! What Creator is this we are supposed to worship who has a special time and place to end suffering, and then too bad if you are next in line." It had been so long since I had articulated or pondered any of this. But now you were listening to me; more than this you walked right up to me. Eye to eye we stood. I breathed deeply into my body, to calm myself. I was thirty-seven years old, and I felt as though I was having the first real conversation of my life.

I stepped away from you, sat down. As I hugged my knees to my chest, I leaned back against the wall. "Jesus, all day, I pray and chant and weave and scribe, every day except Shabbat. If I stop and think about my life for too long, if I think about what used to be in my heart... I can hardly face Our Creator, all these rules that do not... I almost stopped going up to the mountain."

Sitting down next to me, close but not touching, "What are you talking about, Mary? What mountain?"

"Jesus, I cannot know what it is like being king to those rebels out there. When I hear you speak, my troubles seem small indeed. But I can tell you that the last time I ever felt anything real, anything complete and beautiful before right now," a small visit into your eyes, "was when you touched my hand the last time we met. I lived on that for a while, a long while, but then when you did not come back..." I continued with my lips pressed against my knees, "Since then I try not to disappoint. There is a hole inside me where there is supposed to be faith. I am supposed to want to serve my people, and I do want to serve them. But the idea of being queen! I feel so powerless here to change anything, and I do not really think I would feel any less powerless in Jerusalem, even if we managed to 'take it back,' as Hannah says, whatever that means. She says we will restore Astarte's altar, but to me it would just be a pile of rocks so help me, Mother, so help me."

I wished for the relief of tears at that moment, but they did not come. I did find your hand in mine, as solid as anything I had ever known, maybe slightly more.

"Jesus, I feel like a traitor in my heart... You, Judas, Elizabeth, everyone here, they seem never to doubt for a moment. This tradition of rebels for hundreds of years, since Young King Joshua forbade worship on all the high places…"

"High places!" letting go my hand. "Mary, what do you think that was all about? The One True God? The worship of Astarte? Your Young King Joshua, and the Holy Ones of yore in the desert, you can be fairly certain that they were not so much worried about who was being worshipped where, but rather into whose coffers the coins of tithing flowed."

You made a sweeping gesture with your long arms, "Listen to me, Mary, the truth of history is written in blood, but that blood gets washed away by the rain, or dried into dust by the sun and scattered by the wind. It is only the conquerors' words that are carved into temples and monuments of stone. They are hollow and their authors' vanity rings loud. Here is the truth: men and women and children out there are dying by the sword or from hunger every day, because no one is as brave as you to talk about doubt, everyone acts so deplorably certain. They pretend, maybe even fool themselves into believing, that all these wars are not about land and the control of that land."

"So brave as you" – these words echoed in my head. Your hands pulled on mine, and you lifted me to stand. You took me in your arms. The gentleness shining in your eyes warmed me like the sun warms the sky.

Silence surrounded us, but what I felt inside was louder than anything I had ever heard. Your chin came to rest on my shoulder, my chin on yours, a perfect fit. Another cough from someone sleeping below. We stiffened; air moved between us. "Jesus?"

"Yes Mary," your hand on my hair.

"Why did you come here, to Magdala?"

"Because I had a dream, and you were in it."

I pulled back so I could see your face. "You believe in dreams, then."

You looked down. "It was a dream of peace. I sat beside you and I was happy. I was peaceful."

"That was reason enough to bring you down from your mountains?"

A hurt look surfaced in your eyes; you walked away and again began pacing. "What do you think it is like up there in my mountains, as you call them?"

"Oh Jesus, I am sorry, I did not..."

"Of course you did not. You know, Mary, you are not quite what I expected either. I thought I would come here and be refreshed by the cool wind of your serenity; I thought that you held the piece I was missing, that you would help me accept this kingship."

"That is exactly what I was thinking about you."

"Oh? Well we were both wrong, then. You seem to be as confused and unconvinced as I am. The confounded Oracle would have me be the One who '*flies*'! I will tell you when I fly, Mary. I fly when we descend on a cohort of soldiers and leave nothing but limbs, I fly when we find a tax collector taking an ill-advised nap in the woods, with his head resting on his sack of gold, thinking that will protect it, little does it protect him when I fly upon him and sever that fat head."

You gestured as if you held a sword in one hand and in the other a head by its hair, your eyes shining and your lips white.

"Jesus!"

"What? How do you think we keep you safe here in your little limestone cave? Do you think a stern warning from Quedeshah Hannah would keep our enemies away? What do you think you are living on here? The bits of incense and weaving that get sold in

Tarichaea? Your weekly laying on of hands?"

My insides turned to stone.

"Come on Mary! Or do you think you are living on manna from heaven, you just wake up and there is bread and olive oil and Shabbat meat?"

I had never seen anyone look at me the way you looked at me right then. How had valley tenderness given way to such lightning contempt? I had not felt this small since that day a man's hand protested sundown. So what if you called me brave, if you could look at me this way? Why had I bothered trying to bring you to Magdala? What had I been thinking? Why should anything ever be different?

"You know, Jesus, I am just a woman who weaves and prays and tries to be good to the women she lives with. That is it. That is all I have. And you, you are just a man trying to do his best to figure how to lead our people out of the darkness of Roman oppression.

"You and me, a man and a woman. That is who we are. I do not know what it is like to fight a battle, and you do not know what it is like to face all the sick each week with just two hands and face the other priestesses every day with an empty heart. And neither of us can imagine any solution that could change the lives of our people for the better, oracle or no oracle. So no, I do not think we live on manna from heaven, and you should be more careful about what you dream."

Arms at your side, you stepped forward. "I am sorry, Mary, I am so sorry. You should think you have manna from heaven, that is part of why we do what we do. You just have to understand, the price of that manna."

"You think I do not know? You think I can live here more than thirty years and be so sheltered? Even the walls of Jericho came down, Jesus. You do not know what I have lived, you presumptuous, arrogant..."

Stepping forward again, "I am so sorry, you are right, I do not know, I do not..."

I kept my distance, "How do you live with this, Jesus? What do you tell Judas?" Refusing your proffered hand, your softened face,

I turned toward the Lake, "Since Judas believes in the 'confounded Oracle' as you call it… Or is he too just a head chopper, is he too…"

"Mary, it is a lot easier to believe that someone else is to be the Anointed One, than to believe it of yourself." We sighed deeply at the same time; our eyes met and turned away quickly from too much truth. "Judas is free to strategize and plan, because he can simply believe in me. Like I told you he makes much of the fact that I have never been wounded in any of our expeditions, as if some special force protected me, try as I might to get myself killed every time."

Meeting your gaze for a flash, I thought, so, this feeling too we have shared.

You went on, "They will not let me believe in myself as a man, as a leader, they need me to believe that the divine fate of our people rests in my hands, our hands. And Mary," your voice broke. I turned to watch you speak to the ground, your face in your hands, "When you see what is actually happening, there is no hope, no hope. They all look to me for something, and you are right, I am just a head chopper. I do not think we can win. I fight just to keep the light in their eyes lit. I cannot bear to be the one to tell them how hopeless…"

Coming over to you, my head bent close to yours, I tried to bring up the words I had been swallowing all these years – words that were now pouring out of your heart. "Jesus, could the light in their eyes be enough?"

You were crying now in earnest, shaking your head "no." As you settled some, you said so softly, "We are losing. There is no hope. They want us to be king and queen, when being king and queen means waging war all the time. A war that has no end, can you imagine. Why do you think I stayed away from here so long? It was not Judas's doing. The Oracle, this whole plan with the Parthians, it is not enough, it is ultimately meaningless."

"But what else can we do, Jesus? You do not want to fight anymore, and I do not want to follow the Law. But you are here, on Shavuot. They want us to do the marriage ritual now, to fulfill the Oracle: the anointed King and the anointing Queen. What do we do? Will you leave me to my healing and go wage this war without end, without me?"

Almost more to yourself than to me, "Endless, and ultimately useless. Would you have us be king and queen of an endless war?" You looked up at me with a face so naked I found myself weeping as I shook my head "no." Your forehead to mine, hand at my nape, you whispered prayerfully, "Mary. Mary. I do not want to leave without you. I see now the reason I came here. I see that perhaps indeed you have the missing piece I have been seeking. We are only a man and a woman. Everyone near and dear thinks we are going to save the world. Everyone except us. But we cannot just run away; where would we go? Where is it any different, really?"

"There has to be another way," I whispered. As I said these words, I felt the colors move though me, I felt music and light despite being on the roof with you, my feet nowhere near the earth they normally needed. "Jesus, do you feel that?"

"Do I feel inexplicably wonderful? Am I longing to discover what it would be to love you, not just with my body but with my whole life?"

"Yes. I suppose that is it. Yes."

"Yes Mary, I feel that." You held me close, no space between us. Into my ear, you whispered, "Maybe, Mary, what if we were indeed the chosen ones of the Oracle." I stiffened, and you held me tighter, "Wait, listen. Our births were so carefully planned, and yet they did not happen the way anyone expected – '*Born of love, not fate.*' Our lives were minutely arranged, yet here we are, embracing each other in the middle of the night. The Law says we should not even have seen each other, and yet no lightning has come to stop us. We were raised to become one thing, but in our souls we have become another. Before we met or spoke, we have become the same thing, yes? Two people who value life, and love? Is that not in the precious Oracle '*then two become one again*'?"

You loosened your hold on me, and I watched a smile grow on your face as you spoke, "Mary, is it not possible that no one has a blessed inkling what the Oracle means, because no one counted on us longing for a love that has no end, rather than for war? What if, in this foul miserable life, such a love is the greatest miracle, the greatest peace, this peace they say will *'come into the hearth of all'*? What do you think, Mary? Would that be enough for you?"

I nodded, then gasped as your open smile pressed itself to mine, and the night receded behind you. The roof no longer under our feet, we floated across the stars like angels, and now your thick hard phallus pressed against my yielding womb through our thin tunics, my thighs suddenly moist with anticipation. We sank into each other; even with our eyes closed we were inside each other's mind.

We fell softly together to our knees and laid back flat on the rough moonlit roof still faintly warm from sunlight, our breath finding matching slowing rhythms. Hearing a dove coo called me back to my priestess self for a moment, and I had to ask,

"Jesus, what shall we do about our ritual?"

"For now let us listen, and pay attention to signs."

"Like what?"

The dove flew over us just then, called into the night, then dropped its waste a few paces from our heads.

We burst into irrepressible laughter. Our bodies shook, clutched each other, shushed each other, turned away then grasped each other again. All the while I felt the jangling of this rock in the pit of my stomach, this rock that you had not put there but you had loosened after all my years of learning not to notice it.

Oh my love. Do you remember.

Years before, when Salome took Zebedee into the sacred tent, and later when Dinah received Cleopas, I sang and danced and banged the round drum, but I knew this was no wedding. A husband-and-wife marriage was something reserved for the folks for whom we prayed, something for the people on whom I laid my hands each Shabbat. A priestess could not be burdened with a husband to mind and a child to raise, at least not until late in her years. She must be wholly devoted to Our Creator, her life an instrument of worship, of healing, of justice. I knew all this, had always known it.

But all this knowing fell away when I stood before you in the cedar grove for our Sacred Marriage Ritual, on your second night in Magdala. As was the tradition, we appeared before all, dressed in matching seamless white tunics embroidered with gold, vine leaves in your hair, and in mine a headdress of flowers and gold coins. In my most holy moment as priestess, where I fulfilled the most sacred sacrament – the experience of which was meant to forever inform my life of devotion, indeed my intended life as ruler – my heart sang with the feelings a wife has for her husband. I wanted only to be alone with you again as we had been the night before under the stars. I was heedless of tomorrow; I simply could not see it, blinded as I was by what some might call lust.

More than lust of the flesh, I ached with lust in my heart, for I wanted you to be mine. No, that was not it, I did not want to possess you – I wanted you free as the air, free of everyone's ambitions for the nation of Israel. I wanted to wrap my legs around your sinewy waist and fly away like a pair of doves, never to be found again, fly off into the bright moon, with you who spoke my heart.

The necessary words fell from our mouths as we walked through

the seven gates, along the path through the grove to the white bil-
lowing Sacred Marriage tent just beyond the small altar. The
multi-colored gates, fragrant with the heavy perfume of flowers they
bore, gently fell apart around us, for what we were doing could never
be undone.

We spoke the beautiful words of what I had once called Zanna's
up-and-down song, the liturgy for this holiest of acts: receiving the
Lover into the literal and metaphoric Holy of Holies, the inner sanc-
tum, the heavenly gates. We had sung the words on mornings of
the full moon up at the baths, we had sung them in the dark of new
moon in the grove. But I had not heard them until the night of our
ritual,

> *Let him kiss me with the kisses of his mouth,*
> *for this love is better than wine.*
> *the King hath brought me into his chambers:*
> *we will be glad and rejoice.*
> *A bundle of myrrh is my well-beloved unto me;*
> *he shall lie all night between my breasts.*
> *My beloved is unto me as a cluster of camphor*
> *in the vineyards of En Gedi.*
> *Behold, thou art fair, my beloved, yea, pleasant:*
> *also our bed is green.*

The familiar chant, a dry recitation all these years, now held me
rapt. We stepped through the gate and faced each other, stepped and
turned, and even when our eyes left each other our gaze did not.

> *your scent will intoxicate me through the night...*
> *you have the eyes of a dove...*
> *I am feverish with love... he calls to me... hurry my love...*
> *your eyes... your hair... your lips are like a thread of scarlet...*

Were we making love or still standing out under the sky and our
mothers' eyes? Were we standing apart or were our lips touching?

you are a fountain... drunk with love... drenched with dew...
my heart beats out of my chest... fingers wet...
there I give my love to you... come with me...
this is my beloved...
my beloved is mine and I am his...

I could not think, I only wanted you, and you seemed the same,
your tunic gently raised at your loins...

rising like the morning star...
your thighs like jewels...
your navel a round goblet...
your belly... your breasts... your neck...
my beloved longs for me...

Only for me. The way we were on the roof the night before. All
mine. I did not want to give you back to these people, to the mountains. Would you stay, or take me with you?

come my beloved...
there I will make love to you...
I have saved the best for you..
love fierce as death...
for my love I am a city of peace...
let us run away, my wild stag

Yes, let us run away, I thought. It was only a short distance from
the edge of the grove to the sacred tent beyond the altar, each step
excruciatingly slow.

At the flapping entrance to our lovingly embroidered sanctuary, I removed your sandals. Someone handed me the alabaster jar,
once empty under my pillow, now filled with fragrant spikenard. I
anointed your feet, your hands, your head, each touch of skin a kiss,
an entire lovemaking unto itself. Then you took the oil from me,

brazenly. I wondered vaguely, like a whisper, was this blasphemy? And my next thought: Could any tender thing either of us did in this moment be blasphemous? You proceeded to anoint me too, my forehead, my throat. When your fingers brushed my feet, taking off my sandals, I shuddered.

We walked into the tent, without looking back, without hearing the tambourines or song, which must have reached crescendo by now, or did they stop when you took the oil from me?

Inside, we barely noticed the thick rugs, soft pillows, bowls of dates and figs, moon cakes, and jugs of dark wine. I tied the tent flaps closed with careful knots, amazed that my fingers could be so dexterous when my whole being was consumed by the infinitesimal space between my back and your front, as you stood right behind me, inhaling, not touching me, exhaling, not touching me.

As my eyes adjusted to the faint light of a small lamp in the center of the room, I slipped away from you and knelt on the pillows to pour us some wine with trembling hands. You came close and dropped to your knees facing me, took the silver chalice full of wine from my hand. You dipped your finger into the wine and painted my lips with it; the touch of your wine-wet finger on my lips was liquid fire.

Tears of pure longing ran down my face. You removed my crown of gold coins and flowers and tossed it aside, easily pulled my tunic down over both shoulders till it dropped to my narrow hips. I was breathing hard now, my breasts moving deeply up and down, your open gaze on my skin more penetrating than touch. At least that was what I thought until your feather-light fingers traced the contours of my cheek, my throat, my breast, my waist. Was I screaming? My whole body was shaking now. With a single overhead gesture you removed your tunic, knocking off your crown of vines. You were kneeling and naked and erect before me. I wanted to fly into you, fling my arms around you, but with a wide soft hand you softly pushed me back, pushed me off balance, till I fell on the bed of pillows and you fell onto me, your mouth on my belly first then down to my second mouth where I drooled for you.

I never knew this utter falling away of everything. Nobody told

me. Yes there were the new moon stories, and yes I knew, I was created in bliss. But I never knew. Until then. Then you lifted me back
up and kissed me with your mouth slick with me and we fell back
onto the bed together this time, rolling over all the pillows, knocking
over the wine, until hardness found softness, erect found yielding,
thirst found moist, easily and urgently as water rushing downhill.

I had known climaxes before, at my own hand, deep in the night
when all were asleep around me, but never expected this sweet meld-
ing of hearts, this longing to be with you again tomorrow night, and
the next, and the next.

We fell apart and lay back on the bed of pillows. I closed my
eyes and found there the eyes of the husband, the one of the black
hand raised in protest. I saw the burning in that face otherwise worn
threadbare from care and hardship, the naked, desperate longing
conveyed to me up the stairs. He had been ready to risk anything for
his wife, did indeed risk everything he had.

I turned to look at you as you slumbered – the soft dark mass
of your beard, the darker one of your chest, its gentle rise as you
breathed, your eyes closed, your densely black hair spilling around
your face onto the pale pillow.

My heart beat a steady rhythm: always, forever. The idea of being
apart from you was simply not comprehensible. I looked at your
hands. The idea of them holding my breasts was thrilling and right.
The idea of them soiled with the blood they had shed was inadmis-
sible. Nestled into your perfect fit of body, I fought sleep, hoping we
would never wake into the day that would transform us into the king
and queen the world we knew meant for us to be.

Did I sleep, or was I awake? All I knew was my mother Muriel
came to me. I had never seen her face before but I knew her immediately, her dainty hands on my chest and shoulders, shaking me hard
to wake me from my bottomless slumber. "Get up! Get your man,
get out now! Wake up, wake Jesus, get out now. Now."

I clawed myself out of dreaming, and without thinking or hesitation, I pulled you. You were still half-asleep as we crossed our tent's
threshold. I grabbed our tunics. We slipped them over our bodies still

pungent with each other's scent. No time for ablutions; the pressure in my heart said "go!"

Dazed from ritual and lovemaking and sleep as I was, I had no thought but to show you my mountaintop. As my mother had called me out, and that was the only place I ever felt her spirit, I assumed that was what she meant… why she came to me.

There was no logic in my mind, no sequence, just the urge to show you the one place in this world that had been all mine, now that I was yours and you were mine, now that nothing could come between us ever again.

W e were in the thickest part of the woods behind the grove, having trouble finding our path up to my mountaintop, despite the bright moon. Our giggling bare feet stopped mid-step at the sound of a blood-stilling scream. Tightening our grip on each other's hands, we turned in unison toward the compound below, from whence the sound came – now more came, metal on metal. Your body tensed to pouncing stillness, you patted your sides – no weapon, not even a belt. All the same you lunged toward the compound.

I held you back, "Jesus, do not leave me here alone."

Your eyes shallow as shadows squinted as if seeing me for the first time, "Yes, of course, this way."

You led us toward the caves along the slope, deeper into the woods. Suddenly three foul-smelling unbearded men leapt out of the darkness and grabbed us. We struggled, then you were pinned, face to the ground, your hand twisted behind your back. One man held me from behind and the other laughed and ripped my tunic open, mauled me, pawed me. My blood boiled. He licked my teeth. I kicked my knee hard into his groin. You, roaring, threw off your captor and grabbed his sword.

I was thrown down; my attacker turned on you but you swung the sword around as he came at you and cut open his throat. Then you swung the sword back and severed the arm of the man behind you, then you spun around again and plunged it in through the eye of the one still rolling on the ground from my kick. A brief silence fell; we heard more clashing of swords from the compound. You pulled the bloody blade from my assailant's head and offered me your free hand.

I got to my feet with your help, clutching my tunic closed against whose eyes I did not know. We broke into a run, up and across we went. You brought us to the deepest cave you knew. We crouched at the mouth of the hollow, from where we had a partial view of the grove. Despite the pale blue blanket of moon spread across the land, we could see nothing moving, though we heard harsh metal and broken voices. We stood craning our necks, squinting, pulling back in at a sudden gust of air, then creeping out again.

The noise died out after a few moments, or was it an hour? No, the moon had hardly moved. Or had it? Our hearing strained. The complete silence was worse than the noise.

You turned to me, opened your mouth to speak, but your expression hardened at the sound of footsteps nearing. You rolled your body back against the cave wall, pushed me in deeper, and raised the bloody sword with both hands.

If Judas had not called out our names the moment he did, you might have killed him.

"Over here Judas!" We answered him with loud whispers that echoed throughout the cave.

He arrived at the mouth of the cave and stopped, drops of moonlight pouring down his face, his eyes lost in the shimmering night. Behind him stood a half-dozen or so bloody, swords-drawn, wildly-bearded men whose faces I could not make out.

I rushed to Judas, banging the top of my head hard on the low ceiling of the cave, knocking myself dizzy, needing to sit down. As I got my bearings with your steady arm around me, we approached Judas together, and the guards gathered silently behind him.

"What happened Judas, what happened?" I asked him. "We heard... We were..." not knowing how to say what we heard, certainly not knowing how to explain what we were doing, out in the night.

Judas stepped into you like a pillar, his arms heavy, hard. As I clutched my tunic closed as best as I could, you opened to his embrace. He caught his breath, "All thanks be to Our Creator that you are both safe. Truly Astarte is watching over you. All thanks be to Our Creator." I strained to keep still, knowing we would not get any answers out of him until he was ready. At last he stepped back, looked at us with tears streaming down his face. "I do not know what I would have done if anything had happened to either of you. Tonight of all nights..."

Then he noticed my torn tunic. Following his gaze, I saw the muddy imprint left on my chest by my assailant.

Judas asked, "Did they...?"

You answered him calmly, "They tried."

"And you?"

Your voice a pit, a moonless night, a running water stilled, "Not a scratch, dear brother, what do you expect?"

Judas untied his coarse rope belt and offered it to me. I cinched closed my torn garment, as I asked,

"Judas, we are fine, but the others, what happened?" As an answer, he sighed and pushed the hair off his face, and in doing so covered his brow with blood. I reached for his hand; it was sticky, but I sensed no wound. "Judas, whose blood is this?"

He turned to scan the slope he had just climbed. The men he came with dispersed, finding the best spots to hide and guard us, behind some boxwood shrub, some limestone rock, some mustard tree.

Our friend then rested his shoulder against the wall of the cave, his short lean frame silhouetted by the bright moonlit Lake behind him. His chest rose and fell rapidly as if he were still catching his breath.

Your hand on his shoulder, you asked, "Judas, what happened?"

"None of our men have been badly injured, Jesus, they fought well and bravely and left many pig soldiers dead." He spat. "But we were outnumbered. It looks like they are expecting reinforcements, too."

As he fell silent, you pressed him, "What of the women?"

"Salome's sons, Yacob and Nathan, are guarding your mother and Elizabeth, in the cave behind the library."

"Are they alright?" I asked, picturing ten grown women piled together in that small space. "How will they all fit? Are they trapped in there?"

Judas answered, "There is another way in, did you know? Through the back, it opens into a much bigger cave, just over there," pointing down the dark mountainside. "They are safe, hiding for the night. Our men rolled the boulder to block the opening; it cannot be moved from the other side as there is no room for leverage, if the soldiers think to go in that far. Salome too, and the woman from Tiberias."

"Joanna?"

"Yes, and Dinah, and my Zanna and our Abigail."

The blood curdling scream we heard echoed again, this time from inside my head. Deafening. "And Hannah?" Silence but for Judas's slight, rapid breath. "Answer me, Judas? Hannah? And Tabitha? Ariella?"

Time slowed to perfect stillness. It seemed to take hours for Judas's head to pivot to one side, then the other; it looked as if he were engaging in some strange dance, instead of merely shaking his head "no."

I had time to see each tiny line around his eyes, to count his eyebrow hairs if I had wanted to, to notice the blood caking on his tunic and blood still gleaming on the thick hilt of his sheathed dagger.

His voice, steady but soft now, reeled off the names of my sisters-in-Astarte, those who had walked into the cave, and those who had been borne. Maryanna, Elizabeth, Salome, Dinah, Joanna, Zanna and Abigail walking. Hannah, Tabitha, Ariella, carried deep in the mountain, prone.

Their murdered bodies had been covered from head to toe with the veils of the tent Elizabeth had run up to claim from the grove. Judas's voice rising with these names, and falling with those names, his face blank.

You held my hand. Our most vulnerable: my Hannah our eldest, sweet strange Tabitha who made funny faces at me and never thought quite straight, and dear Ariella who likely had died trying to protect the simple one she had adopted.

Through their faces which danced before my eyes, I saw Judas reach into his tunic. He pulled from his neck a thin strip of something that shimmered in the night's light. It was not until I felt the heat of the cylindrical shape in my warming hand that I understood what was being handed to me.

Judas sputtered, "I tried to save her from one of those pigs, I almost slashed off his arm with its foul rose and serpent tattoo." He spat again. "I was too late. I wounded him badly, but he ran off. I could have chased him, but I did not want to let Quedeshah Hannah's body hit the ground. She was still alive when I caught her on the steps of the grove. She said to give this to you." Squeezing the signet tightly, I found relief in the increasingly searing pain in my palm. Pressing my burned fist to my cold muddy breast, I dropped my heavy head. "Quedeshah Hannah also said…"

I knew Judas was telling me something important, some message Hannah had given him for me, but I heard it without hearing. The cave spun around me, my legs failed me, and I fell to my knees on the silent, unyielding ground. "Hannah," her name in my mouth a faithless plea, a moan, "Hannah."

When I said her name a second time, my throat opened to a hot gush of sobs pushing up through my whole body. I opened my mouth to wail, and immediately your wide warm hand covered it. There was no tenderness in your touch, only function.

"There is no time for this, Mary; daylight is coming," you said with an eye on the horizon. "We are not safe here. On your feet, now, Mary."

I opened my mouth, but no sound came out.

"Now!" you commanded, and grabbing my wrist you pulled me.

The signet was still in my hand as I ran behind you along these gentle slopes that had surrounded my childhood. I wrested my hand free and rapidly pulled the silver cord over my head, lest it fall and touch the ground. I thought for a flash of the ritual I had always expected would accompany the passing of this cord over my head and imagined the satisfaction that now belonged to another life. Grabbing my arm again, you hurried me along toward the woods.

The stifled wailing turned into a stone in the pit of my stomach, and I thought of the stopped wailing of the night of waking up twice, to which we never did return, and it occurred to me that the greatest tragedy of war may be the loss of grieving.

Judas was far ahead, the moon on his tunic ghostly pale as it wound its way through brush and stone.

After moments of frantic running, we gathered at a small clearing that turned into a path through the woods. We paused to catch our breath. I looked back and tried to make out Magdala in the setting moon's light.

The silver cord at my nape vibrated then. I stared down at the small dark cylinder between my breasts, held it up to the light of the moon, and saw the caked blood. I heard Hannah's voice, "You will no longer want to run from the fire, but directly into it."

I turned to you. "I want to go see."

Judas stepped between us, waiving his darkened hands in my face, "Mary!" he whispered violently. "Can you not hear? All that banging?"

Suddenly I heard it. What was that? How had I not heard this before? Since the screaming stopped, it seemed there had been only silence, footsteps, Judas's words, and then yours. "Magdala is crawling with stinking soldiers," Judas hissed. "There is nothing there to go back to. Your sisters and mothers are worried to distraction about you. No one knew where you had gone. We must rejoin them immediately."

"I have to go back and see," I insisted.

You moved Judas from between us, your gesture not without violence, your voice tinged with the slightest edge, "You knew enough to run before those pigs even got close to us, Mary! Now you do not know enough to stay away?"

I turned away from you and ran, climbing, taking the longer way around, back over to the ridge of Mount Arbel, the steep cliff up to the ledge being too treacherous for nighttime ascent. I ran and sprinted as though I could turn back the night, as though I could be back in the tent, where I would be a sober and responsible priestess of the Sacred Marriage, and choose to discuss my dream in the morning with Hannah, at the edge of the mighty oak where incense cones were made and dreams unraveled. My legs flew of their own

will across the ridge of Mount Arbel, certain I would tumble and fall
at any moment and yet staying my course.

You and Judas came after me, full speed, and your men's grunting
breath followed right behind you. I checked to see how close they
were and tripped, falling face down. My cheek met not a rock but a
patch of yielding earth.

You caught up with me quickly, crouched to my side, and lifted
me up roughly. Judas pleaded with me, "You have to stop this madness at once! Why are you running into their hands! You will get us
all killed!"

"Woman, listen to Judas, he is right. You will get us all killed. Pull
yourself together," you ordered.

"Jesus, I have to see." I grabbed your tunic at the neck, and suddenly it was Deborah's cavernous morning prayer voice that came out
of me. "I am wearing the signet and I know things and you have to
trust me. I have to see."

You took my hand from your throat and brushed earth from my
face. Calling to your men, "We are going up on the ridge to survey
the damage, to make sure no one has been left behind." The moonlit
men looked at each other, pulled on their beards, but said not a word.
"We will stay well on this side of the ridge until we get to the plateau,
so that we can see without being seen."

No longer winged, each step along the slope of Mount Arbel filled
my limbs with sand. The signet danced wildly between my breasts,
my bare feet struggled up along the ridge on this route that was not
a path. But you led the way, and we followed.

At last we reached the wide rocky plateau, once the shelter of my
deepest peace. This was not how I had intended to get there tonight.
Oh, the distance between this path and that. At the top you signaled
to us all to get down. I laid down belly to the earth, between you and
Judas. I welcomed the warmth of each of your bodies near mine.

In the aquatic light of the enormous moon setting serenely over
the Lake, at first all I could see were bodies of dead armored soldiers
strewn about our sacred grove. Judas's bloodstained hand pointed
further down to more soldiers, these very much alive, busy back and

forth like ants. Several two-mule carts were being loaded by soldiers with heavy somethings that thudded and knocked as they dropped. What could they be taking away? Enormous gray piles. We did not have that much of any one thing. Then the wall of the kitchen crumbled. You, ever at the ready, smothered my yelp with your large hand.

"Now! Do you see!" Judas whispered hoarsely.

Nothing to come back to, indeed: the walls that had confined and secured my life were being taken apart, their stones piled on carts going to the edges of the world, who knew where or what the bloody pig Romans had in mind for them. Or were they Herodians? What difference did it make? Bloody disgusting pigs.

There was no more place for us, now hardly a trace of us. Like the Tower Wise King Solomon had built for Astarte, once tall and mighty in Jerusalem, today a wisp of legend.

My body melded with the solid mountaintop, as my rooted rhythmic life was carted away by animals. How lightly I had run from it in the dawning moon!

A strange nausea, a hollow sickness filled my mouth as if the central thread of Magdala were tied to my navel, now being pulled out from the inside. In my fleeing, had I pulled that thread undone, unraveled? Was the thread broken, the last bit of it hanging from my neck?

Then Judas spoke into the night, "All praise to Astarte, all praise to Yahweh, that you two made it out in time."

You murmured softly into my ear, "All praise to you, my love, who pulled us out."

I turned to look at you and found for a flash the man I was kissing hours ago, the flash quickly yielding to a stone mask.

"All praise to Muriel," I replied. "It was she."

As I uttered these words, a strange glow emanated from where the back of the barn used to be. Fire! They had found the scrolls. They were burning our scrolls. All those generations and years and hours of patient copying. They were burning our story. They were burning our Law. And the women, hiding in the cave just beyond; I could feel they were safe, but how frightening the smell of smoke so close must have been. I opened my mouth to scream, but it was another sound that rent the night, a sharp cracking then a thunderous crashing.

Thus fell in a single moment our mighty oak, which had survived so much wind, storm, and drought, this gentle tree which had shaded generations of holy women and provided the fragrant mystery of my childhood. I imagined I felt the tender turned-up earth around the roots, confused as they discovered the naked sky. I felt as though my tunic had been ripped from my throat again, and I too stood there naked, paralyzed, a tree made into wood. I wondered if the women inside the mountain could hear that, if they felt the crash, huddled together as they must have been over each other and over those who could not huddle.

The signet throbbed at my breast. Behind closed eyes, inside my mind's eye, I saw the other women, the living and the dead, even Judith and Deborah came to me in this moment, others too whose faces I had never seen: Muriel, Rebecca, and others whose names I did not know. Then I saw Maryanna and Elizabeth weeping over the prone shapes under the ritual marriage tent veils.

I opened my eyes to find Judas and you staring at me in dread. I knew not what you saw. I pushed out words with the same effort required to pull oneself out of a nightmare in the deadest sleep, "We must rejoin the others."

"Let us go. Right now." I did not know if it was you or Judas speaking anymore, or which one was giving me the hand I should not really have needed to stand once again on my mountaintop. I let you pull my body up, and my physical form walked along with you, back down the ridge whence we came.

But I left a piece of myself on that ledge to lay there all night, belly to belly with that soft dark soil, to watch each and every stone be loaded by armored devils. I marked each stone with my mind, blessed each one. I had stood witness to the dying tree, which the scum of the earth stepped around like so much dung. This much, this little I could do for the holy place in which I would never offer ablutions, in which I would never lead a chant, and yet where all my moons' blood had been shed.

But I was not my own, and so I followed you.

Neither were you your own; that was yesterday's dream.

I watched your feet move at your command, right, left. You said you loathed killing, but you did not hesitate to kill. You dreamed of me, melted me with kisses on rooftop and grove, but the moment the world was present, you became like any other man.

Hannah's voice echoed inside me again, "You will no longer want to run from the fire, but directly into it."

It was my body that decided to run off the path directly into the thick woods, away from what you seemed to have become so quickly, away from what I could never be. I ran, though low branches tore at my tunic and scratched my legs; I ran with raw bare feet; I ran and ran until my foot tripped on something soft, and I went flying, landing cheek to earth for the second time that night.

Scrambling to my feet, I found myself in a brightly moonlit clearing. As my eyes adjusted to the light, I saw why I had tripped.

In a few steps, I was standing over a fallen soldier with a rose and serpent tattoo, covered in blood. His own blood and my Hannah's. My Hannah.

I fell to my knees near the collapsed killer in the forest clearing. The full pale moon drenched us; I wished it could wash us clean of this night. From the tree line, voices around me grew loud, and big heavy words were thrown this way and that, but they did not reach me. I could not hear them through the booming drum of my heart beat; I could not hear them above the faint gurgling breath of the dying one before me.

I touched, briefly, with trembling fingertips, the cold and sticky torn chain mail that covered the chest of the alien man. On my knees, with my head bent over the wounded one between us, I felt you standing still at the edge of the clearing. Your blank stare cooled the crown of my head. I would have given anything to feel its fire again.

Judas stepped forward. Your men hesitated for a moment between their frozen leader and your moving lieutenant, chose the latter, and moved in. I felt all this without needing to lift my eyes. Judas in front, the men behind, slowly neared.

They stopped as I raised my hand for the first time with the authority of Hannah and Deborah and all those who had come before. Hand bent back at the wrist, palm exposed, I forgot in this moment the markings of the signet newly burned again into tender flesh. The scar may or may not have been visible to these men, may or may not have been meaningful.

The gesture itself certainly was. With it, a circle was cast around me and the man. The high priestess without an altar and the beaten body flirting with death. The promise of the nation of Israel and a bloody Roman. A woman who had no idea where she was going and a man who had no choice.

A gentle warm breeze wrapped the faint scent of piney fennel around us. The familiar fragrance evoked the life that was gone, and yet persisted, for it had crashed me into this battered soldier with the rose and serpent tattoo.

As I thought of all that was no more, I realized I was looking around for a rock large enough to smash his head in. I could taste in my throat, I could feel in my arms, my hands, how satisfying that would be. What a fine moment, what a pleasing, cracking sound it might make.

I also imagined leaving him there. Surely, he would die like that, like any other animal carcass; perhaps he would yet be sensate as the carrions began to pick at his helpless flesh. My mouth watered at the idea of his pain, of his total degradation. Desire. I felt wrapped in a deep intimacy with this stranger, so unlike the one into which you and I had melted, before our world was torn, and yet reminiscent of it. As savagely and hungrily as I had wanted to taste your life, I now wanted to taste his death.

Desire. It did not matter that his death would not have changed anything. It would not have brought Hannah back, nor restored the oak nor the scrolls nor any of Magdala. It would however have brought a moment of satisfaction in the doing, perhaps, and maybe another as I told Elizabeth and Maryanna how I had personally avenged their mother's death. I imagined the savage comfort that news might have brought to Elizabeth's grieving eyes.

In the midst of this desire I found myself breathing in, eight counts, held eight, breathed out eight. And again. How well Hannah had taught me. Tears streamed down my face as this breath brought me back to that sunlit and heart-broken moment, when she had taught my five-year-old self how to come to peace with all I could not have, embodied then in the signet that had swung at her neck.

My body shook in full sobs now, feeling the coveted object swing between my breasts. Willingly I would have given it back, if I could have seen her again, said good bye, said thank you, said sorry. Handing me the signet, Judas had told me Hannah had given him her last words, to tell me. What were they? I had heard them without hearing. I focused, breathing deeply. When the words came to me, they were in Hannah's voice: "I knew I would die. Tell Mary. Tell her I know she will be overwhelmed with desire. Remember, there is nothing in you not from Our Creator."

Could this desire to kill be from Our Creator? Why not? How many others had this man killed? How many would I be avenging? With each weekly laying on of hands, how much of the people's pain had I felt, had been caused by him and his kind? His kind. What made him different from us, from you? I had not believed in your bloodlust until I had seen it in your eyes tonight – you had defended us, to be sure, but you had liked it. Maybe I would like it too. Maybe that was what had been missing: I could have been using my hands not only to heal and weave and spin and scribe, but to help rid this land of these demon pigs. Not fit work for a woman, to be sure, but a queen, perhaps.

And then I heard your voice from the night before, on the rooftop now rubble, but your voice was not rubble, it was clear and solid in my ears even as you stood silent and still at the edge of the clearing:

"Would you have us be King and Queen of an endless war?"

Behind closed eyes I had a vision of an endless line of men and women standing over each other, smashing each other's skulls in with stones, one after another after another, until no one was left. How foolish. How mad. Foolish and mad as the sacred oak becoming wood, the seers blind, and the lovers untouchable. The scrolls were ash. There was no ritual to dictate my action, no Law to govern something no one had foreseen.

What could I do, not as queen, priestess, nation's hope, but as woman there in that circle I had cast, with this dying man who could be any man. In another forest there may have been, there could yet be, a Roman woman standing over you.

My love. My love! My heart gushed open and my head lifted – you were ten paces from me and standing in the moon's shade, yet I was certain I felt your gaze shine back the spark that must have come into mine. What could be more mad than letting myself be guided by my love for you? What could be more mad than everything that had happened up to now? If this moment could be anything, why not catch the sweetest wind?

The dying man's face was blue in places, mostly around his shorn hair, and all of it swollen to distortion. Here in the dark of night, when the sun had set over all Creation, I took his icy hand in mine. As my skin made contact with his, the voices around me got louder and the circle that sealed them out, stronger. I raised the limp hand and pressed it to my hot cheek. I reached my other hand under his armor through the shoulder hole, where I felt the slight heat of his flesh through his tunic drenched with thinly flowing blood.

I closed my eyes, rolled my body back into a squat so that my bare feet had full contact with the earth. Then, as they had never done with any witness, there without my little tent, the warm gentle tingling colors came up with full joy through my soles and through my body and out my hands and into him, and back through me into the earth again.

The dark blue swelling on the man's uncovered head receded, his breathing deepened, and the bleeding beneath his skin shored up. Under my hands, the man passed from unconsciousness into a sleep from which he would soon wake.

"As I have awakened, dearest Hannah," I whispered to myself, pressing the bloody signet to my lips. "As I have."

I rose and stood by the man's head, my bare feet kissed by the cool forest floor, soft and prickly.

Judas's hot booming voice rang out, his dagger drawn, pointed down. "Are you completely mad? What in the name of Creation are you doing? If you do not want blood splattered all over you, step back."

"No Judas," reaching out a protective hand, palm down, over the sleeping one. "It is over. Put away your weapon."

"What do you mean: it is over?" Judas asked, slowly stepping closer, his dagger down at his side. "Nothing is over! He is a soldier! This is war!"

"I am not at war any more."

"Nor I."

This last from you – my man, my mate – as you came to stand by my side and take my hand in yours. Nothing could have been more unexpected, or more natural. My body warmed as you pressed your shoulder against mine.

"You too? Jesus! Are you mad too?" Judas looked back at the men. Not wanting to upset them, he whispered, "Brother, what is happening here?"

"Do you not see, Judas?" as you squeezed my hand, "Mary has found a way out of this madness. This is what is next, Judas. No more war, no more killing – instead, we heal, we make peace. War will burn us out, Judas. This is something we can actually do for our people that will help." Turning to me, "Bless you, Mary, bless you a thousand times as often as you have healed. Bless you."

"Jesus!" Judas pushed your shoulder so you would turn back to him, "What in hell are you talking about? What have you let this woman do to you? The people need healing, no doubt, but they need the tax collectors off their backs, they need the Romans gone. Are you going to heal some pig coming at you with a sword?"

You took him in, your breath steady, your hand firmly in mine. "I do not know what I would do if someone attacked us now. I would try to stop him, disarm him. What would I do if you came at me with a sword, Judas? It is the same."

"If I came at you with a sword! My brother, my whole life I have lived to protect you! How can you imagine such a thing? How can you say it is the same?"

"I do not know how to explain this right now, Judas, but I promise you I will find a way."

"Why are you short of words now? You never lacked for great speeches to encourage our men, or tender words for grieving families! Why can you not explain something so simple as why you do not let me kill this pig?"

As you threw your own sword to the ground, you told him, "Judas, sheathe your weapon, brother, or throw it away. For now the best I can tell you is: all is well."

"All is well? All is well? After all that has just happened?" waving his dagger toward Magdala, stomping back and forth and staring at your sword on the ground.

"Judas, shh, calm down," as he attempted to shrug off the hand you placed on his shoulder, "can you not see Mary has done a brave and brilliant thing? Think about it; it is just what we need. A way to restore peace to the land. Everything is all right."

"Everything is all right as the end of the world goes, sure! What has this woman done to you?" Judas took a deep breath. The men at the clearing's edge had their hands poised on the hilt of their swords, watching their leaders argue. Judas saw this and said, "All right. Fine. All I know right now is that we need to get off this mountainside. Some of those pig soldiers may still be looking for you, that is," looking at me, "those who are not busy destroying the sacred compound."

You answered him, indicating the sleeping man, "They will be looking for him too."

"I do not think so. They left him for dead after they – "

"You mean we did not do this? Was it his own men who – "

"Yes, I saw it, they beat him to a pulp because he would not – "

" – You saw this?" I asked as you overlapped,

"Would not what, Judas?"

"Does it matter? He is an accursed Roman centurion!" Judas leaned in to whisper, "Mary healed him, fine, she is a woman mad with grief, but Jesus, come on, let us get out of here now! What are we doing standing around talking!"

"You are right Judas. We are ready to go, just help us carry him."

"Carry him?" Judas backed away from us, breathing in very hard and deep. "Are you telling me that I was born to this life, that I have lived all that I have lived, after all we have seen, Jesus – like my father Joseph – Jesus," his voice breaking, "after the battles we have fought side by side," tapping your chest, "just to hear you ask for mercy for a scabrous pig of a Roman soldier? What, in the name of all that is holy, are you talking about? Brother? Have you gone soft? Have you gone mad?"

Judas peered into our eyes and must have found a steadiness there, for at last he sheathed his dagger. After staring at the prone man, taking in his rosy cheeks, placid expression, and his tattoo, Judas lifted his square thickly-bearded jaw to look down his chin at us. He leaned in, whispered, "Mary," with a small glance over his shoulder at the others behind him, "please, has some demon possessed you? Do you not realize... This pig is the one who..."

I smiled at him, as reassuringly as I could. "Yes Judas, I know."

"Jesus," he pleaded, not meeting your eyes, "if you have not gone suddenly mad since an hour ago, if you are not possessed, please, make sense of this to me."

Squaring your body to his, you clasped the back of his head with both hands. He lifted his face to your words, "Judas, my brother, my friend. Would you tell me, in truth, after all the battles we have fought side by side, after all we have seen, can you make sense of war? Are you saying that you need me to explain peace?" Your forehead touching his, "Judas, do you really need me to make sense of peace?"

"Yes, Jesus, I really do need you to make sense of peace!" Judas cried out, breaking away from you. "Just this night you killed three men, and now you are protecting the very one who..."

"We will kill no more, Judas." Your smile spread as you spoke, "There is nothing to be gained in it, everything to be lost."

"Nothing to be gained? Nothing to be gained?" Judas looked

again at the men behind him. "All right, all right. How about, in the name of Creation, we get out of this clearing, how about we get to safety? Remember safety, cover? Then we can talk about peace all you want? What do you say?"

You took Judas in your arms, embraced him, "Yes, Judas, that is the thing." Then you called out to your men, "Come on everyone, let us rejoin the others."

Their relieved faces tensed again when you asked, "Who will help me carry him?" Turning to me, "He will not wake up for a while, will he?"

"I do not know," I answered, looking at our new friend. "He will wake up when he is done."

Judas's jaw trembled so badly that he had to hold his chin with his fist, "You really want us to take him?"

"Of course. We cannot leave him out here. He is defenseless until he wakes up. You are the one who said his own men beat him and left him as we found him. He has nowhere to go."

Judas's face closed completely. A cloud passed across the moon. In the new darkness he looked at you, waiting for other instructions, I supposed, but you were simply smiling. Was it you or me or the sleeping man who had been healed tonight, I could hardly say.

Judas picked up your sword and handed it to you. When you refused it, he tucked it into his belt next to his own. You wrapped a friendly arm around his shoulders and started walking down the mountain with him, whispering things I could not hear. I did not need to know what you were saying, for I now knew what was in your heart.

Your armed men looked to me, and so I tried to lift the sleeping man by myself. He was much bigger than I. After watching me grunt and pull, without succeeding to get even a good grip, two men came forward to help. I saw their faces filthy under ragged beards, their lowered eyes. One had forearms so thick they were almost square; the other was leaner and shorter. They lifted the helpless man easily between them and followed me down the mountain path. Ahead of us your white tunic glowed, easy to follow.

Through the awakening acacia tree forest, larks singing gaily all around us, we walked down toward the valley, following your flowing gait I had come to know, so well, so fast.

We passed through another clearing, this one steep enough to offer a view of the road across the open field below. The silhouette of a caravan of three mule-drawn wagons headed north, piled high with pieces of our shattered walls. Beyond them in the paling night and incipient morning fog, the Lake blended blue-gray with the dark far shore. Fishermen came in, their night torches still burning. I could not tell if they noticed the caravan. Did they see anything beyond the return of their night's work? Likely they were keeping their heads down, the best way to live a long life in a land so long occupied by foreigners.

Nothing moved in the valley but the fishermen and the slow, steady wagons. There was enough light now for me to see Judas hesitate. He looked at the caravan and back at you, as if waiting for a signal. But you just carried on as before; I could feel you smiling from here.

I stepped forward without looking. My foot landed on a sharp stone, and I winced. Without thinking, I pulled my hurt foot up on my knee and put my hand over the small cut. The colors went through me more quietly than ever. Had I always been able to heal myself? I had never tried. Did it really matter? This I knew, anything was possible. Now, with you, everything was possible.

Someone behind me whispered loudly, "We must get them shoes," and suddenly my heart flowed at this kindness. This is all we need, I thought, for all the world to look at each other and think, we must get them shoes. Someone else said, "I know the shoemaker in Tarichaea. He will be glad to help." Glad to help. Of course he would be.

You and Judas stopped ahead, at the edge of the forest, where we all gathered. "The cave is only about twenty paces away," Judas told us reassuringly. "Praise Astarte we have reached it before sunrise."

It felt right that we would all gather inside the mountain. At that moment I felt that I never again wanted the shelter of the houses that people made. I wanted only those Our Creator had made, those only

Our Creator could destroy.

Judas ran ahead, and the cave swallowed him in its shadows. The mouth of the hollow was tall enough for us to follow him in without having to stoop. Where was everyone? I wanted to embrace them all, the living and the dead. I burned to kiss every cheek. As my eyes adjusted I saw the back of the cave, where the mountain curved into a narrow tunnel. I heard a steady, almost rhythmic pounding, and I realized this cave was like an ear, like a drum, and the sound was that of our limestone walls still being taken apart. Our round-faced Zanna emerged from the tunnel; letting out a muffled cry, she ran into Judas's arms.

After kissing her mouth and forehead, he untangled himself with a sober smile and asked her, "Wife, how is our Abigail?"

She nodded her dear head, caressing him with her eyes all the while.

"Joanna?" he continued.

"Gone with Ezra, to the city of Tiberias, just as you two decided," she answered, finding her voice.

Judas seemed satisfied with these answers and disappeared through the tunnel, toward where, I supposed, everyone else was hiding. Zanna rushed to us, arms open. She wailed softly, gathering you and me together, pulling us a bit deeper into the cave, her thick hands pulling our heads down to hers, kissing us, squeezing us. I smelled her sweet bread scent soured with fear as she spoke,

"Mary, Jesus, praise Astarte you two are all right."

I loved her so much in that moment; I never wanted to let her go.

"We are fine, sweet Zanna, never better," you told her. Towering over her, you smoothed away her hair, as if you could brush the worry off her flush, upraised face with your long brown fingers. She fingered your festal tunic, now splattered with blood, torn at the shoulder, and sullied along the legs from walking through the brush. She looked at mine, torn and belted. Her mouth tightened with displeasure,

"Look at you! Let me see if I can find two clean tunics for you," and she hurried back along Judas's footsteps.

We did not know if she heard us say, "In fact we will need three, dear Zanna."

Alone together for a moment, you turned to me, your face radiant and serene, answering the question in my eyes, "Yes, I hear that pounding too."

"We may not be able to stay here much longer."

"It will take them a while to take Magdala apart."

"But, Jesus, what if they find the secret room behind – "

"My love, they will take very long to find what they are not looking for. Besides, the Romans are methodical. If they are taking up the walls, it means they have decided that there is no greater loot. I have often thought Magdala would make an excellent outpost, what with its view of the Valley. It seems the Romans are more interested in removing any trace of its existence."

Before I could answer you, your men arrived and fanned out to the defensive posts you had taught them so well to find – around the mouth of the cave, behind whatever shelter of rock or bush they could find. The two men carrying our sleeper were last.

"Where does this go?" they asked crudely.

"That will do, right there," I pointed to a spot on the ground, against the wall of the cave, near which dripped a steady, tiny flow of water.

They set the man down, letting him drop the last arms' length, and walked out to join the other armed men. The sleeping man did not wake. Zanna came back carrying clean tunics and cloaks, followed by a frantic cloud of white formed by Elizabeth, Maryanna and Salome. For a flash I saw us through their eyes. Disheveled, bloody, barefoot, peaceful. After a moment of quiet, I heard again the pounding of rock being dropped on rock.

"Thank Astarte you are alive, my goodness, what happened to you two?" Maryanna's voice was heavy and raw.

"Where have you been?" Elizabeth bellowed.

"Praise Our Creator you are not hurt," whispered Salome.

I rushed into the arms of the two sisters, "Elizabeth! Maryanna!

How good it is to see you!" Between them I reached for Salome, who took my hand and pressed it in hers. "Look at us! Jesus and I are dirty, but we are fine. I had a dream of my mother Muriel, and we are fine. And you, how are you? This has been such an extraordinary night."

Maryanna hugged me back, but Elizabeth did not return my embrace at all; it hardly seemed that she was breathing.

"An extraordinary night?" the elder sister repeated, retreating from my touch. "That is what you call this?"

"Oh Elizabeth," I said, reaching for her as again she pulled away, "Hannah. Our Hannah."

"Our Hannah, yes," the seer said harshly, "and Tabitha, and Ariella, and the oak! And the scrolls! And everything!"

"Yes, Elizabeth, but at least we are here now, together. I have much to tell you. Everything has changed."

I wanted to tell them all that had happened in the clearing, but I did not know how to articulate it, especially to Elizabeth.

"Everything has changed?" again saying my words back to me. "That is what you have to say about this night?"

I remained silent, unable to summon the right words. Your mother brushed past her sister and fell into you, wrapped herself around you. There, resting her head on your chest, she wept. I saw in your eyes what you felt in her touch: not sorrow, but terror. You took her hands in yours, kissed them, and unwrapped yourself of them.

Facing her, you said soothingly, "Thank you Mother. Go back inside now, where it is safe, you too my sweet Zanna," but neither left. Maryanna remained near you, her eyes feverish. Salome came forward and draped an arm around the graying musician. Quietly she asked me,

"Mary, what happened to you? Where were you?"

I met Salome's eyes, let her see my joy. I was about to answer her when Zanna handed me the clean tunics and cloaks. "Mary, child, why did you say you needed three?"

You answered her for me, by turning and pointing to the man on the ground. The three priestesses had not seen him until this moment. When they did, they and Zanna gasped as one, and Elizabeth exclaimed,

"What is a bloody Roman doing here? Have they found our hiding place?" At these words Zanna fled to the back of the cave.

"We brought him here, Elizabeth," you explained, busying yourself with removing the sleeper's armor, a task made difficult by his inability to cooperate. You said to me as much as anyone, "We need to change him into civilian clothes. His life is not worth much if we leave him in uniform."

All eyes were on you, except Salome's, which kept searching mine. "Salome," I told her, "there in the forest, in the dark of night, with everyone all around, I healed him," pointing to the man, "or maybe he healed me. I am not really sure what happened, but I finally understand, there is another way to live."

As I spoke I longed for Hannah. She was the only one who could understand what had happened to me, what this meant to me: all those rocks I had thrown off the mountaintop, for this moment.

Releasing Maryanna, Salome grasped my hands and faced me; her brow knitting, she asked again, "Mary, what happened to you? Are you telling me you healed a Roman? Why? What does all this mean?"

Addressing everyone present, I offered what I could, "Elizabeth, Salome, Maryanna, I do not know how to explain it. I wish I had told you my heart all these years, as I told it to Hannah, and then perhaps this moment would make more sense to you. I never understood how I could be the queen the Oracle says I am, but now I have an idea. There is a different sort of a peace from what everyone expects."

"But do you not care? About Hannah? What has happened to you?" Salome asked a third time, the furrow in her forehead deepening.

"Oh Salome," I began to answer, but Judas came in yelling, red as a pomegranate,

"What is going on out here?" Judas's words echoed off the walls around us. He lowered his voice. "What is everyone doing out here? Do you not hear what is going on?" He quieted for a moment so we could hear the clanging. "And what the...?" as he saw you, now wrestling with the man's bloody tunic. "Jesus! What has happened to you? Like a woman, tending a sick man? And you, Mary, should you not be more concerned with attending to Hannah's body than this pig's?"

I spoke to him very softly, "This man is alive, Judas. He needs our help now. Hannah can wait a little while. My mother came to me in a dream; surely Deborah is watching over her daughter Hannah. What if, for a moment, the living tend the living, and let the dead attend to the dead?"

"Let the dead attend the dead?" As she spoke, Elizabeth seemed to exhale for the first time since seeing the sleeping man. I moved to help you – you were lifting the man up, trying to pull the clean tunic on over his head, but you needed both your hands just to keep him up right. Our seer exclaimed, "How could you bring a Roman here?"

Judas answered Elizabeth for us, "That's not just any Roman. That is Hannah's murderer they are caring for so tenderly."

Before anyone could respond to that you asked, "And we, Judas, how many have we killed?"

In the long silence that followed your question, the pounding from the compound stopped, then resumed.

"What blasphemy is this?" Elizabeth asked, her voice pale as her face.

"You call this man a pig, I call him Simon," you announced, the man's head bobbing in your lap as you guided his arms through his sleeves. "Simon, who, if he accepts it, will receive his new name today and begin his new life. Simon means 'rock,' and this man represents the rock that has been rolled away from the gate to my heart. Simon."

"We were so worried over you," Elizabeth said quietly, staring at you, "with good reason. You are neither dead, nor captured – far worse, you have been possessed." Some fire returned to her stony face. "Look, Salome, Maryanna, look at them. They are touched. Possessed. We must not go near them. We must take precautions. Come inside, quickly, we must consult privately." She motioned to the two women, but they did not follow her.

Watching you shift the man from side to side, working his tunic down onto his body, Salome blurted out, unexpectedly, "They are not possessed, they are transformed." Using her new moon sing-song voice, she recited,

"They will be one, then two,
and two will be one again,
and they will see what none other see,
and shine this, and tell this."

Elizabeth stared at her. "How can you quote the Oracle at a time like this? This has nothing to do with..."

"Hannah. Hannah spoke with me last night. She told me," said Salome.

"When did my mother speak to you?" Elizabeth hissed.

"When Jesus and Mary went into the tent after the ritual, Hannah told me everything was about to change and – "

Elizabeth interrupted Salome, "Well of course everything was going to change, Salome. After the anointing, and the Sacred Marriage of the two..."

Judas muttered, "Enough of this, enough of this," and stormed back inside.

Elizabeth reprised her own words, "...after the Sacred Marriage of the two of the Oracle, we would come into the time of..."

"That is not what she meant," Salome replied quietly.

"How can you presume to know what she meant? There is nothing in the Oracle about healing murderers, is there?"

"But if they see what no one else can see..."

After tossing aside the remains of the centurion's armor and tunic, you rested the newly-named Simon's head gently on the ground and stood.

"We see what all can see," you said serenely to Salome. "This is a man. A man who has made mistakes in the eyes of Our Creator and mistakes against man. Same as me. Same as all of you."

Elizabeth began to speak, but you raised your hand. "Not all mistakes are visible, beautiful Elizabeth, my dear mother's sister. Some wrongs are just in our hearts, such as when we covet."

Her eyes darkened with hurt. The air shrank, as it does before a storm. She remained quiet, staring at you.

You opened your arms wide, "My dear aunt, everybody wants something they do not have. I have seen too many battles fought for gold or land. Indeed, I have fought too many such battles myself. I am done."

"You will not fight for us, Jesus? Even after what they have done to us, to Magdala?" your mother asked.

"Mother, let us find a blessing in the destruction of Magdala, that we may never again be tempted to mistake the worship of Our Creator for the worship of one place. May we see Creation's glory under every tree and under every rock."

Maryanna asked, "But where will we go now?"

Elizabeth answered her before you could, "As soon as it is safe to leave here, we will go to Zebedee, to the town of Cana."

"What about those who cannot leave?" Judas suddenly called out in his whisper-shout, as Zanna, Dinah, and Abigail followed him out of the tunnel. How could they not have, when he carried Hannah's rigid corpse in his arms.

With her body wrapped tightly in the remains of the Sacred Marriage tent, she seemed small as a child. Red blood, stilled in its pouring, had stained brown the center of the fine white linen in which she was wrapped. Far from the dark stain, her white hair spilled out freely. Hannah.

Coming forward, I caressed her cloud-white locks. My moon lady. The women all drew in a collective breath as my fingers wove through the hair I had never touched, hair through which Hannah's fingers would never run again.

Judas stepped back, as Elizabeth exclaimed, "What are you doing? You bring a murderer to our sanctuary, now you touch the dead with your bare hands! You endanger us and defile yourself!"

"Those are the rules we made up, Elizabeth," I answered, not removing my hand from Hannah's hair. "This night, I have come to understand that nothing in Creation can defile Creation." I pulled back the tent veil to see Hannah's face; I was not prepared for the white mask, even less for the faint smile. Tears flowed down my face as I said, "You see Judas, look at her face, even as she died she knew we would be all right."

Elizabeth glared at me. "How dare you treat my mother so unceremoniously, Mary? She was your high priestess too. Is this how you honor her, her sacrifice? Indeed you are possessed." At Elizabeth's signal, Judas carried Hannah's body back into the tunnel.

I watched him go, then said, "Elizabeth, if I am possessed, then I am possessed with love. I wish with all my heart that Hannah could speak now, because she knew how to make sense of me. She would help you see that what has happened to me is not against you, but rather something for us to celebrate together. Hannah taught me, 'Nothing is in you that is not of Our Creator.'"

"This is blasphemy!" Elizabeth shouted.

You came and put your arm around my shoulders. I took your hand and kissed it.

"Elizabeth," I told her, "your mother Hannah spoke no blasphemy." I pleaded, "Do you not see? All that we truly are is an expression of Creation."

"The only mistake is forgetting that," you said and raised my hand to your lips.

Elizabeth cried out, "How can you touch her when she is defiled, and now you are too!"

Dinah, who had been silent until now, spoke in a voice tender with sorrow, "If you are defiled, Mary, it will be at least one week before you can say the prayers over our dead – my little sister Ariella, and our Hannah, and our Tabitha. And where shall we bury them? Who will say the words of release into Our Great Mother Goddess's womb? Who shall lead the ritual?"

"That cave seems a fine place to bury Hannah, and Tabitha and Ariella too," I answered, pointing toward the tunnel. "Can we not leave them in the inner cave, buried deep in the mountain as they are?"

"Without ritual? Without prayer?" Dinah insisted.

Elizabeth answered her, "Maryanna and Salome and I are here, Dinah."

"Yes, but Mary should do it," Dinah answered, pointing at the signet at my neck. "She is the high priestess now."

At this reminder, Elizabeth turned almost as pale as her mother.

"Elizabeth," I offered, stepping forward, causing her to step back, bumping into Judas who had returned empty-handed, "we both know it should have been you. I do not understand the Law, no matter how many times I have copied it. What kind of high priestess would I make."

I pulled the silver cord off my neck. Gazing at the signet, this object I had coveted for so long, I held it in my hand just one more time to feel its heat. It burned in a flash, quickly, completely. I opened my palm, and there was no ash even, nothing left but the silver cord and our symbol seared once more into my palm. I met Elizabeth's gaze. I longed to put my arms around her, but she moved away.

"What have you done!" she seethed, stepping away from the remaining cord that I held out to her.

"At least now, we will always know where it is," I offered.

"You defiled, possessed creature who was not even born of a proper Sacred Marriage! I am the only one left who dreamed the Oracle; I am now the only authority here. I never accepted that you were the one of the Oracle, how could you be! You have used your holy healing gift for a blasphemous purpose, you mock our dead, and you have now destroyed our sacred symbol. Mary, you must prepare to offer atonement for these terrible acts, or be banished. Jesus, you may stay, as long as you observe the seven days of ritual cleansing and eat and sleep apart from us."

"Elizabeth, listen to me," I pleaded, "the world we knew is gone. We cannot bring Hannah back. We cannot bring Magdala back. We can only go forward. Jesus and I have found a new way to see things, Elizabeth. We do not have to live in fear anymore. We can make a new world together. Let me try to explain..."

But she turned majestically, her long smooth hair swooping behind her, and departed into the tiny cave deep in the mountain that for now constituted her entire domain.

No one moved. No one spoke. I felt your warmth beside me. You whispered in my ear, "Where you go I will go..."

"And your people shall be my people..." I replied, continuing the quote from the Book of Ruth, gratefully recollecting the ancient story of outcasts who find their way. But my throat tightened all the same. Opening my hands before me, "These are my people, Jesus. These are the women I have known all my life."

No one moved. No one spoke.

"Well then my brother and sisters," addressing everyone, squeezing my shoulder, "it seems we have broken too many rules, and by staying we will be breaking another. We do not wish to cause any more distress, so we will be off now. Who will join us?"

"My brother, you are leaving?" Judas asked. Withheld tears racking his voice, "You led thousands up in the hills, and now you leave because of a woman? Where will you go? What about your men? What kind of man have you become on this cursed night? What kind of man?"

"Come with us and find out, my brother."

"You will be the one who finds out, Jesus, and then you will be back. I know it." Judas stood, arms crossed in front of his chest, jaw clenched, eyes tearing.

"Maryanna, Salome, Zanna..." I reached out both hands, but these women who had been my world shirked away instinctively. "That is right, I forget, I am defiled. But I do not feel defiled. What I have always known, no longer makes sense to me." I clasped my hands together, "Come with me, come with us."

"Mary," Maryanna's voice so small, "why not simply atone? If not for us, what of the people of the Valley who count on us? To whom will they turn for solace?"

"Maryanna," I got close enough to touch her soft pale cheek, but did not, "we will go out into the Valley and be their solace. Why should they come to us, always? We will go to them."

Silence.

"Come my love. We will find our way together." You took my

hand firmly in yours and drew me toward the mouth of the cave. As we passed Salome, I stopped, indicating Simon. "Would you look after him, when he wakes up?"

Eyes in my eyes, alive as they never had been across her loom, she boldly put her hands on my shoulders. "Mary. Mary." Then a wisp of doubt clouded her gaze. "But he will want to know what happened. What shall I tell him?"

"You will know what to say when the time comes," tucking the empty silver cord in her palm. "Mostly listen. I promise that will be enough."

"Do you think he might still want to hurt us?"

"Oh Salome, I can tell you this: at worse, he will do you no harm."

Zanna had bundled the two fresh tunics and cloaks and slid them now under my other arm, careful not to touch me as she did so. I wished I could plant a kiss on her sweet cheek, but I did not want to get her into trouble she did not want. For a moment I was a child of five, sitting by the road in Bethany in the middle of the night. Emotion constrained my voice. "Zanna..."

Silently, she stepped back.

You pulled me forward, and we advanced together into the dawning day.

We walked down the rest of Mount Arbel, under a round new sun, past frolicking yellow butterflies and wild flowers of every color. Down at the shore, an abandoned fishing boat, consisting of a broken flat bottom, rose and dropped gently with the liquid breath of the Lake, now empty of fishermen. Without a word, we waded in and made a splashy climb onto the rotting wood, where we huddled together. Soon we were far out on the morning water, as smooth and reflective as the brass bowl of the eternal flame once was.

Looking at the expanse of water all around us two, alone in all the world, I burst into tears. "What have we done?"

"We have done all that we could do Mary."

"What will happen now?"

"I do not know. No one knows. But this I do know: we are free. Free as no one I have ever known."

I thought how much I had longed for this up on my mountain-top, and I sobbed even harder.

"Mary, do not forget what you have done. This morning, you ended the war."

"Men are yet fighting!"

"Yes, but now they have a choice. What you have done, I do not think anyone has done before. Your deed will be spoken of, from generation to generation. I feel certain that in time, all will be well."

You stroked my back as I wept and wept until I was done. What else could I do? Breathing more freely now, I untangled myself from you, let my feet drop into the water and lay back flat on our little boat.

"We are floating like Martha's cart!" I laughed out loud and could not explain. You kissed my laughing mouth. My face warmed with morning sun. We kissed again and again. Lying flat on the cool wet wood, we drifted.

I asked myself, what happens now? And I answered myself, we are free, that is all. Free, free fall, the fall of man, man falling into woman, woman's bottomless pit receiving him. The sun rose behind your shoulder, flashing, blinding me, your thick dark hair aglow. Was this me drifting out on a small raft leaving everything I ever counted on and everyone who ever counted on me? Was this me so transparent with happiness I was not sure I existed any more?

Our small craft jolted to a stop as it became snagged by the reeds near the mouth of the Jordan, where the river receives the Lake. You sat up, smoothed your hair back from your face with both hands, and looked around. The Lake was long and shimmering before us. I felt had never seen it; it seemed larger than I had ever understood it to be. I dipped a hand in to splash some water on my face; next thing I knew you had jumped in the water and pulled me in with you. Holding the raft with one hand you grabbed me with the other. My legs wrapped around you. I became your lake, you were my firm boulder to stand on, your mouth on my throat bent back in bliss, my hair floating amid the watercress, your hand grasping me like tree roots hold the earth.

You carried me thus toward the shore, until you found an underwater rock large enough for us to stand on. Cool water swirled around our ankles. We removed our torn bloodied clothes and threw them far into the Lake. When we unfolded the clean tunics Zanna had given me, we discovered a good strong knife that she had hidden in there, bless her heart.

"I am famished," I whispered, realizing that with our fasting for Shavuot, neither of us had eaten for two days.

"Me too."

We kissed. You moved me sideways into your arms and carried me to shore.

I saw our worn bare feet. I knew what had been lost and destroyed. I felt how alone we were as we moved into the dense green brush, without shelter or a morsel of bread. But how much more did I see, know, feel.

Remember our cave in the wilderness, love? It was not even a proper cave, not an open mouth in a mountainside, rather a nook, a curved elbow, the space under the chin of the infinite, enormous hills of barren rock which our people call the Wilderness.

How many days did we walk before finding its shade and steady stream of water? I do not know. I remember no hardship; we were heady with freedom and with each other. In this shelter at last we were not hiding from anyone. Here, you had not a sword but a knife, and it was not bloody but dusty from digging up roots and cutting them into bits small enough for us to chew.

For the first time in my life, I was not waiting. I was not in between. I was right where I was, neither before nor after nor away from anything. Like the tiny trickle of water at the back of our stony shelter, I felt no hesitation, no need even for direction. I was present simply in the taste of us intertwined, your mouth as available to me as my own; your hands possessing me and freeing me at once; our minds and hearts drifting up into the icy starry night, unraveling all we had been told. In each other's presence, we found at last the simplicity of truth, the power of it, the bliss of it.

Some may wonder, how did our mortal bodies withstand the physical hardship of the rocky barren wilderness we called home? I cannot say. I only know that nothing touched our minds but the moment-to-moment reality of each other's being. Even our talk was not of the past.

We were so full of music together, so full of color, that when we did choose words to communicate, which was not often, it was about how you felt my soul open to yours when you touched the inside of my palm, and about the symmetry of the sun warming my back as you delved into my inner heat. Our thoughts were little on our own survival; it does bear wondering how we did not freeze, burn, or starve to death. Perhaps we did, love. Perhaps we died there.

Perhaps, then, all that came after, happened only in the dream of our souls flying up together, as we always knew they should, would, had to. Perhaps even this writing is in that dream, perhaps there is no need for me to find you because we have already turned to dust in the back of the only place we ever both called home. I like that. I like to think of our dust scattering across the wilderness, I like to think of us at last intermingled, inextricably blended with each other and the world.

If this is so, then this writing does not exist. More reason to tell the whole truth, yes?

I woke one morning to the sight of Zanna's plump silhouette. Was I back in Magdala, or Bethany? No: I felt your sleeping legs tangled with mine. Then I saw another face, a man I vaguely recognized from somewhere, where? And who was that, Joanna? And then, in the deep pink morning light, nearing more slowly, standing apart, Salome. Salome? I jerked myself up, waking you.

"Look they are alive, they are alive!" Zanna almost jumped up and down as she spoke, outside in the light with the others. "Salome, you were right. Oh look at you two! What a frightful mess!" The familiarity of Zanna's chatter tore at something. I buried my face in your chest, wanting to stay there, but her voice pulled me, despite your hand on the back of my head, holding me.

"Child, come out now, do not be shy!" Zanna carried on enthusiastically. "I do not care how you look! Do you not know how happy we are to find you alive? We have been looking for you for over a month! Let me tend to you, come! Do not be silly, I used to give you your bath and I have wiped both your bottoms! Come!"

What kept them at the outer edge of our shelter? What kept Zanna with her outstretched arms from entering? Did they think we were mad? Did they still think we were royal? Or did we simply smell very bad?

I laughed at this thought, caught your shining eyes, and tripped open your fountain laughter. Whatever spell was there broke, and Zanna descended upon us, then Joanna. Only Salome and the familiar man stayed out. And someone else, who was that almost hiding behind Salome? Abigail? Somewhere nearby, a mule brayed.

Zanna's rough yet tender hands on my face, pushed my hair back, as she demanded now, "Let me look at you."

Joanna poured water from her leather pouch into a small bowl, then stared oddly at the sack. "The more I pour, the more it fills up! Look!" She opened the flap completely, held it upside down: water poured continuously. She blushed in confusion, making her blue eyes seem even bluer.

Somehow the flow of water seemed quite natural to us. I put my hands in its stream and washed my face. Oh, that felt so good. I had not felt this much water on my face in how long? Did Zanna say a month? I took some more water and sprinkled you. Smiling, you came to wash your face in the pouch turned stream.

When Joanna turned the pouch back upright, the flow stopped. She was still perplexed and turned it up and down again. Zanna gave it a try, looked almost cross, then gave it back to Joanna.

Salome said quietly from the edge, " '*They will not know want.*' "

You jumped up and out into the morning sun. You stayed still for a moment, eyes closed, hands in your hair, head tilted back. Then, turning your gaze to the red-and-silver-haired priestess, "Is that why you are here, Salome, because of the Oracle?" Your voice deepening, "Well, you may as well not have bothered. We are through with all that."

Her hands clasped before her, Salome remained where she stood. A small smile hovered at the corners of her mouth, which by looking at the back of your head I could tell you did not return. You continued, "It is all meaningless. The Law, your rituals. Do you hear me? The only meaning is the path of the heart. The only meaning is depth of intimacy with Our Creator, which can only be found through depth of intimacy with each other, made in the image of Our Creator." You reached back for me; I came to you and took your proffered hand. "That is the only progress we can ever make," you continued. "War is the opposite of this, and I will lead no more war," your voice broke. "No more wars except against the fear we each harbor within. Hear me."

Salome kept her eyes in yours as she said, " '*and they will see what none other see, and shine this, and tell this. Peace will come into the hearth of all.*' "

Your reply stayed in your open mouth, your features still shaped by your revolt, but softened, surprised even. Calmly, Salome continued, "Jesus, we came here to join you and Mary. We are here to be with you, not to make you be with us. If you would have us live under this rock with you, or some other place, then that is where we will stay."

You squinted at her, insisting, "But... they want a king and..."

"That is just it," Salome smiled fully now, more brightly than I had even seen her do. "The promise of the Oracle is really about you two; it is you and Mary whom we should heed and not the other way around. The others seem to have forgotten this. Perhaps in time they will remember."

Salome's gaze shifted to just beyond us; we followed it to a man with a short fair beard, the same tunic and cloak as ours, pale arms. How could someone so foreign-looking seem so familiar to me? Then, as he came hesitatingly toward us, I noticed his rose and serpent tattoo.

"Simon!" you opened your arms wide, and he rushed into them. His head only reached as high as your shoulders. He dissolved into tears, his cheek against your chest. Through his shaking, with one arm around him, you wrapped your free arm around me.

"Simon, this is Mary. It was she who – "

I interrupted you, " – It was us, Simon, it was Jesus and me. One could not have done it without the other."

As Simon sobbed against your chest, you pulled me nearer, and with only your eyes you kissed me deeply, completely. Colors flew all through me like rainbows gone dancing mad.

"Well, now that everybody is together again," Zanna called out through our embrace as she pulled on her blue cloak dusty with road and crossed the sunlight toward the shade where a burdened mule rested, "tell me, when was the last time you two had some real food? What have you been eating, anyway?"

Joanna answered her, with her throaty laugh, "Can you not see Zanna, they have been feasting on each other!" And we all chuckled, you and me too, our mouths apart but joined by a common giggle.

Simon raised his head and kissed your cheek, and Abigail, who had remained apart until now, came forward and joined her mother.

We all gathered in our shelter for a long slow feast of bread, olives, almonds, dried fish, and dried figs. Abigail brought out a small jar of oil, Joanna a larger one of wine. All these containers flowed like the water pouch, as if they were without bottom. But before I could eat or drink, I had to know, "What of the other women of Magdala?"

The travelers all looked at each other. It was Joanna who answered me, "Elizabeth, Maryanna, and Dinah are well and safe. Let us eat now, and later I will tell you everything."

Indeed, everyone was quite hungry and ate avidly. We sat in a circle in our shady cave, around an abundance of food that felt strange to me, intoxicating. My body soon became sleepy and satisfied, and I fell into a heavy slumber.

When I opened my eyes again, the day was waning. Zanna lit a small lamp and placed it in the middle of the cave. Then she set herself down behind me to begin what would be the very long task of oiling and combing out my bird's nest of hair, through which I had barely run my fingers since we left Magdala. Abigail settled in beside me, holding the jar of oil for her mother. You reclined on your elbows, on my other side, just beyond my reach. Salome and Simon talked softly to each other, across from us. Joanna to our right, leaning against the cave's back wall with her legs tucked under her, faced the setting night. In addition to food, our friends had brought thick blankets for us, in which we were each gratefully wrapped.

Rising from where she had settled lazily in the deepest corner of the cave, her orange cloak fresh as sunlight, Joanna stood, the small light of the lamp flickering over her face.

"Mary, you asked me how were the other women. Now I will tell you. The night the soldiers came to Magdala, Judas came to us where we were all hiding, in the inner cave behind the scroll room. Judas was so upset that he could not find you and Jesus. I suggested using that to our advantage: I offered to go to Tiberias, to go back to court and plant the rumor that you two were dead, to throw off any Roman plans still in the making. Judas agreed. Off I went, into the night. That I was successful in this, is thanks to my beloved husband Chuza, who has Herod Antipas's ear and complete trust.

"When I returned to Magdala, you and Jesus were already gone. I found Elizabeth and Maryanna engaged in a veritable shouting match. Judas was practically purple from trying to yell louder than everyone, eager to get them organized to leave for Cana as soon as possible, and 'quietly for the sake of Our Creator if you please.' Elizabeth insisted this was all Maryanna's fault, something to do with Zacharias, a man they both loved, I gathered. Maryanna insisted it was Our Creator's will. And Dinah kept quoting all the relevant texts she could summon, trying to reconcile the two priestesses.

"When I arrived, everyone spoke at once, wanting me to take sides. Somehow I got them calm enough to move back into the inner cave. Judas stayed out in the front to stand guard. Once inside, I looked at each pale, stricken face; only Salome was shining, so I asked her to speak first. Everyone seemed affected by the new timber of her voice – either that or by the sight of our awakened Simon holding her hand."

Salome blushed at these words; Simon emboldened, took her hand anew, causing her to cheeks to redden even more deeply. A silent glow spread among us, one that came not from the oil lamp but the human one before us. Simon sat as close to Salome as he could; his eyes followed her every gesture; he watched her mouth as she sipped water from her cup. Easily twenty years his elder, her hair now equally silver and red, Salome seemed quite at ease with Simon's attentiveness. You spoke earlier of "depth of intimacy" with each other. Indeed.

"Salome refused to leave for Cana without Simon," Joanna continued. "She would not leave his side. No one else wanted him to come with them. As I am blessed to know what it is to be happily in love, I did not hesitate when I heard Salome's position.

" 'Who is with Salome?' I asked Elizabeth and the others gathered in the deep cave of Mount Arbel. 'Who is with Salome, and Simon, and me?' When I spoke these words, Elizabeth looked at Maryanna and Dinah. Dinah did not move, but Maryanna took a step forward." From this moment in her telling, Joanna began to perform the exchange that ensued, modulating her voice and her posture to convey the presence of the different speakers.

" 'Sister,' Elizabeth glowered at the blind seer, 'you have always done as you wanted, is it not time you thought of others? You cannot think as a mother at a time like this; Magdala needs you to be a priestess first.' Seeing her sister hesitate, the tall seer nearly wept, 'Maryanna, are you going to leave me alone to tend to Mother and grieve her? Will I have no kin left?' "

Joanna gestured emphatically with both hands, conveying Elizabeth's distress. "I suppose Maryanna had never heard this note in her sister's voice, indeed perhaps no one had. She embraced her towering sister with her tender arms, crooning, 'Elizabeth, I will never abandon you. Sister, I will stay by your side.'

" 'Me too, Elizabeth,' Dinah chimed in, coming to the sisters with open hands, but not daring to touch them, 'though I am not your kin, I stand with you as priestess of Magdala, to which I owe everything.'

"Then Zanna crossed the small space toward Maryanna and kissed the back of the musician's head. Zanna came to me, and quiet Abigail followed her. 'Very well then,' I told them. 'My carriage is still waiting outside. Let us go.'

" 'Where are you going?' Elizabeth asked, disentangling herself from her sister. 'Why, Elizabeth,' I answered her, 'clearly we will not be welcome with you in Cana. Instead, we will go find Jesus and Mary.' The seer's fury returned, 'Do you know something we do not know? Do you know where they went?' 'Oh Elizabeth,' Salome responded, 'All we know is how to listen. If you had listened, you would know where they are. Or rather, you would know who they are, and that would be enough.' And so we left."

Joanna joined her hands together and dropped her head, eyes closed. She stood perfectly still for a moment.

"They may yet understand," you offered.

"Oh, I doubt that, Jesus," Joanna said, raising her head, "you did not see the look on their faces."

"I have seen many looks on many faces, Joanna. You should never give up on anyone. You never know."

Joanna looked at you, then at Simon, and conceded. "You are right, Jesus. I cannot know. I do know that they would not come with us." Then, returning to her story, "Once we reached my carriage, we had no idea where to go. It was Salome who showed the way."

We all turned to Salome, who spoke quietly, directly to me. "When Hannah drew me aside on the night of your Sacred Marriage Ritual, she entrusted me with the divination stones, along with a simplistic method of reading them – they gave us 'yes' and 'no' answers."

Before sitting back down, Joanna added, "One does not speak of what the stones tell. We are here together. That is enough." Silence fell upon our circle. Zanna finished with my hair. She kissed my head and draped my now shiny curls over my shoulders. After holding her hand to my cheek, I sprung from her grasp. I slid back into the lush welcome of your arms, where I belonged, and, staring into the tiny flame of our lamp, fell sound asleep.

The night had set on seven of us; the sun rose on eight. At the mouth of the cave, a stranger lay stretched out on the hard cold ground, about ten paces from us, his face turned away. Bony arms and bare feet protruded from under his moth-eaten cloak. I turned to find you awake, propped up on your side, observing the forlorn man. No one else had stirred. I leaned my body into yours; your arm went around me; you kissed the top of my head, inhaled me, and whispered, "The poor wretch. How do you think we should wake him, love? With food? With song? Or should we just begin our day and let him come to?"

I rolled over to face you under our blanket, looking around one more time to make sure everyone was still asleep. "I think we should begin our day, love," and I rolled my hips slightly to press into yours. I smiled to find you ready.

This was the first time we had ever made love quietly, the first time our moans and screams had not bounced off the walls of the cave, and there was something more concentrated about it, as though all the energy that usually left our bodies through sound was now being redirected into each other. Perhaps this was why we both climaxed so quickly, the intensity so different from the expansiveness to which we had become accustomed.

Soon after we became still, Zanna began to stir. As was her wont, she started her day by checking on the food supply. She opened the linen square in which she had wrapped the leftover bread.

She cried out, "It is just like the water!" Looking around she found us staring at her, "Look, you two, it is as if we had not eaten last night!" She lifted the perfectly whole loaf of bread so we could see. "All praise be to Astarte, all praise be to Salome and Joanna, who brought us here."

Her face glowed, but her hands shook. This affected her much more deeply than the bottomless water pouch had. That had perplexed her, but this – the making of the bread had been her taskmaster all her life. I leapt up to be at her side, as her tears welled in her eyes, "But then, Mary, whatever will you need me for, what can I do..."

I quieted her, "Shh, Zanna," her dear head nestled in my arm against my breasts. "Shh. We had no bread before you came. You brought this bread. You are the bringer of the bread."

"Yes, but what about now that I have brought it?"

"Shh, Zanna, you need not be useful. You were made in Our Creator's image – surely that is enough? Does Our Creator worry about making bread? No, see, that is better, there is a smile. All right now. It will be your task to distribute the bread. Make sure those who come get what they need. All right? Now look, for example, there is a fellow who looks like he could use a bit of bread, why do we not offer him some?"

While I was steadying Zanna, you had roused the others and gathered them to sit around the still-sleeping stranger. Salome softly sang the Song of Songs to him, the one song everyone knew. Only the man's ragged cloak protected him from the air and earth; he wore neither tunic nor belt. Angry blisters of leprosy covered his calves and feet.

He woke to find Zanna offering him some bread glistening with dark green olive oil. Trying to get up, he winced in pain, and managed only to half-sit as he supported his torso on his elbow and forearm.

Zanna fed the bread directly into his mouth; he accepted, though it seemed less from hunger than from being too startled to do anything else. Joanna rose to get the water pouch. I prepared to lay my hands on the stranger, but you were already there.

The others, including the man himself, gasped slightly as your bare hands made contact with his blistered legs. When you closed your eyes, I closed mine and I felt the colors and the music as if it had been my hands on the man. What was this? Had I transferred something to you or had it been in you all along, hidden behind your sword? Or was it born the moment you felt the man's need? It did not matter. It was as natural and right as the ever-flowing water pouch, as the sun's morning caress over the harsh wilderness around us, as Salome's song, in which Joanna, Zanna and Abigail now joined.

I opened my eyes and needed not even meet yours to feel them. Yes my love. Yes.

The stranger touched his own smooth legs and feet after you let him go, not believing what he saw and felt. Partially chewed bread in his gaping mouth, he looked around, taking us all in, one by one. It was Abigail who started laughing, nervously I think, but then it infected us all, including the healed man – though he made no sound, his eyes began to sparkle. Such merriment in the middle of the stone quiet wilderness!

I did not grow weary of waking up each day to find new faces staring at us in our cave, or still asleep on the unyielding ground. We never knew how these outcasts found us in the wilderness. It felt as if we were still floating on our little boat on the Lake, only now we were floating on a sea of fellowship, abundance of food, and mirth. It seemed our joy could only grow along with our number. Everyone who came was healed and stayed with us as long as they wished.

It sounds like a dream now, and maybe we had to wake up.

Who better to wake us than your loyal Judas? Armed he came, with swords and certainty. Judas believed he could fit our new life into his old plan. This was as foolish as pouring new wine into old wineskins. The new wine causes the old wineskins to burst, and both are lost.

A cloaked man crossed from shadow into light, from the night into our circle of flame-lit revelry, just outside our wilderness cave. Simon was standing by the small careful fire we had built – some gracious soul brought wood! What a luxury! The rest of us were all sitting; you and I ensconced, everyone close around, listening.

Simon had taken to regaling us with fantastic stories about his homeland, a place where it rained almost every day, and the whole land was covered with lush vegetation. We were so entranced with his telling that we paid no mind to the cloaked man's approach. Many people had been coming out of nowhere and finding us here in our wilderness; more showed up each day. We were at least fifty this night.

It was not until the stranger grabbed Simon's arm, lifted his wrist to the light, and pulled back his tunic to reveal the rose and serpent tattoo, that we recognized the stranger as Judas. At his belt, two bare swords glinted in the flame.

Zanna, seated as usual on the other side of me, made a small noise and dug her nails into my forearm. She never spoke of what it might have cost her to leave Judas, when she chose to come find us. I put my arm around her shoulders and held her close.

You characteristically jumped up and embraced your step-brother, who was thus made to drop Simon's arm, "Judas, my brother! You have come to join us at last!"

He hugged you back but pulled away abruptly, "Jesus, my brother, I am relieved to find you well. Though not surprised, not a scratch, right?" He grinned at you and reached up and pinched your cheek. "I have been looking for you for two months now. And praise Astarte, I found you tonight! I overheard a Roman patrol; they are planning

263

to break up this little party you have here and arrest everyone. You know how the Romans feel about large gatherings. They will be here at day break. We must prepare to leave."

"I do not think they will arrest us, Judas. Look at what is happening here. Look at the faces around you! Not even a patrol could resist us!" you affirmed with your arms open wide.

Over the sound of the crackling fire, men's and women's whispers spread like smoke. Judas ignored the crowd and spoke only to you. "Yes, my brother, I see what is happening here. You sit around a fire laughing while your mother and aunt hide, trembling, in Zebedee's house in Cana. Do you not think it is time for vengeance, brother! We must avenge what happened in Magdala. Your men are angry, more ready than ever to fight."

"I will not fight, Judas. I have found peace. I will not give it up for anything. I want only to share it."

"What happened to the man who gave those great speeches when we were up in the mountains, Jesus?" Judas felt everyone's attention on him and began to address us all. "I remember every word you spoke: '*This generation will be held responsible for the blood of all the prophets that has been shed since the beginning of the world, from the blood of Abel to the blood of Zacharias, who was killed between the altar and the sanctuary. Yes, I tell you, this generation will be held responsible for it all.*' Are we not still that generation?"

"Yes, but we are much more than that, we are – "

" – At least take back this sword, Jesus. I cannot bear to see you unarmed, it is as if you were naked. Take it." Judas pulled one of the swords from his belt, the same you had dropped in the moonlit clearing.

You held open your cloak, "Look, Judas, I wear no belt on my tunic, nothing to hold a sword. Indeed, I am naked! Naked as Our Creator made me, free as I was made."

I could hear the smile in your voice, but since your back was to me I could not see the look on your face when Judas swung his open hand and slapped you hard enough to make you turn.

He cried out, "Stop this, Jesus!"

Zanna moved to step in, but instinctively I held her back.

Rubbing your jaw, you got down on your knees. A chorus of shocked exclamations died quickly into silence as you turned your face and offered Judas your other cheek.

"Go ahead Judas, hit me again. I will not fight, you or anyone."

Overlapping your words, Judas wailed, "Get up Jesus! What in the holy name are you doing?" and pushed your shoulder.

You held out your hand to him. He stared at it for a long time in this gathering now taut with stillness. At last he put the sword back in his belt and accepted your hand. You pulled him down onto his knees and into your arms, where he collapsed in tears.

"Judas, my brother, I told you, I will not go to war. Not even with you. Not even with you," as you stroked his head.

Murmurs rose from all around the fire. "He turned the other cheek."

"Did you see that? He offered himself up."

"He turned the other cheek!"

"Did the stranger say a patrol is coming?"

"Is this Jesus a man or a woman?"

"What kind of man?"

"Not go to war. How will anything change?"

"Look at the warrior weeping like a woman."

"He said a Roman patrol is coming."

Quietly people disappeared into the enveloping darkness – some alone, some in groups of two or three. They carried nothing, for they had nothing, only the life they were seeking to preserve.

Zanna pressed her shoulder into mine as she watched her husband cry into my husband's hair, an arm's length away. After hesitating a moment, her hand mid-air, she reached and caressed her husband's brow. At her touch, Judas pulled back, startled. He wiped his face and stood.

He now spoke to you in a quiet, flat voice that might as well have come from the arid wilderness itself. "Jesus. My brother. Do you not realize the danger. People are looking for you, to kill you. Do you not care."

You rose, asking, "So what is death? Do you not believe we will find ourselves in the lap of Our Creator, once we are buried in the earth? Do you not..."

"Since when do the Romans bury their foes? You will find your head on a stick more likely, the rest of you left to rot. That is, if they do not make you a slave... that is, those they do not rape and..."

Sensing the fear on Zanna's face, and right beside her, on Salome's, I raised my hand. "Enough." I stood to continue, "It seems that no matter where we go, how far away from others we dwell, those who need our healing and care will gather. The Romans track crowds. Whether or not we go with Judas, we need to keep moving."

"We will stay with you, if you want to stay here," Salome said, her quaking voice belying her words.

Your eyebrows were arched in real surprise. "Mary, you would give in to the Romans? Do you not want to talk to them, make sense to them, like we did with Simon?"

Simon stepped forward, blushing deeply at this reminder. He said fiercely, "With or without a sword, I will stand at your side, and face what comes."

"Do you not see, Jesus?" I ventured, "This is not about giving in to anyone. War is all around us. If we stay in one place too long, war will find us. Not because of who we were born to be, but because of who we have become. If we wish to avoid fighting, it seems that we must keep moving."

At this point four young men neared the dwindling light of our fire, and I recognized Salome's and Dinah's sons, the two Yacobs, Nathan and Gad. They must have come with Judas. Their barely bearded faces were battle-weary, but their hands were firm on the hilts of their swords.

"Look at them, Jesus," I asked you. "They will meet the patrol, and kill and die for us. They will not let us talk with them. We must care for those who are near, who trust us, stand ready to die for us, those who – "

" – Speaking of which," Judas interrupted, "think of the rest of your men, Jesus. Some think you are dead, while others are still loyal to you. Some are trying to take your place, and they are beginning to fight each other."

"My men are fighting each other!" Color drained from your face. You began pacing, beyond the glow of the fire, out into the night. "This is madness."

"Yes, Jesus, madness." Judas's voice gathered momentum, "Our people are left unprotected in the villages and the farms, while your men argue with each other up in the mountains about what to do next. Meanwhile we are standing here in the dark wilderness arguing about whether or not to defend our women and children from a ten-man patrol, us with only five fighters! You are right; this is madness."

"I will wage no more war, Judas," you insisted, from the darkness where we could not see you.

"All right," Judas acquiesced, grinning strangely to himself, "No more fighting. But at least come and talk to your men. Tell them all this yourself; let them see you and hear your words from your mouth. You are the one who gathered them, and they have risked their lives for you again and again. You owe them this much."

We heard your pacing still out there in the dark, and then you returned to us by the fire. The hairs on the back of my neck stood up. "Jesus, the last time Judas took you up into the mountains, I did not see you again for seventeen years. I am ready to leave the wilderness, but not part from you."

"Mary," as you took my hands, "You just spoke of caring for those who would die for us. I have to go speak to my men. My love, please understand."

The determination in your dark brown eyes made it clear there was no stopping you. "But Jesus," I asked all the same, "what can you possibly give me to keep my mind and heart at peace while I wait for your return?"

"That is easy. I give you my hand. We will go together."

"You are bringing the women? There?" Judas choked.

"I thought you wanted us to leave the wilderness, is that not what you said? My brother Judas, I tell you again, I am not going to war.

I will talk with our brothers, yes. What I have to say will be heard by all."

"Very well," Judas muttered, seemingly resigned.

After kicking apart the sticks of the dwindling fire, Judas counted and found only twelve people. There were the four who came with him – the two Yacobs, Nathan and Gad – Zanna, Abigail, Simon, Salome, Joanna, you and me. Also firmly standing his ground was the first man you had healed, the former leper, who had yet to speak a word, even to tell us his name. Simon had adopted him as a younger brother and taken to calling him Andrew, which he told us simply meant, "man."

"The men are gathered in the hills," Judas said to us twelve, "above the town of Gamala; we will go along the busy road, up north through the town of Capernaum, then across the north end of the Lake. We will leave before first light." We all mumbled our assent. "So, now that that is settled," Judas's expression softened, "have you been alright? What have you been living on?"

"Judas," Zanna cleared her throat, nervous and shy, "you must be hungry."

"Well yes," not looking at her, turning to his men, "in fact the five of us are quite famished. We have been in the wilderness two days looking for you, ran out of bread and water yesterday. Whatever you have, I know that living in the wilderness you cannot have fresh – "

"Oh Judas," Zanna interrupted more boldly now, "I have something to show you."

The sky was still inky with night when we reached the road, which was surprisingly close. The seemingly endless dunes of solid rock had blocked the view and noise of the nearby thoroughfare, which reminded me of the road I had taken with Salome all those years ago. This time, however, we were on foot.

Our first stop was the shoemaker, as Judas insisted that you and I needed sandals. Never mind that we could heal each other; Judas's face got so red at the idea of us walking around "barefoot like beggars," as he put it, that we gave in to him easily. He had some coins in his pouch for the wizened old man who kept a stand by the roadside for the many passersby.

When we entered the fray of travelers, we were properly shod, but it was my senses which longed for a layer of protection. We shared the five-pace-wide road with every kind of person – merchant, soldier, beggar, children, peasants drawing their carts of chickens for the market, half-naked slaves carrying private carriages, horses, mules, sheep, and goats.

With the constant din, and the concentrated smell of man and beast as the heat of the day grew, I was grateful for our group which moved around us like a tight knot.

At first you did not leave my side. "It is all right Mary," you assured me, sensing my tension, "you will get used to it. You have been living in isolation for so long. Welcome to the rest of the world. Thinking of going back into the wilderness?" you teased, your hand firmly in mine.

Watching my sandaled feet walk along the smooth paved road, I shook my head "no," but inside I was wondering, where were we going? After you saw your men, could the likes of us ever settle in

some quiet place and be left alone? If not, then what? Did those walking with us expect us to know this, or did they have their own ideas
of where we should be heading? I did not know how to give voice to
these questions. Instead I focused on my breathing and allowed the
rhythm of our walking to carry me.

"Look how tall he is," Zanna ribbed me, as later in the day you
walked on ahead, arguing with Judas. In the midst of a crowd, most
men's heads only came up to your shoulders. I had never noticed
such comparisons before. Zanna continued, "It is makes him easy to
follow, you know? We always know where he is."

Just then someone called out from a small tangle of bedraggled-
looking men coming from the opposite direction, pointing at you,
"Look at him, is that the prophet? The one who preaches in the river
Jordan?"

Judas turned on his heals and grabbed the interlocutor by his
rough hewn cloak, "What did you say?" We all stopped and gathered
around.

"What? Hands off, you!" the man barked back.

Judas released him with a push, and the man straightened his garment. As you came between him and Judas, the man narrowed his
eyes at you and said, "No, you are not him, but you are tall and hand-
some as the prophet John, that was all I meant to say," sticking his
chest out as his fellow travelers neared and stood shoulder to shoulder with him. "Only now that I am closer, I see, you are not so..."

"Not so what?" you asked.

"Well, you are a calmer sort, I can see it in your face."

You looked off into the distance, "My brother John..."

"Aha!" The traveler said to his companions, "you see! I told you.
The brother."

You asked more, "Have you seen him yourself? Where is he?"

"Well, you know," puffing up even more, now that he had a full
audience. Others on the road were stopping too, some to listen,
others complaining about the delay. "I wouldn't go there myself; it
is too dangerous. The prophet John has been blessing the people in
the river Jordan. Anyone who will come to him. But everyone knows

that. Everyone talks about him."

Zanna, Salome, and I all caught our breath at once. Blessing people in the Jordan! Back in Magdala, we had heard for a few years now of people coming to Q'mran from far and wide to hear your brother John speak. Elizabeth had been both proud and anxious for her son. But we had not heard of John leaving Q'mran, nor certainly of doing of anything so confrontational as this. Already the Romans patrols looked for unsanctioned crowds, in order to scatter them. But performing the mikvah, the full ritual immersion, in the Jordan river and crossing into Israel, this was the living embodiment of a well-known, generations-old symbol of taking Israel back from its occupier. A fine provocateur John had proved to be. But what was he hoping to achieve?

The man in the road continued, "Not only that, but the prophet John says that the Messiah we have been waiting for is among us, the one who will restore righteous rule to our land. This is not John, but John is here to ensure that everyone knows about it. He told us to keep our eyes open for the Messiah, the Anointed One, was near."

One of the man's companions asked, "Are you the Promised One, the one John is talking about in the Wilderness?"

The first man asked directly, "Are you the Messiah?"

Judas shoved the stranger hard and said, "Do not be a fool! When the Messiah is here, when the Anointed One is before you, you will know, the whole nation will know, you will not have to ask. Now move along, you are blocking the way."

And your step-brother took you by the arm and moved us all forward. No one spoke for a long time.

As night fell, we stopped at the outskirts of the city of Beit She'an. There we found shelter for the night in an abandoned barn. Truly our countrymen were being crushed to death by taxes – why else would such a large shelter be empty of animals, alongside such a busy road?

You and I chose a corner and were beginning to settle down on our blanket, apart from the others, when Judas came to find us. The small lamp he carried flickered anxiously beside his jaw that seemed to be getting squarer by the day. "Tomorrow we need to make haste; if we do not stop we can reach Capernaum by the end of the week."

"Have you sent word to our men in Gamala, brother?"

I felt an unfamiliar twinge. You were not at all bothered by his intrusion into our sleeping space. I made myself remember how many years you had spent the night with him.

"Yes of course I have sent word. But more important, we need to move quickly," Judas warned. "Your brother John is becoming a danger to us, telling people to look for you. Does he know how close to the truth he is getting? He may well be a madman, as I have heard tell he has become, but he will get us arrested or killed all the same. We need to get you out of this region, as far from him as possible."

"At least once we reach Capernaum..." Judas's eyes shifted to me – was he speaking to me really or just avoiding looking at you? "The town is full of people moving through it, and most of all it is north-ernmost on the Lake, with many easy exits – onto the water, into the farms, around to the hills of Gamala..."

"Why would we need an exit, Judas?" you asked. "You do not seem to remember that we are not at war anymore."

Judas's face closed like a fist, but he did not move; instead he set his eyes back into yours. "You may not be at war, Jesus, but that does not mean that no one is trying to kill you. Even some of your own men, who feel you have abandoned them, deserted."

"That is why we are going there, Judas," your long arm and hand gesturing an invitation to invisible people. "I cannot bear to have someone who has placed their trust in me feel that I have abandoned them. Once the men hear me, once they see us, their hearts will not stay so hard," you added, poking Judas's chest with your finger, your meaning clear.

"We will see what we will see," Judas answered as he ignored your gesture. "First, we must get you far from the range of John's influence. The talk we heard on the road today, I also heard earlier, while I was still looking for you. John preaches about one who will come after him and baptize with fire. You and I both know that Herod Antipas will stop at nothing to find out who this 'fire baptizer' is.

Herod Antipas is no fool, and neither are his spies. People are getting arrested just for going to see him, arrested and tortured.

"Soldier are knocking on doors, and if they find no husband, they assume he is with John and take the wife for questioning. Do you hear me? They lay their hands on our women!" Earnestly shaking his head, "It is horrible, Jesus." Then, eyeing me, "I will spare you the details. First I have to get you away from here. We are not in a position to take Herod Antipas on just yet."

You had wrung my hand to almost breaking at the words "arrested and tortured." After Judas fell silent, you whispered, "If only people, all people, could see what we see, could see themselves through our eyes for one moment, this would be no more." Then you decided, "We will go see John. It is time he and I met. Let us see if we can put things to rest that way."

"Are you mad, Jesus, you are going right into the lion's den!" Judas exclaimed. "Not only is he dangerous to you by himself, but you cannot go near him – he is being watched."

"All the better. Then what happens there will become known all the faster."

We set out the next day to find John. It was not difficult. Word of him flew like chaff on the wind around the sun-beaten travelers we met on the road.

What was difficult was watching Zanna avoiding Judas. They had not exchanged three words since his arrival that bright night in the wilderness. Private conversation was especially difficult as his four intent young men-at-arms shadowed Judas everywhere, and rarely addressed anyone but their square-jawed leader.

But Zanna watched Judas all day long. He slept alone at night, when he was not pacing and keeping watch. He did not lay with her on her blanket. I tried putting my arm around her when we walked, but she just sighed, kissed my hand, and unwrapped herself of me.

We soon learned that John was preaching a half-day's walk from our shelter in Beit She'an. It was mid-afternoon when we arrived at the verdant strip along the river Jordan, our senses delighted by such teaming life after our trek from the road through the familiar but miserly wilderness. After hot gray rock, here was deep green shade full of strident bird calls and redolent with loamy black soil. The cool air refreshed us like a bath.

You were the first to come upon the three men standing by the edge of the water. They were dressed in fine, pure white tunics and cloaks, standing with their sandaled toes touching the river, watching John. Your half-brother was half-naked, hip-deep in the middle of the flowing river, his brown sunlit back smooth as he preached ferociously to the motley crowd on the far shore.

You approached the men in white, who were positioned perhaps unwittingly in order of height, each one's head reaching the ears of the one beside him.

"Greetings, friends."

They turned as one to look at you, a quick up-and-down appraisal of your tattered tunic, unkempt beard, crooked cloak. For a moment I saw you as they did. I had not thought I could love you more than I already did.

When they did not answer you, you spoke again, impervious, smiling. "Are you here to be immersed in the Jordan?"

They remained silent. We were now all gathered around you. One of Judas's four, Salome's son Yacob, told you, "These men are of the Essenes, from Q'mran. They are John's elders."

"Ah, I see," I heard sparkling mischief in your voice. "So, what do you think of men abandoning their families to come for a dip in the river?"

You received an unsmiling response from the shortest of the three, furthest from you, "They are here to purify themselves, for the End of Days are upon us."

"We are made in Our Creator's image. What could be more pure than that?" you asked.

"We become sullied in this world," asserted the short man.

Judas waded into the river to confront them, "And you wish men to purify themselves by letting their families go hungry and unprotected?"

"If we purify our spirits," the man in white replied, "our children will be able to honor us all their lives."

"If they live!" Judas fumed. "Do you not know that soldiers are looking for rebels in every home, that their wives and children become conspicuous by the husband's absence?"

"That is not our concern, we..."

"How is that not your concern?" Judas interrupted the man who had not yet deigned to look at him. "Are not holy men supposed to protect the meek and seek no honor for themselves?"

The short man in white rested a gaze full of authority on his feisty interlocutor, "Holy men are supposed to protect the souls of ordinary men from the eternal fire of Our Creator's wrath, which will soon rain down upon us."

"Repent," chimed in the tallest one who had not yet spoken. "The End is near."

While Judas argued with these men, you started toward the middle of the murky brown river. Though we were well into the dry season, this stretch of water covered deep holes. You tripped and fell in several times as you made your way.

I came in after you. As I entered, the water rushed against my legs, and for a moment, I forgot myself and wanted to immerse myself in the cool rushing river, to feel the dust of the road and of the past days and weeks and months be carried off in the swift current. The longing was so great that I experienced a moment of complete disorientation – what was I doing there? But then, where else was there for me, for us?

My heart raced. To calm myself I breathed deeply and followed you step by step, as you had found your footing. Those who had been walking with us remained at the river's edge. As you approached John, your shadow preceded you, shading his bare back in mid-river while he harangued the ragged group of thirty or so who listened intently, squinting and shading their eyes against the setting sun. John spun around as if your shadow had pressed upon him.

His wild uncovered hair, black and dense as yours, framed his unfocused darting eyes and pale open mouth. You rested your hand on his shoulder high as yours – the first time you touched him.

Born of one father and two sisters, so close together, having never met. Yet the smell of kindred blood was unmistakable. I thought of Elizabeth; my heart clutched for her as I imagined her seeing her son this way: his deranged expression, his once fine camel-hair cloak in tatters, the elegant leather belt around his waist, shredding and stained. I wondered if she could see him with her inner sight, what that did to her, had done to her.

John knocked your hand off – on purpose? – as he returned to his followers, "Look, the Lamb of God, who takes away the wrongs of the world! This is the one I meant, when I said, 'A man who comes after me has surpassed me because he was before me.' I myself do not know him, but the reason I come purifying with water is that he may be revealed to Israel."

"John…"

I could hear your whisper as if it had been in my ear… Did everyone? Was it the water, or the stillness of incipient twilight that carried your words?

"Brother John, let me partake in your work," your hand on his shoulder again; as you turned him back around, you caught a whiff of the hatred steaming off his face. Nonetheless you continued, "Would you honor me by immersing me?"

"Is it not you who should immerse me, little brother?" John sneered. "Is that not how our mothers decided it should be? The younger brother comes before the older?"

You answered in your softest voice, "That is not how Our Creator – "

"Are you saying I have not been passed over? Am I not the eldest?"

"Yes you are, John, and that is why I am here now to receive this blessing from you, my older brother," and you bowed your head.

Two paces away from you, the river pushed at my legs, but I stood firm. John glanced at me, his gaze bottomless. Closing his eyes, he cupped running water in his long smooth hands, so like yours, and poured it over your head. But then, instead of guiding your immersion by pressing your shoulders gently down, he pushed your neck down hard and fast, and held you there as you struggled. He was stronger than he looked.

You shook him off before I could reach you. Someone splashed in behind me; I knew it was Judas. The cold river pressed my tunic to my legs as I circled my arms around your heaving torso. Outraged, my glare held the self-proclaimed scorned son's damaged gaze.

He laughed heartily and faced his followers once more, "Behold, a Holy Dove comes to him. Proof that this is the Chosen Son, in whom Our Creator is well pleased."

As you caught your breath, I answered him loudly, "Our Creator is well pleased in all Creation, in all the sons and daughters, you and," pointing to the crowd, "you and you, and all who live on the earth."

John laughed more stridently, almost hysterically.

Taking a deep full breath, you said, " 'Our Creator is my light and my salvation, whom shall I fear?' "

"Yes, brother Jesus, you do well to remind us of that psalm; you would do well to remember the last line, 'Wait on Our Creator, and be of good courage, wait on Our Creator.' Why are you in such a hurry to push your own will along?"

You opened your mouth to answer the senseless accusation, but John had departed. He waded upstream, shoulders stooped, waving to his followers to do the same, which they did silently along the far shore.

Judas grabbed your arm, "Have you seen enough? Can we go now?"

Without a word, you wrapped your arms around each our shoulders, and we three waded back to shore.

I pondered John's name for me – a Holy Dove indeed. I had only heard that phrase used of the women in Jerusalem, those whom Judith had gathered. It irked me that the world had a name for us, which I did not use, that there was a system into which I was presumed to fit, that even a wild man standing half-naked in the river could throw an epithet at me and render me invisible as a woman helping the man she loves.

As only little daylight remained, we chose a spot to sleep nearby, in a small clearing veiled by thick cluster of willow trees. No one spoke aloud; only whispers darted about in the darkness. Though Judas had been against it, he and his men had been expecting something of your meeting with John, I was not sure what, but surely not this. As night set, you stared into the blackness. You did not speak of your brother's silly act of boyish violence against you. You who talked about everything were silent. When we slept, your arm went around me, but still I felt alone.

In the morning you rose and dashed off to find your brother, as if your life depended on it. We all followed you to where we had seen John the day before. There, a few frightened stragglers came out from dense bushes and told us: John had almost been arrested that night. While you had been silently staring out at the river, he had barely eluded Herod Antipas's personal guard by running off, alone, back into the rocky Wilderness.

Judas spat into the water, "Serves him right, after the way he treated you."

"Judas," you retorted, "how can you see a speck of dust in my brother's eye and while a great boulder blocks your sight? First take the boulder out of your eye, and then you will see well enough to remove the speck from your brother's eye."

"What boulder? Jesus, when have I ever raised a hand against you? How can you say such things? In front of all these people!"

You answered warmly, "Judas, it is true, you are a valiant protector. Fret not, my brother, I know your love for me and for my beloved. But you do have a boulder in your eye. Let us walk on and see if we can remove it together, shall we?"

After we returned to the road, just north of Beit She'an, Judas set a brisk pace. We now headed toward the land we knew. Though Judas led us intentionally along the very busiest road, full of beggars and cripples who were heading for the many salutary waters of the mountains along the Lake, he scowled and scolded whenever we stopped to help them.

We were so susceptible to the pull of sickness, the pull of despair. Despite the crushing heat, if someone ailing so much as brushed past us, we paused and healed, as naturally as we breathed. Often as not, the ones we helped made their way with us, for a little while at least.

Our familiars paused when we did. Zanna, Abigail, Salome, and Joanna were never far from me, often even tried to walk encircling me so that no one did touch me accidentally, and I appreciated that but refused it. All day on the road we did this dance of them keeping me in and me trying to get out.

Likewise, Judas tried to rush you along, aided by his four faithful. Rarely leaving your side during the day were Simon, and his adopted brother Andrew, who seemed to accept his new name, just as Simon had never questioned his own. As they were both completely displaced and without family, at least none of which they wished to speak, Joanna took to calling them "ben Yonah," Hebrew for "sons of the Dove," since, as she put it, "It may well be said that they have been reborn to be in our service, in Our Creator's service."

After a while Judas finally noticed that many of those we healed would join and follow us, and he stopped complaining. What did he want to do, we wondered, make us king and queen of the rabble of the road? These folks did not know they were part of any plan and drifted in and out of our group without warning, often disappearing after the abundant breakfast made possible by Zanna's bread, Abigail's oil and Joanna's water and wine.

During that hot journey, as often as not we slept under the open sky, close by other groups of travelers for safety. How I savored those nights, which were the only time, only a few hours at that, when I had you all to myself.

We shared a blanket, set somewhat apart from the others. You always fell asleep so easily. I marveled at that, as I was more like Judas whom I could hear tossing and turning just beyond whatever ledge or tree or stony dune sheltered us. More frequently, I could hear him pacing, his sandals raspy against the dry earth.

You slept on your back, one arm tucked under your head, one

wide hand on your chest, your dear face turned toward me. With only my gaze, I kissed your hand as it rose and fell under the motion of your breathing. Against the satisfaction of watching over your sleep, burned the childish desire to wake you, just to see your shining eyes open and take me in smiling, as they always did.

Eight counts I breathed in, eight counts held, eight counts exhaled – until at last sleep would find me too.

We arrived at the shore of the Lake and passed Tiberias. The city's gates were bursting with activity, its marble palace high enough to be seen from the road. The bustling city showed no sign that it was built over graves, beloved bones.

I asked Joanna if she wanted to leave us, and go visit her husband, but she replied only that there would be plenty of time for that. As I pondered her answer, my eyes caressed the familiar shape of the land, and they inevitably came to rest on Mount Arbel. The red scar of our compound, unsettled earth, nothing more. I had never seen it from the road, from so far down. My head spun. I gasped and reached for your hand which was nowhere near – where were you? – just as an old woman was knocked over in front of me by a passing merchant, pushing his cart of newly shorn wool. The finely cloaked merchant did not turn around when we called to him, though I was fairly sure I saw his fat hands cling more tightly to his wooden cart, his thick sandals slap more heavily and quickly against the paved stone road as he disappeared into the dense crowd ahead.

The woman's hair shone bright white. Hannah. Not Hannah. She was all right, she just needed to be set back on her feet. But her thin sandals had ripped open in the fall and would no longer stay on her calloused bony feet. She sighed and picked them up, put them in her reed basket full of piping white and yellow chicks, none of which had fallen out. She pressed my hand in thanks, under her breath said, "Bless you Quedeshah Magdala," pulled her undyed wool cloak over her head as she disappeared into the crowd.

Quedeshah Magdala. Was she one of the throngs who had come up to see me on Shabbat? Or on the full moon only? What story was now told of the women of Magdala? That other world. Right there: I could point to the dip in the mountain where it had been. I turned away. My vision blurred with the glare of the sun off the Lake. Blinded, I found Zanna steadying me, calling out to you and Judas. You were too far ahead to hear, the road too noisy, your argument with Judas too engaged.

Helped by Zanna and Salome, I regained my footing and walked along, head down and watching my feet. I urgently wanted to know: what had they done with Hannah's body? Where had they buried her? My mouth filled with ash; I coughed and sputtered. Joanna appeared with a mule she had just purchased. She helped me sit astride it, facing the Lake. Once again I found myself turning my back on Magdala with a throbbing heart. And where were you? How was it for you, passing here? Was it ordinary for you, another battle site among so many?

Abigail emerged beside me, pulling you by the hand. I exhaled. You walked between me and the Lake, diverting my gaze from the torn mountainside. Your touch helped settle me.

"We did well to leave, Mary. Remember, you saved us, in every possible way."

"Yes, Jesus, but it was us, it was never me – it is always us."

After a long silence, moving forward holding hands, you began to speak of nothing, of now, of everything, "My love, have you noticed these two newcomers? They have been walking with us for days now."

You pointed out two men dressed like shepherds, with rough wool cloaks pulled over their heads. "They hail from among those who told us of John's near-arrest – one is a foreigner named Phillip, the other is Bartholomew, from the countryside around Jerusalem. They had been following my brother John, now they cling to us. Do you think they will find in us what they seek?"

I did not answer you, but I thought to myself, they think we are leaders, which is hardly what we do. On the road, we simply offered ourselves to each other, to the sun, to whomever called us out, loudly or silently, in their need. I supposed that in this poverty-ridden, drought-parched, war-torn land, all that passersby normally did to each other was take, demand, extract, steal. I supposed that in our giving, people found a direction.

Is this reaching you, my love? Across the din of Jerusalem, this fever-ish exultant carnivorous city, do you hear the tale I am weaving? Do you hear all that was not told then, that was not known then?

Can you feel again the time on the road when we were innocent, we were free as bees flitting through a field of flowers, eating and pol-linating at once? Can you feel the time of the colors moving through us freely, of music never quite vanished, stronger when we made love and when we healed, softer when we simply walked or ate?

I had forgotten until I wrote it about my faintness at seeing where Magdala once stood. It seems that much is remembered in telling. Perhaps at the very least, then, this writing will serve to tell the story of Magdala in which so many stories were written, but never its own. It has as much sorrow and loss as any other story I transcribed there.

I wonder now, how much of our love was love, and how much of it was losing our fear and sorrow in each other's gaze? Can what we lived be called love the same as that of a man and woman who live together all their lives? I want to find out. I pray to Our Creator that I may find out.

Oh Jesus, I can still see your proud walk ahead of me on that road, I can still feel you take my hand, your touch a haven that reminded me of the truth: Our Creator is found in our love for all Creation, and nowhere else.

I feel I have not yet begun to love you, or maybe I have, just now.

Let me reach you. Let me in. Stay close. Do not drift further from me. My husband, come back.

Come back to me.

When we reached Capernaum, we had to wait to enter along with the crowd, through the narrow black basalt mouth of the bustling town gate. Amidst the comings and goings, there was one pocket of stillness – the line of people waiting to see the Temple-tax collector at his post.

The Temple priest who would become known to us as Matthew sat in the mid-day heat in his small, partly shaded booth, two sleepy Herodian soldiers guarding either side of him in the full sun. He did not meet people's eyes as they brought him the Temple tithe. He did not lift his gaze to them at all, nor did he seem to see the leathery hands, some with missing fingers, carefully dropping onto his table thin coins for a faraway Temple they had never seen nor cared to – a tax paid simply in the hope, not certainty, of avoiding a visit from the brutal and corrupt Herodian tax enforcers.

The tax-man-priest sat with stooped shoulders under his fine red wool cloak and watched the stamped metal disks appear on the ledge of his wooden booth. A flap of fabric across the top kept his carefully turbaned head but not his rounded back from the mid-day sun. He counted out the coins twice with pale, painstaking fingers, and then made a mark on his scroll with his long reed dipped in a tiny red clay jar of ink.

You saw him too and immediately got on the line of taxpayers. Those of us who had not gone through the gate with Judas stayed with me at the gate and watched you. When it was your turn, you squatted before the priest's booth, forcing him to break rhythm, to see you. Then you placed your hand upturned, open and empty, on his narrow counter, not asking, but more like a flower waiting for the butterfly that would be his hand. There was too much noise around the bustling gate for me to hear what you whispered; I could only guess at what words you chose. Was it your voice that softened his suspicious frown?

When you pointed with your other hand, his eyes darted from you to the rest of us gathered a few paces away. He spoke to you then, a gush like a spring river; you closed your eyes and listened, your hand closed around his as it unexpectedly came to rest in yours. The sudden laughter that burst out of him like a hidden bird from a leafy tree drew us all to gather around him and the light spilling off his long face, pouring from the eyes of a limber child awakening inside the stiffened man. He got up so quickly he knocked his booth over. Ink and paper fell to the ground, and coins scattered noisily. The soldiers woke up.

As the tax-man-priest walked off with you, your arms around each other's waists, the people still on the tax line calling at our backs, "What about the Temple tithe?"

The soldiers shouted, "Where are you going? What about the money?"

"What about the money indeed!" the priest called back merrily.

When we found Judas, he was red-faced, his jaw jutting out harshly, pacing by the town's central fountain; did he know he was marching in rhythm to the water's pulse?

"Where have you been? And who is this now?" His arms crossed, taking in the man's Temple-red cloak, "A Temple priest, great, and here to collect taxes no doubt!" Without another word, Judas turned and furiously led us up through the main street. There a market teamed with buyers and sellers of linens in more colors and hues than I had ever seen in one place. Through the air redolent with spices, prices were shouted out over the loud wailing of babes. Many of those who had entered Capernaum with us dispersed here, drawn to this temptation and that. By the time we emerged through the other side of the market, we had lost nearly every one who joined us on the road since Beit She'an.

A small area of tranquility marked the open space between the market's crowd behind us and a building before us so vast it required six wide round columns to hold up its roof overhang, in whose shade small clusters of people congregated.

"What is that?" I asked.

"It is the town hall, the meeting place," Judas answered. "Ask your so-called Simon, he knows all about it."

Simon started casually, "We call it the synagogue, that is the Greek word for meeting place. The people are gathered in the shaded area called the portico." But he paused when we reached it, resting his hand on one of the black basalt pillars, his voice catching, murmuring, "My poor mother..."

" 'Poor mother!' " Judas practically foamed at the mouth as he spoke, stepping up close to you. I offered him some water from my pouch, but he did not seem to see me. "This man's dear Roman mother is so 'poor' she paid for the rebuilding of this town hall, when it was another pile of rubble along the trail of yet another Roman war. And where do you think a Roman centurion's mother got the money? They destroy our towns, then use the taxes they wring *from* us to build something *for* us, as if it were some wonderful gift! You call him Simon. You do not know his name! It is probably Julius! Jesus, do you not see!

"They are not even Herodians, not even our own people on the wrong side. They are not one of us. Do you not remember, Jesus, what the Romans did to us? When will you wake up and see the people following you and lead them," tapping your chest, "for Our Creator's sake?" He gripped your tunic collar, his voice both bellicose and begging. "How can you keep making friends with Romans and tax collectors?"

Your large brown hands enfolded his tight white-knuckled ones. "I see, Judas, and I remember. I remember how we fought and killed." You closed your eyes. After a deep breath, you pulled him close and kissed the top of his head. "But there is simply no more war in me. Consider this story."

"I do not want to hear another bloody story, Jesus! We have brought this pig home to his mother, now let us get out of here! Let us go rally your men in the hills of Gamala, then get to Cana to see your mother, and Elizabeth, and the others. We will tell them how people flock to you, without you even trying." Judas leaned into you, pushing you under the portico, away from us, as he urged you, "It is time to start the revolution, to take back what is ours."

You went into the shade willingly, but you firmly resisted his plea, "But I am taking back what is ours. That is what Mary and I have been doing. Judas, I love you, and I have been very patient with you, listening to your constant call to war, and now I need you to be patient with me."

Judas yelled right into your face, "Patient with you! What else have I been? And how can you say you love me while you love that pig, Simon as you call him? Tell me that? How can you do this to me?"

"Come in and listen and I will tell you."

You gestured for us all to enter the town hall with you. In the welcome cool of the stone building, a few people gathered on stone benches against the wall stopped their conversation to assess the newcomers.

"Consider this story, Judas, all of you," your gesture including us and the strangers there as well. "Perhaps it will help make things clear.

"There was a man who had two sons. The younger one said to his father, 'Father, give me my share of the estate.' So the old man divided his property between them.

"Not long after that, the younger son got together all he had, set off for a distant country and there squandered his wealth in wild living. After he had spent everything, there was a severe famine in that whole country. He went and hired himself out to a farmer, who sent him to the fields to feed the pigs. He longed to fill his stomach with the pods that the pigs were eating, but no one gave him anything.

"When he came to his senses, he said to himself, how many of my father's hired men have food to spare, and here I am starving to death! I will set out and go back to my father and say to him: Father, I have wronged Our Creator and I have wronged you. I am no longer worthy to be called your son; make me like one of your hired men. So he got up and went to his father.

"While the young man was still a long way off, his father saw him and was filled with compassion; the old man ran to his son, threw his arms around him, and kissed him. The son said to him, 'Father, I have wronged Our Creator and I have wronged you. I am no longer worthy to be called your son.'

"But the father said to his servants, 'Quick! Bring the best robe and put it on him. Put a ring on his finger and sandals on his feet. Bring the fattened calf and kill it. Let us have a feast and celebrate. For this son of mine was dead and is alive again; he was lost and now is found.' So they began to celebrate.

"Meanwhile, the older son was in the field. When he came near the house, he heard music and dancing. So he called one of the servants and asked him what was going on. 'Your brother has come home,' the servant replied, 'and your father has killed the fattened calf because he has him back safe and sound.'

"The older brother became angry and refused to go in. So his father went out and pleaded with him. But he answered his father, 'Look! All these years I have been slaving for you and never disobeyed your orders. Yet you never gave me even a young goat so I could celebrate with my friends. But when this son of yours who has squandered your property with prostitutes comes home, you kill the fattened calf for him!'

" 'My son,' the father said, 'you are always with me, and everything I have is yours. But we had to celebrate and be glad, because this brother of yours was dead and is alive again; he was lost and now is found.'

"Now Judas..."

"Yes, Jesus, I get it, I am the older brother in this tale. Well," he looked like he was prepared to spit on you; instead he turned to Simon and spat at his feet, "no matter what you say, I will never call this man my brother," and stormed out.

As Judas left, you called to his back, "Call him what you like, he is what he is."

Judas dismissed your last remark with a flip of his hand as he exited into the white hot sun.

As you followed him out, I went to our pale and trembling Simon whose eyes were fixed on the doorway through which Judas had just passed. Speaking softly, so as not to be intelligible to those around us, I asked, "Tell me, Simon, what of your mother?"

Looking at me, visibly relieved I was speaking to him, answering as quietly as I had spoken to him, "She was very ill when I last saw her."

"Where is she now?"

"If she lives yet, and if they have let her stay on without me there, she would be where I left her, yonder," he said, pointing outside to the building about thirty paces across from the town hall: Roman headquarters with four columns, flanked by armored guards with spears.

"Well then," taking a step forward, I gestured to Simon to follow me, "let us go see her."

"I cannot go in there," Simon blocked my path. "If they have kept her there, they will surely throw her out if they learn I lived. They will think I deserted. I cannot. They will know me."

While we were speaking, you returned with your arm around Judas's shoulders.

"Mary!" Judas whisper-shouted, "do you not see, that is just it! They will know him, and you do not. You cannot go in there. These are the people who cut down your oak."

Tears sprang to my eyes, surprising me. The oak. Its smell filled my nose. Hannah, my Hannah.

Judas saw he was affecting me. "Do you not remember? Do you not see? If you will not let me," cutting gesture of his finger across his throat, "at least you must leave him here. This is where he belongs. You cannot let him be among us. Today he speaks gently to you, next week he will kill you."

Wanting no more cutting of any kind, not in my name, your hand on Judas's shoulder, you spoke for me, "But all we have is today, right my friend?"

Needing air, I headed out, and everyone followed. As we arrived under the portico, Simon stepped in front of me again, this time no longer pale but rather blushing. "Forgive me, Mary, forgive me. I do know the power of your healing, and the power of your heart. In fact, I will walk right in there with you if you want. But the truth is, though I am not worthy, I know you need say but one word, standing right here, and if my mother is still alive, she will be healed."

I let my hand hover over Simon's shoulder, "And so it shall be, as you say it is." I faced the Roman headquarters, closed my eyes and held my hands open before me. I felt Simon's mother cold, lonely, and ailing in the house; I felt the colors fly out of me.

As I did this, you asked Judas, "You keep asking me to see... Did you hear what Simon just said? Why do you not listen?"

"Simon speaks from fear..." Judas replied.

Your voice booming, "He speaks from faith! You think faith like that could be gone next week?"

Noticing the guard across the way watching us, you smiled, and addressed the nearly empty square, "Who in this land has more faith than this man?

"Judas, until you can see a man for who he is, you will be more blind than that poor beggar yonder. Him I can heal with a touch, but only you can change your own heart, my brother. Only you."

"You are wrong Jesus. Once a Roman always a Roman. It is *your* heart that has changed and turned against your people, and I will not leave your side until I have turned it back."

Heralded by his unwashed ripeness which interrupted us and turned our heads, the blind beggar approached and called out, "Did I hear something about someone healing me with a touch?"

Smiles broke out all around; even Judas cracked a grin.

That night we gathered in the taxman's ample house, where Joanna and Yacob joined us, back from the Roman headquarters. As the wife of Herod's steward, Joanna had the authority to inquire of the guard as to the health of the missing centurion's mother.

Joanna's beaming face, a radiant oval under her sun-faded orange veil, flowered as she shared the news of Simon's mother's perfect health, telling us, "She was ailing in bed one moment and the next scolding the servant in the kitchen for using too much salt!"

Across the room from each other, across the astonished laughter and uncomfortable shifting of those who had gathered with us for the evening meal, yours and my eyes met along the wave of a single thought – healing without touching – how much more could we do?

I had never attempted this, never considered it since the day of the black hand, when the possibility had arisen and was quashed by Elizabeth, who could not bear to see a rule broken.

Pondering this, I realized I had been moved by Simon's trust, and then I realized that on the day of the black hand, I had been stirred by that husband's love for his wife. My ability to heal at a distance seemed to have something to do with a third person, but I did not yet understand what that was.

More disturbing to me was my relief at not having to go into the Roman headquarters, past those guards. Judas's words had affected me, not by prejudicing me against Simon, but by making the enemy seem real, and dangerous. I wanted to come and talk with you, but just then the taxman embraced you and took your eyes from mine.

Your long arm around the tax-man-priest's now squared shoulders, with a cup of wine in your hand you blessed him, called him a "gift from Our Creator," and named him thus, Matthew. Your cheeks afire above your black beard, your eyes glowed all over him.

I did not hear the rest of your words, for I was seized by a terrible fear. I wanted to scramble over the thick rugs covered with abundant fragrant dishes, climb over those seated here and there with their merry laughter and full cups of wine, past the one whose sight had just returned and those who had never lost theirs. I could smell you from all the way across the room, and I wanted to fall against you, take your hand and run, away from all this, back into the wilderness, back where we would be safe, back where there were no Romans nor

Herodians nor followers nor strangers.

My heart was beating in my throat when you turned to me, still deeply smiling over the joy in your newfound friendship.

I will never forget the words you said then: "Whoever tries to keep his life will lose it, and whoever loses his life will preserve it."

I burst out laughing at our harmony. I did not know what you had been saying before to lead up to these words, nor what you actually intended by them, but I knew what I heard. You had spoken directly to my fear. I heard that there were no Romans nor Herodians nor followers nor strangers in that room with us nor anywhere in Capernaum nor in the whole of Israel nor anywhere at all.

I heard that there was only one life, one Creation: we could either chose to see ourselves and everyone as part of that one Creation, or we could chose to cut ourselves off from it by clinging to the idea of our separate fragile life.

That was our choice, and indeed the only real choice we ever had, moment to moment.

Oh, my love, who would have thought on that night of abundant companionship, revelation, and revelry that either of us could ever be so alone as we are tonight? That I could want for just one person to believe in me, with me?

Am I a worthy vessel to be creating this amulet? Or am I simply a sorry widow disbelieving the end of love? Does love end, Jesus? If death is stronger than love, how is it I can feel you behind me, all around me? How is it I can hear you?

I still feel your eyes across the room for me and me alone; you are about to speak the exact words I next need to hear, words that will lead me out of this enveloping darkness.

Show me. Talk to me.

It is cold and dark in this library. I can still smell you in my hair. Your red blood now brown is splattered across my tunic from that moment when the soldier held a rusty thick nail to your wrist and –

I cannot write that part. Not yet. Perhaps never. Do I have to? I am afraid I will faint, and you know I cannot stop until I am done.

Who would wake me?

We intended to leave Capernaum early the next morning, before sunrise. We were at least a day's walk away from Gamala, which you were eager to reach. After quick and quiet ablutions from a jug of water, we tiptoed gingerly over the sleeping bodies strewn about Matthew's home, amidst empty bowls full of olive pits and discarded wine jugs resting quietly on their sides. Our fingers on our lips, we silently nudged those who had been with us since the Wilderness and motioned them to come with us. Despite these efforts, everyone around us stirred and followed us out.

Dozens more slept outside the house, many without a rug between them and the stone-paved street, some without even a cloak. They too followed, clamoring praise, calling for healing, waking a whole other group who had been sleeping on the roof, waking the whole neighborhood. They did not ask where we were going.

Simon caught up with us at the front of the growing crowd. "What do you want to do with all these people?" Before we could answer, Judas called out to us and urged us down a narrow street, toward a small town gate being opened by the night watchman.

Perhaps the soldier thought he was still dreaming as we flooded past his side gate, most of us ragged, unwashed, and road-weary, and amidst these Matthew in his fresh red cloak and Joanna whose silk was faded but still flowing. How many more would come with us?

Straight out the gate lay the open road. We crossed it and climbed the hill above the town, pulling the people as if they were a royal train. When we reached a wild olive tree alone at the top, we turned to find a sea of people gathering beneath us.

"I am hungry," you said to me. "All these people, they must be hungry too."

I took your hand. The sun crossed the horizon and rose over the purple mountains across the Lake's perfect reflection of the sky, its blue so close it seemed we could touch it. The morning's first rays touched and warmed our faces and the backs of those still climbing. Matthew mingled with our familiars and sat with them around us.

The people gradually ceased in their ascent and came to rest where they were on the dry grass. You called out, for all to hear, "You must all be hungry. Come, let us feed you."

The people looked at each other, then at Zanna as she began distributing bread from her basket. Salome brought us some fish, and she handed some out to the crowd too. Seeing the abundance, people took some and then passed the flat bread and dried fish on down the hill, in silence. They saw the size of the baskets and the impossible quantity of bread and fish coming out, and they did not stir.

As they ate and shared, you watched them all, your gaze caressing each one.

You spoke again, your voice a deep and sweet honey, "You! You are the salt of the earth. If the salt loses its saltiness, how can it be made salty again? It is no longer good for anything, except to be thrown out and trampled by men."

Someone cried out, "That is what we are, we are trampled by men. And what can we do about it?"

And another, "How does all this food appear from two baskets of food! Is this some strange magic?"

Calls from up the hillside chimed together, "Is this a holy act or the work of a devil?"

"What other miracles can you perform? Can you make the Romans disappear?"

"We pay three taxes: one to the Temple, a bigger one to Herod and the greatest to Rome: can you make even one of them disappear?"

"Can you make the Roman Emperor Tiberius give back our taxes of grain and of gold?"

You called back, quoting the sacred texts, " 'Do not worry over evildoers, and do not be angry against the unjust, for they will soon be cut down like the grass and wither as the green herb.' "

Someone called out, "Yes, we all know the psalms, those lovely songs; that one you just quoted ends thus, 'Our Creator will help the righteous, and deliver them from the wicked, and save them, because the righteous trust in Our Creator.' Are you calling out those words to tell us that you are here to do Our Creator's Will, and deliver us from the wicked?"

And another, "Why else would you stand up there on the hilltop?"

You paced back and forth as they spoke, listening and nodding, your hand pulling softly at your beard. When they quieted at last you declared, "I stand up here though I am no more than you, and you are the light of the world! We should all stand on a hilltop! A city on a hill cannot be hidden. Neither do people light a lamp and put it under a bowl. Instead they put it on its stand, and it gives light to everyone in the house. You want deliverance: you must first free your occupied hearts, and let your light shine before all, that they may see your good deeds and praise Our Creator in heaven."

Near us at the top of the hill, a scrawny, bearded young man, wearing nothing but a threadbare tunic, called in response, "Who cares about good deeds when our bellies ring with hunger!"

"Is this why you followed us, because you are hungry?" you asked him.

"Is there some other reason why we do everything we do, from dawn until dusk?" the young man answered, and others across the dry rocky hillside responded with "Hear hear!" and "Amen!" and "So it is!"

Your voice filled, "You hunger for bread from wheat, but what about the bread of life that feeds your spirit?"

Someone bellowed out, "If we have no bread, then we have no life or spirit either!"

"Amen!" again was heard from all parts. Judas came to stand near me, his eyes gleaming. It seemed he was thinking: at last, the revolution begins. But his gaze clouded as it followed Salome, who handed Abigail her basket and came to stand at your side.

Salome's words rang out over the crowded hillside, "My brothers and sisters, hear me. You speak of bread and of hunger, and you forget the power of Our Creator."

A man crowed, "What is the woman doing? Make her sit down."

I exclaimed as loudly as I could, not being used to addressing a crowd, "She is a priestess of Magdala, a daughter of this land. Hear her."

A hush fell over the crowd with these words. Then I heard a child ask her mother, "What is Magdala?"

So soon! How quickly would the generations forget we ever existed? True, there was nothing left of us but our own bodies – not one scroll, not one stone. You saw my agitation and came to stand by my side. Together we took a deep breath.

Salome's head fell back, red and white hair falling off her narrow shoulders, her brown face and palms raised to the paling sky, reminding me suddenly and blindingly of Deborah. Then Hannah. Not Hannah.

"You are humble folk," Salome sing-songed out, loudly, as she used to up in our new moon grove. "Blessed are the humble, for theirs is the might of Our Great Mother Goddess and Our Great Father God. You mourn. Blessed are those who mourn, for they will be comforted. You have no weapon. Blessed are the gentle, for they will inherit the earth. You hunger. Blessed are those who hunger and thirst for justice, for they will be filled with power. More than this: Blessed are the merciful, for they will be shown mercy. Blessed are the pure in heart, for they will see Our Creator with their own eyes. Blessed are the peacemakers, for they will be called the Sons and Daughters of Our Creator. Blessed are those who are persecuted because of righteousness, for theirs is the reign of heaven."

A loud shout boomed out, "How can you say, 'blessed are the persecuted!' How blessed can it be to have your eyes poked out or your head lobbed off by some scurvy pig!"

Gusts of angry words pushed up the hillside. Salome dropped her arms, and I went to her, taking her trembling hand in mine.

I straightened myself to my tallest height, before offering, "Maybe you will hear it this way, those whose ears are open to hear: Blessed

are you when your righteousness burns so bright that no act of violence can dim it."

People booed in earnest now, their discontent no longer gust
but gale, softened only, I imagine, by their filling stomachs. Salome
retreated to sit by Simon's welcoming side. The same strong, angry
voice from before shouted, "That is right, sit down fancy lady, and
you, what do you know of righteousness in your finely woven tunic?
What do you know of violence?"

You must have seen the blood rush to my face. Your cool hand on
my forearm, your speech louder, sharper than before, "These women
have seen violence enough, as you can see from the angry scar in the
earth which was once their home. All their lives, these women have
spoken the truth, and you should heed them."

The man retorted, "If you have all seen so much violence, why do
you refuse our call to fight?"

You answered him, "You have heard it said to the people long
ago, 'Do not murder, because anyone who murders will be subject
to judgment.' But I tell you that anyone who even looks down on
another will be subject to judgment. It is well known that anyone
who puts a curse on another must answer to his elders. But I tell you,
anyone who says 'You fool!' will be in danger of the wrath of Our
Creator."

Your interlocutor called out, "You fool," pointing his finger at
us.

I could not see his expression. Could you? All I knew was that
you burst out laughing, clapping your hands together, and walked
through the crowd down to him.

About a third of the way down the hill, the man with the angry
voice stood up. A heavily mended cloak draped his broad, bony
shoulders. His jet black hair stuck out in all directions, as did his
beard. With the sun directly behind his head, I could not make out
his features, even when I shaded my eyes with my hand.

"Well done!" you sang out, "Well done!" When you reached him,
you offered your embrace but he demurred. You patted his shoulder
instead. "What is your name, my brother?"

"I am not your brother."

"No, rather you would be my twin."

"Your twin?"

"Yes, my twin, for you accept the rules of no man. Would you do me the favor of walking with us?"

"Where are you going?"

"Wherever we go, I think I will need you to remind me that I am a fool. To remind me there is no wrath greater than my own foolishness. I forget myself sometimes, and you, if you would, can remind me."

"And what would I get for this great service?"

"As much as you can eat and drink, and my eternal friendship, and the companionship of those you see up on the hill."

"What about those women? They talk such foolishness!"

But already he was walking with you back up the hill, toward us. You smiled that wide smile I recognized by its corners, as the bright sun behind you cast your face in dark shadow.

"Those women? They saved my life, you know. They are not so much foolish as strange. You will get used to them after a while."

As you approached I realized the man's face was as dark as his beard. I had never seen such a person. The white of his eyes glistened as he walked by. He harrumphed, dropped next to a surprised Joanna – no more stunned than the rest of us at what had just transpired – and took a long draft from the wine jug she offered.

He wiped his mouth with the back of his hand and said, "You too, are you one of the foolish strange women?"

She grinned irresistibly. "One of the most foolish, the most strange, and I am keeper of the wine," she said and winked at him.

The man laughed out loud, his teeth bright white.

"All right tall man," he decided, "I will walk with you." His expression turned inward for a moment, his dark hands picked at the dry golden green grass, "Nothing holds me to any place." Then he asked, brightening again, "What shall I call you?"

"Jesus. I am called Jesus. What shall I call you?"

"I am called..." He sighed so deeply, I thought he was going to cry.

"What did you call me before? Twin?"

"The name Thomas means twin. We will call you Thomas."

After this latest exchange, the gathering on the hill grew into an increasingly rowdy mob. Every time one of us tried to speak, someone shouted out, "You fool!" evoking peals of bitter laughter.

Worse, a woman cried out for all to hear, "If they are not here to deliver us, then they cannot be here in the name of Our Creator. They must be some sort of devils, feeding all of us from just two small baskets."

The hairs on the back of my neck rose. Judas must have sensed something too, for he motioned to our group to follow him immediately down the hill. The crowd on the hill gathered momentum more slowly, pushing us like the cold wind of a distant storm.

Arriving breathless at the Lake shore, Judas negotiated urgently with one of the fishermen just back from his night's work, to take us across the water. Where did Judas get the gold he pulled from the pouch at his belt, I wondered? The wind-carved face of the fisherman was unmoved; he did not want women on his boat. It was bad luck. However, more gold seemed to solve the problem.

I was so disoriented by the morning's events that I could barely take in the foreign reality of the boat, with its tidily piled nets and coiled serpents of rope. The stench of fish was welcome, steadying, and simple. Better than the dark clouds of men and women moving down the hill, or Judas, yelling at us as we waded to the boat and then from the shore where he remained with his four men-at-arms, "Wasted a perfect opportunity! All for what? For another good-for-nothing who deserves not one moment of your time, much less your friendship! When will you remember who you are? When?"

From the deck of the slow-moving vessel, your arm around me, we watched his compact form on the shore, hands on his hips, getting smaller and smaller. My head on your shoulder, I longed for tears that only came when I realized I was watching Mount Arbel recede too. As we sped across the water, seeing my mountain all in one piece, I had not recognized it right away. I could barely make out where Magdala had been.

I discovered that the mountains were not purple across the Lake, as they had always seemed to be; the slopes were the same pale gold and green as they were on the side I knew.

We set up camp in an olive grove that had been picked clean, in the hills above the town of Beitsaida. In addition to some shelter, the grove provided us with much dead wood from where the branches had been beaten free of their fruit. Though the wood burned slowly, it burned, and made a soul-warming fire.

And my soul did need warming. It seemed to me that no matter what we gave, the people wanted more. It was not enough to be healed, blessed, and fed. On the way down the hill I heard many behind us cry out for the revolution Judas extolled. Why did everyone want war? They still believed in it, even those who had suffered most terribly. But it was not so with those we met directly. What had Salome done for Simon, what had you done for Matthew, that we could not do for a crowd?

Back on that hill, you tried to give the people what you believed they needed, and that was no longer the simple free overflow of our love, no longer about you and me being us, hand in hand.

In the evenings in Beitsaida, Thomas told us of his travels across the land and sea as a slave in the Roman army. He captivated us with tales of foreign lands, strange foods, fantastic constructions called "pyramids." Your deepening friendship with him embodied the change I was observing in you. You were so willing to shed your pride again and again, on the chance that the shedding would let someone in, would let someone shine. But you were trying to prove something too – all those years in the mountains, you had never shed a drop of blood, and now it seemed you longed to bleed for the people, to establish how much you loved them. The people seemed to become more important to you than I was, than we were. I felt you far away, even when you looked right at me.

The new moon came, and though my moon blood did not, all the same I slept at night with Salome, Abigail, Zanna and Joanna, apart from you, not on our square brown blanket.

On our third night in Beitsaida, we had settled down in our usual circle to eat our evening meal of fish and bread and sweet olive oil, when Judas and his four appeared out of the darkness and sat without a word beyond, "Greetings."

Your step-brother waited until our unusually silent meal was eaten to deliver his news: your brother John had been arrested by Herod Antipas for his so-called "seditious actions" and for allegedly "fomenting a rebellion." Judas concluded his report by saying, "It happened to your brother, Jesus, it could happen to you next. Will you at last let the reality of the world penetrate your thick skull?"

Simon, who normally never entered these discussions, countered, "The reality of the world must be penetrated by Jesus' mind, not the other way around."

"What are we going to do?" Thomas asked you, ignoring Simon. "Shall we go break your brother out of prison?"

"That is not so easy," Judas informed us. "They have taken John down to the mighty Fort of Machaerus, from which no one returns. But we have now a solid reason to go to war with Herod Antipas! Not that we needed one more, but the people love John, they are moved by him, inspired.

"Jesus, they will rally around you for his liberation. His mother Elizabeth's hopes are hanging on you. I went to Cana to confer with her and the others when we heard. You should have seen their faces, Jesus. Your mother Maryanna is so worried about you. She asks you personally to come to Cana, at least come and talk. Let her see you. I, as your brother, ask you the same."

"Who is my mother, and who are my brothers?" You indicated all of us around you, "Here are my mothers and my brothers. Those seeking to dwell in the presence of Our Creator are my brothers and sisters and mothers."

"Jesus, you speak such hurtful nonsense!" Judas replied. "Are you not moved at least to pity your blood kin, to offer them your strong arm and restore justice to your tribe, your family, your nation?"

"You speak not of justice but of more violence, Judas. Do not confuse the two. It is not my strong arm they need, but my heart of hearts." You turned to me, "My beloved, shall we set out tomorrow to go speak together to my men in Gamala?"

Before I could answer, Judas jumped up. "That is it, that is brilliant! Rally the men around a clear cause: avenging John! All the people will hear of it, and join us and – "

You held up your hand, "Peace Judas. I was speaking to Mary." Grinning slightly, sadly, "For all the affection I have for you, Judas, I do not think I have ever called you 'my beloved.' "

Judas sat back down, blushing furiously.

"My love," I answered with my hand on yours, "what do you hope to gain from talking to your men, as you still call them?"

"Why Mary! You heard what Judas said the other day! They are fighting among themselves. They need clear leadership in order to be at peace with each other."

"And you think that talking to them will bring that about."

"What else?"

"Jesus, you saw what happened on the hill with the people, those we fed. As soon as the talk turned from war, they lost interest, even prepared to turn their war on us. Why would it be different with the men you have trained to fight and kill all their lives?"

"Precisely because I trained them. I am the one who put that poison in their hearts, I am the only one who can remove it."

"No, my love, only they can remove it, and it seems they have no mind to."

"Do not worry, Mary," as you took my other hand, "I could not resist you, remember? I was transformed by the call of your spirit, that night in the clearing. Perhaps my men will fall under your spell as well."

I rose, freeing my hands, unable to smile back. "Like the people we just fled?" pointing across the darkened Lake. "What happened that night in the clearing is that I saw a man and healed his body. Simon's transformation happened when he woke up. And Matthew's happened when you heard him, and touched him. I am beginning to believe that no crowd can receive us the same as one man, nor can we see the many gathered as we see one man."

You threw a small branch on the fire, where it hissed and moaned. "What else would you have us do, Mary? Sit here in this olive grove for the rest of our lives?"

"In Magdala, it was I who asked you what we should do. You said that we should listen, remember?" My face warmed at the memory. In the dark I could not tell if yours did too. "This much is clear, Jesus, we cannot know what is next, with all this talking. Rather, the quiet all around us may hold some answer."

My heart in my throat, I walked out into the night that had settled, expecting you to follow me, but you did not. My arms wrapped around myself against the sharp cold, I paced around the perimeter of our camp until my feet hurt, and then I collapsed on the rug with Zanna and Joanna, twisting and turning into no sleep at all.

But I must have slept, because I dreamt – of my brother's death. I had not seen my brother Lazarus since I was little, when I left Bethany in the middle of the night. In my dream, my sister Martha prayed over Lazarus's blackened body, her own body bent like an old woman. I heard his gasping breath, then silence, then her wailing.

I woke up covered in a cold sweat, knowing I had to leave right away. I crossed our camp in the faint dawn and shook you awake. But unlike the last time I woke you to come with me, you refused, saying, "It is only a dream."

I could only ask again, "Come with me."

When daylight came, seeing the blanket rolled up under my arm, you tried to reason with me, "You are only going because of the news of John, because of our talk last night. You are worried about my men. Do you not trust me, Mary? I assure you, at worst, they would never harm us."

"Of course I trust you, Jesus. Will you trust me? Come with me."

Back at the women's new moon blanket, I woke Joanna. She listened with sleepy eyes, then embraced me and pressed her tearful cheeks to mine, but she said nothing, either way. When I asked Zanna to come with me, she agreed right away.

Learning that Abigail, Salome, Simon and Andrew had volunteered to come too, you said, "Mary, Lazarus may well be dead by the time you get there. What good can you do?"

Doing my best to remain calm, I replied, "Why are you going to speak of peace to armed men restless for war? Is this to appease Judas, or your own doubts? Does this truly come from the depths of your heart? I know this much: we cannot guide what our hearts tell us, for this is how Our Creator speaks to us. We can only listen; these are your own wise words which you have already forgotten." I took both your hands in mine, "I can only ask you to listen to your heart. Do what it tells you. That is what I am doing. I am going to Bethany."

When Judas heard of my plan, he seethed, "We are at the end of summer! It is the time of the pilgrimage for the holy days; the roads will be full of travelers and thieves making their way up to Jerusalem. I cannot keep both of you safe if you part."

"Judas, my ever vigilant Judas," surprising myself with the tenderness welling in my own voice, "Our Creator will keep us safe. No one knows who we are. We will be fine, just another group of pilgrims."

He turned on his heels without another word and went to confer with his four.

When Zanna, Salome, and the others gathered with me at the side of the road, ready to leave, you asked me, "Why is Lazarus more your brother than anyone we meet on the road?"

You held my unyielding body for a long time and kissed my hair.

At last I answered, "Why is he less?"

There was something I kept from you, for fear it would not have swayed you, for fear you would not have understood: for the first time since it had vanished to smoke, I felt the solid presence of the signet at my breast – the signet I had worn too briefly for it to make such an impression. Still I felt it. Still it called and pulled me up and out and away, not from outside me, but from inside my very soul.

Separating from you. What was I thinking? I was not thinking. I felt the pull in my breast and in my womb and I had to go. I had to go.

I sat alone in the house and waited. Mourners had been visiting and bringing food for four days, people I hardly knew, mostly friends of Martha and Ruth, since Lazarus himself had few friends. Not even I could be counted among them, but sisterhood was irreversible, so there I sat. In just a few days, I had taken on a role among these people whom I could not abandon like so many picked flowers falling from my lap.

I sat alone though I was surrounded by people. Simply no one was there with me; they were there for me, sharing stories of my brother's life, of my father Jacob's death, making meaningful eye contact with each other when they let their voices drift away from the mention of my mother Muriel. Full praise went to Martha, who had taken care of the embalming, after Lazarus had coughed up the last of his black blood.

I sat and prayed alongside the mourners, who did not seem to know who I was. As far as I could tell, they did not know Martha had a sister, let alone one who was a priestess of Magdala. Their polite verbosity thinly veiled their palpable refusal to include me in their conversation.

I sat in the middle of the big room from which I once had been banned. When I was not praying, I watched Ruth's daughter Morah, who had come back to live there when her husband rejected her for barrenness, long ago. She knelt by the door, washing people's feet and directing them toward the pitcher of water where they could wash their hands. She looked exactly like her mother had when I had left, only somehow she had managed to keep most of her teeth. Our ancient indefatigable Ruth, Zanna's erstwhile ally in all things, shuffled back and forth from the door to the kitchen, welcoming the slow steady stream of mourners, accepting the offerings they brought: warm fragrant round breads, bowls of cool brown eggs, glistening green olives, and smooth plump figs – all things round, to remind us of the circle of life and death. Ruth set these out on the familiar low round table, in wide earthen bowls, for all to partake.

I sat and I waited. I did not ponder, and I did not wonder. I was stuck there like Lazarus was stuck in his tomb: I could not open my mind to the possibility that you would not come, despite how we parted. And so I could not open my mind.

While I listened absently to the mourners, I stared at the unmarred surface of the table which shone from under the abundance of full chipped bowls; it whispered to me of the child I had been. A child who had peeked at me, on the road down here, a road I traveled with Salome again, as it had been all those years before, but now with Zanna, Abigail, Simon, and Andrew too.

I did not fully understand what I was doing on that road, moving further and further away from you with every step. Nor did I know how *not* to do this. I felt the empty space at my breast where the signet had hung so briefly. I felt the emptiness of my hands without yours. So empty, I could have floated up and away, and yet I walked the hot stone road, my thin sandals slapping time.

Those who had come with me had now set up camp in the old olive grove, outside the courtyard gate. As I sat at the table under which I once hid, I watched Martha scrutinize Ruth's every motion with a scalding eye. My sister seemed ready to pounce at the slightest infraction of Shiva, the ritual observance of grief, yet she was powerless to participate, certainly to touch food or be in the kitchen, needing to wait three more days before she could be ritually cleansed from her contact with Lazarus's corpse.

Her husband Amos had gone to Jerusalem the night of Lazarus's death, heavy with coins, to purchase at the Temple some water mixed with the ashes of the red heifer. According to the Jerusalem Temple customs, which prevailed in Bethany, only this mixture would complete Martha's ritual cleansing; in Magdala, a week apart in the birthing cave and a full immersion at the bath would have been sufficient.

We had not seen nor heard from Amos, despite Jerusalem being less than half a day's walk away. Not that Martha was surprised. Not that she could not guess what Amos was likely up to. While she sat coolly nailed to her stool, daintily picking among the olives those she could grasp without touching the others, I felt her submerged hot need to flip the whole table over and holler to the mute walls and ceiling until she was hoarse. I knew that need too well.

Unlike those gathered around me I was not sitting on a wooden stool but on a hammered iron chest, which, with the table and the house itself, was one of the last traces of our family's vanished wealth. The precious chest, with its fine linen lining, held no greater treasure than Lazarus's clothes, most of them threadbare, and his charcoal etchings, the one expression of his soul that made me feel related to him. Martha had been ready to throw this all away when he died.

When I had arrived, weary from walking for three days almost without sleep, Martha greeted me numbly, as if she had known I would come. She took me to Lazarus's embalmed body. I held my hands over him, and that was when I knew.

I felt in my hands what was possible. But I could not do it alone; I needed you. You were the only one who would believe with me, who would even try. I reached out to you in my mind, but I did not have months to wait for my call to reach you in your dreams. I gave Salome a written message for you. I told her simply, "I need him to get this." She sent it by carrier pigeon, which she found in the village. I counted on Matthew to read you the contents.

When I had seen Martha emptying Lazarus's metal chest, ready to cast his things into the fire, I had stopped her. Even as I lent an ear to the mourners' rhythmic tales of yore, Martha's harsh words resonated in my mind.

"What is this stubbornness? You will not give up on Lazarus who is rotting dead, and you will not give up on your vagabond husband either. You sent word, and what have you heard? Listen to me. Your husband is not coming. He does not care. If you do not know when to give up on a man, you will get even crazier than you already are."

But I had wrenched the metal chest from my sister's grip all the same and had sat on it since. I had slept curled up on its hard coolness, my feet hanging off the edge, leaving it only when absolutely necessary.

Through the wide open door, the afternoon sun bounced from the courtyard into the room full of mourners. It would soon be sunset, time for the visitors to go. A hush fell as a hunched wizened couple arrived bearing bread and some news that had to be whispered into Ruth's ear. After letting them in, our faithful servant shaded her worn eyes to gaze out where the azure sky met the pale dusty road, beyond the courtyard gate. Fresh bread tucked like an infant in the nook of her arm, she motioned with her free hand to Martha, who stepped unsmiling out of the circle of mourners. But before my sister could reproach her servant for not taking the bread directly to the table, she received a whispered report that sent her dashing out the door like the young girl I never saw grow up. She returned out of breath, her youthful sprint having taxed her creaking lungs, her breath heavy and thick.

She stepped around to whisper into my ear from behind, pulling back my hair with surprising gentleness, pressing her cracked lips directly onto my eager ear, "Jesus is here, with the rest of your friends. He said it was all right to touch me, and for me to touch you. He said there is no defilement. Also, he has asked for you."

I barely registered my sister's quick kiss, the first ever. With a nod and pressed palms, I excused myself from the others and walked steadily to the door, grateful with each step for Salome's training which had taught me to move with poise under all circumstances, under the guise of teaching me to count and add. How much I had learned at that loom.

I did not speak; I did not dare open my mouth lest my heart spill out onto the floor for everyone to see how fast it was beating, how immense it was becoming, how full of holes it was.

I calmly crossed the threshold, ducking slightly with the habit I had acquired of late from so many bumps on my head. My gaze scanned those gathered at the gate.

I saw you. My feet stopped. You ran to me through the gate and wrapped your arms around me; I found your eyes broken-hearted, open-hearted.

You said, "Never again will I choose anything over you. Forgive me, my beloved."

"Yes. A thousand times, yes. Yes."

I buried my face in your neck and breathed in your musk as I would a pine forest. I pulled back to return the smile I found wide and easy like a cool breeze. Then, overcome with the relief of seeing you, I closed my eyes, drank in your body's nearness like a strong wine. Feeling the full weight of the past week, of being apart from you, of opposing my will to yours, I fell to my knees and wept.

You laid a trembling hand on my sobbing head. As I cried, your own tears fell onto my hair like fat rain drops, and I pressed myself into you and held you.

After a little while, we drew a deep breath together, and you lifted me to stand at your side. "Mary, your message said you needed me."

"Yes, Jesus, come with me."

Holding hands, we headed out to the family tomb where Lazarus had been laid. Martha appeared at our side, clearly intent on joining us. I did not mind. You had come; we were together. That was all that mattered.

My sister did not follow us into the tomb where you and I joined hands over Lazarus's lifeless form. This time there were no colors nor music, only the steady beating of our two hearts, then three.

We stood in awe as Lazarus opened his eyes, got up and walked unsteadily out of the family burial cave, shielding his bright eyes from the setting light of the day. His embalming linens awkwardly hugged his emaciated form as he made his way. Martha kept her distance. You and I assisted him through the olive grove into the courtyard, and into the stunned silence of all our friends and the few straggling mourners gathered there.

As I write of our friends' silence, I realize that no one has come to check on me or try to talk sense into me, for a long while. Have they forgotten me in this stone room? As they seem to have forgotten you in your sealed tomb?

When I think of those three beating hearts. There is something else I should write. Does this thought belong here? Here it is: the new moon has not called forth my blood since the last time in Magdala, before our ritual. How long ago was that? Although at thirty-seven years of age, it could be my days of bleeding are ending. Then again, if we could heal the dead, does anything have to end?

Our friends seem to think so. Despite what they saw that day, they have refused to come with me to your tomb and lay hands on you with me – they would rather try to flee Jerusalem without you.

I understand now that you and I were able to heal Lazarus only because we both believed we could. Our agreement on what was possible was essential. One could not have raised Lazarus without the other.

That blessed day, did we overcome death, or fear? Loyal and loving as they are, it seems that none of our friends will consider overcoming either.

And so I sit and write. Here without you, here within these thoughts of you, I burn like this tiny lamp – it should be out of oil by now, but it is not. I do not know how long I have been working on this amulet. It feels like days and days. Yet the flame of this small lamp has not wavered. Is this again proof that we are those who "*will not know want*"? Or is it you, my love, letting me know you are with me somehow? Or is it some angel? Have you become some angel? Have you flown from my reach?

No matter now, I must complete this tale. I cannot know its power until it is done.

As night set on the day we healed Lazarus, we all gathered for the evening meal in the main room. The last of the mourners had long gone. Martha and Ruth had arranged all the rooms and the barn so that all of us could sleep within the gate. Our usually animated group was silent. We were under the spell of watching Lazarus eat his bread. He chewed slowly, dreamily. What could be said, in such a presence? It was not until Martha took him up to his room that the spell broke.

Simon spoke first, "Truly, Jesus and Mary, there is nothing you cannot do."

Your voice full of unshed tears, "There is much we cannot do, my dear Simon. We can pull a man back from death, yes, that is a great, astonishing gift from Our Creator." You shook your head, your eyes on your hands where they rested on the table. "You would think I had every power. But I return to you now from a terrible failure. In Gamala, I could not touch the heart of even one of my men. They wanted to hear none of my talk of peace – nothing but a call to arms. When they saw me, those who loved me felt betrayed that I was alive and had not come to them sooner. Those who wanted power accused me of being a demon, taking my form only to turn them from their path of righteous war. Judas, bless his heart, took only one side, mine. We did not stay among the men in the hills of Gamala long enough to break bread.

"Judas and his four escorted me away as soon as the first sword was bared and raised in rally. No one had yet pointed a weapon at me, but we did not take any chances."

Your step-brother's square face was gray, drawn. He had come to your aid, yes, but he seemed to have died inside with what he had

witnessed. As he stared into space, it seemed perhaps it was he who
had just emerged from a tomb.

After your account, the evening settled into a contemplative
silence, aided by the day's stunning events and the fatigue of travel.

By the next morning, however, the bustle and racket were over-
whelming: the entire olive grove outside the courtyard walls was
aswarm with the living and their dead, those who could speak calling
out for healing for those who could not. The mourners must have
shared the news, which had spread like a wild fire can in this end of
the dry season. Judas, still on edge from the events in Gamala, stood
with his four inside the front gate, their hands resting on the hilts
of sheathed swords, at their feet a gathered pile of rocks to slingshot
anyone trying to climb the wall.

I found a spot in the wall where I could see into the grove,
through a small space between two stones. There I saw more kinds
of people than I had ever seen in all my life, even in all our walking.
There were the rich with servants and fancy flowing tents, and the
poor with only a small blanket on which to sit. There were Parthians
with shaved faces and multicolored cloaks. There were traveling sto-
rytellers who claimed to have seen Lazarus fly out of the burial cave
and who were willing to share full details of the story for a coin or
two. Some men seemed to gather with fellow tradesmen; others were
encamped together with women, children and elders.

The road to Jerusalem from Jericho comes through the town of
Bethany. Pilgrims made their way down the road from there, from
everywhere, with a single destination: the Holy City. I supposed the
story of Lazarus had waylaid many of them on their pilgrimage for
Sukkoth, the feast of Booths, which was imminent. Most had brought
with them their makeshift abode, according to the Sukkoth custom
to sleep out under the sky, to remember to thank Our Creator for our
shelter. Some of the people gathered in the olive grove had no shelter
at all, and perhaps lived nearby.

Periodically a clamor of "Lazarus! Lazarus! We want Lazarus!" would rise up and die again like a chance breeze.

You and I had had enough of crowds, and now we felt trapped. We knew no good could come of acceding to these people's wishes, which we were not at all certain we could do. These healings happened through us, not by our own power. Even if we were able to heal another's dead, we knew now that this would lift us into a place of power and leadership we did not want. We decided the best we could do was to wait inside the gate until after Sukkoth, when most of the people would have gone back to the fields and labor, and by which time the excitement would have died down, we hoped.

But word of our deed grew. The beauty of that moment when Lazarus's eyelids fluttered vanished quickly. People came in droves, angry, demanding, entitled. As days passed, there were ever more of those who had not walked there but been borne – the dead, in varying stages of decomposition, from the freshly deceased to what looked like exhumed bones.

The stench of the dead intensified every morning, like the crowds, like the noise. Shouting, fighting, horrible cries of pain and sorrow seeped through the walls like mud. We never ventured outside the gate. Outside gate, inside the gate. *Us* and *them*. Did every path lead there?

Then Judas received a letter. We were all huddled in the big room, despite the heat, to avoid the terrible smell coming from beyond the gate. The room was thick with the smoke of incense, local crude sticks nothing like the delicate fragrances which Elizabeth and Hannah had blended under the tree. The tree. No tree.

Your step-brother stormed in so excitedly, at first I thought we were under attack. But no – he waved a small scroll over his head. He had recognized the symbol of Magdala on the seal. He handed it to me to read. I looked at the mark in the wax seal: Elizabeth must have had a new signet made. I cracked the small wax circle and opened the scroll. Recognized Dinah's handwriting, I read the letter aloud.

"Greetings all. The last seer of Magdala, Elizabeth, her sister, Maryanna, and I, Dinah, have come up to Jerusalem, after receiving word from Judas that Mary and Jesus were going to Bethany, not coming to us in Cana. We are staying in the great mansion of Joseph of Arimathea, Elizabeth's old friend, the one who brought her to Q'mran all those years ago. As you know, Joseph is a great and powerful ally of Magdala. Maybe you do not know, he is also a member of the Sanhedrin, the Holy Council, the last remnant of Hebrew rule which the people obey willingly. Joseph has obtained the Council's agreement to see Mary and Jesus in order to consider supporting us in their claim to the throne.

"Elizabeth spoke directly to the entire Council. She told them how Mary and Jesus have gathered crowds throughout the land, have healed the sick and restored hope to the despairing. She told the Council that Mary and Jesus show no fear in the face of Romans, Herodians or bandits. She declared that Mary and Jesus are the long awaited unifying King and Queen. Mary and Jesus must come now to Jerusalem for the Council to meet them. Send word that you have received this letter. Tell us when to expect you.

"All praise to Our Great Mother Goddess, and Our Great Father God. After all that has happened, our day is at hand."

With each word I read, my heart sank more deeply, and Judas's face shone more brightly. As soon as I finished reading and rolled the scroll up, he reached for it, saying,

"I know just how we should proceed. If you two could raise one more person outside these gates, the whole crowd would follow you anywhere, and we could make a triumphant entry into Jerusalem. That would really show the Council."

"Judas, we will not go to the Council," you told him. "Do you not see? At best, they want to make an idol out of me, out of us," your large hand enfolding mine where it rested on my knee, "and then use that idol to make people go to war. We will not be a part of that."

"I am not talking about idolatry, Jesus! We are talking about kingship!" he said, waving Elizabeth's letter. "It is all arranged."

"Judas," I said, "nothing is arranged. We are not who you think we are. Raising the dead... It can be a miracle. But it is not enough. I overheard one family outside, quarrelling over who would keep their farm if their dead father were revived."

You opened both hands wide, palms up, "What sense renewed life of the body, when in their hearts they will continue as the walking dead? You say that you want us to heal someone, so that people will be so impressed they will follow us to Jerusalem. Then they will be asked to follow us into war. Heal one dead, so that untold numbers will kill and die. No."

"What then are we doing here?" Judas pleaded, tossing the scroll onto the long rug on which we all sat. "What is our mission?"

"We are not on any mission," you said. "Is what happened in Gamala not enough for you? If we have a mission, it is this: to love each other the best way we know how. We raised Lazarus. We are not magicians. Nor are we a King or a Queen, or anyone, but Mary and Jesus."

"That does not make any sense, Jesus," Judas insisted.

"Judas," you said softly, "when was the last time you talked to your wife Zanna and your daughter Abigail, who are right here with us? Or better yet, when is the last time you let them speak to you? Who is not making any sense?"

Judas's jaw clenched tightly as he looked away. Lazarus, who had mostly been a silent shadow to our group, leaned in and spoke with a soft low voice that still startled, its ordinary sound coming from one now so alien, "Jesus, what does it mean that your great deed of power and love is generating so much fighting, right outside for all to see?"

You answered him, "Thank you, Lazarus, for this beautiful question. Here is how I can answer you. A farmer goes out to sow his seed. As he scatters it, some falls along the path, and the birds come and eat it up. Some falls on rocky places, without much soil. It springs up quickly, because the soil is shallow, but when the sun comes up, the plants are scorched, and they wither because they have no root. Other seed falls among thorns, which grows up and chokes the plants. Still other seed falls on good soil," you smiled into Lazarus, he blushed and dropped his head, "where it produces a crop that is much bigger than what was sown. He who has ears, let him hear."

Judas fumed, "Why must you speak in parables? You are a warrior, not a teacher."

"All right Judas, how do you like this?" I leaned in and looked him square in the eyes. "When people see an act of love without truly understanding it, only thinking of how to get more, it is as if a devil has come and snatched away what could have started to grow in their heart.

"This is the seed sown along the path. There are some who received the seed that fell on rocky places – these are the people who see and hear and at once receive the experience with joy. But since there is no depth, the joy lasts only a short time.

"When things get difficult and complicated, these people disappear, like so many we have met on the road. The one who receives the seed that fell among the thorns is the one who hears what is being said, but he is so preoccupied with his house, his health, and his money that he may as well have heard nothing."

You leaned forward toward Judas across the thick rug and finished my thought, "But the one who receives the seed that fell on good soil is the man who hears what is being said and understands it. His understanding grows, and others are drawn to him because of his new depth, his new possibilities."

Right back into your face, without blinking, Judas asked, "And the rest are the walking dead?"

"Yes, Judas my brother, they may as well be."

After all that talk, we did end up in Jerusalem. But not the way anyone had planned.

It started with you jumping onto the wall, the day after we received Dinah's letter. We were at the well – the well of the floating cart of yore – drawing water for our morning ablutions, when you broke from my side and before I knew it, you were up on the courtyard wall.

I immediately looked for Judas – where was he? His men? Who would protect you up there? I heard the camp of unwashed, hundreds beginning to stir with the new day's light.

"Good morning to you, my brothers and sisters! Peace be unto you!" You paced back and forth on the narrow wall, balancing carefully.

I saw Judas at the gate send two of his men to keep the crowds back as best they could. I ran to my eye-hole in the wall, not far from where you stood.

A man I could hear but not see, called out, "Are you going to come out now and share this power you have? Or do you think you are too good for us?"

You ignored his taunt, "You who bring your dead to this place, you bring them so that they will be raised, like our brother Lazarus was, but what of your own soul?"

At the far edge of the camp, a thickly veiled woman who held the lifeless body of a small child in her arms called out, "This boy was my soul! If you restore him, you will restore me too!"

You turned toward her, crouched down on the wall, "Woman, if you do not feel your soul within you now, if this child returned you would suck his life out again."

She shrieked, "What kind of a devil are you to say such things!" People started pushing to get to the wall. Joanna appeared out of nowhere, took my hand and pulled me in to the main room, where Salome and Zanna were already huddled with Martha and Lazarus. I refused to let them close the door, so I could still hear and see as much of what was happening as possible. Thomas, Matthew, Simon, Phillip, Bartholomew and Andrew went out to the gate to assist Judas and his four.

"I am not possessed by a demon," you called out. You paced back and forth along the wall, your loose hair falling down your back to your waist. "I follow the commandments; I do not kill, nor do I covet nor bear false witness. You come here seeking solace – you think that if your dead were alive, all would be well. But I tell you, until you make peace in your soul, nothing will ever be well for long.

"And what's more... Those with ears, open them to my words! Those with hearts, open them to my meaning: if you make peace in your soul..."

"How can you suggest we make peace in our souls! With all that you see around you!" someone called out.

"I will tell you. It is so simple. Love each other. Love each other as I love you. Love each other as Our Creator loves you for having given you life and the means to sustain it. Greater love has no one than this, that he lay down his life for those he loves, and nothing but this will bring you to the door of the house of Our Creator."

"You do not love us!" a man called out. "You do not offer us your life! Look at her, I hold her up for you to see, my beautiful Naomi, I just want you to bring back my beautiful young wife, look at her..."

You did look, crouching down. "I do love you. I love each and every man and woman here, dead and alive. I offer you my life for I come here seeking nothing for myself. I seek only to give you the best I have to offer, my peace and my love. And you, whom do you love? You say you love this woman, but unless you love me, unless you love your father and your brother, the Roman and the tax collector, you love no one."

You stood straight up again, held your hands open at your sides, your long arms stretched out. "I say to you, who have ears to hear, and hearts to understand: once you love each other, friend and enemy alike, as Our Creator loves you, for having given you life, once you do this, once you listen to my words and take them into your hearts, you will taste bitterness no more, and you will not know death."

"Are you greater than our father Abraham and our mother Sarah?" another man called out. "They died, and so did all the prophets and all the kings and all the queens. Yet you say that if anyone listens to your word, he will never taste death. Are you greater than Abraham and Sarah? Who do you think you are?"

"I am like you, my brother, no more than the son of man."

I did not see what hit you, but something knocked you right in the middle of the stomach as a cry rang out, "Come here and heal our dead, Son of Man, or leave us alone with your devil talk!"

Something else was thrown, hitting your head, and you lost your balance, fell off the wall, into our side of the courtyard, praise Astarte.

We could not longer wait patiently, peacefully, inside. It was time for us to go.

This is how I remember this time, and I hope I am not leaving anything out. I am sure the emotion of all that has come since has colored my memory of those days. But after you fell off the wall, I remember only being with you and sleeping with you intertwined on our blanket, not enough distance possible from the others, in that big room full of incense smoke, to do anything but hold each other, and whisper, and gaze. Those sublime nothings which are everything.

I only remember some of the words we said when we decided to leave.

You said, "You were right Mary, in reminding me: we are here to listen. The crowds mock us, but each man and woman alone, these we can touch, and they in turn can touch others, as Salome did with Simon."

I said, "I do not want to be king or queen of anything, of anyone. But staying in one place, we can only attract crowds, and amass power, political power. Constant motion seems to be the only way of life for us."

We traveled together like children through all the possibilities. We talked all night. What to tell, who to tell, when to tell.

To begin, we would have to do what Judas wanted. We decided that the members of the Council were only placating Joseph of Arimathea. Why would they want to share their power? Once we met with them, they would quickly find some reason to dismiss Elizabeth's claim. By giving in to what was being asked of us, we would be set free – for good, this time, we hoped.

Those who wished could come with us. We would make our way all around the world, go to all the places Thomas talked about, and maybe more. Healing people along the way, as much as we could without starting another debacle like that outside the gate. Moving on, ever on. Sharing what we had learned about love, about Our Creator, and deepening that knowledge with kindred spirits. We would find out what it meant to love and honor Our Creator, not just for the Hebrews, but also for the Romans and the Greeks and the Parthians and the Egyptians.

We decided to start in Egypt, the most ancient land of all – the home of the great Library – with its many ideas and possibilities.

We wanted to hear the different truths being proclaimed everywhere, hoping that in time we could formulate a truth that could be true everywhere, all the time. As true as the history that you said was written in blood, as true as my body's quiver at your touch, as true as the penetrating heat of the sun on the rock.

Was it Our Great Mother Goddess Astarte who cleared us of any doubt, so we could fly as we did? So we would crash as we did, as in the Greek story of Icarus, the boy who flew too close to the sun?

Unlike Icarus, I did not die, I am just here at the bottom of the ocean trying to figure out how to build a new pair of wings. Nothing in us not from Her. All I have here in the way of wing material is my love for you. Could that be enough?

Perhaps the core belief about the Sacred Marriage – that the world gains all its strength and fertility from the sacred union of two lovers – perhaps this belief is the unifying truth, and it was right here for us all along. But we went and looked for it anyway, did we not.

It seemed so simple, lying there in your arms in Bethany, talking about Jerusalem, thinking about how there were so many people to love, so much to discover together hand in hand.

I thought we were drunk on love. I see now we were drunk on hubris.

Oh my love.

The day after you were knocked off the wall, we woke before the light. At the well we did our best to wash the sleepless night off our faces, splashing great quantities of cold water over our eyes, napes, and throats. Then we gathered everyone in the courtyard, including Judas, forcing him to abandon his gate vigil for a while. We also called Thomas down from the roof where he was guarding us from intrusions from the other roofs of the village.

I looked at each weary face and told them, "As you know, tomorrow is the first day of Sukkoth. We are going to Jerusalem. We will meet with the Council as our mothers have requested. We would like all of you to come with us."

"Praise Our Creator! Praise Yahweh and Praise Astarte!" Judas beamed with joy and shock as he embraced you, letting tears fall freely into his beard. "I knew you would come around. I have been praying and praying. I knew."

You held him tightly and said nothing.

"But what about the people outside?" Simon asked, indicating the courtyard gate with his chin.

"We will walk through them, all together, and invite them to Jerusalem with us," you said. "That is where most of them mean to go anyway."

"Will you perform any more healings?"

"Not the way they would like, but yes, in a manner."

"And you think they will simply let you through?" Simon persisted.

"Shall we all come? Me too? What of Ruth?" Martha asked.

"Yes, everyone who wishes."

"But what then of the house? Who will look after it? Will we be gone long? Should we bring food, clothes? What will we need?"

I sighed deeply. Martha had not been with us in the Wilderness, nor on the road; she did not know how it was with us. I pondered how to explain without frightening her.

Salome saw my concern. She put her arm around Martha's shoulder, drew her near. "Of course, you worry about clothes, my sister," Salome said. "But think of this, think of how the lilies of the field grow. They do not spin or weave, yet they are dressed as beautifully as any queen. If that is how Our Creator clothes the grass in the field, which is here today and tomorrow is thrown into the fire, do you not think Our Creator will do even more for you?"

Martha's dark almond-shaped eyes – like our father's – grew round and scared. I could see she thought we had gone completely mad. Zanna brought clarity, "Bring whatever you think you will need, Martha, but no more than you can carry. Who knows when or if we will come back here."

And so we left. You and I walked in the middle of the others. I marveled at the family we had gathered. We headed for Jerusalem amidst Zanna, Abigail, Salome, Joanna, Ruth, Morah, Simon, Andrew, Martha, Lazarus, Matthew, Phillip, Bartholomew, Thomas, Judas and his four.

The just-waking crowd watched us go, calling out but not attacking. Perhaps there were too many of us at once. Perhaps they were too stunned by our casual exit – why had we not tried this before? We safely reached the road which was already bustling with early risers on their way to Jerusalem. We blended easily into the thick crowd. Your hand in mine, the sun at our backs.

On the road to Jerusalem, Martha walked right in front of us, talking with a stout blue-turbaned man who had fallen in step with us. She did not know we were right behind her, well within hearing. She leaned her furrowed face toward her listener's ear and said,

"Miracles like that, people coming back from the dead and such, yes, it is very exciting, but let me tell you, nothing is as miraculous as the look on Jesus' and Mary's faces. Sometimes I feel that they are locked in a lover's embrace, when they are across the room from each

other, not even looking at each other. In my short life, that is something I have seen quite a bit less of than the walking dead. Life is just
a heartbeat, on and off and on and off until it does not come back on
again. But love like that, it goes on and on and on into the stars and
back again. That is the real miracle here."

I did not hear the man's reaction. A rush of emotion filled my ears
like a roar. I gripped your hand in mine and thought of what it took
for us to get from that dark smoky room to the bright open road.

When we rounded the Mount of Olives, we were stopped in our
tracks. Both of us had heard of the Temple's splendor, but neither of
us had ever seen it. Beneath the gold crown set aflame by the sun,
the white stone of the sanctuary building blinded. What stunned me
most was the vastness of the courtyard around it – I had never seen,
never imagined, that there could be a single structure bigger than any
one town we had visited.

Joanna laughed at us, "Yes, it takes your breath away, does it not?
Well come on then, you want to get there, yes? You will not get there
by staring at it! Although that might be better, considering the crowds
get denser from here," stepping aside to let a rickety carriage go by.
She took my hand in her cool one as we started walking again.

"Have you been inside the Temple, Joanna?"

"Yes, once, but only as far as the Outer Courtyard."

"The Outer Courtyard?"

"What you see from here is the Temple itself, in the middle of the
square, and all the surrounding porticos. Those porticos frame the
courtyards. Imagine a grape. The walls with the porticos are the skin.
The Outer Courtyard is the pulp."

"And the seed is Temple?"

"Just about, although my image of the grape does not quite work
proportionately, because there is more. Let us see. Imagine an egg."

"The porticos are the shell, the egg white is the Outer Courtyard
and the yolk is the Temple."

"Right, except the yolk is the Women's Court, and inside that is the Court of the Israelites where the Great Altar is, then inside that is the Priest's sanctuary, and inside that is the Holy of Holies."

Hannah's voice and her hands in my hair under the oak tree came back to me: the Women's Court, her vision for us, and her dreams for this place. How I longed to tell her it was all right now. We did not need that now. But instead a sob pushed up and out my throat. So much lost, for what. I held your hand more tightly; you squeezed back.

"Joanna, how do you know so much?" you asked her.

"That is easy. Anyone can come into the Outer Courtyard. Only Hebrews, men and women, can come into the Women's Court. Only Hebrew men in the court of the Israelites and, you guessed it, only priests in the Priest's sanctuary. As to how I know all this... well," her smile warmed us as much as the Temple blinded, "you forget my gift, Jesus. When Herod Antipas sent Andronicus on official business to Jerusalem, my husband took me with him. All I had to do was stand at the majestic stone gate to the Women's Court – and believe me, you do not want to do more than that, there is a sign right there that Andronicus read to me, 'No foreigner shall enter the protective enclosure around the sanctuary. And whoever is caught will only have himself to blame for his own ensuing death.' Quite clear, yes?

"So I stood at the gate and let the priests brush by me. All I needed was a few accidental sweeps of their robes across my feet, and I knew what was inside those gates. More than that, I learned that there are many secret passageways, in and out of every part of the Temple complex. Many rooms underground, that only a very few get to see, full of remarkable treasure, and confiscated texts. And other goings on no one would suspect."

Listening to Joanna, looking at the Temple and the vast courtyard around it, my heart raced – never had I seen such an edifice built by human hands.

Soon the crowd got too dense and rowdy for conversation to continue. It was all we could do to hold hands until we arrived at the eastern gate of the city. There, my awe at master-builders' skills was shoved aside by the sweaty throngs, pushy pilgrims with all they owned on their backs, and children holding on to their parents legs for dear life. The air was filled with cries of "Mama!" and of mothers calling back frantically for their lost children. A sea of people breathed each other's exhale, the pitiless sun weighing on us like a boulder. Merchants thrusted their wares at us from every possible nook and cranny between unwashed human bodies, seemingly disembodied hands holding out worn leather gourds stinking of acrid wine, small filthy stones inscribed as amulets and used, smelly sandals, possibly yanked off someone not far away. My own sandals felt thin between my feet and the sharp uneven street.

I glued myself to you, your arm around my waist a veritable lifeline. We were taller than almost everyone around us, making it easy for our friends to follow. We made our way up the steps. Once inside the Temple platform itself, the ground under my feet was smoother. The density of the crowd eased. But in catching my breath I found myself dizzy at the immensity around us. You brought me to sit in the shade, under a wide portico, just beyond the edge of the vast courtyard bustling with activity. The stone floor and wall were cool and soothing; I pressed my palms to the solid ground and closed my eyes.

Little by little our friends found us. Joanna sat near me – did she notice my pallor – and offered me water from our bottomless pouch. I drank and poured some over my steaming brow, over yours too, just for play. Your eyes were closed, and you were startled by cool wetness. Your eyes opened at the same time as your dazzling smile spread. It would never cease to amaze me, your smile itself a gentle rain on my hot dry mind.

We all gathered and sat there for a moment, passing the water pouch and looking around. Judas and his four positioned themselves to guard us – two at the entrance to the portico, two just outside the columns. He stood inside the portico, just beyond us. I could not help but wonder, was he keeping us in or trouble out?

Meanwhile, Joanna explained to me the sights before us. Once inside the precincts of the Great Temple, everyone wanted to get as close as possible to the main altar, so that on the great day they might witness the climax of the Sukkoth celebration.

On the last day of the feast of Booths, the High Priest would pour the water into the drain around the great altar, in remembrance of our covenant with Our Creator, who caused the primordial flood waters to recede under that spot. The water was also poured in thanks for what rain had come in the past year, and in prayer for more to come.

This explained the frenzy of people getting set up, trying to find a good spot for the week's festivities. The vast outer courtyard was full of men, women and children, afire with activity despite the blazing sun. Most families focused on setting up their makeshift shelters of wood and cloth, while the children chased each other through the mass. A few settled groups reposed in self-satisfaction underneath their completed sanctuary. Others still had the materials bundled on their backs, looking here and there for an adequate space to begin their task. Amid these, life in all its boisterousness: singing, chanting, arguing over politics and space, fighting with words and fists, cooking and eating, drinking and dancing and even sleeping.

But where we were under the portico, everything was surprisingly orderly. Just across from us, in a long row, over a dozen portly men each sat behind their own wide blanket, their backs to the portico columns. Each wore a fancy bright blue turban, like the man with whom Martha spoke on the road. Heavy-looking sacks as big as heads were stacked on either side of each man, within arm's reach. Beyond that, scores of different colored coins and various trinkets covered the blanket, so much that its color and pattern could not be perceived. Men and women, some carrying a small animal, formed long lines to talk to the turbaned men.

The turbaned men argued loudly with whomever was in front of them, then handed them a coin or two taken from the big sacks, and yelled, "Next!" People walked away from the carpets cowed, heads down, looking at the coins in their hands. I could not help but be reminded of the people who once lined up to see me, long ago, in a place that was no more. I drank the tiny sip of water my throat let pass.

Except for Thomas, Joanna was the only one among us who had been to Jerusalem before, and she was the only one who had been to the Temple. Seated beside me, her orange cloak sun-faded now to the palest pink, but her eyes more bright sky than ever, I watched her take in the exchanges occurring across from us with a knowing expression.

"Joanna, what is all this? Everything is so push-me-pull-me around here, what is this organized activity people are willing to wait on line for?"

"We are in the alley of the moneychangers," Joanna answered.

"What are the moneychangers?"

"Those men. In the blue turbans. The ones who look like they run the place."

"What do you mean, run the place, is that not what the priests do?"

"Well, it is not so simple. The people come to the Temple to make an offering to Our Creator, yes?"

"Yes."

"But the problem is, they cannot bring any old thing, like they did in Magdala, oil poured from their own kitchen jar into a small jug to bring to you. Everything here has to be pure."

"Pure?"

"Yes pure, blessed, and approved by the priests. There are many rules, all based on the words of Moses, all that Our Creator told him. Only the priests really know them all. Most people want to make an animal offering, bring a sacrifice. It must be a perfect unblemished animal, a dove or a lamb, or a calf if you can afford it. Or money, always an accepted offering. The idea is, the bigger the offering, the closer one brings oneself and one's people to Our Creator."

"Closer?"

"But the trouble is, most people cannot bring these animals with them on their long journey. Or if they do, and it does not fit the Temple's rules, they have to buy a new animal once they get here."

"But these men are not selling..."

"No, they are the moneychangers. You cannot transact with a Temple priest with just any kind of money from anywhere. It has to be the holy Temple money. The people argue because the money-changers can set whatever kind of rate they want for that exchange. If a person is not happy, they can go wait on line for another money-changer, but they all agree together on an exchange rate beforehand, so it does not really make any difference which one you see."

"And what about the people who already have an animal, why do they need the special Temple money?"

"They need to pay to have the animal examined by a priest, to make sure it is suitable for sacrifice."

"And if it is not suitable?"

"Then they have to buy one, or try to sell that one and make an offering of money."

I took a deep breath. To think there had only been one rule – sundown – that had governed the healing I dispensed. Was that why the women of Magdala had clung to it so? Why had no one told me about this business of the Temple before? Had they known? They must have. What had they thought of this? It fell to Joanna to explain. Not Hannah. Not Hannah. I thought of Hannah's words, "You will be one who finds the spirit of the Law and brings its understanding to a new generation."

What could I bring to a whole city of people who thought they could not be close to Our Creator without haggling with some fat blue turbaned man who would not even deign to look at their faces?

As did everyone in our group, you listened attentively to my exchange with Joanna, your hand squeezing mine ever more tightly with every new bit of information. Our eyes met, with the same question in them: where to begin? Behind you, Matthew grinned at us from the other side of Thomas. You followed my gaze and looked at the once-taxman's happy face. You said, "That is where we will begin. As we did with him."

As we rose, I said, "We will be right back."

Judas rushed over, "Oh good, are you ready to go? Can we leave this chaos and make our way to Joseph of Arimathea's house? We did not answer their letter, but still, he must be expecting us; they are all expecting us."

"Just one thing, Judas," you said with that look in your eye, your hand on his shoulder.

"Oh no, Jesus, come on! This is the Temple, you cannot cause a scene here! This place is guarded all the time, look!"

He pointed out from under the portico toward the far corner, where a huge square tower surveyed all the Temple courtyards. "That is the Antonia Fortress! Full of Roman soldiers. They are on high alert during the festivals, armed and watching our every move. Come on, look, they are even walking around down here, patrolling the outer courtyard – "

" – Judas," you raised a hand to interrupt his speech. "We will do all that you ask. We are here, are we not? And yes, after this we will go with you, just as you like. All will be well. You worry too much."

We went to get on line with everyone, but we paused at new sound – one of the moneychangers laughing. We followed the cackle to find the man pointing at a little raisin of an old woman, all doubled over, stone-still with her hand still out.

"Two mites?" the turbaned man said through his muffled chuckle. "Two mites? There is no Temple currency small enough for you, old hag. Go home and wait for death, that is the best for you. Stay out of trouble for you have no way to atone for any more sins!"

The people around her started laughing too, pointing. The old woman stood as if nailed to the spot. We went to her; I put my arm around her frail birdlike shoulders, closed her crinkly hand over her small treasure. She turned to me a face trampled by time and misery, surrounded by pure white locks that peeked out from under her moth-eaten cloak. Hannah. Not Hannah.

You took in everyone laughing. You raised a hand high above your head, "I tell you the truth, this poor widow has offered more than all of you who laugh. You have brought what you can spare, but she has offered all she has to live on. But even the greatest offering anyone can bring Our Creator means nothing without the offering of compassion! Where is yours?"

The moneychanger who had rejected the old woman shook his head without looking at you, "Hebrew, take your mother and go home. We have business to do here. Next!"

You went right up to him; walking over his blanket and coins. He rose slowly, his attitude more annoyed than afraid, though I saw no weapon at his side. His eyes reached only your chin, and he had to tilt his head to meet your eyes, but meet them he did with full contempt. He turned instinctively, so his back would not be to the wall.

The other moneychangers saw something happening and stopped their dealing for a moment. Those closest to us stood too. Judas was suddenly on the other side of me, and I saw two of his men just on the other side of the moneychanger, right outside the columns.

"My brother," you said to the moneychanger, "you say you are doing business, but this is supposed to be a house of prayer. Is it not?" You turned and repeated, "Is it not?" and found eyes all around staring at you, but no one offering to answer you.

"You say you are doing business," I cried out, "but you are robbing these people!" The old woman broke away from my grasp and disappeared into the crowd.

The moneychanger did not look at me, rather said to you, "Hebrew, control your woman and get off my blanket, or I will call the guards."

"Why should I silence her when she speaks the truth!" You turned from him, addressed everyone under the portico, "These men steal from you, extort money, cheat you, and you line up thinking only of how to try to get more from them! How do you expect to get closer to Our Creator this way, if all you have in your heart is 'how much?' and not 'why?'"

I had not seen you so passionate since our rooftop night, your voice cracking, rising, "If you truly want to live by Our Creator's Will, if you truly want to know It, you would all be better off in solitude and silence and devoting yourselves in your hearts," shouting now, "not here where everyone can see how much you give, and where nothing is really sacrificed, where it is all one big spectacle!"

You turned back to the moneychanger who had not moved. "You

want me to get off your blanket, fine, I will get off it!"

You took one big step off it, bent over, and yanked the blanket, sending coins flying everywhere.

"You do not know what treasure is!" you called out. "You value what is valueless!"

"Guard!" the blue turbaned man shouted with his bright red face. "Guard! Thief!"

Together we yanked another blanket, and one more.

Judas right behind us shouted, "Look out!"

Armed soldiers ran toward us, swords drawn. We were willing to stand our ground, hand in hand, but we were caught up in the flow of people running in away from the guards like water running downstream.

"This way," Joanna urged as she pulled my arm and led us through a door on the inner side of the portico, down a complex set of stairs. It was just you and me and her. "Come this way," and she led us farther and farther down.

My heart pounding in my chest, your pulse in my hand, we raced through the cool darkness and suddenly Joanna pushed a door, and we were in the street, in the sunlight, outside the Temple precinct.

Joanna shaded her hand with her eye and pointed, "See that hill over there? See the olive grove beyond the city wall? That is Gethsemane, the oil press and olive garden; Joseph of Arimathea owns them," put a finger over your lips, "do not ask me how I know, just go, you will be safe there. Here," handing me the water pouch, "I will find Judas, and the others. Go wait there. Do not move from there until one of us comes, all right?"

She started off then came back, "You are in more trouble than you know." Her eyes darkened for a moment, then brightened with tenderness, "And I could not love you more right now if I were Our Creator Herself."

She kissed us both on the cheek and disappeared among the passersby down the narrow street, her pink cloak bobbing in and out until we could see her no more.

We did not speak as we made our way, still hand in hand, through the incoming pilgrims and merchants. The crowds thinned as we went down into the valley past all the tombs deeply nestled into the hillside, and up the hill across the way to where Joanna had directed us. It was not the noisy crowd that stilled our tongues, nor the steep climb which kept my heart pounding.

The small building that housed the olive press looked dark and cool, but without a word we agreed we wanted sky and ground. We sat in the grove at the foot of a thick olive tree, its branches light from the recent harvest. Its long narrow leaves fluttered in the faint breeze which cooled our sweaty bodies.

You sat with your back against the tree. Sitting between your legs, I leaned into you. The soft rise of your breath lifted me. Your heavy hand rested on my hair, not moving.

"Jesus, let us not wait, let us go, this is our chance."

"Mary, beloved, so impatient. We cannot abandon those who trust us. Without our word, what are we?"

"Yes of course you are right. But…"

"There is nothing to be afraid of. The trouble at the Temple has simplified everything. The Council will never agree to meet with us now. It is over. Judas will be furious, but in the end this may be what he needs to let us go, to let his plan go. We just need to give him time to have his say."

"Yes, Jesus, but what about what Joanna said. That we are in trouble. The soldiers…"

"What have soldiers do to with us, my love. They chased us off, now they can go back to sleep."

"Is this the life we are to lead, Jesus, always running from angry crowds or soldiers?"

"I do not know my love," kissing the top of my head. "I can tell you this is so much better than oneself being that angry soldier. I suppose we will have to keep moving, even faster than we had planned. Never fret – as you well know, Mary, indeed as I learned from watching you, Our Creator provides all that we need."

Judas's face was so distorted when he arrived, I almost did not recognize him. The sun had just set behind our hill, but not the day. Beyond him, all our friends were gathered, everyone except Joanna. Judas slapped your shoulder, "Jesus the untouchable, you stubborn mule, get up you lucky donkey, you!" I realized now his face was distorted with joy. "Just like in the mountains, brother, no one can touch you!"

"Judas, my brother, what are you talking about?" you asked. "Were we really such a success with the moneychangers?"

I felt you stretch behind me. I got up and stretched too. "Changed everyone's mind about money, have we?" I asked. "Where is Joanna?"

"Never mind Joanna, she is fine, she is at Joseph's house, but you, you are more than fine, you are amazing!"

"All right, Judas, tell us what happened. I can see you are bursting." You had risen now and reached out for the water pouch, which I handed to you, having forgotten I was holding it. You splashed your face with water, drank. I did the same, after you. "Out with it, come on now."

"Jesus, it is all happening. The chief of the Sanhedrin Council, Caiphas himself, is sending his personal escort to meet you, and take both you and Mary to their meeting house. You will not meet with them tonight of course, it is too late, we will have to wait until sun up, but that is the only place you will be safe right now, until they figure out how to work this to our best advantage."

"They still want to meet with us, after being chased out of the

Temple?" your voice catching. I wondered, did you need another drink? The water pouch got handed around. Everyone was parched. No one was speaking. Salome came to me, put her arm around my waist. Something was not right.

Judas jubilated, "Yes, Jesus, in fact they loved what you did in the Temple! They have been wanting someone to stand up to those moneychangers for years! Those blue-turbaned men, they are foreigners, and as much as they cheat the people, they cheat the priests twice as much. But everyone has been afraid of them, they present such a united front, and they have a good deal with the Romans, too. They are holding the Temple hostage, essentially.

"Not only that, someone noticed your unseamed cloak, the likes of which are reserved for the Temple's Chief Priest in these parts. The Romans keep those sacramental garments under lock and key except for the festivals, and here you are, from who knows where, dressed like a chief priest, stirring things up! And best of all, it is not just political," tapping your chest, "you want to help the people get closer to Our Creator!"

Your voice in your beard, "I would like to help people realize how close to Our Creator they already are..."

"Yes. Yes, save it for your speeches, you know that talk is wasted on..."

"So what exactly happened after we left you?" your eyes on the ground, listening with your whole body.

"Well since I could not find you, I went straight to Joseph's house, bringing everyone," Judas indicated our friends with his hand, "figuring you had gotten arrested, and that Joseph was the only one who could help. Joanna got there after us, and she told us that you were up here, safe. Joseph was very interested by what you did with the moneychangers, and he sent word to the high priest, Caiphas, the head of the Council, who has been trying to get leverage against the moneychangers for years. He sent word that he was very interested too, and that he wanted to speak with you as soon as possible."

Why did this tale make my heart race? Why were my hands icy cold? "Why can we not spend the night here, Judas?" I asked. "Why does he want us there?"

"You will not be safe here, Mary. The Romans patrol these hills at night, looking for anyone who seems even slightly seditious. Without any children among us, and not even the barest makings of a Sukkoth shelter, we do not exactly look like pilgrims. It is best this way. The rest of us will stay at Joseph's – "

"Why can we not be there with you?"

"Because the Romans are still looking for you. They are going around house to house, with the moneychanger you confronted to identify you. Did you think that would just go away?"

You laughed a little. Just a little. "Yes, I suppose we did."

"Can Joseph not hide us? I have heard he has an enormous house."

"Yes, but the Council meeting house is even better, because no foreigners can set foot there, just like the inner courts of the Temple."

You hugged Judas tightly, pressed his head into your chest. "You did well, my brother. You did well. Bless you for your persistence." You lifted his head with both hands, kissed his cheek, then the other. Looking right into his eyes, "I know you love me. All right? Remember this, I know everything you have done is because you love me."

Judas pushed you away, wiped the tears from his face, and cackled a bit, "Do not forget that when you are king!" Then simply exultant again, "Caiphas, man! The Chief Priest, the head of the Council. This is it!"

You pushed him back, and the two of you sparred lightly for a moment. You were acting like everything was fine. You went around and greeted everyone, tousling hair, slapping shoulders. Salome held me tighter. I asked her, "Why is Joanna not here? Did she sense something? Did she say something?" But Salome had no answer for me.

"I am hungry!" you declared loudly, hands on your belly. "Let us eat."

Abigail and Zanna stepped forward and unrolled blankets. Kneeling down, they set out our food baskets.

Judas put his arm on Zanna's shoulder. It was the first time I had seen them touch since the cave on Mount Arbel. She looked up, then rose and melted into his arms, burying her face in his neck.

"I am sorry," I heard him whisper. "I am so sorry. I have been an ass. But that is over now. Shh. That is over now." Zanna's shoulders heaved with sobs. Abigail watched her parents for a moment, then with bright pink cheeks, she wrapped her arms around them.

The setting night found us all eating, seated on the soft ground around the blanket covered in food and drink. You handed me a different pouch from the water one. I took a drink, spat it out; my throat would not let it go down.

"What is it my love, something wrong with the wine?" I drank again, took a tiny sip, and passed it around. You cleared your throat. "This meal, this night. I want you to remember this. After tonight everything will be different."

I was reassured by these words. I thought they meant that soon we would be on our way.

"What do you mean, different?" Simon asked.

"Are you really going to be king?" Matthew asked.

"Who knows? What matters is that you remember this night as it is, with its soft air, abundant wine and food, and happy fellowship. When you find yourself like this again, think of me. Whenever two of you are gathered and speak of me, there I will be."

"Jesus?"

"Yes, Thomas."

"Enough with this strange talk, all right? I want to ask you a serious question."

"All right."

"Do you pray?"

"Of course I pray."

"I never see you pray."

"I pray all the time, Thomas, I am always in conversation with Our Creator, whether I am talking to you, or making love with my beloved, or drinking wine."

"Well that is good for you, Jesus. But what about a man like me, who cannot pray all the time because his mind is too busy. When I want to pray, what should I say? You seem to know Our Creator pretty well, what are the right words?"

"Whatever is in your heart, Thomas, there you can always find the right words," I suggested.

"Mary, you are very kind, but I was not asking you, I was asking Jesus."

"She is right, Thomas, there are no special words."

"All right Jesus, I see you want to make this difficult for me. Let us say right now, you were going to say a prayer, of this moment right now, what would you say?"

You took my hand, "I would say, *Blessed are You Our Creator who dwells where love is found.*" And you turned to me.

I offered, "*Love is Your only Name; Love is the only power; Love is the only presence, in us as it is in You.*"

You added, "*Each day You give us all that we need. Your Presence lifts us away from our battles with ourselves and our battles with others.*"

"*Never let us forget Your Love,*" I clasped your hand.

"*Never let us forget our love,*" you answered, deep into my eyes.

Thomas chimed in, "The power of these words! Would that they remain with me, etched in my heart."

"For all time," Simon added quietly.

"May it be so," you said at last, and kissed me.

We all looked at each other, shimmering in the ensuing silence.

Then you called out into the darkening night, "Pass the wine! Who has the wine?" and our gathering flowed over with eager talk.

Into this liveliness came the guards. You kissed me again, lightly, and pressed my shoulder down for me to stay put.

Stay put?

Judas went with you and greeted the men whom I could hear but not see at the entrance to the olive grove. Those of us sitting together all strained to hear words eaten up by the night.

When you came back, I rose, asking, "Shall we go?"

"Not us, Mary, it is enough that I go," you answered.

"But why? They want us both."

You took me a bit away from the others. "Listen to me, Mary. I will not stay there all night. I will get this settled quickly so we can leave by morning. If we are both there... You know, with a woman, it will take longer, as they will stand on ceremony."

"Do you think I do not know you are lying to me?" I slapped your chest. "Jesus! What is it?"

You held my head in both your hands. "Woman, let me do this thing for you. Let me do this thing. There is nothing I would not do for you. Nothing."

You kissed my shocked mouth, hard, and walked off into the night.

Salome came up to me and said, "He will be back soon." I held her and hung on her words of straw until the night made those words bloody and they were wrenched from my useless hands.

How did you know?

How did you know the high priest Caiphas's intention? How did you know he meant to arrest you, deliver you to the Romans like the dog he is? The rest of the members of the Council knew nothing. It was just Caiphas, acting alone. For what favor? What advantage did he hope to gain from the bloody Pontius Pilate, the Roman governor of Jerusalem, in exchange for the trouble-maker from the Temple?

What difference does it make. I know not nor care to know.

Joseph explained all this to me, when they brought me to his house in a panic after the news reached us in the grove that you had been taken straight to the Antonia fortress.

What difference does it make.

You knew if I had gone with you I would be dead too, or worse, and then what. What difference to be here without you, than anywhere else without you. If I were dead maybe we would be together. But likely they would not have killed me. Those Romans like to take slaves.

What did Judas say that let you know?

Had you heard of Caiphas? Did it all sound too good to be true? You knew if you had resisted, there would have been bloodshed. Blood on your hands, again.

But you said "for me," nothing you would not do "for me." Is this what you have done for me, let me live without you? Do you think you have spared me some suffering this way?

I now must write the part I dread most.

A skull-shaped hill, barren and round, outside Jerusalem's city walls. A hill covered with trees of death. Men dying on the high crosses to which they were nailed, some naked and writhing, others long dead and rotting, for all to see. You among them, accused like a criminal, hanging on a cross like a common rabble-rouser, dying. Within my reach and yet beyond it.

Those accursed Roman pigs. When they nailed your wrists, your blood splattered on me.

The soldiers walking back and forth in front of us, in front of you and the others being crucified; soldiers calling out to each other as they nailed flesh and heaved crosses, complaining about their wives and joking crudely about the women they would rather know.

Your poor mother, who had not laid eyes on you since we departed bold and dawn-lit from the cave on Mount Arbel, how she wept, quietly, so as not to call attention to her sorrow. Her body shaking silently beside mine, my arm around her on one side and on the other whose? Dinah's? Salome's? I do not know, one or the other behind us embracing us all – each of us so deep inside our own loss, so alone and yet joined as we knelt at the foot of your cross, each of us alone and joined as the strings on one of the lutes Maryanna used to make.

How unsettling and grounding it felt to be with these women again, good and hollow and familiar and strange and comforting and heartbreaking. Everything had changed and nothing had changed. At last, we were able to weep together, all that we had not cried for all these years, for Hannah, and for Deborah and for Judith and for Rachel and for Tabitha and for Ariella and for Zacharias too. This welcome unwelcome gift to us, this opening of the time for gathering and grieving.

And then you cried out, barely loud enough for us to hear, "Oh My Creator, why have You forsaken me?" – the call to remember that first verse of the psalm of David which in the end concludes, "This triumph of Our Creator shall be told for all time, and the people will come and speak of Our Creator's Power to each new generation being born."

You so generous, your faith so complete, even in your torment, even then you called out to comfort us... But the quality of your voice, gurgling with blood, hoarse with pain, pushed me over the edge and I fainted, to wake here, in Joseph of Arimathea's palace, in this house of marble and despair, in this house where the only plan is to leave Jerusalem as quickly as possible.

They say your tomb is guarded by soldiers. Even that is a grace: Joseph had to go to Pontius Pilate, with gold in both hands, to buy the privilege of taking your body off the cross, so it would not be left to rot there, as everyone else's is.

How can they stand to be themselves, those cowardly, accursed Roman pigs.

Oh I know my love, I can hear your voice inside me: "They are not pigs because they are Roman, they are not pigs at all, they do not know what they do. They are blind; they need to be healed just like the whole rest of the world needs to be healed."

Do you think I do not know that?

The whole world does need to be healed. Even if they killed you, tortured you, like so many others have been killed and tortured – and how many did you kill, in your day?

The world needs to be healed. And I am a healer. I am here to heal. Then what am I doing in this room all alone, when the very people who followed us everywhere and trusted us with their lives are right here? They are desperate for tender ministrations I am sure. They need me. I have been thinking about how they would not help me, when it is I who should be helping them.

My love, I have been selfish and blind!

Perhaps I was blinded by the sight of your mangled body. Perhaps I needed to tell our whole story to come to this point, to open my eyes: our love is not only about you and me.

Perhaps this is how your spirit comes to me, as I never doubted it would. Perhaps I am the one this amulet was meant to heal. I will open the doors and call out down these endless hallways. I will ask our friends to take me with them, let me do with them whatever they need done.

Jesus, I leave you now in the care of Our Creator, in Whose Care we all are, whether we understand the mysterious ways in which She moves, or whether we suffer them like blind fate.

I love you. Your life goes on within me. You and me became us, and now I am me again, if I ever was before. I have done all I can, Jesus, and now, once again I must attend to the living.

May Our Creator help me live with that being enough.

My love! Just as I opened the door, I found Salome and Dinah and Joanna standing there! They have agreed to come with me to you. Their trick to get past the guards at your tomb: embalming oils. We will say we are there to care for your corpse. Indeed! And best of all, it was your mother Maryanna who came up with the plan.

But first, I told them I need to add these final words. Did this writing raise their hearts, or only mine? Perhaps their coming had nothing to do with this writing or me at all. I will never know. It no longer matters.

May Our Creator bless me with the capacity simply to welcome the grace of their faith.

They tell me it is Sunday. I have not eaten or slept since I began writing. Three days since I have seen you.

You should see their faces my love, so bright with fear and courage.

My love, I am on fire. I fly to you.

Come what may.

SELECTED BIBIOGRAPHY

(for more complete list go to: www.valerie-gross.com)

The Song of Songs: A New Translation, by Ariel Bloch & Chana Bloch. Pub.: University of California Press, 1998

Jesus - A Revolutionary Biography, by John Dominic Crossan. Pub.: HarperOne, 1995

Prayers of the Cosmos: Meditations on the Aramaic Words of Jesus, by Neal Douglas-Klotz. Pub.: HarperSanFrancisco, 1990

Misquoting Jesus: The Story Behind Who Changed the Bible and Why, by Bart Ehrman. Pub.: HarperSanFrancisco, 2005

Galilee: History, Politics, People, by Richard Horsley. Pub.: Continuum, 1995

Inanna: Queen of Heaven and Earth, Samuel Noah Kramer and Diane Wolkstein. Pub.: HarperCollins, 1983

The Gnostic Gospels, by Elaine Pagels. Pub.: Random House, 2004

Hebrew Goddess, by Raphael Patai. Pub.: Wayne State University Press, 1990

The Nag Hammadi Library, General Editor: James M. Robinson. Pub.: Harper & Row, 1988

"Protest and Profanation: Agrarian Revolt and the Little Tradition, Parts I & II" by James C. Scott. Pub.: *Theory and Society*, Volume 4, No. 1 & 2, Spring and Summer, 1977

The Woman with the Alabaster Jar, by Margaret Starbird. Pub.: Bear & Co., 1993

The Rise of Christianity: How the Obscure, Marginal Jesus Movement Became the Dominant Religious Force in the Western World in a Few Centuries, by Rodney Stark. Pub.: Princeton University Press, 1996

When God Was a Woman, by Merlin Stone. Pub.: Harcourt Brace, 1976

Sarah the Priestess, The First Matriarch of Genesis, Savina J. Teubal. Pub.: Swallow Press, 1984

The Woman's Encyclopedia of Myths and Secrets, by Barbara Walker. Pub.: HarperOne, 1983

Complete Works of Josephus Flavius, Trans.: William Whiston. Pub.: Hendrickson Publishers, 1987

www.magdalathebook.com

Also available online:
- Print out the Book Group guide
- Listen to author interviews

- Contact Valerie to share your thoughts or ask her whatever you'd like to know

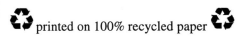 printed on 100% recycled paper